ALSO BY THOMAS POWERS

Heisenberg's War: The Secret History of the German Bomb

Thinking About the Next War

The Man Who Kept the Secrets: Richard Helms and the CIA

The War at Home: Vietnam and the American People

Diana: The Making of a Terrorist

THE CONFIRMATION

THE CONFIRMATION

THOMAS POWERS

Alfred A. Knopf
New York
2000

THIS IS A BORZOI BOOK
PUBLISHED BY ALFRED A. KNOPF

 Published in the United States by Alfred A. Knopf, a division of Random House, Inc., New York, and simultaneously in Canada by Random House of Canada Limited, Toronto. Distributed by Random House, Inc., New York.

www.aaknopf.com

Library of Congress Cataloging-in-Publication Data
Powers, Thomas, 1940–
The confirmation / by Thomas Powers.—1st ed.
p. cm.
ISBN 0-375-40020-6
I. Title.
PS3566.O96 C66 2000
813'.54—DC21 99-049237

Manufactured in the United States of America
First Edition

This book

is for my sister, Susan.

NOTE TO THE READER

The Confirmation takes place in a parallel universe. It reproduces as nearly as I could manage the manners and attitudes, the historical context, and the institutional relationships of the CIA and other American intelligence organizations as they operate in the real world. Several well-known public figures from the recent past, not all of them dead, make brief appearances in this book under their real names, as they might have if the story had been true. But the story is entirely my own invention, and all the characters—real and imagined alike—have been used fictitiously, without intent to describe the actual conduct of any person.

THE CONFIRMATION

I

The secret of anger management, the young therapist Lisa Benson explained to Dean Cutter at their first meeting, was to avoid situations that he knew were going to make him angry. She was not dismissing the importance of alcohol; the fact he was sitting in her office under court order was all the evidence he needed of that. But she had read the report of the arresting officer, and she could tell him he was a very lucky man not to be facing a charge of felonious assault.

"I can explain," said Dean Cutter.

"Of course you can explain. Explaining is one thing I'm sure you're very good at. What I want to help you do is to stop explaining and change."

The way she said it, like he was some kid.

"Look—" Dean began.

"I'm going to put this as clearly as I can," she said. "You have been ordered to attend twelve sessions of group counseling for alcohol abuse. In my opinion you have got to work on anger, too, and my opinion counts. If you take this seriously and come to class and do the work, you'll get your license back. But you're going to have to stop explaining things away and take an honest look at your life."

Tough little bitch. The way she looked at him: It's up to you, asshole.

Story of his life. Dean hated being lectured, being told it was his own fault, "You're not performing up to your potential," all that we're-just-trying-to-help crap. Mrs. Solloway, Miss Coates, Mrs. Noonan, and the others—all through grade school, middle school, high school—until he couldn't stand it and quit going. "You're fucking up, soldier"; the black drill sergeant during basic training at Fort Gordon, Georgia, was Mrs. Noonan in combat fatigues. "You get over that wall or you're going to be cleaning out the grease pit behind the mess hall for the next three years. It's up to you."

Even in the Gulf: "Don't come crying to me, soldier. You're supposed to remember your own asthma inhaler."

Maybe he did bring his troubles on himself. But he hated being told what was wrong with him, how to do right, pull himself together. He hated the way this woman young enough to be his daughter sat behind her desk, thoughtfully tapping her chin with a yellow pencil, waiting for him to decide if he wanted to learn to control his anger and his drinking or would rather take the bus to work every night for the next three years.

"Perhaps you can give me an example," she said. "Describe some situation that you know from experience is likely to end up making you angry."

He wanted to say, Have you got all day, lady?

But she was right. It was his choice. If he wanted his license back he had to kiss ass, answer questions, go through the drill, so he told her truthfully that he did not think he had ever read the newspaper or listened to a news broadcast or watched one of the Sunday morning talk shows without getting angry. She asked what it was: their tone of voice? the things they said? the way they looked? Maybe the fact they were on television and he wasn't?

Dean had to admit she was pretty smart. They talked about it. He had opinions about all these things in the news. He wanted to tell the people on TV that they were missing the point, getting things wrong—but of course they paid no attention. They didn't know he existed.

"I can understand that," Lisa Benson said. "So why do you turn on the tube every chance you get? Do you *like* getting angry?"

He said no. He said she was right. Yelling at the tube was something he could easily drop right out of his life and save himself a whole lot of aggravation. But that was a lie, and he knew it was a lie. Being angry made him feel powerful and dangerous.

He took the bus home to his apartment in Southeast, and watched the idiots on the networks and CNN all Friday night, and was madder than hell all day Saturday because the weather was lousy and his boots had cracked and let in water and slush at the toe and he had to stand in the freezing cold at the bus stop for half an hour to get to work. Naturally he was late. The early man, a black guy called Jimmy, was pissed, said he was tired of it, said this time he was telling the district manager.

"Run to teacher!" Dean spat.

Late Saturday night, just before closing, Russell the ex-marine showed up and pushed Dean's buttons with a rap about who really runs this country.

At first glance Russell looked a little like one of those vets you saw down at the Vietnam Memorial on the Mall: skinny guys in tattered green army jackets with gray ponytails. But Russell wasn't burned out with drugs and booze, his boots were spit-shined, his fatigues were pressed, he was clean-shaven. There was nothing slack about Russell. He looked like he'd just walked in from a year in the desert: blazing eyes, straight back, never a wasted word.

Russell had a way of talking backwards.

"You're not wondering why I limp, fuck no," Russell would say. "I never stepped on a mine on Highway One. It quit hurting years ago. The VA can't do enough for me. It's an honor to sacrifice the use of your leg for your country. I'd be happy to give them another. Please, feel sorry for me. Pity is what I want."

Dean had not mentioned Russell to the therapist. He had not known Russell long, but he knew Russell would not appreciate the mention of his name to anyone in authority, even a lady therapist barely out of school. Russell wasn't like anyone Dean had ever known. He understood the way things worked in this country, and in ten minutes he could have Dean panting with fury with a point-by-point on all the damage the people who run things had done to America since they turned their backs on the boys they sent to Vietnam.

"But we're easy," Russell said. "We've forgotten what they put us through, am I right? We like turning the other cheek."

Russell was a cold sonofabitch. He was always under control. He thought things through, he knew who the enemy was, he was in touch with people who were ready to act.

But the lady therapist was right about Dean. Anger was the story of his life. Sometimes he got so angry he broke beer bottles against the wall of his apartment. The amber stains remained. Three weeks back, as Lisa Benson informed Dean that she had read in his file, he rear-ended a rusted-out Ford Taurus at a stoplight at the corner of New York Avenue and Fifth Street. Far from apologizing, he had taken from the trunk of his car an iron bar, kept there for precisely such an occasion, and had methodically smashed the windows of the car he had hit because the other driver had had plenty of time to get through the light but was chickenshit and slowed down and then slammed on his brakes when Dean hit the horn, thereby causing the accident and pissing Dean off, to put it mildly. He had started with the windshield and proceeded around the car, smashing the rest of the windows. The bar was heavy and folded the windows right in, turning them into white sheets of fractured glass.

All this had been observed by a District of Columbia policeman from his cruiser a block away. But not observed, and not included in the officer's report, was the fact that the Hispanic driver of the car, his wife next to him in the front seat, and their three children in the back all cowered in terror as Dean smashed their windows. Little dark people as fragile as birds; Dean made eye contact with each one of them as he worked his way around the car. They openly showed the fear he might kill them, and Dean was in fact thinking about hauling the driver out into the street and beating him to death when the DC police officer with his hand on his gun commanded him to desist. Dean did not describe any of that to his therapist. On the contrary, he lied and said the whole thing filled him with shame and remorse.

They talked about it. He admitted he went too far sometimes. But in Dean's view, despite the rare lapse, he already had his anger pretty well managed. Usually he just got pissed and lashed out verbally. Isn't that what healthy people were supposed to do—express their feelings?

Got her that time, he thought.

"Are you familiar with the word *minimization*?" she had asked.

But the truth was, the aches and pains and disappointments of life weighed heavily, and telling somebody where to get off wasn't enough. Dean was hurting Sunday morning when he flicked on *Meet the Press* on NBC; the program made him angry beyond the power of words to relieve. The guest was vaguely familiar—Dean had seen the face on TV before—not a tall man, maybe in his fifties, trim, well-dressed, good-looking in the way of men in shaving commercials, but his hair was silvery white. The comfortable look of the man, like he had been in front of television cameras every day of his life, began to make Dean angry. He was fidgeting on the couch in front of the tube, trying to get his leg comfortable; it was as if he had pulled something.

"This is a big day for you," said the interviewer, Walter Moss. "Late yesterday the White House announced that President Anderson has chosen you to be the next director of the Central Intelligence Agency. I know you've been in the business a long time: arms control specialist for the National Security Council, special assistant to William Casey for Nicaragua for a year, chief intelligence analyst, and now, today, acting director of the Agency since Patrick Delaney announced he was stepping down. Mister Cabot, you've taken your share of hard knocks."

CABOT: Goes with the territory, Walter.

MOSS: Lot of tough questions up there on the Hill during Iran-Contra, as I recall.

CABOT: We're not going into all that, I hope.

MOSS: Maybe one or two small points. But first I want to ask you: How does it feel to be moving into the top job?

Central Intelligence Agency. Director. Fucking intelligence analyst. Top job. Every word made Dean angrier. Know-it-all Lisa Benson was certainly right about one thing. If you don't want to get angry, don't watch this fucking crap.

CABOT: Don't jump the gun, Walter. I'm not director yet. I've got to be confirmed first.

MOSS: We've watched some major confirmation fights in this town, but I don't see one here.

CABOT: I'm not expecting to breeze through. Somebody is always opposed—that's politics.

MOSS: But not Senator Harrison Hawkins. As chairman of the intelligence oversight committee, he'll be running your confirmation hearings, and it's no secret he thinks you walk on water.

CABOT: Well, I think *he* walks on water. [*Laughter*] We've worked very closely with Senator Hawkins and his committee, especially on POW/MIA issues. That's a subject very close to the senator's heart. He feels this country owes it to the boys we sent over there and to their families. And I agree.

MOSS: But MIAs are not exactly the burning issue of the day.

CABOT: No.

MOSS: Your attention is going to be focused on what, the mess in the Balkans? The Middle East? Outlaw nations with nuclear weapons? Figuring out what's going on in Russia? There's a world of trouble out there, am I right?

CABOT: I'll be busy, Walter.

One sentence. That's what the MIAs got, one sentence.

After another freezing wait for the bus and forty minutes of stop-and-start, Dean arrived at Blockbuster Video ten minutes late. Jimmy, the early man, was already gone. The district manager was behind the register, big Greek guy called Niko. He looked pissed. "You own a watch, Cutter?"

Dean wanted to smash the guy's face, but he knew that would never happen. Niko lifted weights and worked out and was three inches taller than Dean, and each extra inch weighed a good ten–fifteen pounds of muscle. Dean wasn't crazy. If he wanted to bring the sweat to Niko's brow and a quiver to his lips he would need to show him a gun. Which one of these days he just might do. Dean had some serious guns: pistols, from a huge blue-black .357 magnum that would crack the engine block of a car to a little matte-black seven-shot Italian Beretta .380 automatic. Five guns, all right there in his apartment, in his bureau, bottom drawer, waiting.

Dean explained about the bus.

"Get an earlier bus," said Niko. "I'm not warning you again."

By the time Russell showed up around midnight, Dean's anger was almost out of control. He had told one customer to get the fuck out. Russell barely said hello before Dean began talking about the CIA guy who said MIAs were not exactly Topic A. Old news. Go through the motions and forget it.

"You're talking about Frank Cabot," said Russell.

"That's the guy. What the fuck did *he* ever do for MIAs?" Dean was fuming.

"Cabot's just telling the truth," said Russell. "They gave up looking years ago. But why should we care? They weren't our buddies."

"I care," said Dean. "I knew one of those MIAs."

When Dean was in Accokeek Middle School, the big brother of a girl he knew went missing in Vietnam. Such a great guy. Just a goddam great guy. All the kids in the neighborhood looked up to Jason Dyer. On hot summer days he used to fill his pickup truck with kids and take them to the beach.

"I'm going off to war," he said one day to Dean. "The government's going to pay me to hunt little yellow men." He drew the eight-year-old boy close. "Be a good kid," he whispered. "I'll send you an ear."

And he did. Dean had it in his bureau, wrapped in Kleenex in a little box. That ear made him the most popular kid in school for a week.

But then the army came one day to tell Jason's family he had gone missing. They never found him. His kid sister, Stacy, still cried about him. What did Frank Cabot or anybody else in the CIA ever do for Jason Dyer? They had secret agents everywhere, spy satellites, geniuses breaking codes—they could have done something. If they wanted to.

Russell listened to this without comment. After Dean finally cooled down and stopped, Russell said, "I don't suppose this makes you mad enough to do something. You just want to bitch about it when you're feeling mean, am I right? Not actually *do* something?"

"What could I do? I'm just one guy."

"Sometimes one guy is enough," said Russell. "One guy with balls. Did you ever hear of John Hinckley? How about James Earl Ray? Or Lee Harvey Oswald?"

Cutter had heard of Oswald.

2

In nearly two years of working for the CIA, Brad Cameron had heard a lot of talk about keeping secrets, but it wasn't until Saturday night after his friend Hugh Diamond had called to say Turn on the news that he began to realize just how secret a secret could be. Now it was Monday morning, February 18th; a heavy wet snow fell out of the sky. Brad was on the first leg of his daily four-mile run and he was still stunned by the news.

He was amazed that he had utterly failed to see it coming. It wasn't a big secret in the larger scheme of things, but it was sure as hell tightly held at the Agency. Thinking back over the previous weeks, Brad could identify no hint of a clue, and he was certainly in an ideal position to have picked up *something.* The fact the president picked Frank Cabot to be the acting Director of Central Intelligence meant nothing, according to Hugh; acting DCIs were usually an interim choice while the White House looked for a serious candidate. But Brad had been reporting to Cabot twice a month for the last year; he was going out with Cabot's niece, Jenny Moore; and he had been invited to dinner twice at Cabot's home in McLean in the last six weeks while everybody at the Agency was trying to guess the president's pick for DCI. Brad had even listened to Cabot and his wife, Kitty, only ten days ago, the night before Jenny took off for a conference in California, as they weighed his hopes against the chances of the chief of the Directorate of Operations, Joe Flint. Flint was not a man Cabot would have enjoyed working for; he made no secret of that. Cabot had a shot, but no one at the dinner table treated it as more than a shot. Not one word escaped Cabot to suggest he had a pretty damned good idea the president had made up his mind.

"Did it come as a surprise?" Walter Moss had asked on *Meet the Press* while Brad watched Sunday morning.

"Not as a surprise," said Cabot. "We'd been talking. But you've been around this town a long time, Walter. No appointment is firm until it comes from the president's lips. So I found out pretty much at the same moment that the rest of the world did."

. . .

Brad liked Cabot's way of talking, his modesty. But the truth was he'd been talking to the White House for weeks; it was a done deal, yet he told no one. Not even his wife had known ten days ago. Now Brad's life was about to change, and he didn't need a wise if exotic bird like Hugh Diamond to explain why. It was all right there on the front page of the morning's *Washington Post,* face out in the newspaper vending machines Brad passed every block or two on his way down Nineteenth through the freezing slush toward the Mall. Two columns, off-lead, befitting big news in a company town:

ANDERSON SIDES WITH OLD BOYS,
PICKS COLD WAR PRO FOR CIA

The light changed and Brad Cameron jogged across the street toward the Mall, head down against the wet snow. By now it was seven or a little later. Brad ran every morning, summer and winter, sun or rain, no matter how cold it got and, more to the point, no matter how hot. Brad's third summer in Washington was coming up; he hated the 100-degree days with a humidity reading one point short of being underwater. Brad was a true child of New England; what he loved were winters on snowshoes and summers in the cool pine forests of Maine. These Washington summers gave him serious pause. But whatever the weather he ran eight-minute miles till his body glowed pink and his yellow hair lay flat with sweat. He'd been running since he was sent off to boarding school in midterm when he was ten years old. Running gave him a feeling of peace.

Franklin S. Cabot. Years passed before most young new intelligence officers had a word alone with the man running the CIA. Some never did. Brad saw him every week or so to report the status of news—usually none—about members of the U.S. military services carried for thirty years on the Pentagon's official roster of those reported Missing in Action in Vietnam. Frank Cabot was very, very attentive to this subject, and it hadn't taken Brad long to understand why—MIAs were the passion of the chairman of the Senate's Select Committee on Intelligence.

Cabot had been friendly even before Jenny came into Brad's life. He had none of the bluff swagger of some officers in the upper ranks of the CIA who were plainly anticipating greater things. His businesslike manner did not change during the weeks while the naming of the new Director of Central Intelligence had been the principal smoke-break and lunchtime game at the Agency, ever since Patrick Delaney had announced on New Year's Day that he was resigning as DCI to spend more time with his family. He was running the outfit one week, gone the next. The rumor was he rubbed the president the wrong way. But even after Cabot was named acting director, no one called him a front-runner. Too quiet, too professional, too identified with the Cold War, too . . . pick your reason. Perhaps it was his calm style; he didn't seem ready to die or kill for the job.

Over lunch in the cafeteria, or on the second floor where Brad had a windowless cubicle in the East Asia Division, or down in Records in the subbasement where Brad spent two or three afternoons a week reading MIA files at one of the big oak tables, or in the halls and on the way out to one of the far parking lots, the names were floated and then picked apart. In the bowels of the Agency many believed that the natural and logical choice for Director of Central Intelligence was Joe Flint, Deputy Director for Operations, venerable old boy, once the fair-haired protégé of the legendary Allen Dulles. The fair hair was thin now, but Flint had the respect of the professionals. In addition, he had done at least one important favor for every president since John F. Kennedy. They loved him on the Hill, they hated him at Harvard, he had never been caught in a lie, it was widely accepted in Washington that among many other exploits he had personally recruited the secretary of a member of the old Soviet Politburo in 1979, and he had no enemies at the Pentagon. Flint had earned his shot at the job.

But Joe Flint had at least one blot in his copybook. A dozen years back he had informed an unmarried but pregnant case officer working for him in the Tel Aviv station that he was going to ship her home unless she got an abortion. God knows what was going through his mind. She got a lawyer, and the CIA's general counsel unwisely asked this lawyer for a couple of days to consider their offer to settle.

The next day *The Washington Post* ran a front-page story by Faith Osborne reporting the awful facts. Osborne had a way with stories about the treatment of women by men in Washington. First she reported the crime. Then she reported the inadequate and self-serving official response to the crime. Then she reported the spreading national indignation of politically active organizations at attempts to cover up the crime. Faith Osborne kept Joe Flint's name on the front page for a week, and despite Flint's eventual apology—and a cash settlement sufficient to send the infant to the private school, college, and law school of his choice—it was considered something of a miracle, much later, when Flint was appointed the Agency's Deputy Director for Operations and actually assumed the post.

"But that was all years ago," said Brad at lunch one day with Hugh. Brad had seen Flint only once, in the auditorium, at a memorial service for a recently deceased old boy. Flint was just about the last of his generation—he had joined up during the Korean War—but there was no stoop to his shoulders, no slack to his chin or gut. Sitting in the second row of the Bubble, exchanging an occasional word with Deputy Director for Intelligence Frank Cabot, next to him, a rival of many years' standing, Flint looked weathered but vigorous. Everything was still new to Brad at the time; he gawked when he saw these legends in the flesh.

Flint had risen in his turn and spoke of the deceased briefly but with feeling as a man you could trust with your life; he knew, he had done it.

"Few people recognized him in the halls," said Flint. "Fewer knew his role in creating this agency. Running a secret intelligence organization requires silence while other men are giving press conferences. You young men and women out there—we were like you once, fresh out of college, full of ambition and love of country, ready to lay down our lives. Some of us did; you've all seen their names and stars in the main hall. But trust me, the time will come when it will seem easier to die than to hold your tongue."

Flint made a strong impression. He seemed like the sort of man Brad's father had known in the Agency just after the Korean War. Some flap ended his dad's career: Brad's mother was vague; his uncle Max said the simple answer was Joe McCarthy. That was as close as Brad could get. After leaving the Agency, Brad's father went to law school, married late, and died at sixty when Brad was only ten. But Uncle Max often said how much his father's Agency years meant to him. He invited Brad home often for weekends during the bleak boarding-school years and helped him get into college. It was Uncle Max who introduced him, one memorable night at the St. Botolph Club, to the correct method for making a martini and brought him as a teenager to Washington to meet some of his father's old Agency friends. In the absence of Brad's mother, whose chief talent was for marrying rich husbands, Uncle Max had exerted a powerful influence on Brad's life.

"Flint will never be DCI," said Hugh Diamond. "Faith Osborne isn't the only one with a long memory in this town. That kid is probably a cute little tyke with freckles by now and you can bet the rent money that Faith knows exactly where to find him. Trust me. Flint's days are numbered. The new DCI is going to want his own DDO."

Hugh had taken Brad under his wing soon after his first day on the job, explained the world to him, warned him where the footing was treacherous. He'd been around forever, knew everybody, broke the rules when they gave him trouble. "I'm going to tell you the secret of intelligence forecasting," he said, one day early on. "The bad news is always true. When you know that, you know the worst."

Diamond wrote off all the obvious candidates for DCI with precision. "Who's left?" asked Brad.

"Who's left!" exclaimed Hugh. "The phone lines are humming with candidates calling the president's friends right this minute, and the friends of his friends, and the guys who only went to kindergarten with the friends of his friends. Many roads lead to the seventh floor: guys who used to sell rockets to Uncle Sam, guys who won hearts and minds in Vietnam, guys who made a hundred million bucks in the computer business, guys who run study groups on nonproliferation for the Council on Foreign Relations, guys who spotted Anderson in the primaries. . . ."

In six weeks of talk Brad heard Cabot's name seriously argued only once. "Cabot's a decent guy," said a reports writer visiting from Russia. "They trust him on the Hill, Hawkins loves him, he actually knows something about computers, he's never been trashed by the *Post* or the *Times*—what's wrong with Cabot?"

"For one thing," said Hugh, "Cabot was a life member of the Don't-Trust-the-Russians Club."

"Nobody around here got that right."

"He's too careful, too bland, too smooth."

"From what I see," said the reports writer, "around here smooth is good."

"All right," said Hugh, "make your best case."

"I met Cabot once," said the reports writer. "He was kicking tires in the Moscow station. He had a free night, and we played chess. I'll tell you something about Cabot. He thinks three moves ahead."

"Who won?" asked Diamond.

"The next DCI," said the reports writer.

By the time Brad reached Constitution the wet flakes were coming down so heavily he could barely see the Lincoln Memorial. Brad was running alone. None of the other regulars were out; it was too cold and wet and miserable. The capital of the world's most powerful nation was dragging to a halt in four inches of wet snow. Brad's sneakers and sweatpants were already soaked through from the slush. But he quit thinking of the misery when he started around the Reflecting Pool. He was into his second wind and beginning to feel good. He liked running alone and there was plenty in his life to think about. His girlfriend, Jenny, was just back from a conference on the traffic in endangered animals and animal parts, her passion; they had a date for dinner at nine. Hugh had suggested a new restaurant in Adams-Morgan—Italian, not too expensive. Not least, Brad had finally pried a whole new category of MIA files out of the DDO after months of pressing and getting nothing but one-word refusals from Flint's office. Brad knew Grafton Morse on Hawkins's staff would take a cool, realistic interest in this. For Brad it prompted bigger hopes; he sometimes daydreamed of finding an honest-to-God MIA.

Brad was as ambitious as any other young man freshly arrived in Washington, and he understood perfectly that Cabot as DCI was going to make a considerable difference in his own life. Nobody could have planned so much luck. It wasn't just the fact Cabot was Jenny's uncle. It was Cabot who had picked Brad from East Asia to handle MIA reports. Cabot and Senator Hawkins had been close for years, even before Hawkins took over the intelligence committee. They'd been to hell and back on the MIA issue. When fuzzy photos of grizzled "American POWs" sweeping streets in Hanoi landed on the front page of the *National Enquirer,* it was Brad who pulled the information together and briefed Cabot, who went up to the Hill personally and told the old senator it was another false alarm.

In spite of his hopes of glory, Brad believed the alarms would always be false. Too much time had gone by. Anybody left behind when the prisoners came home in 1973 would be long dead by now. And if by the grace of God and the confusions of bureaucracy some forlorn American soldier had managed to survive, the brutal truth was Hanoi would kill him on discovery before admitting they had been lying for thirty years. Everybody knew this at CIA and the Pentagon. Brad was pretty sure even Senator Hawkins in his heart knew this, but the senator had taken an oath he would never vote one penny of American aid to Vietnam until every American mother's heart was at rest—if knowing the worst after three decades of prayer could be called a kind of rest.

From time to time, when the evidence looked particularly strong on first arrival, it had been Brad's job to break the mother's heart. The scene was always the senator's wood-paneled office, maintained at an even 78 degrees Fahrenheit the year round. The mothers arrived full of anxious hope and left crushed. It was the depth of their feeling that moved Brad; his own mother did not believe in gush. In time Brad came to understand that his job was to end what began thirty years earlier with a message from the president of the United States. Brad sometimes imagined the birth of hope after the first shock of the grim news: "Missing, not dead—thank God."

How little they knew. On receiving the terrible news it was only human nature to ask, "What happened?" For most grieving survivors a few bare facts were enough; others wanted more, a body or proof of a body. Brad counted his day a success when he could prove someone irrevocably dead and thereby end a family's agony. From Hugh Diamond's point of view, the job was ideal: face time with important figures like Cabot and Hawkins, very little that could go wrong. But Brad found it hard to be the breaker of so many mothers' hearts.

It was bleak work in its way but he began to feel at home in Washington once a college friend introduced him to Jenny Moore. Brad thought she was beautiful. She believed in her work at the Earth Defense Trust, she was a tireless hiker and runner, and at the end of six months she had assured Brad that no man meant more to her, but she did not want to think about marriage for the time being.

Now Brad was far from sure Jenny was going to like being the niece of the DCI. Something about the idea of Uncle Frank on the Sunday talk shows, testifying in the Senate, running the entire intelligence community made Brad uneasy. Jenny was skittish. She hated being ignored but she didn't like to be the center of attention either. Praise made her ill-tempered. She had no talent for gracious small talk. The next time she walked into a room crowded with political types, the well-wishers were going to start sidling up in a steady stream to bask in the warm glow of reflected success: "I've always admired your Uncle Frank; you must be so proud."

Jenny was devoted to her Aunt Kitty, who was like a second mother, and she liked her Uncle Frank, who had been around forever. She would be pleased for him. This job was what he wanted, there was no doubt about that. But Brad had a feeling Jenny was not going to like the bright lights.

When Brad had completed his circuit of the Mall he recrossed Constitution and turned north on 18th toward Connecticut. The snow was still heavy, the traffic was moving at a crawl through the slush, and he quit waiting for the lights but simply dashed between cars. His heart was really pumping and he felt he could run forever. But as soon as he crossed L Street he slowed down and walked until he turned into the bright morning warmth of the Mayflower Hotel to get the paper. It was still early; the lobby traffic was mainly men without ties heading for breakfast. Brad was reaching for the top copy of *The Washington Post* when another hand reached to pull it away.

"Sorry," said the man. He handed the paper to Brad and took another. "I didn't see you."

"Thanks," said Brad.

There was something familiar about the face: sharp-featured, skin a bit rough with old acne scars, eyes of a startling blue, slick dark hair combed straight back. He was wearing a gray overcoat with a black velvet collar, reading glasses on the end of his nose, a cord around his neck. He started to turn away.

"Hey, Mr. Tater!" called the woman at the newsstand.

"Sorry," the man said again. "Thinking about the fate of the nation."

He smiled, extracted a dollar from his glossy buffalo-hide billfold, held out his hand for the change, and then headed across the lobby, scanning the front page.

"Should I know him?" Brad asked the woman at the newsstand.

"He buys the paper here most mornings," the woman said, making change for Brad's dollar. "Plus you might have seen him on one of the talk shows. George Tater. Reporter for the *Times.*"

"Doesn't ring a bell," said Brad.

"He was famous a few years ago," said the woman. "I can't remember what for."

3

George Tater at fifty-five was a man who liked people to do things for him. He never shined his own shoes, changed his own bed, did his own taxes, or made himself a meal more complicated than a bowl of cornflakes. He did not know how to change the bag on a vacuum cleaner or load a washing machine. He had never balanced a checkbook. His accountant paid his rent, utility, and credit card bills. For a time during his brief marriage in the late 1970s, he had sometimes helped his wife carry in the groceries. She did the shopping on Thursday nights on her way home from work. Soon Tater began working late on Thursday nights.

In the twenty years since the marriage had ended, Tater had never brought anything into the house heavier than a quart of milk, a pound of coffee, a box of cigars, and bottles of wine, gin, and vermouth. He had a maid in to clean on Mondays and Thursdays, his laundry was picked up and delivered, and he ate all his meals out. He owned a razor but preferred a barber.

At the far side of the Mayflower lobby, George Tater pushed his way through the door marked OFFICES in slender gold letters and made his way one flight upstairs to the place of business of Salvatore Morelli. The girl with the dark red lipstick, sitting at the desk flipping pages of the *Post,* looked up. "Good morning, Mr. Tater. Manicure today?"

"Not today, Cherry," said Tater. "Thanks."

He made his way to the far barber chair, a classic edifice of porcelain and worn leather padding on a fat chrome piston.

"Morning, Sally," said Tater, taking a seat.

"Bobby's going to do you today, Mr. Tater."

"Nice story about you guys in the *Post,*" said Tater. "But I never saw the president sitting in one of these chairs."

"They got that wrong," said Salvatore Morelli. "The president likes to get his hair cut in the Oval Office."

Morelli was short, thick, bald, with reddish skin and the heavy hands and thick fingers of a stonemason. He had emigrated to the United States from his native Calabria in the 1950s to carve Gothic fretwork for the Cathedral of St. John the Divine in New York City. The promised job failed to come through, and after some months Morelli found work shining shoes in the barbershop of the Hotel Roosevelt. Soon he was cutting hair. One of his steady customers ran for Congress, got elected, and urged Morelli to follow him to the nation's capital. That was thirty years ago, and Morelli had been one flight up at the Mayflower ever since.

George Tater arrived a little after seven-thirty four or five mornings a week, when he was in Washington, because he hated to shave and because you never knew who would be sitting in the other chair.

Bobby Morelli was just like his old man—knew when to talk and when to shut up—except he had never thickened up with hard physical labor. He pinned a crisp linen neck cloth snugly beneath Tater's chin and then swung the dropcloth around so it opened wide and flat and settled down softly over Tater's lap. Next he wrapped Tater's face in a hot towel—so hot it almost hurt, but not quite. Tater felt himself drifting away on the steam, with its faint aroma of cologne. But his mind was working.

Tater was on the prowl. He'd picked up a bit of a story about the Banca del Lavoro affair two months back, but it was mostly old news. Bill Safire responded with a column in *The New York Times,* sent Tater a glowing note, and took him out for a two-inch porterhouse at the Palm. No one else cared. A few months before that, Tater had been on the front page with a long-secret Israeli rescue of a downed pilot held prisoner in a basement in Beirut ever since Israel invaded Lebanon in 1982. The story took a lot of work and two trips to Israel, where Tater was always treated with cool circumspection as a reporter who could not be trusted to view things in a friendly light. But the rescue was essentially a one-day story—no follow-up. By the end of the week everybody at the *Times* had clapped him on the shoulder and said "Great story!" and that was it.

And before that—nothing for a year or more. He'd get a tip, get on the phone, get on the shuttle, meet somebody for drinks, fill his pockets with scraps of paper recording scrawled names and phone numbers, rush about looking for all the world like a reporter in pursuit of a story. Then one morning he'd wake up and admit to himself he was getting nowhere. This wasted year left Tater restless and short-tempered, full of vague pains and complaints, coming and going between Washington and New York, calling old sources, buttonholing people at parties.

"What is this?" said Morrie Bloom, who became Tater's editor at the *Times* after a string of blockbuster stories for the city desk. When Tater moved down to Washington he said he wanted to go on working with Bloom, and the powers that be broke all the usual rules and said okay. Everybody in the Washington bureau reported to a Washington editor—except Tater. Bloom understood Tater inside and out. They spoke daily, and Bloom prodded him without mercy. "We've got a front page every day, George," he said.

Tater made no excuses. Other reporters covered a beat: the White House, the Hill, race, drugs, the breakup of the Soviet Union, the hunt for a grand unified field theory in physics, whatever. Tater had no patience for looking into anything that didn't promise a story—not just a piece in the paper but an honest-to-God story. Tater himself did not like theorizing about the news business. He never made speeches or wrote articles for the *Columbia Journalism Review* or tried to explain what makes a story to classrooms of awestruck young faces. But Morrie Bloom at the *Times* and fellow reporters on the street who had heard Tater in full cry knew perfectly well what got his juices flowing.

The last really good story Tater had worked on was Aldrich Ames, the infamous spy who wrecked the career of one CIA director and nearly destroyed the Agency. Tater was the first to report Ames's flunked polygraph tests, the names of some of the Russian spies he had betrayed, and the failure of the CIA's mole committee to track him down year after year. From Day One of the Ames story, Tater was convinced there had to be a second spy in the Agency, some high official who had helped Ames acquire the bushels of secret papers he had passed on to the Russians. But there was no name, no incident, no date, no muffled voice on the phone late at night willing to contribute some fact to go on—nothing Tater could build a story around. The failure rankled still. He thought about it sometimes at night, the end of his cigar glowing in the dark.

Tater's idea of a story was quite exact. The major elements were a well-defended secret, something powerful men would run risks to protect, which at the same time threatened the placid assumption of the public that we live in a fundamentally decent world. The perfect Tater story upset everybody. As a young reporter in 1971 he had won a Pulitzer Prize with a string of pieces spread out over two weeks uncovering a secret American bombing raid on a town in Cambodia. A hundred civilians had died in ten minutes. But what made the story a sensation was Tater's proof that the raid had been personally ordered by President Nixon, that an air force chief of staff had knowingly delivered falsified documents covering up Nixon's role to the Senate Foreign Relations Committee, and that the chairman of the committee told him to do it—a fact Tater published several days *after* the chairman had expressed in the strongest possible terms the deep sense of personal betrayal he felt at this gross deception of the American people.

Some historians thought the story played an important role in the impeachment proceedings against Richard Nixon three years later. Tater didn't give a damn what the historians thought. What warmed him even after so many years were memories of the day the air force general hung his head in federal court and in a broken whisper pled guilty to six counts of perjury, the awful words—"guilty . . . guilty . . . guilty"—coming like the final gasps of a dying man. And the day when the wife of the chairman of the Senate Foreign Relations Committee, dressed in dark gray and dabbing at her eyes, announced that her husband had been admitted to Walter Reed Army Medical Center for treatment for exhaustion, the first stop on his road back to South Carolina. And the day, sweetest of all, when Nixon's press officer, his voice husky with the enormity of the confession, told not only the entire White House press corps but the whole country assembled in their taverns and living rooms, "Mr. Tater, I apologize. I was misinformed. You are correct. On the point you raised, the president, I am afraid, was not completely candid."

The glory of those moments had not dimmed in a quarter century. *That* was a story.

. . .

Musing on past triumphs only made the prospect of another aimless day more painful. Tater would go next to his office at the *Times* Washington bureau and check his messages. Then he would drink coffee and flip through the papers—*The Boston Globe,* the *Los Angeles Times, The* (London) *Times,* whatever else was lying on the big table by the front door. Then he would call someone for lunch—but whom? Tater hated to waste his lunch, an ideal time for nosing around in a man's professional life. But you needed a clue to get going properly, a trace scent of something in the wind. . . . For days past he had rummaged in his Rolodex for an hour each morning, hunting for a lunch partner who might conceivably tell him something.

Faintly through the towel, now rapidly cooling, came the sound of the door, then the voice of the elder Morelli: "Good morning, Senator. How are you today? Is it warm enough? Cherry, turn up the heat a little. Young Harry was in last week. Says he's going to be running your office back home."

Tater's mind was instantly focused on the question of identification: *young Harry? who's Harry? Senator Harry . . . Harrison. Senator Harrison Hawkins. Ahhhh.*

Bobby Morelli lifted the towel from Tater's pink face and, standing behind the big porcelain chair, began to rub Tater's jaw vigorously with both hands. Bobby's hands did not have the strength of the elder Morelli's but he was no slouch. Tater loved this part, just lying back, letting someone work on him. When Bobby was done he began to build up a lather in the shaving mug, using a big English brush of badger bristles. If the second barber chair had been empty at this point Bobby would have opened a conversation. Not today.

In a firm voice Tater said, "Nice to see you, Senator."

The tall white-haired man rolled slowly over in the next chair to look at him. He squinted, needing glasses.

Tater said, "George Tater."

"Of course," said the senator. "Getting old. Can't see anything anymore. Hard to get around."

"Come on," said Tater. "I was at that hearing a couple of weeks back when you gave Akins hell about MIAs."

"Akins, yes. . . ."

"You were like a prophet out of the Old Testament. He learned the meaning of the word *wrath* that day."

"He deserved it. He didn't think that photo proved anything. My God.

It proved there were Americans in Hanoi in 1975. *Two years* after they all came home."

"I thought that photo was a fake," said Tater.

"It was—but they didn't know it at State until much later. They sat on that photo for a year."

"Why?"

"You know, I don't understand it. Walter Akins is an honest man and a pretty good secretary of state. He was still in law school when that Nixon gang negotiated the end of the war. He didn't leave all those kids over there."

"It's been over twenty-five years," said Tater. "Those kids are in their fifties now. What do you think, Senator? Is there anybody still alive waiting to come home?"

"You want my honest opinion?"

"Yes," said Tater.

"I don't know. I really don't know."

"What I'm wondering is, have you got any evidence you can't prove one way or the other? Have you got any really good cases?"

"We have lots of good cases. Dozens."

"Yeah?"

"Absolutely. Some visiting agricultural expert says he saw a white man planting rice in the Red River delta. We ask questions. Hanoi says no such man. But our guy says he saw him, it was a white man, and the man looked at him in a desperate way. How can we ignore that?"

"Who was this agricultural expert?" asked Tater. "I don't remember reading about him."

Senator Hawkins rolled over in his chair to squint at Tater for a moment. "You know, George, I don't think I've ever seen your byline on an MIA piece. Why the sudden interest?"

"Truth?" asked George Tater. "I'm looking for a story—something I can get my teeth into. Nobody's been writing about MIAs lately. Maybe there's a new angle. If you were me, where would you start looking?"

"That's easy," said the senator, holding his head back while the elder Morelli drew a straight razor up beneath his chin. He had to speak through clenched teeth. "Get in touch with the National League of Families. If you'll call my office I'll have Grafton Morse give you chapter and verse. These are impressive people; they've been waiting for their men for twenty-five years. You'll get some heartbreaking stories from that outfit, believe me."

Tater was silent for a moment. In his view, heartbreaking was not a story. "You think State has been sitting on evidence?"

"They take their sweet time, but they hand it over eventually."

"Do the Russians know anything?"

"They might have once. They don't anymore."

"What about the CIA? Are they forthcoming?"

"They are. It was different before the Soviet Union collapsed, but they can't do enough for us now."

"Have they got a line into Hanoi?"

"I would say they keep pretty close tabs."

For a moment Tater was silent. The sound of snipping scissors filled the room. Finally Tater found the question he wanted. "What's Frank Cabot think—any chance?"

"Oh, you know, Cabot's a professional; the evidence says what the evidence says."

"Good man?"

"You mean am I going to give him a hard time over confirmation? No story there, I'm afraid. Ha-ha! You're going to have to keep looking. Frank Cabot and I are old friends. We've been to hell and back on the MIA issue. I trust him completely. I think he's a fine choice for DCI. You can take my word for it, George—Frank Cabot has no enemies on my committee."

4

When Senator Hawkins, freshly shaved and clipped, emerged from the side entrance of the Mayflower shortly before 8 a.m., his lean long-boned frame was bundled up in a fur hat of Russian sable, a cashmere scarf, fur-lined gloves, and his grandfather's greatcoat with the bearskin collar. Still, he shivered. He squinted against the snow as he crossed a dozen feet of slushy sidewalk to the car. Lamarr held the door open as the senator climbed in, then limped around to the driver's side. While the senator had been getting his hair cut, Lamarr had kept the motor running and the car heater turned on high. The temperature within was probably 80 degrees or more. Still the senator hugged himself in his greatcoat. "We're just two Georgia peaches, Lamarr," he said as the car eased away from the curb. "We don't thrive in this brutal northern weather."

"Big office or little office, Senator?" asked Lamarr.

"Big office, Lamarr—I've got paperwork today."

Hawkins took off his right glove, opened his greatcoat, and slid his hand in under his shirt between two buttons, resting three fingers directly over his heart. Sometimes an hour or so after breakfast Hawkins felt a kind of jingly-tingly feeling in his chest. Occasionally his right jaw would ache as well. He might also feel an uncomfortable pressure in his ears. Senator Hawkins had suffered a mild but nonetheless frightening heart attack a few years back, and he feared these sensations might be an early warning of a second event. His doctor back home in Savannah, a childhood friend named Wade Tilton, insisted that these symptoms resembled no kind of angina he'd ever seen. But the senator would not be reassured. When he seemed to be trembling inside—as he felt himself trembling now—it made him feel better to take his pulse, check the artery in his neck, or lay three fingers over his heart. He believed he had learned to perform these checks so casually and naturally that no one ever noticed.

Lamarr said, "Senator—it's kind of cold here in Washington right now. How about a quick trip home to check on the constituents? Just till this mess clears up."

"I've got too much work, Lamarr," said the senator. "In Washington everybody wants something, and this week they all seem to want it from *me.* Now the president says he wants Frank Cabot confirmed as DCI by March fifteenth. I can't boss the FBI around and tell senators what they can ask, but presidents don't understand problems of that sort. They just know what they want."

Hawkins was not a confiding man, but he was in the custom of telling Lamarr freely just about whatever was on his mind. Lamarr Stebbins was a local boy from back home, second son of a Savannah policeman, blindingly handsome as a youth, the only player ever to pitch a no-hitter for the Savannah High School baseball team, who lost part of a foot to frostbite in Korea. When Lamarr returned to Savannah, Harrison Hawkins was two years out of law school and running for Congress. Nobody got to be a sergeant in the Savannah Police Department without knowing something about politics, and Lamarr's father paid a call on the young Hawkins to request a job for his son. "My boy Lamarr is a steady driver and knows when to keep his mouth shut," said Sergeant Stebbins. "Also, he never forgets a name or a face." Young though he was, Hawkins realized this was not a trivial gift. He hired Lamarr, and they had been together ever since. It would be forty-six years in June.

The senator's heart skipped a beat. He slipped his hand from beneath his shirt and his coat, then felt his wrist for a pulse. A casual observer, which Lamarr was not, might have thought the senator had simply folded his hands in his lap.

"Young Harry says that fellow Wendell Dorsey could give you trouble in the primary," said Lamarr.

"I know, I know. Maybe we'll go down this weekend," said the senator. "Drinks at the Oglethorpe on Saturday, church on Sunday."

"Young Harry says Dorsey has been trashing big government and farm subsidies," said Lamarr. "You might give a talk on Monday. Mention the words *tobacco* and *cotton* and *peanuts.* Get on the evening news."

Lamarr knew plenty about politicking.

"Well, maybe," said the senator. "If I can get Cabot moving through channels."

The lobby of the Russell Office Building was nearly empty, a fact explained partly by the hour—8:15 a.m.—but mainly by the weather. The guards at the door all expressed surprise that the senator had made his way through "the blizzard"; a few flakes of snow survived the heat of the lobby on his hat and collar. One guard, a black woman with magenta lipstick, wished him a good morning and added that as far as she knew, there was only one other senator in the building. Hawkins inquired who that might be.

"Senator MacLaverty," she said.

"Ahhhh," said Hawkins.

He was not surprised. Brian MacLaverty, long known as "the other senator from Massachusetts," was the second-ranking Democrat on the Select Committee on Intelligence. If Senator Hawkins were to be defeated in the Georgia primary in June, or if he were to lose in the general election in November, or if he were to die suddenly of a heart attack (something Hawkins feared was far more likely), MacLaverty would succeed him as chairman of the committee.

When Hawkins got to his desk and checked his messages, sure enough, there was a handwritten note from MacLaverty:

Would like to see you this a.m.; will you be free at ten?

This irritated Hawkins. Of course he would be free at ten; he never made appointments before eleven and MacLaverty knew it. The senator snorted in disgust. His secretary, Rhoda Pratt, and his chief administrative assistant, Grafton Morse, waited patiently in front of the senator's desk while he sorted through mail and messages. "Shall I tell Mac okay?" asked Rhoda.

"Wait till we see what else we've got."

He knew he'd say yes, and Rhoda and Grafton both knew he would say yes, and Hawkins knew they knew. It was a moment of perfect communication and far from rare.

Lots of letters from home: please contact the Department of Agriculture; or Commerce; or the Bureau of Tobacco, Alcohol, and Firearms; et cetera, et cetera. He knew what they wanted at a glance. Also in abundance: invitations he would never accept but ought to regret personally. Invitations he just might conceivably accept. Congratulations on the brilliance of certain remarks made upon the Senate floor, or in any event so reported in the *Congressional Record.* Message from his wife, Lydia: Please remind Lamarr to pick up the cleaning. They had been married forever and left messages for each other half a dozen times a day. Message from young Harry reporting a maximum contribution from the PAC run by officers of the First National Bank of Savannah. Two or three heartbreaking letters from the wives or children of men who might have but did not return from Vietnam thirty years ago. Rhoda personally selected these letters from the many that began flooding in every winter as the anniversary came and went of the POWs' return. These Hawkins set aside to read carefully later; he would answer each one in longhand. Over the years he had written hundreds of such letters. Another message from Lydia: Please don't forget we are scheduled for dinner with the Wilsons at seven-thirty. *Please return call* from the president's chief of staff, Peter Schleicher.

Hawkins leaned back in his chair, thinking. He placed his right hand over his heart and lightly tapped his fingers once or twice.

"Will you get Schleicher on the phone? Then ask Senator MacLaverty if he'd like to stop by for coffee at ten."

Hawkins had no great liking but plenty of respect for the White House chief of staff. Peter Schleicher had worked for Norman Anderson since the early 1970s and had led him out of two or three scrapes over the years that might have blocked his long march to the White House. Hawkins met Schleicher first when Anderson was in the Senate and learned to trust the single-minded young man absolutely—within certain well-defined limits. If Schleicher, for example, said the vote on a certain bill was going to be 51 for, 44 against, with 5 still undecided, Hawkins knew it would pass. Schleicher could count. But if Schleicher said Anderson himself was leaning in this direction or that, Hawkins knew the vote was up for grabs and Schleicher was still looking for the drift of public sentiment. Therein lay the seeds of Hawkins's dislike. In the senator's view, those who serve elected officials were supposed to think sometimes of the good of the country. Schleicher concerned himself only with what would be good for Anderson. In addition, Schleicher was annoying on the phone.

"Thanks for calling back, Senator," said Schleicher, a few moments later. "The president has asked me to follow up on Cabot's nomination."

That was one annoying habit right there; it was always the president wants this, that, or the other—never Schleicher himself making the request. Nine times out of ten it was utter horseradish, but that tenth time was serious.

"Justice promises a quick FBI check; Cabot has been vetted and fluttered for years. There are no black marks on his record that we know of. The president wants this to sail through; he wants Cabot to be at the Brussels conference on terrorism next month with all flags flying, and that gives us less than six weeks. So the president hopes you will keep the pressure on."

"Of course," said Hawkins, preparing to enter upon a few general remarks.

"*But,*" said Schleicher. That was his second annoying habit. "The president is worried about Brian. He's worried Brian has got some ancient grievance or annoyance with Cabot that will slow down the hearings—"

Hawkins interrupted. "Is the president worried about anything in particular?"

"No no no no no—"

"Does the president know something I should know?"

"Of course not. We wouldn't have picked him. What's worrying the president is the Russia thing."

"What Russia thing?"

"All those years of beating the drum about the Russian strategic threat: pinpoint missile accuracy, 'backfire' bombers, Russian spies in the French government, Russian military spending, Russian spies in the German government—watch out for Gorbachev, it might be a trick—all that. You know how Brian feels about that."

"We all worried about the Russians," said Hawkins. "Nobody predicted the Soviet collapse. You can tell the president he needn't worry about Cabot's record as an analyst. He called them as he saw them. That's why I'm behind Cabot a hundred percent. Senator MacLaverty will ask a few questions to prove he's the smartest boy in the class, but that'll be the extent of it."

"Then press on," said Schleicher. "Keep us posted."

"Of course," said Hawkins, preparing to remark that he would be seeing MacLaverty in an hour's time.

"Thank you, Senator," said Schleicher and broke the connection without waiting for parting pleasantries. Hawkins found that the man's most annoying habit of all.

Just to one side of Senator Hawkins's desk was a deep, comfortable wing chair covered in red satin with mahogany ball-and-claw feet. It had been made in Savannah for the senator's great-great-great-great-something in the 1750s. Hawkins asked his assistant if he would mind changing the wing chair for the other chair, an armchair called a "great chair" from the Plymouth Bay Colony in the mid-seventeenth century, all knobs and spindles with a straight back and a hard oak seat, very rare, very valuable, very uncomfortable.

When Rhoda opened the door to show in Senator MacLaverty promptly at 10 a.m., Hawkins rose with a big smile, gestured toward the old armchair and said, "Please. Make yourself comfortable."

"Thanks."

"Can we offer you something? Coffee?"

When the chair had ceased creaking, and the coffee had been brought and served, and the door to the office had been quietly closed by Rhoda, and reports of health had been sought and given, and inquiry of wives had been made and answered, MacLaverty said, "Cabot."

It was no idle inquiry MacLaverty had in mind.

MacLaverty was a good deal younger than Hawkins, but they had been colleagues for more than fifteen years and understood each other well. Hawkins, for example, knew that MacLaverty had grown up in South Boston, had attended Boston College, had considered the priesthood, had a campaign war chest of more than a million dollars contributed by Boston real estate interests, fancied himself as an expert on China, and understood that he would never be president, which was more than you could say for a lot of senators.

Hawkins liked MacLaverty well enough but he was wary of him. Mac wanted the committee chair so much it was like a body scent. Sometimes

Hawkins wondered why he bothered to run again. He'd been in Washington for more than forty years, in the Senate for eighteen. There was no future for him here, just more of the same. If he went home to stay he could sip iced tea and read novels. But he told no one about these hesitations, not even Grafton Morse, who had been with him every day he'd spent in the Senate. Once or twice, Hawkins had been on the verge of telling Lydia he was thinking about going home and what did she think? But he never quite put it into words. He was afraid she'd jump at the idea and one thing would lead to another and he'd be on his way out of town before he really knew what he wanted.

But there was another reason he said nothing. Hawkins had learned a few things during his years in Washington, and at the top of the list was the importance of keeping your own counsel. If you want to make up your own mind in your own good time, keep it to yourself. One word in the papers and Hawkins would be fighting for his life. So Hawkins pondered on his own whether he should run again or go home to Georgia, because he feared it would somehow get back to Brian MacLaverty, who would use it as a weapon to bring him down. Everything was a weapon to guys like Mac. The confirmation of Frank Cabot would become a weapon in Mac's hands, if Hawkins let him find a way.

"Cabot is very much on the president's mind," said Hawkins. "I spoke to Schleicher this morning. The president is concerned that you will oppose Cabot on the basis of 'some ancient grievance or annoyance'—his words."

"Schleicher's words."

"Of course. But offered as the president's."

"Schleicher thinks I would try to hold up Cabot's confirmation just because I guessed wrong in New Hampshire?"

"Fears it, anyway. But I told him Frank Cabot has no enemies on this committee and we would move with dispatch."

"Of course," said MacLaverty, "but deliberately. The Director of Central Intelligence is a very sensitive post. This is the one man who must understand what is going on in the world. He's got to have a *feel* for it."

"Well, Brian, I don't think I would push that too hard. The DCI can't assign himself the job of knowing everything. That's why he's got twenty thousand people working for him."

"The big issues. The most important issues."

"Economic rivalries around the Pacific rim—I agree."

"Whether Russia is going to come apart completely."

"That's a big question, certainly."

"Do you know what my deepest fear is?" asked MacLaverty. "Do you know what I worry I'm going to find some morning in a banner headline across the top of the front page?"

MacLaverty leaned forward and looked at him intently. Hawkins was pretty sure the answer was going to be China.

"China!" said MacLaverty. "One of these days the Chinese army is going to cross the Amur River and make a grab for Siberia."

"Brian, please."

"China has got the world's fastest-growing economy; Russia is coming apart. And Frank Cabot was the last man in the CIA to see what was happening. We can't ignore this, Harry."

"Cabot's cautious," said Hawkins, "but he's a very able man."

"I think we've got to look into this."

"You can ask any questions you like. You know that."

"Harry, I want two days. I want the right to call three or four witnesses."

"Two days to explore it? Or two days to try to kill it?"

"Two days to explore it with an open mind."

"Oh, no," said Hawkins. "Oh, no. An intelligence analyst has got to feel free to say what he thinks. I'm not going to let anyone destroy Frank Cabot's career because he got something wrong. That would wreck the Agency for sure. I won't allow it. You can have two days to explore any question you like. You can call any witnesses you like. You can express any point of view you like. But I want your word you'll vote with the majority at the end."

"What if I feel that in good conscience I must abstain?"

"In that case, no witnesses."

"You drive a hard bargain, Harry."

"I'm trying to be fair to both of you. He's a good man. He deserves his chance."

"I should sit here and argue this out for the rest of the day. I don't think you're looking into this deeply enough."

"Fair enough. I'll tell Rhoda to cancel my appointments. I'll listen to anything you've got to say for as long as you care to say it. If you make the argument, I'll change my mind."

The great chair creaked as Senator MacLaverty shifted from one buttock to the other and back again.

"I'll take the deal," he said. "You have my word. I'll vote with the majority in the end."

. . .

After MacLaverty left, Senator Hawkins took his pulse and then buzzed Rhoda. "Sugarplum," he said, "would you please ring up Frank Cabot's office to see if he can stop by here around five this evening? And would you please tell Lamarr we'll be leaving on the late side tonight, so he'll need to pick up that cleaning now? And would you please let Mrs. Hawkins know that I will meet her at the Wilsons' at seven-thirty?"

Then the senator turned to the letters from the wives and children of MIAs and gave his full attention to their ancient grief.

5

The phone calls of congratulation had been coming in all morning, beginning at 10 a.m. when Frank Cabot told his secretary, Jane, to open the floodgates. In the four hours since he'd reached the CIA's main gate in the swirling snow at six, leaving Kitty at home in bed dead to the world, Frank Cabot had done all the real work he would get done this day—a steady reading of cables, signing of letters, initialing of reports, dictating of memos, returning of calls. He leaned back in his chair thoughtfully for twenty minutes at one point, listening while Bob Chase, the national intelligence officer for China, laid out his side of a quarrel with the air force about the accuracy of a new Chinese missile system. Not many people understood the argument and fewer cared. Cabot qualified on both counts and was the ideal one-man audience, having been through it all himself.

The NIO explained the dispute with great urgency while the sky grew bright over the Virginia woods surrounding CIA headquarters. Later in the week, Cabot and Chase would cross the river for a meeting at the White House with the National Security Council, where the Agency would have to defend its views before the president, and Cabot had not yet quite decided what those views were going to be—piss on the air force estimate or let them have it their way. The president's chief of staff, Peter Schleicher, would be calling to schedule the NSC meeting, and Cabot would drag out of him what the White House really wanted. Once that was clear, Cabot would decide how to play it. Until then Cabot was the ideal listener.

This was how most CIA officers knew Frank Cabot—those who knew him at all. He liked to push his oak swivel chair back, cross his legs, and tap his lips with a forefinger while he listened and asked the occasional question. His hair was white, but his face looked a dozen years younger than his age by the calendar—fifty-nine next birthday, in April. Cabot had listened to hundreds of briefings, and he came away from every last one of them with the answer to one question at least clear in his mind: Was the evidence open to interpretation, yes or no? Almost always the answer was yes. That fact gave Cabot quite a lot of wiggle room. Bob Chase departed at the end of his twenty minutes thinking Cabot was the greatest guy in the world.

Cabot sometimes said that the flower of his young manhood in the early 1970s had been devoted to divining the CEP—circular error of probability—of a Soviet heavy-missile system that the Americans called the SS-18. An early guess based on the rumblings of Cabot's gut and long nights passed in bull sessions with the Agency's telemetry nerds had been right on the money; a Soviet defector from the Kharkov Technical Institute had confirmed it. The Secretary of Defense had given Cabot a gold watch fob engraved with the CEP number—300.

"Dear God," Kitty had groaned over a nightcap when he tried to explain the argument. "What difference does it make?"

The difference, Cabot patiently explained at the time—until he realized his wife had quit listening—the difference was that Russian missiles carrying one-megaton thermonuclear warheads landed at least half the time within 300 feet of the target, not 600 feet, which meant they were targeted upon the very hardest of American aim points, which were American missiles in their hardened silos.

Or to put it another way, as Cabot had confessed late Saturday night to his friend and mentor Otis Jones, the difference was that the men who had argued for 600 feet now had offices without windows, while Frank Cabot was about to be the next DCI.

Jones had smiled thinly, the creases in his ancient cheeks deep enough to grip a dime. He had been around a long, long time. There were those who said Jones was nearing a hundred; others said he had not yet cracked ninety. Jones only raised his eyebrows when asked, which few dared. "I don't doubt the CEP helped," Jones said. "But what made the difference, Frank, was that small favor you did for the president when it counted."

That was Otis Jones to the core; he never forgot a favor and he never forgot an injury. Jones had been the very first to congratulate Cabot, if you didn't count Peter Schleicher, who told him what the president had in mind when he called to make the appointment, and if you didn't count

President Norman Anderson himself, who said thanks weren't necessary, Cabot's nomination was well deserved. Otis Jones had invited Cabot over for a drink that very night. How Jones knew was left unexplained, as always, but Cabot was not surprised. Jones had known what was going on in Washington for decades. With powerful friends in both parties and a reputation for discretion, he'd held some sort of job in almost every administration since the fourth term of Franklin Delano Roosevelt, and between jobs he'd been the sort of lawyer who never writes a brief, never appears in court, never shows up in a roomful of lawyers until the arguments have all been resolved. The work performed by Otis Jones was of a more delicate nature. He offered the name of someone who might help. He asked for a word with the man who could make a problem go away. He arranged a quiet lunch at the Metropolitan Club or a quiet dinner someplace where the woodwork was dark and the first language of the headwaiter was French or Italian. He penned short notes. He made phone calls. At the end of the year the partner's check made out to Otis Jones was always one of the two or three largest at a firm noted for the high monetary value it placed on access.

Cabot could hardly recall now when Jones had first entered his life—sometime in the early seventies when Cabot, a junior analyst in the Russia Division of the DDI, was beginning to make a name for himself as a hawk in the tiny circle of estimate writers cleared to see all sources of intelligence on Soviet missile accuracy. The intelligence battles of those years drew blood, and Jones was at the heart of them. He had an office in the Pentagon. He had known Nixon for years, he got along with Henry Kissinger, he never tired of warning the community of strategic thinkers that the Soviets were assembling the weapons and technology required for a bolt-out-of-the-blue first strike. Jones at the time was a lean tennis-playing sixty with the intricate wrinkle pattern of a man who spent summers on sailboats. He was not a tall man but his back was straight. He was unfailingly polite but never backed off an argument. Jones had no prepossessing title. His office was small; only one secretary reported to him. But the first time Cabot watched Jones run a meeting he knew the man would never fail to recognize an ally or a foe.

Jones did not use flattering words or make promises, but he drew men to him all the same. Cabot lingered after that first meeting and they spoke for a moment alone, sensing a community of interest that went beyond a command of technical detail. A week later Jones invited Cabot for lunch at the Cosmos Club. There was nothing like the Cosmos Club in Columbus, Ohio, where young Cabot had grown up with a banker for a father, but he was completely at ease at a table near the window in a room filled with famous faces and names he had only read about. There was no mystery about what Jones was up to; he was inviting Cabot to rise, and Cabot was accepting. They began to exchange notes and memos. They spoke frequently on the phone. One day the Deputy Director for Intelligence asked Cabot in a respectful tone what Jones thought about a certain point then raising temperatures in the Pentagon, and Cabot realized he had been taken under the wing of a powerful mentor.

Jones lived alone now in a big apartment filled with Empire furniture out on Massachusetts Avenue. His wife had been dead for a decade. His two daughters had married well. A Filipino ran his household but it was Jones himself, still erect in his late eighties, who welcomed Cabot at the door, took his coat, poured him a couple of fingers of twenty-five-year-old single-malt whisky, and led him to the fire.

"You've been up to the Hill many, many times," Jones said. "You've testified to everything under the sun, Frank. But you've never been confirmed. In a confirmation hearing there may be a great deal of talk but only one word matters—yea or nay."

Frank Cabot was born the same year Otis Jones joined the U.S. Strategic Bombing Survey: 1943. Cabot's only memory of the war was of the excitement throughout the house on the day his father returned from Italy. He remembered sitting on the beaming man's lap surrounded by familiar happy faces, and of course the two-year-old Frank thought everybody was thrilled with *him*. He had thought so ever since.

Dad prospered as a banker, made a lot of friends in real estate, moved the family from a big house to a bigger one, bought a second car, bought a third car. Whatever might make a boy happy was Frank's until he was sixteen, when things changed. It took Frank quite a while to understand what had happened.

Shopping centers were the coming thing, but Dad's business friends failed to guess correctly where the new exit on the interstate was going to be built. That was as far as his mother would say by way of explanation. Frank figured out soon enough the problem had been more acute. It wasn't just a bad guess; his father had tried to make it happen and failed. Jail was avoided only narrowly. A year later his parents separated, and a year after that his father was found dead in a California hotel.

Frank's mother worked as a legal secretary, raised her only child like a prince, and told him there was no limit to what he could do. He excelled in the local schools, got a full scholarship to Ohio State University, and went on to graduate studies in Russian at Stanford. There his doctoral thesis on the origins of the Cold War received high honors. In the air force his time was divided between Washington and Strategic Air Command headquarters in Omaha. Cabot never made a real friend until he got to college, and he never had a serious girl until he moved up to Washington after training by the CIA at the facility in Camp Peary, Virginia, which everyone called the Farm. It was December, the month Richard Nixon bombed the living daylights out of the capital of North Vietnam, and Cabot called the phone number of a girl a college friend said he might like. She came to the door wearing a coat as red as her lipstick. That night at a Christmas party in Georgetown given by the boss of his boss at the Agency, Cabot found himself sitting next to Catherine Ann Moore on a silk-covered sofa beneath a Winslow Homer in a gold frame and felt in his soul that he was making all the right choices.

Cabot thanked one caller after another in more or less the same words between ten and noon Monday, the day the news of his nomination as DCI appeared on the front page of *The Washington Post.* To his niece, Jenny, just back from a trip to California, Cabot confessed he had allowed himself to dream of this day ever since he had joined the CIA. He also took pleasure in thinking that his father, whose life had taken a wrong turn, would have been proud of him.

But most of Frank Cabot's callers were friends from college and air force days, old boys who had helped Cabot on the way up, military men whose budgets might depend on CIA estimates, and the scholars and diplomats who always came to listen when Cabot flew up for a breakfast meeting at the Council on Foreign Relations in New York City. Jane weeded out the people he didn't need or didn't want to talk to. She knew unerringly which journalists could be brushed off with a promise to pass on best wishes and which wielded the sort of power no Washington official could ignore. Most of the latter were titans of the airwaves with perfect teeth and personal publicists. But one or two journalists who mattered still actually put words on paper. Just before noon, Jane said, "Mr. Cabot, you need to set aside a few minutes for George Tater of the *Times.* I promised him you'd call back before twelve-thirty."

"Now's fine," he said, full of the glow of congratulations.

Cabot had never been the subject of a full-scale Tater story, but he had known men who were and had watched the lives of several destroyed by a week of headlines. There was always a rough justice to it; Tater picked his targets and did his homework. But it was a blood sport. Cabot didn't like it. Some men in town fed Tater stories to keep him at bay, but not Cabot. He answered a question with a question and then listened.

"The buzz is all good," said Tater on the phone. "They're all saying you're the right man for the job. You've got a lot of friends in this town."

"Thanks, George," said Cabot. "That's good to hear. Because if I have any enemies I know you'll find them."

"Ha-ha," said Tater. "Which enemies are you thinking about, Frank?"

"Ha-ha," said Cabot. "My enemies have all retired from the air force. Without the Russians we haven't got anything to argue about."

"They weren't all in the air force. Some were out at Langley."

"Oh, we argue," said Cabot, "but we're not enemies. Hawkins tells me not to worry. We've gotten to be pretty good friends over the years. He says he can explain anything to God except leaving one of our boys behind in Southeast Asia. But I've worked damned hard for him on that issue and I'm hoping the hearings will go smoothly."

"How about Brian MacLaverty?"

"Oh, you know the drill. Mac will find half a dozen ways to ask me how the Soviet Union could go broke and split up into seventeen pieces without my actually noticing. I'll give him my straightest face and confess I got it wrong, like everybody else in the world paid to think about the Russians. And he'll accept my explanations or he won't. But Mac's the person to ask about that—what does he tell you?"

"He says he'll have questions," said Tater, hurrying on. "Nobody rifling the till down at Langley? Nobody selling nukes to Iraq?"

"I'll call you first, George."

"No medals from Moscow? No secret trips with Aldrich Ames?"

"Who's Aldrich Ames?"

"Ha-ha," said Tater again. "No Swiss bank accounts? No secret wife in London?"

"Just one wife, George."

"I don't think I've ever met Mrs. Cabot."

"We aren't partygoers."

"Spook?"

"She's never worked for the Agency. I met her at a party in Georgetown. I'd just finished training. We talked about Winslow Homer. I fell in love. I'm telling you this on deep background, George."

"Ha-ha," said George Tater. "Kids?"

"Two boys now in New York City. One's on a tenure track in art history at NYU, the other is making a crazy amount of money on Wall Street."

"Spoken like a proud father," said Tater. "So what's going to be the tough question in the hearings?"

"I have no idea," said Cabot. "If you find out, let me know."

Among her classmates, Kitty Moore had a reputation as a quiet hard-working girl. She rarely went on dates and spent long hours in the studio. In Cabot's opinion she was the prettiest girl in town; he was crazy about her blue-green eyes, ash-blond hair, and milk-white skin. He liked her careless dress, distracted manner, and way of talking about what to put on a blank canvas. Catherine Anne Moore had been drawing and painting since her first Christmas stocking had included a box of crayons. She had talent. She drew with the stiff simplicity of an Edward Hopper, and she had an eye for domestic detail like Mary Cassatt. She sometimes said the best years of her life were spent in front of an easel before she knew what people were willing to look at. This was a way of saying that the kind of thing she painted was not held in high regard at Yale Art School, where Kitty spent two of the years Frank Cabot served in the air force. At Yale, Kitty was broken on the wheel of Josef Albers, who praised her sense of color but not the picture-making. The way he said the word conveyed implacable dislike. Kitty had little talent for theory or argument and she never found the right words to defend her idea of a painting as a kind of witness to life. That wasn't at all what Albers wanted. Inevitably she tried to please. She got as far as stifling her natural gift.

By the time Frank Cabot got out of the air force and finished his CIA training, Kitty was back home in Washington, nothing had taken the place of painting in her life, a bright young lawyer had bored her for a year with the details of a big case before government regulators, and Frank Cabot burned brightly with his passion for America's role in the world. She chose him without hesitation.

Nearly thirty years had gone by. They had moved three times but always to another house in McLean. The boys had grown up, finished college, and moved to New York, one to teach, the other to sell bonds, but they all still spent part of the summer at Kitty's family's place on the Outer Banks of North Carolina. Cabot worked hard and was often late getting home. After the first few years, Kitty rarely joined Cabot for social events in Washington. She began to harbor something of a dislike for the CIA. In Kitty's view, which she did not hide, whatever it was Cabot did there no longer had anything to do with America's mission in the world. This pained Cabot, but he knew there were some things he was never going to be able to explain. They led a quiet life. When Cabot got home in the evening he liked to read. He would listen absently when Kitty would talk about the boys or about the garden or about things that needed to be fixed around the house. At dinner with friends she would sometimes get going about the schools or something in the paper. She liked a drink, but so did he. Cabot felt things were under control.

George Tater was only one among many Washington figures who had never met Kitty. None of the intelligence officers and generals and congressmen and senators and committee staffers and White House staffers who peopled Cabot's working day had met her. Frank Cabot had talked to Senator Harrison Hawkins at least once a week for five years, but Hawkins had never met Kitty. Otis Jones had played a central role in Cabot's life and career since the early 1970s but he'd met Kitty only once, and she had little idea just who Otis Jones was. There was a line down through the middle of Frank Cabot's life; his home and family were on one side and everything else was on the other. It now occurred to Cabot that this fact must have been on his mind for some time—all these people were about to meet Kitty.

Cabot told Jane to hold his calls. He stared out the window for several minutes. The sky was still gray but it had stopped snowing. He could see figures sloshing through the parking lot seven floors below. He picked up the phone.

"Jane? Can you look into something for me? What do wives wear to confirmation hearings?"

Promptly at four fifty-five that afternoon, Frank Cabot's driver drew up in front of the Russell Office Building and Cabot made his way alone to the office of Senator Hawkins, where he was met just inside the door by the senator's secretary, Rhoda.

"Wait!" said Hawkins, as Cabot was about to seat himself in the oak great chair. Then, after it had been exchanged for the wing chair, coffee had been offered but rejected, the door had been closed, and the two men were alone, Hawkins said, "Now, Frank, I have to ask you in all seriousness—even though we've known and trusted each other for years, so please forgive me—is there any reason why you cannot be confirmed as DCI?"

"George Tater wanted to know the same thing."

"That fellow does not rest. I ran into him at Morelli's."

"So he said. I told him no. But we both knew I meant there was no cat with one paw already out of the bag."

"And he went away satisfied?" asked Hawkins.

"He went away," said Cabot. "I have to be honest with you, Harry. I've been in this business for three decades. They don't hire us to be Boy Scouts. I'm on the clean side of the house—I've never recruited agents or delivered bag money or run a secret war. But I've seen information used for purposes that weren't intended. I've sometimes pushed an argument a little beyond the edge of strict civility. Some skins in this town are pretty thin."

"I know that," said Hawkins. "And you've been wrong plenty of times, too. You don't have to worry about that."

"What about MacLaverty? He'll never forget I said the Soviet Communist Party was like Mount Rushmore—you might not like it but it was here to stay."

"Did you say that?"

"I thought it sounded good at the time."

"It does have a ring," said Hawkins. "But I've got a deal with Mac—he gets to call witnesses and grill you for two days, but then he votes with the majority."

"I can take two days."

"The question is, have you done anything that goes beyond permissible hardball as the game is played? Is there anything in your personal life? I have to ask this, Frank. Believe me—you don't want to be caught by surprise."

This question was hardly new to Cabot; he had asked it of himself many times during the weeks of delicate conversation with various assistants to the president, culminating at last in a meeting in the Oval Office. Cabot had been in the intelligence business for thirty years and he had done a great many things intended to remain secret forever, but he could not think of a single one he could be accused of having done on his own hook. The chain of command went straight to the Oval Office, and no president, or anybody working for a president, had ever asked Cabot to do something that was not intended for the good of the country. That's the way he saw it. So it was with conviction that he told Hawkins he felt he was about as clean as a career spook could be.

"I wasn't on that side of the house," he said again. "We don't use poison pens in the estimating business. I was utterly and completely wrong about Russia for three years, but there was nothing secret about it. Everybody in

Washington knew; they've been giving me holy hell ever since. It's all old news. I give you my personal word, Harry—I've tried to argue my views like an honest man—there isn't anything else."

"And your personal life? No business troubles of an inconvenient kind? Everything okay between you and the wife?"

"There are things that cause me pain in my personal life," Cabot said. "But nothing that affects my ability to be a good DCI, nothing that would ever come up in a confirmation hearing, nothing the *National Enquirer* would pay to know—no women on the side, no men on the side, no big loans from missile builders. I smoked dope when I was in college, but I told Tater that ten years ago and he used it in a story at the time."

"I remember that," said Hawkins. " 'If Cabot did it then everybody did it.' "

"Yes. That was a long day at the office."

"You know, Frank," said Hawkins, "I don't believe I've ever met your wife."

"We're not partygoers, Harry. But she's looking forward to the hearings. Front row center—the blonde in blue silk."

"I didn't know you liked blondes."

"There's only been one blonde in my life," said Frank Cabot.

"Well, all right then. That's that. I'll get you through. There's just one thing I want to ask of you in return."

"What's that, Harry?"

"Don't forget the MIAs. You're going to have a lot of people knocking on your door. That young man you've got working with us is great. He's a crackerjack. But if you quit paying attention they'll move him to another job in a minute."

Hawkins stood. There was a letter opener on the blotter on his desk. He turned it slowly with one finger as he talked.

"I was in the House in nineteen sixty-four," he said. "I hurrahed the Tonkin Gulf resolution. I went out to Saigon and got on the evening news talking up the war."

"It's not easy to get everything right," said Cabot.

"These weren't just opinions," said Hawkins. "I voted for that war. I pushed that war. When you're up here, you know, your door is always open to the home folks. I've had many a father and mother sit where you're sitting right now and tell me their boy didn't make it home. Most of them know what happened. Most of them took a flag-draped coffin to the cemetery and consigned their boy to the earth.

"But some of them don't know, Frank. They don't know if their boy is dead in the jungle or locked up somewhere in a bamboo cage. And it preys on their mind. They can't rest until they know. You're going to be one of the busiest men in Washington, Frank—what I'm asking is, don't forget them. Don't forget me."

There were tears in the senator's eyes. Frank Cabot was not surprised. Washington was a crying town. The snapping of a flag in the wind; a reference to *our boys, this hallowed chamber, the burdens of the Oval Office, the little people who make America great, the supreme sacrifice*; memory of the faithful service of the departed; the sound of a bugle blowing taps—all these brought copious tears to the eyes of the men and women who enjoyed the possession of power in Washington. Frank Cabot rarely joined in the tears on such occasions.

But the sight of the lean old senator with his silvery hair and his faintly palsied hand turning the letter opener, the glistening pool of tears in his eyes, the husky timbre of his voice, the pleading words—

Perhaps it was the moment, a profound ambition suddenly within reach, the weariness at the end of a twelve-hour day. With amazement Frank Cabot felt the tears coming to his own eyes. The rush of feeling was completely unexpected. His words caught him by surprise. For his own father at that moment he could have felt no deeper bond.

"Harry," he said, "I will never let you down."

A few minutes later Cabot was being driven through the streets of Washington. He called his office. "Jane," he said, "there's a young fellow working in Far East—Brad Cameron. Will you get hold of him? Tell him to be in my office Wednesday morning at eight. And will you call my wife—tell Kitty I'll be home by nine? I've got a few bases to touch."

Cabot checked his watch, then his pocket diary. All over town people of wealth and power were gathering in clubs, hotels, restaurants, embassies, living rooms. They came to talk, listen, check out the crowd, make an appearance, say a few words, show support, move on. Cabot mapped out a route home, three or four stops, twenty minutes each. He'd shake some hands. Everybody wanted a chance to meet the new DCI. Cabot thought of it as part of the job. He never knew when he might need these people.

6

Jenny Moore's bedroom was one helluva mess. She was only just home from California but her bedroom looked like a scene from an urban riot. Her suitcases were open on the floor, and the drawers of her bureau were all pulled out, and bras and slips and dresses clean and unclean were piled where she'd thrown them on the bed and the chair when she was looking for something to wear last night before going out to dinner with Brad. Now, on Tuesday morning, she needed a completely different outfit for lunch with Aunt Kitty and her favorite suit was still at the cleaners—along with a lot of other stuff she'd forgotten to pick up before leaving for California—and a skirt-and-blouse combination that would be second best was hidden somewhere in the back of her closet. She rummaged vigorously until she remembered—she'd left that skirt and blouse on her last visit home with Mom and Dad in Philadelphia. Jenny came back out into the middle of the bedroom and stood and thought.

She wondered what her friend Meg would advise. Meg was one of those people who always knew what to wear, what to order in a new restaurant, where to find a deal on an apartment, who knew some guy you might be interested in. Meg had been helping Jenny through the smaller crises of life since tenth grade at George School, which was a major crisis. Meg had stayed all four years; Jenny had left only a couple of weeks short of Christmas after a ghastly confrontation with the school's headmaster. She still hated to think about the hour in his office when he accused her of stealing money from another girl. Some fifteen-year-olds would have been struck dumb by the enormity of the charge; Jenny denied it nine ways and insisted on leaving when he refused to believe her. But Meg kept in touch, and three years later they ended up at Bryn Mawr together. Now they were both living in Washington and saw each other three or four times a week.

But looking around the room with Meg's eyes didn't help. In the life of Jennifer Thayer Moore this drill occurred at least once a day, sometimes twice. Jenny didn't like to be hurried and took her sweet time. This was her room and her stuff and her life and she wasn't about to neaten up or hurry just to please somebody else. Last night Brad had asked if she would move in with him—not marry him; he knew she wasn't ready for that—but he wanted to live with her and he wanted her to know it. Jenny was halfway through a *bistecca alla fiorentina* when Brad asked. She was touched. She was pleased. She was alarmed. She promised to think about it and she did think about it, and after about a minute of thinking she panicked. Jenny was not ready to start picking up her stuff and shopping for dinner and paying bills and asking the same person, month in and month out, What do you want to do this weekend?

Brad was wonderful, but Jenny's Aunt Kitty had married young and Jenny knew she regretted it—not the man, not the life lived with the man, but going straight from college to young married life with almost no life of her own in between. Jenny wanted an adventure. A week in California only stirred up deeper longings—for what, she wasn't sure. A husband, kids, and a dog; a house, a yard, and a bunch of friends with the same—someday, not now. Jenny didn't need any advice from Meg about this. She liked Brad well enough, but she still held back some large part of herself.

The digital clock read 11:10. She was meeting Aunt Kitty at Clyde's in Tysons Corner at twelve-thirty. Plenty of time.

At dinner the night before she had explained to Brad the workings of the black market in exotic wildlife. She would be moving into a new job at the Earth Defense Trust, making sure that key aides of key congressmen understood the need for laws governing international commerce in specimens and body parts from endangered species of animals. Gallbladders of bears prized by the Chinese, rhinoceros horns used for dagger handles by potentates along the Persian Gulf, lizard skin for handbags, elephant ivory, Siberian tiger skins, baby chimpanzees—it was quite a list.

"I couldn't believe the amount of money involved," said Jenny. "Millions. Nobody knows how much. But I can tell you where it goes—right into the pockets of politicians. I wish you CIA guys talked about *that* behind all those locked doors."

"We do," said Brad. "And drugs. And arms. And World Bank loans that bounce back to Switzerland. We talk about all that."

"Why don't you *do* something about it?"

Brad spread out his hands and looked pained. Where to begin?

"Oh, I know, I know. You don't make policy; policy is set in the White

House. I'm being unfair. I just don't understand why you want to work with those people."

"Your Uncle Frank is going to be *running* those people," said Brad.

"It's different for Uncle Frank."

"Why isn't it different for me?"

"His work's his whole life. Aunt Kitty says he was worrying about the Russians and their bombs the first time she met him."

"Well, I'm worrying about MIAs. What's the difference?"

"Those MIAs were all abducted by aliens."

"No," said Brad. "We're finding them."

"Dead."

"So far," Brad admitted. "But you never know. One piece of paper is all I need, and I just got fifty cubic feet of raw files from the DDO. Maybe I'll find something in there."

"The DDO?" said Jenny.

"The spooks. The clandestine side of the house. The Deputy Directorate of Operations. We've been having the same old argument for years. The DDO says they have no positive identification of MIAs. We say, What *have* you got? They say, We've asked everybody; they report no positive identification of MIAs. We say, What *do* they report? They say, You don't need to know that. We say, We'd like to make up our own minds. They say, Fuck you.

"But we keep pushing. And last week out of the blue Joe Flint quit stonewalling and handed over those fifty cubic feet of files."

"And you're looking for. . . ?"

"A clue. A hint. You know how it is when you lose your car keys—they're under the book on the table the whole time. Well, it's the same way with each MIA I keep thinking about. We're having dinner here in Washington, and I know he's somewhere in Laos or Vietnam right now, sleeping on a straw mat or cleaning out latrines."

"You really worry about this," said Jenny.

"You really worry about animal parts," said Brad.

"We're worriers."

"But we're not only worriers. We're friends and lovers, too."

"We're friends and lovers," said Jenny, "and I'm ready to go home and prove it."

Kitty Cabot was sitting alone at a table in the sun near the window when Jenny arrived. She had thickened in recent years, but her complexion was a rich creamy rose and her full lips were calm and moist. Some gray had joined the ash-blond hair, but her eyes were clear and her manner quiet; she seemed to be listening and watching carefully. It would be the rare man or woman who did not notice Kitty Cabot on entering a room.

Before Kitty on the red-and-white checked tablecloth was a short stout glass with a maraschino cherry and a slice of orange sitting among the ice cubes. "I thought I'd have a drink while I was waiting," said Kitty. "I'm so glad to see you—you're sweet to wear the pearls. They look so well on you. I loved them too."

As Jenny settled herself a waiter bustled up with a refill for Kitty, whisking the empty away. "My name is Ronald," he said, rolling the *r*. "May I bring you something?" Jenny ordered a glass of white wine and a bottle of Calistoga water. Periodically throughout lunch she would top up her wineglass with bubble water until the wine had faded to vanishing. Jenny didn't like drinking in the middle of the day.

"Are you ready for this?" Jenny asked. "Uncle Frank running the CIA?"

"Nobody can be ready for it," said Kitty. "But Frank's been living for this day."

Jenny did not doubt it.

When the families got together for Christmas or Thanksgiving, Jenny had sensed even as a child that Uncle Frank's mind was always on work. He brought wonderful presents and was very good at making sentimental or amusing toasts at dinner, as required, and he always knew about the things that mattered most in Jenny's life in any given year, but he was never quite a hundred percent there. The phone would ring and he would disappear for twenty minutes or he would get into a deep conversation with Jenny's father, Kitty's brother, about France or the two Germanys or missiles—she was the only kid in the fourth grade who knew what Euromissiles were.

Jenny remembered lots of moments of that kind—family moments interrupted by the demands of a job—but what she remembered best was a birthday party when she was nine or ten. Jenny and her cousin Richard had been born a day apart, in June 1974, and they often celebrated their birthdays together. That year two men came around the side of the house in McLean to the backyard just as Richard was groping his way forward, eyes covered with a blindfold and holding a paper donkey tail. Jenny was standing next to him as Uncle Frank stooped to kiss his son goodbye. Richard pulled down his blindfold with one hand and watched his father depart. "No fair!" shouted the other kids. "That's cheating!"

Aunt Kitty stood there with a strange look on her face, and Jenny looked from Richard to Aunt Kitty and back again. Richard looked like he was about to cry, but two minutes later he was laughing and jumping. It was Aunt Kitty's look that didn't change.

"Things come up he can't ignore," Kitty would say. "I've learned not to mind."

By the time Jenny was sixteen she knew that wasn't true. It was hard for her to be close to Frank, but Aunt Kitty was different. Bryn Mawr had been Kitty's idea, and all through college Jenny came down from Philadelphia frequently for weekends and Kitty would take her to the National Gallery or to plays or modern dance at the Kennedy Center. Kitty sometimes said she would have missed having a daughter if it weren't for Jenny. Once in a great while Uncle Frank came with them, but not often. He had reading to do. He had paperwork to catch up with. It was quiet at the office on Sunday afternoons, a good time to work.

The summer after Jenny's first year at college she went to Italy with Kitty. The boys were out west, so it was just Kitty and Jenny until Uncle Frank joined them in Rome for a couple of days before a conference of some kind being held in Vienna. Jenny and Kitty had been sharing a room in a *pensione* on the Via Margutta near the Spanish Steps. They had dinner at a different restaurant every night—sometimes grand ones like Galeassi in Trastevere but more often little *trattorie* on narrow side streets. They looked at a great many paintings in churches and at statuary in museums. Jenny had no great passionate interest in art, but she loved being with Aunt Kitty and she loved what Aunt Kitty had to say about what she saw.

At the Villa Borghese one afternoon they stood in front of an Etruscan sarcophagus for twenty minutes while Kitty talked about the terra-cotta figures of a man and a woman reclining on a couch. "How old do you think they were?" asked Kitty.

Jenny had no idea. They were adults obviously and they clearly weren't frail with age and they didn't have the dewy bloom of Jenny herself at eighteen, but that was as far as Jenny could go. "Thirty-five?" she guessed. "Forty-five?"

"It's impossible to say, isn't it? And what do you think they thought about each other?"

The figures were gazing into the middle distance. They had faint, mysterious smiles. "They're comfortable together," said Jenny.

"I think so too," said Kitty. "They are very, very comfortable together. They probably had their arguments about sex, money, and how to raise the kids—but they are comfortable together."

When Uncle Frank came, he and Kitty took a room for a Friday and a Saturday night at the Hotel D'Inghilterra a block away. At dinner on Friday night, Uncle Frank asked, "What have you been looking at?"

"Paintings and statues," said Kitty. "What have you been talking about?"

"Whither Europe," said Frank.

"I think," said Kitty, after giving her order to the waiter at Clyde's, "I shall join my niece in a glass of wine."

Kitty asked lots of questions: How was the trip? Had she talked to her mother in Philadelphia? Did she ever hear from her cousins? Was the sauce on the veal too bland? Was she still seeing that young man who worked for Frank? Yes? How was that going?

"He's work obsessed," said Jenny. "But so is everybody else in Washington. He says he loves me and he says he wants to live with me. Fear of commitment is not Brad's problem."

"What are you going to say?" asked Kitty.

"I don't know what to say," said Jenny. "I love him, but he's safe as houses. I still want to see the world."

"Your job seems to be getting you around," said Kitty.

"I mean something with a little more risk," said Jenny, "than conferences in a Best Western motel."

"I get the idea. Dangerous love affairs."

"A dangerous love affair would be just the ticket," said Jenny, "if nobody knew and it ended well. My choices are all so easy. I'd like a couple of hard ones to think about in my old age."

But in fact Jenny loved Brad as he was. She had once listed his virtues for Meg: He didn't talk about himself all the time. He didn't discuss things he planned to buy. He didn't describe elaborate plans for getting close to powerful men. He didn't draw diagrams on restaurant napkins of the layout of his office and how he'd claimed a desk in exactly the right place. His eyes didn't keep flicking toward the front door in restaurants or at parties to see who was coming and going. But he was so earnest about his work.

"I know the type," said Kitty. "They were pouring out of all the best schools in the nineteen fifties, coming to Washington to make the world a better place. Trust me, it rubs off.

"Ronald!" she trilled.

The waiter spun around in mid stride two tables away. Kitty held up her empty wineglass and shook it like a little bell.

"Maybe you're wise to hold back. Being an Agency wife can use a woman up in a hurry. Agency wives aren't supposed to tell anybody anything. It's funny—when you won't tell some woman what your husband does, she quits asking about everything else."

"You've always had lots of friends."

"Frank has lots of friends."

"But aren't they your friends too?"

"Sure—until they go off to Timbuktu. Sometimes they come back together, sometimes not. It's not like real life, Jenny."

"Well, I'm not ready for real life."

"I wonder if Frank is," said Kitty. "He's wanted this job since the day I met him. He told me so. We were sitting on a love seat in Georgetown. I thought he was crazy, but he said I was the most beautiful woman since Cleopatra. Who can resist that?"

"Uncle Frank can handle it," said Jenny.

"I don't know. The cheering stops when you get to the top. Frank thinks he knows what to expect, but he doesn't. They're going to go after him until they get him. I've seen it."

"But Uncle Frank hasn't got any enemies."

Kitty had a deep streak of pessimism. The thread of her own life seemed to have broken many years earlier, and she had watched the battering taken by half a dozen men who had run the CIA.

"The job makes the enemies," she said. "Once Frank takes that seat at the witness table, he's fair game. Getting confirmed can be an ordeal by fire. I've seen it. I get sick wondering where they'll go after him first."

On the way to the car, Jenny made a decision and offered to drive. Kitty declined. In fact she moved steadily and spoke clearly and smiled as if everything were fine. So they got into the big dark-blue Lincoln and left the parking lot. At the corner Kitty waited for the light and then turned right, taking the turn a little wide—wide enough, in fact, to make Jenny think they were about to clip the fender of a car waiting at the intersection. But there was room to spare.

The car picked up speed but Kitty was far from reckless; she held steady at perhaps twenty-eight miles an hour. "I know Frank," Kitty said. "He thinks he's on top of all the problem areas, what people want, how to say exactly what he means to say. What worries me," Kitty said, as she proceeded down the street, "is the stuff he thinks is dead and buried. I wake up at night thinking about it."

She turned to look at her niece. A cold light revealed every line in her face.

"Some little thing," Kitty said.

But Jenny was not watching her aunt's face. A green car was pulling out of a parking lot directly in front of them. Jenny saw everything clearly: a dark-haired woman at the wheel, a small child in back. The face of the other driver was turned away as she waited for a break in the line of oncoming traffic. Jenny tried to speak, but what emerged was like the sound she made as a child when the doctor held her tongue down and told her to say "ah"—a kind of strangled cry.

"What?" said Kitty.

The bumper and then the hood of the Lincoln bit deep into the side of the green car with a roar of collapsing metal. Jenny was thrown forward against her seat belt and snapped back, but Kitty, who never saw a thing, had not fastened her seat belt, and the impact of her head folded the steering wheel in two.

7

"Call me Myrna," said the woman when Brad arrived Tuesday morning. She was sitting at a long oak table in one of the secure reading rooms in the underground warren beneath the CIA known collectively as Records. Beside her was a rolling cart piled high with gray file boxes.

"I come with the files," said Myrna. "It's a package deal."

She had just a trace of an accent. She was stout, short, seventy-something—one of those retirees who hung on forever doing contract work. She wore a print dress and sensible shoes on feet that swung freely beneath her chair.

"Deputy Director Flint sent me down to help."

"That's nice of him," said Brad. "There's a lot of stuff to look through here. But to tell the truth I'm kind of surprised. I thought Mr. Flint didn't want us anywhere near his files."

"I believe Mr. Cabot has explained to him the importance of your work," said Myrna, "and that made all the difference."

"You've been working on MIAs?"

"I'm attached to a special study group," said Myrna.

"Far East?"

"Expediting," said Myrna.

"What's that?"

"Good question," said Myrna. "We often ask ourselves the same thing. And the answer is, How long have you been working for this institution?"

"Two years," said Brad, "almost."

"Hasn't anyone explained to you the primary rule of etiquette in a clandestine organization?"

"What?"

"All these questions. Don't you know we do secret work around here? I'm not supposed to tell you this sort of stuff until you take me out drinking. Such a *yekl* you are. It's my job to make sure you see everything you need to see and copy everything you need to copy. Is this so complicated? Pour yourself a cup of coffee. Take a seat. Get a pencil and a yellow legal pad to write on. Take off your coat. Loosen your tie. Get that box on top, the one that says LIAISON. Let's find this missing person you're looking for."

"Okay, Myrna," said Brad.

Once—only once, for perhaps half a working day—Brad thought he had found an MIA. Not an actual, warm-bodied, English-speaking, dog-tag-wearing former member of the American armed forces missing in action in Southeast Asia, of course, but something that seemed (for a few hours) almost as good: a photograph. A congressman on a junket to Hanoi had gone off with a tour group of French agronomists to inspect dikes in the Red River delta. A Vietnamese government photographer recorded the visit and the congressman was given a sheaf of 8-by-10 glossies on his way out of the country. The photos made their way to the office of the Senate Standing Committee on POWs and MIAs chaired by Harrison Hawkins. There the photos had been handed on by Hawkins's assistant Grafton Morse to Brad, one day the previous October, along with a bundle of other stuff. It took Brad a few days to get to the bundle and then it took him a morning to get to the photographs. Then his heart stopped.

In three of the photographs Brad could see on the edge of the group of distinguished visitors a round-eyed man in black pajamas and a conical hat who was a full head taller than all the other Vietnamese in black pajamas who were carrying hoes and looking interested. In one of the photographs the sun caught the cheek of the big man and revealed the dimple of a deep scar. Brad was sure he had seen that scar before.

By this time Brad Cameron had read the Pentagon's 201 files of every MIA. He had examined thousands of family photos. He had pored over thousands of news photos taken in Vietnam and Laos since 1973. He had collated thousands of snapshots of young men in olive-drab tank tops and crew cuts drinking beer, playing volleyball, hugging skinny Vietnamese girls, and leaning with a familiar proprietary air against planes, tanks, artillery pieces, and helicopters. In three of those photos—high school graduation, 1969; Marine boot camp, 1969; Danang beach party, 1970—a scar was plainly visible on the right cheek of a private first class from Evansville, Indiana, who had unwisely lingered behind a routine patrol in I Corps to take a leak in late 1970 and had not been seen again.

Brad had a good memory. He scouted up the photos of the Marine within an hour and immediately called his boss in the Far East Division, Randy Short, to tell him the spectacular news. Short, alas, had departed for lunch.

At this point the episode turned tender in Brad's memory. Instead of waiting for Short's return or confiding his discovery to some trusted friend, Brad did his best to alert the United States Government. He called a State Department officer to tell him to pull the file and get ready for big news. He called Grafton Morse in Hawkins's office to inform him that a positive ID was on the way. He called Frank Cabot's secretary in the DDI's office to leave a message that a positive ID would be on Cabot's desk before close of business at five. He told half a dozen guys passing his desk on the way to the men's room, "I've got one! I've got one!"

Brad found the memory of these follies unutterably painful. It was worse than his first high school dance at Boston Latin, and that was bad. He was on the verge of dwarfing all previous gaffes by calling an aide to Peter Schleicher in the White House when a merciful Providence at last brought Short back from lunch. Brad laid out the photos on his boss's desk. His hands were trembling with excitement. Silent moments passed.

"One problem," said Short.

Brad looked at him with lips parted.

"Our man's scar is on the *right* cheek."

. . .

The merriment in FE had been decently restrained, but the episode had made Brad cautious all the same. At Myrna's instruction he pulled down the gray file box marked LIAISON and looked at her expectantly.

"Talk to me," she said. "What exactly are we looking for? What makes you think the DDO has it?"

"My job," said Brad, "is to make sure the Agency tells Hawkins's committee everything we know about MIAs."

"And so far that amounts to . . . ?"

"Not too much. That is, nothing positive; we don't know about any MIAs or POWs still being held in Southeast Asia. But Hawkins and his committee hear rumors all the time. They're always very specific: somebody somewhere saw somebody who looks Caucasian. So his aide asks me what we know about the report, and I put the request in writing and send it around."

"You think Flint is holding out?"

"No. But *no* is all I get back: no, nothing found, no positive ID, no substance to report."

"So what's to complain?"

"There's got to be more to the story," said Brad. "I know the DCI on at least five occasions over the years has sent out a book message to all stations ordering a positive request for info on MIAs from all sources. This is bound to generate a ton of paper, and buried in there is what we really know about conditions in Vietnam and Laos and the fate of missing Americans. But Flint has refused to let anybody else have a look at this paper, period."

"You understand the problem?"

"He doesn't want me poking my nose in his business."

"No," said Myrna, "he doesn't want some little *pisher*—forgive me—making a list of every asset run by the Agency in Southeast Asia."

"What's a *pisher*?"

"Forgive me, it's a word that means the opposite of a wise and experienced man who can be trusted to handle the most serious and sensitive information securely and discreetly."

"*Pisher,*" said Brad.

"In here," said Myrna, tapping the gray file box, "is a lot of information that shouldn't fall into the wrong hands."

"Okay. So why has Flint decided to trust me with it now?"

"Good question," said Myrna. "But we haven't got all day. Our best bet is liaison, so we'll start there."

"Why liaison?"

"Such a *doppess.* I'm going to tell you a big secret. I can trust you, right? You're not going to blab it all over the place?"

"They can pull out my fingernails."

"I knew it. You're a good boy. Here's the secret." Myrna leaned forward in her chair and lowered her voice. "The way we find out most of the good stuff—*the other spies tell us*! That's it. Liaison with the Brits, the Israelis, the Australians, the Koreans. We go to their head office and they tell us."

Myrna pulled over the gray box and pulled out a thick sheaf of paper.

"Believe me," she said. "Anything we know, it's in here."

By the end of the first hour the pattern was clear. Some farfetched but not entirely ridiculous report would reach Hawkins in the Senate, and within a day or two it would pass through the hands of the Agency's MIA working group (now Brad, latest in a long line), which would draft a request for information from the DDO, and before the end of a week at most a formal response would come back with a terse paragraph or two signed by Flint or his predecessors over the previous three decades saying *nothing found.* But between the request and the response there were always additional, much fuller, often quite detailed reports to the DDO of contacts with foreign intelligence services. Often the chief of station (COS) himself—in Seoul or Bangkok or London or Sydney or Tel Aviv—would pay a call on his local counterpart. But what surprised Brad most was just how often the COS in Israel would see high officials in the Mossad seeking information on events halfway around the globe. Reports to Flint of these visits were filled with chatty asides and the passing on of good wishes and veiled remarks about ongoing matters of mutual concern. It was soon obvious to Brad that Flint as DDO had a very close and trusting relationship with the Israelis that clearly went back a long way; he'd been deputy DDO, and before that chief of the Middle East Division, and before that chief of station in Beirut and Tel Aviv, and before that a lot of other things, including deputy chief of station in Saigon. In every posting Flint had apparently been up to something with the Israelis, some joint operation, some exchange, some friendly informal relationship that he carried on to the next job.

Some of the earliest contact reports were on yellowing onionskin paper called flimsies, and others appeared to have been printed out on tractor-feed printer paper only that morning. Some had routing slips attached, some not. Many had comments scrawled in the margins. Brad sped through them, stopping whenever his eye caught a watchword—*MIA, Vietnam, prisoner.* As far back as you could go the Israelis seemed to know an awful lot of Russians, and quite a few of those Russians had been to

Hanoi. The Israelis knew a lot of diamond merchants in Amsterdam, and the merchants paid frequent visits to China, where the cutting of low-grade gemstones cost even less than it did in India. These Chinese businessmen seemed to pass surprisingly often through Hanoi as well, or so it appeared from the Mossad contact reports. Indeed, by eleven in the morning Brad had formed the impression that the Israelis knew somebody everywhere, and these somebodies did not hold back what they learned from their friends who had friends in the Mossad, and the Mossad in turn was generous with their friend Joseph Flint. Two or three times Brad remarked on the warmth of these exchanges.

"What's the word for guardian angel?" he asked.

"Now I'm a dictionary," said Myrna. "I think the word you're looking for maybe is *rabbi.* In certain circles the man who looks out for you and protects you and helps you get ahead is a rabbi. Your rabbi is Frank Cabot."

"Me? Cabot?" Brad was amazed.

"So they say," said Myrna. "I have no opinion myself."

"These Israelis," said Brad, "seem to be looking out for Flint. They remember his birthday, they remember his anniversary, they remember his kids, they remember all the good times they had at the *bazouki* place in Athens."

"You've only got half the exchange," said Myrna. "Flint remembers too. In this business all you've got are friends and a pension to look forward to, with maybe a secret medal."

"We want to know about POWs and MIAs. What do they want to know about?"

"Who's who and what's what. So many questions you have."

"Sorry."

"It's okay. We're all young once, thank God."

"How many boxes of this stuff have we got?"

"That cart—a few others. You're afraid you won't live so long? Use a little system. You sent requests? Check the answers, work backwards, don't read every word. You know what you want—it'll jump out at you, believe me. If it's there at all."

Brad followed Myrna's advice, checking Flint's responses to his own requests and making his way slowly back through time. Brad had been on the job not quite two years. Flint had been promoted to DDO nearly four years before that. Before him, other DDOs had handled similar requests in much the same way. The names changed, but the questions and the answers were all the same.

Question from MIA working group: What do you know about X—say, a road-building gang in the mountains near Lai Chau in the northwest of North Vietnam, where someone reported seeing Caucasian laborers?

Report from chief of station in Bangkok: Reliable source in Burma says Russian engineers in Lai Chau have taken to wearing black pajamas but do not *repeat* not use picks and shovels or speak American.

DDO answer to MIA working group: Believe no substance to report of Caucasian laborers.

So it went: the same story, over and over again. You couldn't fault the official reports from the DDO; they passed on accurately the substance of whatever had been learned. But it was the reports from the field, in all their wayward contingency and salty detail, that gave you a feel for the real world where an aging American prisoner of war, taller by a head than the gawking crowds that gathered around every round-eye, would be as conspicuous as a feathered Indian chief at an office picnic. Brad had always known this in a theoretical way. The DDO files made him feel silly. At two in the afternoon he finally took a break for lunch, called Jenny, and left a message on her answering machine of which the substance was: working late, dinner at nine?

In the cafeteria, Brad ran into his friend Hugh Diamond. "Seen the paper today?" asked Hugh. "Cabot can do no wrong. Safire calls him a spook's spook—balls enough to take a risk and be wrong. Translation: Don't give him a hard time for being a doofus about the Russians. The anointing begins."

"You think it's a sure thing?" asked Brad.

"In this town," said Hugh, buttering his bread in his meticulous way, spreading it thin into the corners, "in this town everything's a sure thing, no problem, piece of cake—until the pissing starts. But Cabot's always been a kind of golden boy. Iran-Contra, arms to Iraq, the infamous Aldrich Ames—they never laid a glove on him. So if the president wants him, the president can have him."

He looked over the top of his glasses at Brad.

"What are you finding down there in the bowels of the org?"

"A lot of Vietnamese who look like the boy next door squinting into the sun."

"It's funny work, isn't it? You're the apple of Cabot's eye because you make sure nobody will find people who aren't there."

"I'd like to find one," said Brad.

"We all felt that way once," said Hugh. "The big discovery. The perfect spy. First call on the next leader of Russia. But in this business it's what you find that brings you grief. You'll get a lot farther by telling people it isn't true, it isn't going to happen, there's nothing there, report unfounded."

"No wonder they love me," said Brad. "I haven't found a damned thing in two years."

"Count your blessings," said Hugh.

Back at work following lunch, Brad pulled down another box of liaison paper. Myrna worked across the table, humming to herself. After thirty or forty minutes, Brad finished one box and commenced another. Nothing jumped out at him. So it went. It was peaceful work. Slowly the world of the clandestine service took on character and detail in his mind: the office squabbles, the broken air conditioners in tropic cities, the new guys who didn't work out, the marriages coming apart, the sleek local gentlemen who knew too much of interest to be disturbed in their pursuit of business, the marine guards quietly bailed out of local jails, the stations where nothing happened, the stations where too much happened, the nuances of relationship among men on their way up or on their way down. Running it all over the last six years was Joe Flint. The man exercised control with the ease of a concertmaster.

Then late in the afternoon something in a memo caught Brad's eye. He found himself staring at a scrawled name: "Avi the elder."

Avi the elder.

The memo in its entirety read:

> Wed 6 Jul. Jim called 10 am—says Avi the elder came by w imp news on sens matter, suggests mtg his place this pm—said I was free—?? TT

Brad stared at the memo for the better part of a minute without a trace of conscious thought or question. Then he asked aloud, "What's Avi?"

"Short for Avraham," said Myrna.

Brad checked the dates on a couple of previous documents in the folder. Letter to DDO of July 5. Memo of July 5. Outgoing cable of July 5. All from 1977.

Brad went back to a box he'd already checked, flipped through the folders again, and began going through messages slowly one by one until he found the one he was looking for. Copy of a cable. Deputy chief of station

Tel Aviv J. Y. Flint to DDO, 4 January 1978, report of liaison meeting with Mossad PLO analyst Avraham Lipsky. Third paragraph:

> On separate matter, Avi's father stopped by with further vague news of construction at Kamchatka tracking station from debriefing recent camp arrivals—adds little to what he gave us last fall. Message to you from Avi, the elder: What should he tell his source about the rara avis in Akmolinsk? Source extremely anxious at lack of news and threatens call to new journalist friend on *Ha'aretz.* Suggests mutual friend as channel for answer.

"Where's Akmolinsk?"

"Never heard of it," said Myrna. "Russia, probably."

"Akmolinsk," said Brad. "Akmolinsk."

He reached for the phone and dialed four digits. "Hey, Maria—Brad. Is Hugh there? . . . Hugh? It's Brad. I've got a question. Akmolinsk. Why do I know Akmolinsk? Where is Akmolinsk?"

After he hung up he turned to Myrna. "It used to be the site of a labor camp, on the Ishim River in Kazakhstan. My friend Hugh tells me a lot of writers died there at the beginning of the war. He says prisoners there called it the last stop before the moon."

"So?"

"So what kind of rare bird did they have in Akmolinsk?" He pushed the two documents about Avi the elder across the oak table.

"Such luck you have!" said Myrna. "It's the *Russians* have the MIAs! No wonder we've been getting nowhere."

"The timing's right," said Brad. "Nineteen seventy-seven."

"Sure," said Myrna. "The Vietnamese set up a big prisoner camp in Kazakhstan. Who'd have guessed?"

"All right, all right," said Brad. "Who's TT?"

"Retired. Out in Falls Church someplace."

"But who is he?"

"Terry Tyler. Oldest of the old boys. Flint included him out when Gates was cutting the budget."

"Friend of John Manley?"

"You could say that."

"You know him?"

"I knew him."

"You liked him?"

"I liked him."

"You trusted him?"

"He was my *donstairsiker.* Same apartment building. We didn't work together. He was in the office. I knew him. I liked him. Sure, I trusted him. I trust you. What do you want?"

"His phone number."

"I told you—Falls Church. What a day! I got to go, big date tonight! See you tomorrow." She gathered up coat and bag and was gone.

Brad looked up the number and dialed. Tyler was mute as a post until Brad mentioned Myrna's name. "All right," he said then. "Tonight's fine. But I'm busy till later—my daughter's coming for dinner. Eleven, maybe? Midnight? Don't worry. You come when you're ready, I'll be here. Since I quit drinking I stay up all night."

Before leaving the building Brad stopped upstairs at his desk and called Jenny again. He told the answering machine he was leaving the office and heading home. An hour later he told the answering machine he *was* home and he was getting hungry. At nine he told the answering machine he was going to pick up some dinner at the Chinese take-out place but would be back soon. On his return the phone was ringing.

Jenny's voice was shaking. "I'm at Georgetown Hospital. I'm okay, it's Aunt Kitty—her neck may be broken. She's on a respirator. I'm okay, don't worry. I'm fine.

"But I'm stuck here. My car's at Kitty's. I hate to ask, Brad, I know it's late. Can you pick me up?"

8

As dusk settled over the city that Tuesday evening, George Tater put his notebook in his pocket and left his office in search of a drink. Yesterday's wet snow had turned to rain, and by the time Tater reached the street, Washington was awash in six inches of slush. Traffic moved at its usual crawl. Tater turned up the collar of his double-breasted camel's hair topcoat, pulled the rim of his cap, a gray tweed, down over his eyes, and, squinting into the rain, headed up toward the Hay-Adams. Tater had owned his coat and cap for a dozen years. They had cost a fortune but Tater had no family, no expensive hobbies, and no fears for his old age, which had already been handsomely provided for, and he believed that a man in a two-thousand-dollar suit was always one up on the world.

George Tater was a creature of habit. He was generally dating two or three different women who had already had enough of marriage—women who liked talking as much as they liked sex. But tonight he was alone. He had spent the critical afternoon date-making hours on the phone with the old boys, asking about the intelligence career of Frank Cabot. He took copious notes: born and raised in Columbus, Ohio; Ph.D. in Russian studies at Stanford; Air Force service; something about a big intelligence fight over a Russian missile back in the seventies; longtime intimate of legendary Washington fixer Otis Jones; favorite of the Council on Foreign Relations crowd, et cetera, et cetera. The usual Washington web of friends and jobs. It was Tater's habit to read over his notes and underline the important stuff with a red ballpoint pen. The only name he had underlined by late afternoon was Otis Jones, a man he had been wondering about for years.

Between calls, Tater put his feet up and browsed the *Post*. He paused at the Style section to read Faith Osborne's take on Frank Cabot. She wrote twice a week under the title CITY WOMAN. The *Post* had a strict policy against running photos of columnists, so few in the nation's capital would have recognized Osborne in the street. But Tater had a picture of her in a desk drawer: sensitive mouth, warm direct look, shoulder-length dark hair tucked behind her ears. Some people thought her good-looking. Tater would never have admitted he was one of them. About Faith Osborne he had very mixed feelings. NEW AGE HITS THE CIA, read the headline.

"Jesus Christ," said Tater.

> The Cold War is finally over [Faith began]. What used to be called a decent man has been asked to run the spies.

Tater groaned aloud.

> Cabot has tracked down every rumor of POW/MIAs as if his own son or daughter were among the missing.

"What daughter?" spat out Tater. "There *are* no women MIAs."

> It is no accident that the last remnants of anticommunist paranoia have fled out the back door with the bold march of women in through the front.

"Oh, my God," Tater groaned.

> Human rights, women's rights, and American national interests are all served by President Anderson's nomination of Frank Cabot.

"Give me a fucking *break*!"

Women . . . compassion . . . justice . . . Tater could read no more. He threw the paper violently to the floor. This was classic Osborne, and it made Tater crazy. What was worse, Faith knew it. They had dated for a few months some years back, but they spent all their time arguing. Nothing made Tater madder than lies in good causes; Faith promoted anybody trying to make the world a better place. The endless disagreements soon killed the romance. There was no angry break—it just stopped, and now when they met, which in a town as small as Washington was inevitably often, they both tended toward irony and sarcasm.

By the time Tater felt the stirring of desire for a drink, it was on the late side for calling one of the women he was currently dating and, besides, he was preoccupied with thoughts of Frank Cabot. Boy Scouts did not thrive in Washington; it wasn't sensitivity to women's rights that had elevated Cabot above his meat-eating rivals. Tater knew as a matter of course that some serious careerism lay behind Cabot's nomination. Otis Jones was in it somehow. Cabot must have promised something the president really wanted. Tater could feel a story coming on, the way other men sense the onset of flu. *If I have any enemies I know you'll find them,* Cabot had said over the phone. The voice conveyed the serene good humor of a man free of worry, but in Tater's experience no man could fully resist the impulse to name the thing he feared. Tater had a wolf's nose for the odors of fear, injury, and vulnerability. "I know you'll find them," Cabot had said. His words were like drops of blood in the snow.

But making his way up the street toward the Hay-Adams, bent into the wind, collar turned up around his neck, cap low, high-stepping in a futile attempt to keep the freezing slush from topping over into his shoes, George Tater wasn't thinking about the tender places in Frank Cabot's past. That was unfolding below the level of Tater's consciousness, in the primitive recesses of his brain. What he was thinking about was a drink.

Tater's day was over; he could have exactly what he wanted, as soon as he knew what he wanted.

Martini. Straight up.

After Tater had shaken off his cap, and his coat was hung up on a wooden hanger, and he had one foot comfortably up on the brass rail of the bar, he gazed solemnly for a considerable time at the martini glass in front of him. The glass was beaded with moisture. Three pearl onions pierced by a red toothpick stood in the glass. No bartender ever informed Tater twice that he was in point of fact ordering a Gibson. Tater didn't like the word *Gibson.* He liked the word *martini.* He liked to think about the first taste before he took it.

"George Tater!"

Tater picked up the glass by the stem and took the first drink, sucking it in. It swirled down around the base of his tongue, gently nipping. The teams playing tug-of-war with all the muscles in his back slowly let go, and some part of his mind popped above the sea of quotidian anxiety and smiled. From experience Tater had learned that he could not repeat this sensation for twenty-four hours. He savored it with a tranquil soul.

"Someone told me you were on the West Coast, George, some sort of Hollywood exposé—Sony? MGM?—something like that."

Tater turned to his right with a warm smile. Richard Kramer. Harvard '64. White wine drinker.

"Al Scarpi, maybe. I think he said you were working on something out there. Ran into him at a dinner for Helmut Kohl at the Council—small group—just a few inky wretches from the writing press being polite to a hero of yesteryear. I asked him where you were. I haven't seen your byline for months."

Time magazine. Chief diplomatic correspondent. Hair parted in the middle. Double-breasted suits tailored in London. Another man who believed in the power of clothes, but a little too formal, in Tater's view.

"Waiting for Faith Osborne. Off to the Kennedy Center—visiting Bolshoi group. You working on that Middle East deal, arms and all that?"

Covered the White House two years out of Harvard. Failed to recognize the name of Tater's Texas college. Now traveled the nation and the world and wrote an occasional highly polished twelve-hundred-word essay. The new China. The new Russia. What the president ought to do now. Whither Europe.

"Believe me, I understand," Kramer persisted. "The Russians and the spooks are all quiet as little mice. I had to find a new beat too. Keeping the American Dream alive in the twenty-first century."

Major asshole.

"Don't laugh. The American Dream is what keeps us all going."

Faith Osborne and Richard Kramer. The perfect couple. George Tater spoke. "You working on a big dream piece, Richard?"

"An essay," said Kramer. "Next issue. What's your quarry, George? You haven't done a CIA story in years. You used to be the terror of the Agency—they had guys out there who did nothing but keep track of what you were up to."

"Who told you that?"

"I don't think it's a secret. You're a member of the Council, aren't you?"

"I belong," said Tater. "I don't go."

"Well you *ought* to go. I was part of a little study group that met last spring on the old East Bloc intelligence services. Lot of very solid, useful stuff. Guest speaker simply mentioned in passing that much had changed—for example, the Agency used to track American reporters. One or two of us pressed pretty hard on that and he said yes, he had you in mind. Just a little informal check on who you were calling up and what you were asking about."

"Who was it, Richard?"

"Old boy."

"Tell me, Richard."

"I don't suppose he would mind. Man in the news. Frank Cabot. Soon to be the new DCI. Said they quit worrying when they finally convinced you they weren't a threat to the Constitution."

"I wonder," said George Tater, "why Cabot thinks I was convinced."

He ordered a second martini. Richard Kramer had barely touched his white wine. Tater pulled out a gold cigarette case, tapped an unfiltered cigarette on the bar to settle the tobacco, and lit it with a wooden match. He knew Kramer didn't smoke. The fact was, nobody smoked, which was half the reason Tater still did. He took a long slow drag, let the smoke emerge, sucked the dense swirl back up through his nostrils. The smoke seemed to disappear into his body. When he exhaled at last only pale wisps of smoke emerged.

"You know Cabot?" Tater asked.

"We talk from time to time."

"What do you think?"

"Very solid guy. First-rate education, Stanford and Oxford. Fluent Russian. I met him first in Switzerland in the seventies when he was on the

SALT team. Cabot knew all the Russians, and he knew every draft of every paragraph in the agreement, and you could talk to him. Very straight shooter. A lot of the negotiators would bullshit you, but not Cabot."

"Who brought him into the Agency?" Tater asked.

Kramer looked at Tater for a moment, gently swirled the wine in his glass, took a small sip. "I don't know. I have no idea. Some professor at Stanford, perhaps."

"Who was his boss in Geneva?"

"Otis Jones was running the show."

"Wasn't Jones Assistant Sec Def for International Security Affairs under Reagan?"

"Yes," said Kramer.

"Maybe I'm wrong," said Tater, who liked to rub things in, "but wasn't Cabot the Agency's liaison with the National Security Council during Reagan's first term? Wasn't Jones the one who raised so much hell about Russian violations of the ABM treaty? And weren't Cabot and Jones the last holdouts on the menace of the Russian bear?"

"It all rings a bell," said Richard Kramer, looking into his glass as if a tiny gemstone might be hiding there. "You've been doing your homework."

"So how would you play it?" George Tater asked.

"I don't know: Area studies comes into its own," said Kramer. "New wave of bright young men—analysts with clean hands—rise of the intelligence professionals. That sort of thing."

"Sounds like something for *Time.*"

"Already written," said Kramer.

"Guess I'll have to dig up something different," said Tater.

"Good luck. Cabot's the cleanest man in town. You'll grow old trying, George."

"Maybe," said Tater.

Kramer raised his hand to wave across the room. "Faith!" he called out. Then he turned to George Tater. "Faith's a big fan of Cabot," he said.

"So I read," George Tater said.

"Lays it on a little thick, perhaps," said Richard Kramer.

George Tater smiled thinly. "Nothing fishing waders can't handle."

Faith was making her way across the room, shaking her hair and unbuckling her trench coat, a tall, slender, dark-haired woman carrying a shoulder bag of butter-soft leather with a brilliant brass clasp. She placed a hand on Richard Kramer's arm. "Richard, darling!" She gave him a quick small touch of her cheek. "God, what a night! Very slow going—we can't linger.

She looked coolly at Tater.

"George," she said, with a nod of the head. "I haven't seen you, and I haven't read you since—what? That big bank thing. Whose scent are you trailing now?"

"George has got his periscope on Frank Cabot," said Kramer.

"I didn't say that."

"I suppose," said Osborne, "you've been flailing the air about my Cabot column."

"Oh, no," said Tater. "I love your prose, Faith."

"You are such a hypocrite."

"Nobody else could have written it," said Tater. "Great stuff."

"You are such a liar," said Osborne. "You have *never* finished anything I ever wrote."

"I finished this," said Tater. "But, Faith, I confess—there wasn't much news in it."

"Here's some news," said Osborne. "Cabot's wife was nearly killed in a car crash in Tysons Corner today. She's in Georgetown University Hospital."

"Georgetown," said Tater. "Are you sure?"

"I'm sure."

"Who was driving?" asked Tater.

"I don't know. Some stringer phoned it in from Virginia. They were checking it out when I left the paper. Richard?"

They bustled for a moment with money, coats, hats.

"Thanks, Faith," said Tater.

"Show some mercy," said Osborne.

George Tater watched her cross the room toward the door. He loved the way she walked. She was smart. She knew her way around. If only she took a little interest in *news.*

Tater stood alone at the bar for twenty minutes, slowly finishing his second martini. Then he went out into the hall to find a pay phone. Information gave him the number for Georgetown. When the hospital answered, he asked for the chief of security. A man came on the line.

"This is George Tater. I'm on the national security desk. We have an important security question to deal with here. You folks admitted the wife of a high government official this afternoon—an accident victim, Catherine Cabot. She's probably in intensive care. Her husband is CIA. We may need to make urgent contact with him in the course of the evening. I assume there's no phone by Mrs. Cabot's bed—okay—but there's a waiting room nearby; I'll need the extension for that. . . . And the name of the doctor? . . . Yes. And the attending nurse? . . . Yes. And the nurse on the floor—would you please give them my name and let them know I may be calling, and I may have to come by later in person? . . . That's right, T-A-T-E-R. George Tater. If you need to reach me, here's my number."

Tater then called his answering service and instructed the operator on duty to forward any messages from Georgetown immediately to the cell phone in the pocket of his overcoat. In the restaurant, he ordered a Delmonico steak, rare, and a large bottle of Perrier water.

Boy Scout gets nominated to top job at CIA. Wife nearly kills herself in car accident. Something going on here, thought Tater.

9

During the first hour Frank Cabot talked to half a dozen doctors and nurses, answered the questions of aides, called his office twice, and watched the green spiky lines on the monitor that tracked his wife's pulse, blood pressure, and oxygen saturation. Her hand in his was warm and motionless. If you had asked him who else was in the hospital room and the small waiting room just outside, he could not have told you.

Clear plastic tubes entered Kitty's nostrils, and clear liquids dripped from clear plastic bags into a network of tubing connected to a needle in her arm. A stiff white collar held Kitty's head and neck rigid. One of the drip bags contained a new miracle drug that would keep her from being paralyzed from the neck down—if it worked. Kitty had not moved since her arrival at the hospital, but she was not conscious either and the doctors did not yet know if she had suffered extensive nerve damage or was only comatose. The miracle drug was just in case. Kitty's personal physician, who had been waiting at the door when the ambulance arrived, had assured Cabot that the potential side effects of the drug were small potatoes and he shouldn't worry about them. The danger justified the risk.

Cabot nodded his head and looked as if he were carefully absorbing what the doctor was telling him, but he was not; he was trying to make sense of a feeling that he had been in this room before.

After a while Cabot followed his niece from Kitty's bedside to the couch in the small sitting room next door. There he could still see his wife in bed and watch her breathing. "Are the boys coming?" Jenny asked. She liked her two cousins, trusted their good sense, wished they were already here to squeeze Aunt Kitty's hand.

"They called a little while ago," Cabot answered. "They're catching the last plane. They'll be getting here late tonight. I have a feeling," he added, very much in the manner of a man fully aware of what was going on around him, "that this is going to be a long night."

He had been in this room, he had sat on this couch, he knew just where the nurses' station was down the hall, he had made numerous phone calls from the white phone on the table next to the couch, he had stood next to that same hospital bed for hours—he was sure of all of this. His face knotted in concentration as he tried to remember why this seemed so familiar.

"It's going to be all right, Uncle Frank," said Jenny. "The doctors say the fact she's breathing normally on her own is a very good sign."

"Yes," said Frank Cabot, with a wan, distracted smile.

Then he sighed and really smiled.

Of course! This was Bill Casey's room fifteen years ago. Casey ended his life and his tenure as Director of Central Intelligence in this very room, slowly failing over a period of weeks after a series of strokes and surgery to remove a brain tumor. Bill Casey, last of the gung-ho vets of World War Two, last of the cowboys. It was Casey who led the CIA to war in Afghanistan and Nicaragua and nearly brought the Agency to grief and left Frank Cabot and every other high CIA official with a lot of unanswerable questions that dogged them all through the last third of the 1980s. Casey lay in his bed in that very room while Cabot sat on a stool nearby with a pad and pencil, ready to write down Casey's instructions to the Agency in the event he should understand them.

Not easy! All his adult life Bill Casey had suffered from a unique neurological impairment which made it almost impossible for him to speak clearly. The words bubbled like coffee in a percolator. But like deaf people who hate to be reminded of their deafness, Casey hated to be asked to repeat himself. Once was okay. Twice got you a growl of impatience. Many a promising career in the early 1980s had been cut short at the Agency when some young fellow straight out of Georgetown and ranger school asked "What?" too often. Many an intelligence screwup could be traced back to a blind guess at Casey's intent made by one of these young men afraid to ask "What?" for the third, the fourth, the fifth time. It was a miracle no hard-nosed reporter like George Tater ever got hold of some of those horror stories.

But Bill Casey after a stroke was even worse. He sounded like a man with a mouthful of hot soup. Frank Cabot saw him often during those weeks, but in the first ten minutes of the first visit he decided he was not going to ask "What?" under any circumstances whatsoever and he stuck to it. He caught perhaps one word in three and made up the rest. God only knew what Casey was really trying to say. It was tragic and it was funny at the same time. The man who commanded all the secret resources of the Free World could not have told you what he wanted for breakfast. Cabot smiled, thinking about the weird things he had witnessed in this very room, and shook his head ruefuly.

Someone handed him a cup of coffee. "Thank you," he said. Jenny and the others were all looking at him strangely.

"I was just remembering something," he said.

Then he saw his wife through the door and his heart skipped a beat. "Oh, God," he whispered.

The sight of the uniform brought Cabot fully back to the present. The uniform was standing in the doorway with his hat in his hand, a tall fellow with a craggy face and a blank look, leather jacket ending at his waist just above the hardware store of the modern peace officer: regulation .38 revolver riding high, handcuffs, billy club, citation book, handheld radio. One of Cabot's aides had stopped the officer with a gesture of his hand, but Cabot nodded assent. He knew what was coming. This was not the first time. He had only just straightened out the last mess.

The aide stepped back and the peace officer approached.

"Mr. Cabot?" he asked. "Patrolman John Scully." Cabot nodded and the officer further identified himself. "I need a word with you about Mrs. Cabot."

Cabot's response was a heartbeat slow in coming.

"Can't this wait?" snapped Jenny.

Officer Scully looked at her.

"This is my niece, Jenny," said Frank Cabot.

"Jennifer Cabot?" asked Scully.

"Moore," said Jenny. "Jennifer Moore. Mrs. Cabot is my mother's sister."

"You were in the car this afternoon?"

"Yes."

"Ma'am, I'll have to have a word with you as well."

"It's all right, Jenny," said Cabot. "He's got to do his job."

It was exactly what Cabot expected. Officer Scully was sorry, difficult time, preliminary investigation—waiter at restaurant, other patrons at restaurant, and witness at scene indicated that Mrs. Cabot had been operating her vehicle while intoxicated. Obviously Breathalyzer test could not be performed, but the hospital had blood samples and a judge would allow a test if Cabot was unwilling to permit one himself. Of course, that would mean legal complications with an unavoidable danger of publicity. "I'm sorry, sir," Officer Scully said again.

"I understand," said Cabot. Scully handed him a clipboard with a document for his signature.

Jenny had retreated across the room and Scully followed her. She was clearly angry, but Cabot gave her a little smile and a nod of the head and he could see that she understood. In this life you have to do what you have to do.

And there it all was. The only woman Frank Cabot had ever loved lay in mortal danger in the next room, and the one thing he wanted most in this life—the job he'd been running after for twenty years—was suddenly at risk. Jenny's answers were all short, abrupt: yes, no, I don't know. He knew it would make no difference. It would come to the same thing.

Cabot understood how these things worked. In this town your enemies never attack directly. They bide their time until weakness shows: some ancient indiscretion of youth, some folly of middle age, some stupid joke told in the wrong company, standing by the wrong friend, an investment too good to be true, a brother boasting of access, a child on drugs. The crazy thing was that none of it mattered until your enemies wanted to bring you down. Then a secret dredged up into the light could be lethal. An alcoholic wife offered a fine target.

Cabot had watched the awful spectacle many times. Washington is a town of wolves, not lions. They seek out the weak, they come in numbers, they attack from the side and from behind. Each bite is small but draws blood. They drive you frantic with the pain of small admissions—yes, it happened; yes, I was there; yes, I made the phone call. In this town a man caught in a lie was red meat. Cabot knew his chances hung by a thread. If that little boy in the other car died it was all over. Even if the child lived, a DUI charge against Cabot's wife would send out a signal like blood in the water.

He watched Jenny across the room, fire in her eyes, giving the peace officer hell with every word. But there was nothing she could do. Frank Cabot had hidden his alcoholic wife for years. Otis Jones and one or two others knew—and that was it. The words Officer Scully scratched into his notebook threatened to sink Cabot's nomination. More than anyone else it would depend on Hawkins. The power of a committee chairman was very great. He could brush this embarrassment aside or allow his colleagues to pursue it as they liked.

Frank Cabot bowed his head in shame. His wife was critically injured—no one knew how badly—and he was worrying about his career. But he wasn't only ashamed; he was angry, too.

The inevitable call came a little before nine. "Sir?" said an aide, approaching. "The White House is on the line."

Cabot picked up the white phone on the table by the couch.

"Mr. Cabot?" asked a woman's voice.

Cabot said it was.

"Please hold for Peter Schleicher."

Cabot snorted in disgust. Schleicher never just picked up the phone and called. Schleicher's secretary always placed the call, as if Schleicher's time were too important to waste twenty seconds of it waiting for the acting director of the CIA to come onto the line. But that would change, Cabot promised himself that.

"The president," said Schleicher without greeting, "wanted me to ask how Mrs. Cabot is doing."

Cabot explained.

"We're praying for her," said Schleicher. "The president would like to know what happened, so he can answer any questions if necessary. Was Mrs. Cabot driving?"

Cabot explained.

"There's a child involved?"

Cabot explained.

"But you say the child was sitting in the backseat and wearing a seat belt. How could he get hurt back there?"

Cabot explained.

"Mrs. Cabot . . . *hit them broadside*?"

"Yes," said Cabot. He tried to explain but he knew it sounded lame. You see a car in the road, you stop.

"The president will be distressed," said Schleicher. "We're praying for you. Keep us posted."

Cabot figured that Peter Schleicher would just hang up at that point, and he was right. For a moment he looked at the phone as if a dog had dropped it on the sidewalk. Then he hung up too.

Some minutes later Jenny came to ask if there was anything more she could do; her boyfriend Brad had come and was volunteering to drive her home. Cabot looked up. Young Cameron was standing behind her with a serious expression on his face.

Cabot almost smiled. "Thanks for coming, Brad," he said. "Jenny's had a helluva day. But life goes on. I still want to see you in my office tomorrow morning at eight."

"I'll be there," said the young man. "And, sir—I'm very sorry about Mrs. Cabot, sir."

"I think we've touched bottom now," Cabot said. "It's hard to see how things could get much worse."

Cabot believed this. He knew Otis would have some solid ideas for damage control.

A few moments later there was another quiet tussle at the door and Cabot looked up. He recognized the face immediately. You can't stop the cops and you can't stop the press. "It's all right," he said to the aides, who were blocking the way for the second time that evening. "Come in, George."

George Tater shook the rain from his coat and cap.

10

On the way out to Falls Church in his car, Brad brooded about Jenny. There had been a definite edge in the way she said No, fine, of course, I know you can't help it. "This feels different," he told her. "It doesn't feel like the standard dry hole."

"Fine," said Jenny. "Don't keep him waiting."

"I should be back by one or two."

"I'll be asleep," said Jenny.

"I'll call you tomorrow."

"Fine."

"Noon," said Brad. "We could meet for lunch."

"Fine. You call. We'll see."

. . .

Terry Tyler said he knew James Angleton well. He had worked on the CI Staff for a dozen years, identifying Soviet liaison officers in the services of the Eastern European client states. "Painstaking job," said Tyler. "But file-keeping is the soul of intelligence work. I'm sure you heard that old saw a hundred times when you were training down at the Farm."

"Actually," said Brad, "I didn't. They said computers are the soul of intelligence work."

"Interesting," said Tyler. "Not quite the same thing."

In time Tyler had moved on to an administrative slot in the DDO, but he still saw Jim often and they remained friends even after Bill Colby kicked Jim out of the Agency in December of 1974. There was nothing at all strange about Jim's calling Tyler with a sensitive message from Israeli sources three years later.

"Jim himself was a strange man," Tyler said. "You know about Jim Angleton?"

Brad was in a wing chair in a corner of the small book-lined room. Tyler was sitting behind a cluttered desk. A gooseneck lamp with a green glass shade was bent low in front of him, providing the only light in the room. Both men were drinking from glasses of soda water.

"I've heard the name," said Brad.

"You've heard the name?" said Tyler. "They didn't talk about him in training?"

"That's where I heard the name."

"I suppose it had to happen," said Tyler wearily. "It's all ancient history now. It's hard to know where to begin."

"What I'm really after," said Brad, "is the Israeli story about the American."

"Not so fast," said Tyler. "I'll get to that. You can't hurry Jim Angleton, and he's the one telling this story. Believe me, I'm giving you the short version. Here's what you've got to understand about Jim. For him everything was connected, and he had a very deep knowledge of all those points where the secret services of the Soviet Union were in contact with the outside world. Do you understand what I'm saying? Where intelligence work was concerned, in Jim's mind there was no such thing as an accident and no such thing as a coincidence."

"I understand," said Brad, to help Tyler along.

"Behind this simple story from his Israeli friend—I'll get to it, don't worry—Jim was sure something much bigger would be found, if you only knew how to look for it."

They had talked in Angleton's greenhouse. It was July 1977, not long before midnight, the windows were cranked open, but the air was still heavy and moist among the potted plants, row on row of terra-cotta pots containing orchids—or so Angleton had told him. *Epidendrum nocturnum.* But what did Tyler know? They looked kind of halfhearted to him, a few leaves on spiky stalks, droopy blossoms of greenish white.

"First thing," said Tyler, "Jim was the Agency's chief spy catcher. He got so good at it he began finding spies who weren't there. Long story. I'm surprised nobody told you about this down at the Farm. Ask Myrna."

"I will."

"Second thing, he knew the Israelis. They were closer than close. Ask Myrna about that, too. What Jim told me was this: An Israeli friend of his said the Mossad had been given a reliable report of an American in the Gulag. Of course there were problems galore. There was no easy way to check the story. Besides, the Russians had insisted for years they held no unknown Americans prisoner, and Washington agreed. The books were in balance. So this American: Was he one of ours, or was he a defector? Were we glad to find him—or sorry?"

"I don't understand," said Brad.

"I don't blame you," said Tyler.

He explained that in the mid-1970s there were lots of "Americans" in the Soviet Union. Some had been there for decades, like the handful of aging idealists who had gone to build a Ford auto plant in the homeland of socialism in the 1930s. There were also some friends and colleagues of the atomic spies Julius and Ethel Rosenberg in the 1950s, who had departed for sudden vacations in Mexico one jump ahead of the FBI. Add to them all sorts of people with American passports, maybe valid and maybe not, rounded up by the Red Army in Eastern Europe after the war; army soldiers who went AWOL in Berlin; possibly even crewmen from American intelligence aircraft shot down over Russia in the 1950s before satellites took over the job. Who knew what happened to these fliers? Washington assumed they were dead. Some of their buddies weren't so sure.

"So there were lots of possibilities," Tyler said. "All the Israelis knew was this—a Russian Jew told them he'd met an American in the Gulag."

"Was it true?" asked Brad.

"You're new in the business," said Tyler. "That's not the first question, that's the last question. And most of the time you never know. I can tell you what Jim told me."

Tyler had taken notes while Jim talked.

. . .

The fact it came from Avraham Lipsky made a difference. Jim trusted Lipsky. They went way back. Avi had survived the war in the forests of Poland and then made his way to Italy. There he helped smuggle other survivors out of the DP camps and onto ships bound for Palestine. Jim ran X-2—the counterintelligence branch of the OSS—in Italy at the end of the war, and the two men became close. With money from America, Lipsky's group was buying old freighters and tramp steamers along the Adriatic coast, filling them with Jews from Poland and Hungary, and sending them out at night with false manifests for North African ports. Great Britain was trying to stop the flow of Jewish refugees to Palestine, but Jim knew the Brits after his year in London, and what they told him in a collegial way soon reached Lipsky. Many a rusty tub slipped out of harbor the night before the Brits planned to pounce. Later the Israelis gave Jim a secret medal. Brad could ask Myrna about that if he was curious.

After Israel declared its independence in 1948, Lipsky rose in the intelligence service of the new state. He came from Poland, he had relatives in Russia, he spoke Russian, and he ran an office in the Mossad that maintained secret contact with Jews in Russia. Jim was in the CIA by that time, and the outfit was interested in everybody Lipsky was talking to: Jewish grad students in physics at the Technical Institute in Kharkov; Jewish filmmakers in the Moscow art world, such as it was; Jewish accountants working for Gosplan, the Soviet economic planning agency; Jewish doctors and lab technicians in the secret hospitals where members of the Politburo went to get treated or to die. One way and another over the years, Lipsky and Jim spent a lot of time together. When Lipsky came to the States he stayed with Jim.

In the 1970s, Lipsky's shop was the brains behind a worldwide campaign to get Jews out of Russia. This was not a ratline for secret escape like the one in Italy but a major public effort with a lot of American support to force the Russians to open the gates. The fate of Jews in the Soviet Union was a big part of the story, and Lipsky's people were debriefing every émigré who reached Israel, especially those who had been in the camps. The most heartrending stories went straight to the newspapers. Naturally the debriefers were also asking a few questions of purely intelligence interest, and one day a debriefer came to Lipsky's office with a story that required special handling. "He had been talking to a man let out by mistake," said Jim, surrounded by his orchids in their pots. "This was a Jew from Odessa supposed to die in the camps—a man with a special job."

"Name?" said Tyler, who was taking notes by moonlight.

"Golenpolsky," said Jim. "Lev Golenpolsky. He'd been given ten years for slander of the Soviet State."

Things did not go well for Golenpolsky in prison. He was young; he thought he was a tough guy. He complained in one letter too many to the chairman of the Politburo, and they sent him to a harsh-regime camp in Akmolinsk. There he was assigned to slop duty in the kitchens, one more *zek* to feed the lice of Central Asia. Part of his job twice a day was to carry food to a single prisoner in a separate cell block. The man had his own guards, his own exercise yard. Golenpolsky was under strict orders. He was not to talk to the prisoner or to look him full in the face. He was to go in with the food, wait while he ate, and take everything away.

But of course this was Soviet Russia. The guards were all Kazakhs and could barely speak Russian. They played dominoes in the guardroom and were always drunk by dark, and while they shouted and laughed Golenpolsky sat in the cell with the prisoner and talked to him. Golenpolsky's dream was to be a chemical engineer, and somebody had told him the language of science was English. Golenpolsky knew a little English. And of course the American prisoner, a big sandy-haired guy in his twenties, knew nothing but English. So Golenpolsky got in the habit of talking to the prisoner, hoping to improve his English, and inevitably one night some officer checking on the kitchens wanted to know what was detaining the *zek* Golenpolsky. The officer sent to check caught the pair talking, and next thing Golenpolsky knew *he* was a special prisoner in a cell all by himself getting *his* meals delivered—by an Asiatic who was deaf and dumb. Before they slammed the door they told Golenpolsky that for being such a wise guy he would stay there till he rotted, and he believed them.

"And then the damnedest thing happened," said Tyler. He paused.

"What?" said Brad.

"We're sitting in the dark, Jim and I, and suddenly a wave of heavy scent filled the greenhouse. It was like perfume, but strong. We sat there for a while just breathing it in. 'That's why they call it *nocturnum*,' Jim said. 'You only smell it at night.'

"I said, Come on, Jim, how about the rest of the story? He said he was afraid there wasn't much more to tell. This Golenpolsky spent a couple of years locked up with the American, a sergeant in the army. He'd lost a leg somehow. He'd learned about three words of Russian and had no idea why he was being held prisoner.

"Golenpolsky told him that wasn't hard to figure out. They were keeping him locked up so nobody would find out they were keeping him locked up. But maybe there was more to it than that. I know Jim thought so.

"Then Golenpolsky got lucky. He wrote a letter to Chairman Brezhnev, and somehow he got put on a list of Jews to be given visas to Austria. Typical Russian screwup. Next stop after Vienna was Tel Aviv, and I already told you the rest."

"That's it?" said Brad.

"That's it."

"You never checked it any further than that? No name? No home town? No idea how he got there?"

"What I know stops here. I wrote up a report for the DDO, Larry Winter, that same night, and what he did with it I don't know. I assume he gave it to Admiral Turner."

"And then?"

"I never heard. Maybe the guy was dead by that time. Or maybe he was traded for some spy even I never heard of. Or maybe the Russians said *nyet* and that was the end of it."

"Did Angleton ever ask you what came of it?"

"He asked. But I couldn't tell him anything."

"Doesn't that seem odd to you? We find out the Russians have one of our guys and then . . . nothing?"

"I'm afraid not," said Tyler. "In this business you drop stones down a lot of wells, but it's not often you hear a splash."

"You think it was just bullshit?"

"Not at all. I'm virtually certain it wasn't bullshit," said Tyler. "Angleton knew Lipsky, and Lipsky knew how to ask questions. Jim didn't call me out to his greenhouse in the moonlight to pass on some dumb story with nothing to it. Golenpolsky saw someone in Akmolinsk who wasn't supposed to be there."

"Maybe," said Brad. "But did Golenpolsky know an American when he saw one?"

"I think he did," said Tyler. "This guy was a sergeant in the army, he had an American-sounding name, and he said he dreamed of fast cars and loose women. Plus he had *Mom* tattooed on his arm."

Brad leaned back in his chair "Okay," he said. "That's American enough for me. Can you remember his name?"

"It was twenty-something years ago. I heard the name once. I'm afraid it's gone."

"Well, I can tell you one thing: I'm going to find out what happened to that soldier, but I don't know where to begin."

"You know how things work around here," said Tyler. "I wrote up a report. Nothing in this place is ever thrown away. So my advice to you is—Follow the paper."

11

During the night, more cold rain fell. All the way into the office Wednesday morning, Frank Cabot sat deep in the backseat of the gray government car and with one part of his mind counted the other cars that had gone off the road on the patches of black ice. At 7 a.m. the sky was gray and overcast; traffic was light, leafless trees were black with wet.

Kitty was out of immediate danger. The doctors had promised a prognosis by midday—whether she had suffered nerve damage and how much. There was no point in worrying about it yet so Cabot did not. Instead, he was trying to find the right tone for the conversation he was soon going to have with Harry Hawkins. He was pretty sure Hawkins would never think the troubles of a man's wife ought to be chewed over in a confirmation hearing, but he was not one hundred percent sure. Ever since the first call from the White House two weeks back, Cabot had been trying to identify every potential problem, however slight or remote, that might derail him. Until yesterday it had never occurred to him that Kitty might be it.

At his desk, Cabot half listened as the duty officer summarized the night's cables. No surprises; the world was not at peace but the United States was not at war, which was the next best thing. Jane brought a mug of coffee and reminded him of all the things he had promised to do and the people he had promised to call or see before day's end, beginning with the Agency's MIA liaison officer at eight o'clock. The word was out; Jane knew about Kitty. Cabot filled in a few details. Then he asked her to place a call to Senator Hawkins's car phone.

"Frank!" said Hawkins. "This is about Kitty, am I right?"

When the acting director of the Central Intelligence Agency telephones the chairman of the Senate Intelligence Oversight Committee out of the blue at 7:45 a.m. the latter would like to know promptly just how big a thing was heading his way. "It's Kitty," Cabot assured him. "Important to me but not to the world."

"Ah, Frank," Hawkins sympathized.

Cabot explained quickly, stressing all the signs the doctors had described as encouraging.

"I'll be praying for good news," the senator said. "If there's anything I can do . . . ?"

"Senator?"

"Yes?"

Cabot told him the hard part, leaving nothing out, including the alarming fact that George Tater had the scent of his wife's possible arrest and appeared to think there might be a story in it.

"Have you heard from the White House?" Hawkins asked.

"Peter Schleicher called. I don't think a DUI charge had occurred to him."

"Any chance you can finesse it?"

"Slim—not zero but slim. I spoke to Otis Jones last night. He said he might know somebody."

"Jones is a good man to have on your side," said the senator. "But George Tater can be trouble. What does he know for sure?"

"Not much from me," said Cabot. "God knows how he knew where to find me. I told security no reporters, no cameras, no press, but he breezed right on through. I saw him talking to the investigating officer. Tater knows cops don't make social calls. I think he put it together without too much trouble. So everything's a bit up in the air."

"You take care of Kitty. We can handle the rest."

"Senator?"

"Yes?"

"Two days ago you asked me if there was anything you ought to know about, anything that could blow up in our faces at the hearings. I never thought of this. I was thinking about my own life—was there anything *I* had done?—was there something in *my* past? I wasn't thinking of Kitty."

"I understand, Frank. You don't have to worry about that. This is a personal tragedy, and I'll do everything in my power to see the Committee treats it that way. I may not succeed entirely. There's one or two members who might see an opening here."

"MacLaverty."

"It's possible. But don't start worrying that I feel betrayed. I wasn't asking about your uncle, cousin, father, or wife—I was asking about you. My trust in you is complete."

When Hawkins mentioned the word *father,* Cabot's heart took a small jump. He was pretty sure, after he hung up, that Hawkins meant nothing by it, but once again he wasn't a hundred percent sure. The biggest single event in Cabot's adolescence had been his father's near arrest and public humiliation in a bank scandal. A lot of money went south, and once it was clear there would be no criminal charges, some of the bank's shareholders sued the elder Cabot for civil damages. For more than a year, until the bank's insurance company finally settled out of court, the case was hashed out on local television and in the papers, and on many a morning Cabot had to enter a schoolroom with all eyes and some half-hidden smirks pointed in his direction. His father's failure had even less bearing than Kitty's drinking on Cabot's fitness to run the Agency, but he knew how things worked in Washington; the slightest chink in a man's armor could be enough to admit the blade that killed his hopes.

Frank Cabot's call to Senator Hawkins was only the first of many, but it was the hardest, and when it was over Cabot had nothing to do but get through the day and wait for news and tell people he appreciated their prayers. Very few deserved or needed to know more. Thirty-five years in Washington had taught him how to keep things in their place. Kitty, children, private life were all on hold, and everything else—his work, his hope of confirmation as DCI, the hundred pending decisions of a man running a major agency—was right here, in his office on the seventh floor, on the surface of his desk, requiring his full professional attention.

"It's your eight o'clock," said Jane. "Brad Cameron."

Cabot was in no mood for a young man's awkward sympathy; he told Cameron the latest news from the hospital—stable vital signs, wait and see—and proceeded briskly to the reason for his summons. He explained that Hawkins was planning hearings possibly as early as the middle of next week. Of course there would be questions about MIAs, and Cabot wanted a complete accounting case by case of every report received and the Agency's determination of same over the last five years. He wanted the numbers up to the minute—how many MIAs were on the books in 1973, how many had been accounted for over the years, what cases were still under investigation.

Young Cameron sat forward on the edge of his chair scribbling furiously as Cabot talked. The look on his face was alert and intent. I was like that once, Cabot thought. Everything was the most important thing in the world. One sharp word from Kitty could turn me inside out.

"Sir?" Brad asked. "Do you want current cases?"

"I want everything," said Cabot. "What we know, what we suspect, what we're still trying to find out. Are you in the middle of something?"

"Not the middle—"

"Does Hawkins know?"

"Not yet, sir," said Brad. "I've just learned about this. I think it's serious, but it's hard to say. It's an old case. I've just started tracking the paper."

"Well, you've got till the middle of next week. Get all the help you need from your boss; he knows how I feel about this. Nail it down if you can, but if you can't then give me the status the morning I go into the committee room."

"It's an unusual case," said Brad.

"Whatever," said Cabot. "We need to tell Hawkins when it's solid. No rumors of rumors. Me first, then Hawkins."

"Yessir. I'm not sure it's Vietnam-related. It goes back to nineteen—"

He was getting ready to tell the whole story; Cabot could see it in the young man's face. Cameron had hold of something that was bursting inside him. Cabot knew the look, eyes wide with a puppy's desire to please. Cabot, too, had once been ready to plunge his arm into the fire for the first man who asked.

"Brad," he said, "not now. I want to know everything, but I haven't got time for the whole story today. You put it together and write it up and give it to Jane when it's ready, and we'll go from there. I'm trusting you to handle this for me."

"I won't fail you, sir," Brad said.

"One thing."

"Yessir?"

"Don't let the bastards block you on this one."

"Yessir."

"Whatever it takes."

"Yessir, I understand, sir. Follow it wherever it goes."

"That's the spirit," said Frank Cabot.

12

The acting director knew his man. Brad Cameron would have done anything for Cabot, and he silently vowed, descending in the elevator from the seventh floor, that he would send his boss into the confirmation hearings armed with the mother of all reports. Brad knew exactly what Cabot wanted: answers on paper to questions on paper with no loose ends. In his first months at the Agency, Brad had learned how to write paper designed to blow opponents away—crisp, neat, exhaustive. He had always been good in school, and he was good at this. Once or twice in committee, after Brad had delivered a report, his opponents had been reduced to the shuffling of papers and a mumbled reply. Brad glowed at the clipped little words of a boss's whispered praise: "Nicely put! Good prep! Well done!"

Down the halls and around the corners he went, heading for his cubicle and his desk to do battle with paper.

But what Brad secretly dreamed of was *doing* something—not just of finding the right word at the right moment but of action itself. This was not impossible. It happened. Certain old hands, when they showed up to give a little advice or say hello to buddies, were followed down the halls by awed whispers: guys who had been in the field in Vietnam or Latin America, guys who had taken boats onto the beaches of Cuba, guys who had made brush passes in the streets of Moscow. That's Rip, someone would say; he flew in Guatemala. That's Dave; he punched a KGB colonel in a Vienna coffeehouse. That's Tony; he held off a battalion of NVA regulars with a .50-caliber machine gun on a mountain in Laos. Businesslike men in Cabot's mold ran the Agency—well groomed, well connected, always on their way to a meeting, returning calls, heading for the airport, just back from a conference. But the men with scars and salty stories from the field were folk heroes, and Brad dreamed that one day he too would step out of a plane on his country's business in some part of the world where they don't speak English and you're on your own.

He slipped into his cubicle, checked his messages, and picked up the phone. "Myrna?" he said. "Have you got twenty minutes? Can you meet me in Records?"

As a child on the coast of Maine, Brad had spent long summer days reading about the heroes of the American frontier in the novels of Kenneth Roberts. His favorite was *Northwest Passage,* with its account of the raid on the Abenaki Indians at St. Francis in Canada. He thrilled at the account of Rogers's Rangers making their way without food south through the wilderness from Montreal after the battle. Winter approached; they froze and starved; men died or went mad or lost their way in the trackless forest. It was character that made the difference; some persevered and survived, some fell by the way. All through his childhood, in his bed after lights-out at boarding school or camp, Brad dreamed of feats of bravery and endurance. On weekends now he sometimes ran ten or twelve miles through Rock Creek Park, pushing himself winter and summer, proving to himself—he would have blushed to admit it—that he had what it takes.

Soon after joining the Agency he began to sense he was not alone. It wasn't hard to spot the born spooks: accountants, lawyers, area studies Ph.D.s, Harvard Business School grads set apart by a streak of the romantic. They had all read John le Carré's novel *The Spy Who Came In from the Cold* and Rudyard Kipling's *Kim,* and they spoke with mingled irony and longing of the Great Game. Brad was comfortable at the CIA from the beginning. In a way it was just a bigger boarding school, with more intrigue and whispered secrets but with the same gulf separating the old boys from the new.

"You're a real *macher,*" said Myrna. "Tell me what you got."

"It seems kind of thin by the light of day."

"Tell me," said Myrna.

"I went to see Terry Tyler, who thinks you're the greatest."

"He's a sweetie."

"What he told me was this: In July 1978 an Israeli named Avraham Lipsky went to see a retired CIA officer named James Angleton—"

"Only the most famous spy in the history of the CIA," said Myrna.

"I know, I know. Tyler gave me hell for not knowing all about him. Anyway, Angleton told Tyler that Lipsky came to him privately and unofficially with a report of a POW. The source was a man newly arrived from Russia—a Jew from Odessa named Golenpolsky. He'd been in Akmolinsk, and while he was there—in a separate prison segregated from the rest of the prison population—he met an American."

"Who says, some troublemaker from Odessa? How would he know?"

"The man had a tattoo on one arm that said *Mom*. He told Golenpolsky that what he dreamed about was 'fast cars and loose women.' "

"Okay. Maybe you've got something. What else?"

"A big guy in his twenties or early thirties, sandy hair, missing one leg. And he told Golenpolsky he'd been a sergeant in the U.S. Army."

"Told him how—in Russian?"

"In English. Golenpolsky spoke a little English."

"This is more than twenty years ago," said Myrna.

"I've tracked down a lot of reports," said Brad. "This one sounds different."

"Call it good," said Myrna. "Now what?"

"Well, now I think I ought to go see Larry Winter and ask him what he did with Tyler's report. Tyler said he never heard another word, and apparently Angleton didn't either."

"You mean the DDO in nineteen seventy-seven? I don't think that's a good idea. Not yet."

"Why not? It's the only name I've got," said Brad.

"Let me explain," said Myrna. "Listen to me. Take notes. This is basic. Is Winter glad to see you?"

"I don't understand."

"Here you are, a young fellow, so low on the table of organization Winter needs a chart. But!"

"Yeah?"

"But you arrive at his door on the business of Frank Cabot, the next DCI, no less, to ask Winter why he screwed up."

"How do I know he screwed up?"

"Listen to me. In this business every question that comes out of the blue about things long ago is most likely why you screwed up. Trust me, Winter is not excited to see you. All you bring for him is trouble. He wants you gone. So you've got to be ready for him. You've got to do your homework. Otherwise he says to you, 'I looked into it, nothing there, goodbye, Mr. Cameron.' And that's it. You're out in the hall. You see? You only get to ask once."

"All right. Any ideas?" asked Brad.

"Sure I got ideas," said Myrna. "Come on-a my place."

Up in the elevator they went, down a hall, through double doors with a cipher lock, past a pudgy fellow at a desk named Roy, who logged in their names and identification numbers, down other halls and through other doors, until at last they came to a small office in the windowless interior of the great building, protected by a last cipher lock with a name tag on the door that read MYRNA RASHEVSKY. Inside all was chaos.

"Home," said Myrna.

Brad looked around at the piles of documents, folders, old copies of the classified *National Intelligence Daily,* photographs, computer floppies, books bristling with stick-it notes. . . .

"How do you get away with this?" he asked in wonder.

"We came to an understanding," said Myrna. "My whole office is my safe. If I had to put this all away at night I wouldn't get anything done. Now sit, we're gonna do a little search."

She took a seat at a desk and slid out the keyboard tray of her computer. Brad pulled up a chair beside her.

"You take notes," she said.

Myrna began typing. Screens came and went. Each screen required a new password. Myrna's fingers flew; xxxx came up. After the third or fourth screen, Brad was pretty sure he had picked up Myrna's password. It was FOXY.

"We're in the DDO registry, we've got access to the central files: cases, code names, hostile services, biographical, geographical, you name it, everything's here. But you got to know your way around, and you got to know the way in. Once upon a time, little old ladies like me looked it all up on index cards in Records. If you tried to poke your nose where you shouldn't they slapped your hand. Now—passwords. But they're still watching. Everything we look at goes into the memory, and little bells and whistles go off in security if it's not kosher."

Finally everything was ready.

"Okay," said Myrna. "From the top. Avraham Lipsky." She typed in the name.

PASSWORD?

Myrna typed xxxx. "That's for friendly services," she said. Her fingers flew, giving the passwords for Israel, operational officers, U.S. informants. Once inside the CIA's files containing everything the Agency knew about Avi the elder, Myrna narrowed the search to July 1977. The first screen appeared:

> INS PSPT CNTRL/4 JULY 1977/ARR JFK INTL TWA 126 (TEL AVIV, ATHENS, ROME, LONDON). 9 JULY 1977 DPTR JFK INTL LUFTHANSA (MUNICH).

More typing brought another screen.

5 JULY 1977. LNCHN NOON C. BAKER DDO/ME RE: BLK SEPT PLANS AIR TERROR, REPRT RECENT ARREST CAIRO ARPT MUHAMMAD ALI HASSAN (SYRIAN PSPRT G3547TX 11 NOV 75) W/WEAPON/TCKT ATHENS, CONTL AGENT "PC/MOONGLOW."

Myrna followed the trail.

PC/MOONGLOW. TANCRED PAVELOVICH GORSHKY, MD, CNTRL COMM CLINIC #2, PEREDELKINO, USSR. 21 MAY 1977 REPTS [SOURCE: OT/FLUTE] CONVERSATION PERSONAL SCTY MIKHAIL SUSLOV RE: DISSIDENT CRACKDOWN.

A fourth screen appeared.

7 JULY 1977. WM. MCCARTHY, DDO/ME, REPTS DINNER W/SUBJECT AND DAN POWELL FBI LIAISON RE: CNTRTERROR, MUNICH EPISODE CF: QR/22137-ME.

So it went, down one digital corridor after another, cases, names, meetings, cables, liaison reports, memoranda of conversations. "Interesting," said Myrna after an hour, "very interesting. Avraham Lipsky comes to the United States, spends three days in Washington, sees everybody, tells 'em this, tells 'em that, it all goes into the files. Then—according to you—he tells the former chief of counterintelligence he has learned there is an American in the Gulag; Angleton tells the chief assistant of the DDO, who tells the DDO and—nothing. Not one word in the files. What's this, some kind of mistake? Sure. So we try another route."

She typed in AKMOLINSK.

Back came the answers to her many questions: one-time labor camp on the Ishim River in Kazakhstan, established 1946 to house Axis POWs working on the Magnitogorsk–Pavlodar rail line, under command KGB internal troops until January 1992, transferred to KGB successor organization, etc. List of commanders, Gehlen org interviews with returnees 1949–1956, references in open literature, references to UN debates 1947–1950, U.S. diplomatic démarches 1947–1952. . . .

At that point Myrna took a detour to follow up reference numbers to State Department circulars: June 1947, Akmolinsk one of seven camps allegedly housing Italian POWs; March 1949, Akmolinsk one of four camps allegedly housing Japanese POWs; May 1950, U.S. requests accounting of Japanese POWs in six camps including Akmolinsk. . . .

"What is this?" said Brad. "The war had been over for years."

"Forced labor as reparations," said Myrna. "Moscow sent most of them home in nineteen fifty but not all. Some had worked on projects nobody was supposed to know about. They were finding those people right up until the seventies. Quite a few of them had 'Wallenberg disease.' "

"Wallenberg disease?"

"Raoul Wallenberg. Swedish diplomat who saved Hungarian Jews. Soviets arrested him in nineteen forty-five, denied all knowledge of him for years. Useful rule of thumb: Once Soviets deny having someone, the only way he's going to turn up is dead. That's Wallenberg disease—death in custody, heart failure."

"Are we getting anywhere?" asked Brad.

"I'd say a cautious maybe. Akmolinsk was the parking place for a lot of people the Soviets said they never had. We're talking about creatures of habit here. If they had an awkward American they'd definitely park him someplace like Akmolinsk. This is the first thing I've seen that sounds like maybe Lipsky's man knew what he was talking about."

More typing. Back to Akmolinsk, DDO reports, debriefing of Soviet defectors, one extremely fat file from 1949–1950 built around a German returnee report that Akmolinsk housed a laboratory doing nuclear research, eventually concluded to be unfounded. But not before Myrna had plowed through scores of references to the original Gehlen report, analysis of report, bona fides of source of report pro and con, British comment on report, French queries of report with U.S. denial of report's existence, answers to queries provided by two controlled sources in Ministry of Medium Machine Building (whose identities were thickly defended by passwords). In the end the science and technology desk at Berlin Base concluded that the whole story could be traced back to an overheard reference to Akmolinsk as "a nucleus of research." The full file was probably more than a thousand pages. Myrna skimmed it in about eight minutes and moved on to a name register for inmates, several hundred at least: Germans, Italians, Finns, Hungarians, Japanese, and, in later years, quite a few Russian Jews.

"How about some lunch?" asked Brad.

"Wait," said Myrna. She scrolled down. "No Golenpolsky." She sighed audibly, stared at the screen for a moment, scrolled up, scrolled down. "No Golenpolsky," she said again.

"Damn," said Brad. "It's nearly one. I promised to call Jenny. We've been at this nearly four hours."

"Time flies," said Myrna, "when you smell blood." She tapped a command, and the list of names covered the page again.

GALLOTTI, ENRICO
GARASAYEVA, TATYANA
GAVRILOVICH, YEVGENY
GEKKER, ANATOLY IVANOVICH
GERSHUNI, GRIGORY ALEXANDROVICH
GESSLER, KURT
GEVORKYAN, SOKRAT
GIES, HERMANN
GINZBURG, NIKOLAI P.
GIZZI, PAOLO
GLETKIN, Y. D.

GORLITZ, WALTER

Myrna hit the PAGE DOWN key. Now the screen read:

GLETKIN, Y. D.

GORLITZ, WALTER
GRACHEV, MISHA
GRASSELINI, GIUSEPPE
GRIGORYEV, IGNATI
GRUBER, KARL
ILIN, IVAN P.
INOSHIN, PYOTR
IVANOV, VLADIMIR
KOTOV, P. I.
KRASIKOV, GYORGI

"Look at that," said Myrna. PAGE UP, PAGE DOWN.

"Missing a line," said Brad. "Right where Golenpolsky should be."

"Exactly," said Myrna. "My guess? Somebody wrote to a file, deleted the block, but then neglected to close the space. Maybe Mr. Somebody didn't like to do what he was told."

"Now what?"

"Now I'm going to show you a few things you're not supposed to know. Pay attention." Her fingers flew over the keyboard.

"One set of passwords lets you read the files. A whole other set of passwords lets you write in the files. And a third set lets you into the log of who did what when."

AKMOLINSK/BIO REGSTRY/DDI/DDO/ACCESS 5362QT
01-27-73 DDO/SR/A. P. MOSS/"ABAKUMOV, VIKTOR"/162/8:12 AM

Myrna translated: " 'On January 27, 1973, A. P. Moss'—Arthur Moss, nice guy, smoked Luckies, dead—'entered 162 bytes of info on one Viktor Abakumov into the Akmolinsk name registry at 8:12 a.m.' Why 1973 I don't know; a lot of info started coming out in the early 1970s. If we follow the entry we'll find the source down the line somewhere. For now, let's take a quick look-see for our friend Golenpolsky."

Myrna scrolled to the Gs. The screen showed:

03-?-46 OPC/USSR/J. T. MCCARTHY/"GALLOTTI, ENRICO"/IND
03-?-46 OPC/USSR/J. T. MCCARTHY/"GARASAYEVA, TATYANA"/IND
06-12-64 /DDP/SR/S. O. RESNIK/"GAVRILOVICH, YEVGENY"/82/
4:44 PM
11-11-73/DDO/SR/A. P. MOSS/"GEKKER, A. I."/321/11:20 AM
06-12-64/DDP/SR/S. O. RESNIK/"GERSHUNI, G. A."/112/4:46 PM
02-09-48/OPC/WGER/M. TELL/"GESSLER, KURT"/IND
09-23-58/DDP/SR/H. JONES/"GEVORKYAN, SOKRAT"/IND
01-?-47/OPC/GER/M. TELL/"GIES, HERMANN"/IND
09-23-58/DDP/SR/H. JONES/"GINZBURG, N. P."/IND
04-?-47/OPC/ITAL/S. PRESS/"GIZZI, PAOLO"/IND
10-02-64/DDP/SR/F. X. POWELL/"GLETKIN, Y. D."/216/10:13 AM
XXXX
03-?-46/OPC/USSR/J. T. MCCARTHY/"GUSTAFSSON, S."/IND

"Some sort of security block," said Myrna. "Let's see." She called up a menu, sought help, scrolled till she came to XXXX, asked for a definition, and got BLCK.

"Thanks," said Myrna. "Let's try security override."

She typed a few words.

THIS INFORMATION IS SENSITIVE COMPARTMENTED. SEEK ASSISTANCE.

"We shall call on the high and the mighty," said Myrna.

She typed another few words.

THIS INFORMATION IS SENSITIVE COMPARTMENTED. SEEK ASSISTANCE.

"Don't ever, ever, ever tell anybody you've seen me do this," said Myrna. "I'm about to use my own personal global master key."

"What's the clearance for that?" asked Brad.

"Codeword MYRNA. I invented it myself. Believe me, it opens a lot of doors."

She typed a few words.

The screen flickered, darkened, disappeared into itself. The fan in the hard drive went dead. The keyboard lights went out. The phone rang. Myrna and Brad looked at each other. "Jesus Christ," said Brad. The phone rang again and Myrna picked it up.

"Rashevsky," she said. She held the phone away from her ear so Brad could listen too.

"Myrna? Harold in security. What the hell are you doing? We got bells going off all over the place. The men in soft shoes are about to come charging up there."

"Harold? Tell everybody to sit tight. You come up here. We can sort this out. This is Myrna talking."

She hung up, tried to reboot her computer, and got a screen that read ACCESS DENIED. "Brad," she said, "my advice: Get your *tochis* out of here. Harold knows me, but you he doesn't know. He will have a lot of questions. Trust me."

Brad got up and put his hand on the doorknob. "You'll call?" he said.

"I'll call. Now go."

Brad opened the door but it was too late. Three men blocked his way, breathing heavily. "*Oy*," Myrna said. "Somebody doesn't like us. *Boychik*, let me do the talking."

13

It wasn't Myrna's friend Harold standing at the door, and there was no talking. "Not now," said the man in front when Myrna started to explain. "This office has been sealed under Section Six of the security regulations; you may not take anything with you at this time."

This first man was huge, limbs like stovepipes, a belly swelling the white shirt, meaty hands. He and his two companions all wore shiny gray suits. The companions had crew cuts and did not speak.

"I'll just get my bag," said Myrna.

"Sorry." The big man placed his hand on the bag. "Arrangements will be made for you to retrieve your personal possessions later." He turned to Brad, reached over, plucked Brad's identification badge from his shirt pocket, and compared the smiling young man in the color photo with the bewildered face in front of him. "Mr. Cameron, Miss Rashevsky," the big man said, in a toneless voice that was like the back of a hand, "you are both temporarily suspended with pay under paragraph four of Section Six and are not authorized to be anywhere in this building without escort."

"Wait a minute," said Myrna.

"We will escort you to Security."

"I can explain," said Brad. "I'm a special assistant in the director's office for MIA affairs, and we're—"

"You can explain later."

"The acting director has personally—"

"Not now," said the big man, more sharply this time. "We're sealing this office. We're going to Security. We'll sort everything out there."

"Let me make a phone call," said Brad. He was getting over the shock, beginning to be irritated, ready to be angry. "We can sort this out right now," he said.

But before Brad could put his hand on the phone the crew cuts each took firm hold of one of his arms and started him toward the door.

"Wait," he said. The crew cuts were holding him just above the elbows; their grip was tight and painful. "Hey," he said. "Let go!"

"Mr. Cameron," said the big man, "no phone calls. No detours by your office. No visits to the little boys' room. Do you get the picture?" Brad started to speak again but the man said, "Save it." He took Myrna by the arm, no less firmly than the crew cuts held Brad, and marched the whole party down the hall.

Myrna glanced over at Brad, raised her eyebrows, and said, "*Meshuggener!*"

When they reached Security, Myrna was immediately led off in one direction, Brad in another. Security seemed a puzzle of offices within offices; at each door the crew cuts had to fill out another form. When Brad tried to speak he was cut off or ignored. At first he was sure there was going to be hell to pay when these clowns understood they were seriously getting in the way of something the acting DCI wanted done. Once or twice Brad got it into words—"Look, I'm working personally for Cabot, call his office, this is *his* project; trust me, he hates delay"—but even the officials who heard him out only shrugged and said mildly, "Perhaps," or "We'll see."

Like all other recruits Brad had answered a great many personal questions and had taken a lie detector test on joining the agency, but the security officers vetting him then had been a friendly, unthreatening group. This was different; the crew cuts had hustled him along like men who preferred dragging to asking, and the blank faces at desks revealed so little interest in his explanations they might have been working for some other organization. He told them as seriously as he could that this was all a mistake and couldn't understand why he made no impression.

But at last the crew cuts led him to an office within an office where he found Myrna looking disgusted and shifting uncomfortably on a gray metal chair in front of a gray metal desk with an utterly bare surface. Behind the desk sat a man with an air of calm authority and willingness to listen, a man in his middle years, with pale yellowish skin, slender fingers, thinning hair, rimless spectacles tinted the color of light coffee. He introduced himself as Enzo Popescu, invited Brad to sit, and said he hoped the three of them might have a productive talk.

"I'm sure you're wondering what this is all about. Miss Rashevsky understands perfectly but you are new here. Let me explain. We are very careful in this organization about the security of our files. I'm sure you understand that you and Miss Rashevsky have been knocking on doors, so to speak, that you are not authorized to open. Forgive me, but Miss Rashevsky has a very bad reputation in this office for poking into corners uninvited."

"She was helping me," said Brad.

"She was breaking every rule in the book," said Popescu.

"We're trying to do something for the director's office—for Frank Cabot, actually—"

"Mr. Cameron," Popescu interrupted, "I don't care who's waiting for the results. We don't tolerate computer hackers in this organization. If you want access to protected files, you've got to go through channels."

"Can't you call the director's office—"

"I already have."

"And?"

"Cabot's assistant confirms you're working for him. If he hadn't, this interview would have a different tone."

"Well, can't Cabot give you some kind of okay so we can find what we're looking for?"

"No, he cannot."

"Not even the director?"

"Not even me, Mr. Cameron. You have been trying to gain access to the files of a sensitive internal investigation."

"No," said Brad, "we're trying to do a name check on a Russian named Golenpolsky who spent time in the Gulag."

"Excuse me," said Popescu. "Those were counterintelligence files Miss Rashevsky was trying to open up."

"I don't understand."

"They were keyed to an important internal security investigation of a few years back."

"He means Aldrich Ames," said Myrna.

"Aldrich Ames?" said Brad. "Golenpolsky?"

"I don't want to get into specifics. I'm simply explaining to you that Golenpolsky is not a neutral subject."

"Ames told the Russians everything he knew, and he knew everything," explained Myrna. "They don't let people browse the files anymore."

"We are not discussing Aldrich Ames," said Popescu.

"Ames?" Brad repeated. "It doesn't sound right. Didn't he start working for the Russians back in the mid-eighties?"

"Nineteen eighty-five," said Myrna. "On the job for nine years."

Popescu, growing agitated, turned to Myrna. "Can't you save the history lesson for later?"

"It doesn't fit," insisted Brad. "Golenpolsky was nineteen seventy-seven and had nothing to do with counterintelligence."

"Mr. Cameron," said Popescu, "I'm security. My job is protecting files. This man Golenpolsky means nothing to me. But one thing I can tell you. When you ask about Golenpolsky, you ring a very important bell. And when you ring that bell, you get our attention."

"He means Aldrich Ames," said Myrna again.

14

Dean was the last to arrive for the Wednesday night class in problem drinking. It was on the first floor of an old red-brick elementary school in Southeast, down a long corridor lined with gray steel lockers, past a black man in a green uniform pushing a wide broom over the brown linoleum, to the last room on the right. When Dean opened the door he found himself at the front of the room. Seven or eight people were sprinkled in the first two rows: one woman, the rest guys.

The young therapist Lisa Benson was standing at the blackboard, chalk in hand. At the top of the board she had written the word DENIAL. She turned with the chalk in her hand at the sound of the door.

"You're late, Mr. Cutter," she said. "Why were you late?"

"I had to wait for a bus."

"That's an excuse," she said. "I asked for the reason."

Dean hesitated.

"You were late for a reason," said Benson. "We'd like to know the reason."

"You mean, like I don't want to be here at all and being late is my way of saying fuck you?"

"That sounds about right," said Benson. "And that attitude will not help you complete this course. So I'm going to ask you to apologize to the class and take a seat."

Dean hesitated. He felt his color rising.

"Don't make a federal case out of it," said Benson. "Just say *I'm sorry I was late.* That's all it takes."

"I'm sorry I was late."

"Thank you. Take a seat. I was just starting to explain the concept of denial. 'I haven't got a problem. I can quit drinking whenever I like. I can cut back if I want.' We have a saying in this business: *Denial is not a river in Egypt.* Step one is getting beyond denial, admitting you can't control your drinking. Nobody likes to admit that. What it means is you can't drink anymore. We're spoiling your fun."

A ripple of laughter crossed the room.

"It takes some people years to admit they can't control their drinking," Benson continued. "Other people are stubborn and never admit it. But we won't try to tackle this head-on tonight. We'll work our way up to it. Let's start with introductions. Tell us who you are and why you're here. Not just the DUI, a little bit of your life story. Mr. Dunham, will you begin?"

Dunham was at the far end of the first row, a chubby bald guy wearing a sport jacket and a bright red shirt open at the collar with a gold chain half hidden in the hair of his chest. He explained he was a good-time guy, partied his way through high school, had a lot of buddies. Sometimes it got away from him.

Down the row the life stories came.

When it was Dean's turn, he said, "I can't tell you why I drink. But I can tell you when it started—after I got back from the Gulf War. Do you want me to leave it at that, or do you want to hear about it?"

He was looking at the young therapist. "Tell us whatever you think we need to know," she said.

"Ever since I was a kid I wanted to join the army," Dean said. "There was a guy in my town who went to Vietnam—big brother of a girl I knew. I didn't have a brother or a father or an uncle, so Jason kind of took care of me and I looked up to him the way kids do. The government never explained what happened—just two officers marched up to the door one day and said he was gone and that was it."

"You mean he was killed?" asked the therapist.

"Missing," said Dean. "Missing and presumed dead. Later, one of his buddies told us about it. They had been sent across the border into Laos, which was supposed to be illegal. It was an army unit, but the CIA was running the operation. The rest came back, but not Sergeant Dyer. His sister calls the government every couple of years: no news. The most powerful nation in the world with the biggest spy organization and overhead satellites and those huge computers out in Maryland cracking codes—and they could never find out what happened to an army sergeant left behind in Laos."

The room was silent. The rest of the class was listening intently.

"You seem to know a lot about the CIA," said Lisa Benson.

"Quite a bit," said Dean. "I've made the CIA an object of special study."

"May I ask a question?"

Dean waited.

"What does this have to do with the Gulf War? And what does the Gulf War have to do with the fact you were arrested following a rear-ender three weeks ago with a blood alcohol content of zero point one nine?"

"Is that a rhetorical question or do you actually want me to tell you?"

He could tell he had set her back a bit. She wasn't expecting that sort of language. People often thought he was an illiterate asshole and he took pleasure in proving otherwise.

"Go ahead," said the therapist, "but try and keep to the point."

So Dean explained to the class that he had joined the army as a tribute to Jason Dyer. It hadn't been easy. He'd been in a bit of trouble as a kid, dropped out of school, spent some time on the streets, eventually straightened out, got his General Equivalency Diploma and finally joined the army. His Military Occupational Specialty was gunner in a Bradley Fighting Vehicle. After the first four he re-upped. Then came the Gulf War.

"I went over there in November. We were deployed in Saudi, in the desert west of Kuwait. There was no drinking in Saudi—I mean none. We sat there in the desert eating sand for three months till the ground war began. My buddy was a guy named Floyd from Oklahoma. He said he thought he knew dry and he thought he knew empty, but he said Saudi made Enid, Oklahoma, look like a golf course."

"Mr. Cutter," said the therapist.

"Floyd was my closest friend out there. One of the best friends I ever had. So the war began, and about an hour before daybreak we took off across the desert like cavalry to cut off the Iraqi army. We really covered ground. They said, Don't worry, we know exactly what's out there; the CIA and the NSA have been listening to their communications, and the satellites have been mapping their bunkers; don't worry, we've got it knocked. Forget the biological weapons. Forget the chemical weapons. We know where every Iraqi latrine is—just go.

"So the third day we come to this huge blazing complex of we-don't-know-what. We radioed back, What the hell is that? They say, Don't worry about it—fuel dump, supplies, whatever; the air force hit it this morning. We said, Listen, the smoke is like blocking out the sun; it looks like night. We're not even in it yet, and we can feel it in our eyes and in our throats and in our lungs—it's like acid.

"Don't worry, don't worry.

"So we barrel through it, the whole line of BFVs, and that night we begin to feel like shit. We radio, We got a problem. They say, It's just a little smoke inhalation. But it isn't just smoke; we can hardly breathe. We start to puke. My friend Floyd is sitting beside me; he's shaking, he's pale. When the sun goes down in the desert it's freezing. I think maybe it's just the cold. Floyd says, I ain't cold, man. I'm poisoned.

"Cut the crap.

"No, man. I'm poisoned.

"I get the medic. He says, I don't know. I radio back; they tell me there was nothing in that dump but number-two diesel fuel; we got the best intelligence in the world; your buddy's going to be okay. He just sucked in a little too much smoke.

"And at that exact moment Floyd leans over and pukes—blood. Blood and green crap. He begins to shake all over. The medic starts to jab needles into him. But nothing works, and after a couple of minutes Floyd stops breathing. The medic is pounding on his chest, giving him mouth-to-mouth. Finally he stops. I don't understand it, he says.

"You won't read about this anywhere in the history of the war. It's never been on the news. We were all told later it was smoke inhalation, plain and simple, but it wasn't smoke inhalation. Everybody puked blood that night. Floyd and seven other guys died. That wasn't a fuel dump; that was some kind of Iraqi chemical-weapons depot—bombs, artillery shells, storage tanks. And the CIA knew it. They had photos, they had radio traffic, they had defector reports. They just didn't get around to telling the air force. But you won't read one word about it. That's how we deal with things in this country."

"Mr. Cutter, that is a very affecting story. I'm sure it was a horrible experience. But that was years ago in the Persian Gulf. The rear-ender was last week in Washington, D.C. Forgive me. I don't quite see the connection."

"Puking blood wasn't the end of it. We could hardly eat for weeks. We had blinding headaches, dizziness, numbness in our hands and feet, shortness of breath, blurred vision. They brought every man in the unit back to Fort Detrick, Maryland—for observation, they said. More than two hundred of us. That's where they do research on chemical and biological weapons. The government says we stopped all that, but you tell me: What are all those people doing out there in Fort Detrick? Call up and say you'd like to drop by for a visit, maybe take a few pictures, and see how far you get."

"Mr. Cutter."

"I'm getting there," said Dean. "After a while it got better—not completely, but the numbness and the shortness of breath weren't so bad. Everything except the headaches. The Pentagon will deny it, but there are two hundred guys in this country who get blinding headaches two or three times a month, every month. You can't move, you can't think. The docs at the VA say, This is a migraine of unknown origin, but we'll give you a break and call it a ten percent disability; take two aspirin, and four if it's really bad. Well, aspirin isn't enough. I don't know what the rest of the guys do, but for me, vodka helps. So I keep a bottle of vodka in the freezer, and when I feel that pain begin to grow right back here"—Dean clenched his fist behind his head—"I self-medicate. That's the connection. I drink to control the pain."

After a moment the therapist said, "Well. That's quite a story."

"You asked," said Dean.

"I don't doubt something is causing you pain, Mr. Cutter. But you're saying the government makes you drink. Where's *your* responsibility in all this?"

"My responsibility? You don't believe what I'm telling you, is that right? You don't think the Pentagon would let Floyd and the others die just so they didn't have to admit they fucked up. You don't think they'd abandon two hundred of us with some kind of crippling condition that makes it impossible to live a normal life—just so they didn't have to tell the truth. You *trust* the government?"

"I guess I'd like to know more before I felt comfortable making a judgment."

"Yeah," said Dean. "Well, that's the difference between us. When I've been fucked over I get angry; you pretend nothing's wrong. What did you call it—denial?"

"The government hasn't done anything to me, Mr. Cutter. I don't want to argue with you, but the fact is I don't blame the government for whatever might go wrong in my life."

"Right," said Dean. "Nothing touches you. You don't breathe the air and drink the water. You don't eat the fruit and vegetables they've sprayed with chemicals. You don't drink the milk from cows pumped up with bovine growth hormone. You never think about cancer. Nobody you know ever died of cancer. Tell me something. Does anybody in this room think the government tells the truth about cancer?"

There was a moment of silence.

"Anybody?" repeated Dean.

The therapist collected herself. "I can't sort all that out, Mr. Cutter. But you need to understand something. You are going to have to accept responsibility for what happens in your life. You can do it now, or you can wait till you've really got yourself in trouble."

She was just like all the rest—everything was his fault.

15

In the front hall of Houlihan's, an old Irish steakhouse on a downtown side street where the nineteenth-century row houses somehow escaped the wrecker's ball, a weight-driven mahogany tall clock slowly chimed the hour of ten. Myrna had placed a drink order and departed immediately for the powder room, giving Brad a quiet moment to sort out his thoughts about a depressing, exhilarating, confusing day. Almost two years spent handling secret documents in a secret organization with secret missions had given him a first stirring of confidence that he was beginning to know his way around. Watching Myrna operate for an afternoon showed him he knew nothing.

Popescu had delivered a stern lecture on channels and had extracted from Myrna a solemn promise to make no further attempts to use or refine her homemade global master key. In return Popescu restored to her the use of her own office. To Brad he explained the channels for requesting the file of former Soviet prisoner Lev Golenpolsky. "Myrna knows the drill," Popescu had said.

Indeed she did. But she had told Brad as they were marched back through the halls that neither one of them would live long enough for all that Mickey Mouse. She said it wasn't the usual Office of Security crap that had her steaming. She was just a little bit familiar with the nine-year-long investigation of the Ames case, every last detail of which had been chewed over like a dog's rawhide bone until it was a limp rag of pulp, and she could tell Brad without hesitation or qualification that the Ames Task Force and the FBI and the CIA's Russia Division had never heard from the Counterintelligence Center, much less from Ames's lips, so much as one word that tied into Lev Golenpolsky or Akmolinsk or the Soviet Gulag. "I don't mind telling you," she informed Brad, "I am really mad, and you better believe the Bureau is going to be mad."

Brad had been taken aback by this furious monologue as they returned to Myrna's office. It was nearly five o'clock. Popescu's grilling had worn him out, he had not the first clue about what to do next, and he was full of anxious regret over his failure to telephone Jenny as promised. It had been nagging him all afternoon. Half a dozen times he had been on the verge of asking Popescu for the use of his phone but he held back; he was embarrassed. What could he tell her: that he'd practically been arrested as a foreign agent? What he wanted was a quiet dinner with Jenny, a night in bed, and a bright idea in the morning. What he got was a crash course from Myrna in tracing secrets and extracting information.

"This will only take a minute," Myrna had said when she grabbed the phone. She punched in some numbers as if she were poking a finger into an enemy's eye. "Sy Osgood," she spat out. "Tell him it's his friend Myrna." She spun herself around in her chair.

Myrna's interrogation technique wasn't at all hard to follow. Brad listened transfixed. Myrna told Osgood she'd just spent an interesting afternoon in the Office of Security, where she had learned that the notorious Aldrich Ames had told someone about some CI case that somehow involved a Russian-Jewish émigré named Lev Golenpolsky. Which was very interesting because she had a pretty goddamned good memory, and she did not remember any report of Aldrich Ames saying any such thing to his debriefers from the Office of Security, the Russia Division, or the FBI. Which left only the debriefers from the CIA's Counterintelligence Center. Could Sy contribute any word of explanation about the singularity of that fact?

Brad could not hear Osgood's end of the conversation, but it was evident from Myrna's rolling eyes and snorts of derision that he was offering bogus assurance of amazed ignorance and disbelief mingled with apologies and earnest pleas not to poke her stick any further into this particular hornets' nest. "I've got a need to know, Sy," Myrna shot back. "I am asking you to get Warren on the phone and get back to me pronto."

She had hung up and turned to Brad.

"That's got his blood running. Now you call your sweetheart."

Brad dialed Jenny's number and after eight or nine rings reluctantly admitted to himself that her answering machine was not turned on and Jenny herself was not going to pick up.

Within a very few minutes Myrna's phone rang and she went through the entire routine more or less verbatim a second time with Warren, whom Brad knew to be Warren DeForest, old boy chief of the CIA's Counterintelligence Center.

"No, Warren," she said. "No looking into it overnight. We have a very pressing question here that need not involve the Center's handling of the

Ames case so long as I find out right now, tonight, what Golenpolsky had to do with it. Otherwise I must pursue this subject elsewhere, and you and I both know that everything Ames told anybody is supposed to be in the files of the FBI."

Mention of the FBI brought DeForest to full alert status. The sweet pleadings from the other end doubled in intensity. Myrna was unbending. "Now, Warren," she said, her voice as implacable as a banker's saying the grace period was over, there would be no more extensions, the hour for understanding and forbearance had passed. "Not tomorrow, Warren. I want to know now."

A long moment of silence had followed this implicit promise of doom. At last he spoke. Myrna placed her hand over the receiver and told Brad, "He surrenders, but he'd like to explain in person, okay?"

"Okay," said Brad.

"Ten minutes," said Myrna.

Brad had tried Jenny one more time. Still no answer. He had followed Myrna down the hall.

Back from the powder room with lips a vibrant red, Myrna Rashevsky took a drink from her long-stemmed margarita. Then she removed a cigarette from her bag, lit it, inhaled, sighed.

"I quit smoking thirty years ago," she said. "I liked it but my father hated smoking. He went to a lot of trouble to get me out of Poland—all the way across Russia to Vladivostok, then a boat to South Africa, and another boat to the Dominican Republic. A year it took me to get to Brooklyn. The Germans, the Russians, and those *behayme* in Santo Domingo I survived—so I should die from lung cancer? Every time I lit up I thought of my father. So I quit for him.

"Now I smoke a cigarette once in a while—when I get worked up. You want one?"

"No, thanks," said Brad. "I'm a runner."

"Okay," said Myrna, "no more secrets. I'm not really in expediting. I was on the Ames postmortem. We spent years on that case. And I tell you something's not right here."

They laid out everything they knew: the 1978 memos about Golenpolsky and his report of an American in the Gulag, the details added by Terry Tyler, protection of the Golenpolsky file in Akmolinsk records, a flag to the Ames case, and finally Warren DeForest's explanation of what Ames had to do with it.

DeForest had visibly suffered before spilling the beans. Who was Brad? What was he doing here? Working for Cabot? Oh, my God. That created a bit of a—well . . .

"Look, Myrna, this is going to be a real mess. I think we should save our talk till morning. Will you trust me on this?"

But Myrna was unyielding. DeForest was impeccable in banker's gray and tie, an elegant man of years and much experience, but he hemmed and hawed and grimaced and did not want to say what Myrna was insisting he say. "All right," he said at last. "You've got me, I don't know all the details. I was in London at the time. But I don't doubt for a minute you'll dig up the rest. Here it is. This is why Golenpolsky's name was flagged to the Ames case. It wasn't Golenpolsky per se. I mean, it wasn't anything *about* Golenpolsky. But Golenpolsky was the subject of a conversation between an important official of this organization—I mean the Agency, not the CIC—and another official, a foreign official, a defense official, security official, from another country: the Soviet Union, actually. I don't know all the details, but its essence was a remark by Ames during one of his debriefing sessions here in the CIC. It's interesting you called Sy Osgood—very good guess; actually, it was Sy who was debriefing Ames that day, just the two of them. And Ames mentioned this conversation about Golenpolsky and that was it; really, that was the heart of it."

"Come on, Warren. It's not going to kill you, just say it."

"I told you," said DeForest.

"Who was he, Warren?"

DeForest shrugged. "Man named Kondrashov. Nobody important. Mikhail Kondrashov."

"Not a clerk, I take it."

"Well, I think we had identified him as an officer, possibly, of one of the intelligence organizations. KGB, I believe."

"Okay," said Myrna, "you're halfway home."

"Please?"

"The other name. You know we're not leaving without that."

DeForest sighed. "I guess it's our own fault," he said. "We should have circulated it at the time. Why we didn't I have no idea, actually. I was in London at the time, and when I came aboard in 'ninety-six I confess I didn't pay much attention to all this ancient history."

"Come on, Warren."

"Yes. What Ames told us, as I understand it, is that Golenpolsky was the subject of the meeting with Kondrashov. And the other party—you'll understand all my hesitations immediately—got the wind up here for a minute or two, I can tell you! But I caution you, this completes my knowledge of the matter; you'll have to track down the gory details elsewhere. One way or another it got sorted out, obviously. I mean the questions, whatever they were, must have been answered satisfactorily because the entire matter was laid to rest in a day or two."

"*Warren!*"

"Well, Myrna, the man who went to see Kondrashov, I'm afraid, was our acting boss, the next director of this agency, if all goes well. Frank Cabot."

In the front hall of Houlihan's the weight-driven mahogany tall clock was chiming the hour of midnight. Myrna had been noticeably slowed by the third margarita, but Brad was excited. He was beginning to get the picture. It hadn't come easily, but he now finally understood that his eager-beaver pursuit of Lev Golenpolsky had created a very considerable problem for the man who had put him onto the case. Myrna made him see it.

"What happened at that meeting in Moscow we don't know," she said. "Maybe nothing. It's what should have happened that's going to cause the trouble. Sy Osgood should have written up a complete report of Ames's story, his boss should have signed off on it, and copies should have gone to the Office of Security and the FBI—especially the FBI."

Brad balked at that point. So what? Cabot wasn't a spy; the idea was ridiculous. So the CIC bent a rule. Cabot wasn't running the CIC; it wasn't his fault.

"No, no, no," said Myrna. "You don't get it. Cabot can't be confirmed without a complete background check by the FBI. This was not passed on to the Bureau four years ago like it should have been, so they've got to investigate now. That takes time. That means delay in the hearings. But the hearings are already scheduled for next week. No way they can do this by next week. So Hawkins has got to postpone the hearings. What does he tell the president? What does he tell Senator Brian MacLaverty? What does he tell the reporters? Think about it."

Brad did think about it. Finally he replied with a question: Why tell the FBI at all? They didn't know. DeForest could just keep his mouth shut.

"Oh, no," said Myrna. "DeForest's got to tell them now. Don't you see? *We* know. Once somebody knows . . ."

It wasn't obvious to Brad, so Myrna explained. A secret may lie dormant for years, but once somebody knows, the secret begins to stir, warmed into life by the attentions of the hiders and the revealers. The hiders make some small mistake, the revealers begin to nose about; the hiders panic and try to hide the secret in a new place, the revealers inevitably note the scurrying and begin to draw closer; the hiders grow frantic, the revealers summon help; the hiders issue threats. . . . A secret wants to be known the way a flower wants to bloom or a peach wants to be eaten. It exudes an irresistible must. Once somebody knows. . . .

It was at this moment that Myrna had ordered her third margarita.

"Once somebody knows," she said, licking the salt from the rim of her glass, "it's as wriggly as a snake. There's only one way DeForest can avoid a nasty bite. He's got to do the right thing. He's got to tell Frank Cabot the CIC is going to pass on the Ames report to the FBI. And then he's got to call up the FBI and tell them the CIC has been holding back.

"I don't envy Warren tonight. On the other hand, he doesn't envy us."

"We didn't create this mess."

"Maybe, but we're the *bulbenikim* who turned over the rock."

"What you're saying," said Brad, "is that we're going to be facing a world of trouble tomorrow."

"First Cabot, then us."

"All right," said Brad. "I understand. But there's one thing we're forgetting."

"What's that?"

"Cabot obviously knew about Golenpolsky. And the fact he went to the Russians means he must have taken the story seriously. So what did the Russians tell him? Were they holding the American or not?"

"I don't think I would worry about that right now," said Myrna. "I don't think that's going to be the first question on Cabot's mind when he gets to his desk in the morning."

"Wait a minute. What about the prisoner? That's what this is about."

"Not anymore," said Myrna. "Don't try to give this story a happy ending, Brad. It's unprofessional."

16

George Tater did some of his best thinking, especially in the early phases of a story, while getting his nails done at Salvatore Morelli's. He sensed the Cabot confirmation story beginning to stir now, as he closed his eyes and stretched out his right hand on Thursday morning February 21.

It was a little later than his usual hour. Hawkins had come and gone but Tater had tracked the senator down late the previous evening, following a tip from a friend at the FBI. The tip was short on detail: "It's Cabot. Something has come up, we're in slow gear."

"His wife?" Tater had asked.

But that was all the special agent was at liberty to say, and of course it was more than enough. Hawkins, reached at home after he was already in his pajamas, said nothing to quiet Tater's suspicion that the problem went far beyond Kitty Cabot's still-possible arrest for driving under the influence. But for the moment Tater had no idea what the problem was.

He lay back with his eyes closed, stretched out all but flat on the reclining barber chair, while next to him, wearing a white smock and sitting on a low stool, Cherry began to minister to the cuticles on his right hand. Sally Morelli was in the other barber chair reading *The Daily Racing Form.* At noon he would call in bets. Sally's son, Bobby, had disappeared down the hall. In a sense those in Morelli's at this quietest of moments, the half hour before noon, were what Tater had instead of a family. No man in Washington spent more time in Morelli's than George Tater, whose accountant at Tater's instruction deducted every nickel as a business expense for "research." But it wasn't what Tater learned, much as he valued each gold fleck of information acquired in the course of a waking day, that brought Tater to Morelli's; it was the peace, the acceptance, the prospect of being cared for, the fact nothing was required in return except money.

After Cherry first appeared at Morelli's a year or two back, George Tater made a point of asking her out for a date while she worked on his nails. He liked her black hair, worn in a pageboy with bangs across her forehead; the purple-red and lavender shades of lipstick she favored; the milky-white skin of her inner forearm; the rich and graceful curve of her buttock and thigh in crisp white polished cotton slacks as she sat beside him on a stool. Sometimes as she worked on a nail her pink tongue emerged and played along her upper lip. Cherry spoke quietly, almost demurely, with a slow soft voice, and it took Tater, usually a quick study, five or six weeks to realize that she understood him perfectly: he was a sponge for whatever was being given away. She wouldn't go out with him on a bet. Once that was clear, things went smoothly; Tater tipped generously and Cherry did his nails the way he liked them.

Part of it was simple male vanity, of course. Tater liked to make an impression and he did: expensive clothes, strong face, an unblinking gaze. But he also liked extended attention, being handled, the unhurried filing and buffing of each nail while he lay back and let his mind roam. Sometimes he talked aloud, explaining to Cherry in careful detail just what information he was after and who might have it. More often he reflected in silence, walking his way mentally through a story almost as if he were scripting a film: Tater dialing the phone, Tater approaching the secretary's desk outside some potentate's office, Tater putting his questions to the keeper of the secrets—sometimes elliptical, sometimes as pointed as a sword thrust.

But for the moment, sitting in Morelli's barber chair, what pricked Tater's curiosity was an evasion by Senator Hawkins on the phone the night before. "It's late, George," he had said. "If you want to follow up the MIA thing, we can talk tomorrow."

"I've got something else on my mind, Senator."

"What's that?"

"Cabot's wife," said Tater.

"She's going to be okay," said Hawkins. "There's nothing there."

"Then why the delay in the hearings?"

"What delay?" said the senator. "There's no delay. Who told you there's a delay?"

"I'll be frank with you, Senator. I spoke with the investigating officer. There was a question of alcohol involved."

"Well, I'll be frank with you too, George. I think that's been resolved. I think the other driver was at fault in entering the roadway, so I don't believe there are any charges pending. Anyway, George, it's the man's wife. It's a traffic story. It's beneath you. You aren't planning to hound this man about his wife, are you?"

"So the hearings are on schedule for next week?"

"Of course. Or the week after. We'll let you know when the dates are firmed up."

"On Monday you told me next week."

"On Monday I hadn't talked to the Bureau. They say next week or the week after. The FBI can't do a special inquiry in ten minutes, you know. We're talking about the Director of Central Intelligence here."

"The FBI has to do a SPIN on Cabot?"

"Of course. The Bureau will treat this like any other sensitive appointment. They won't sign off until they've dotted every *i* and crossed every *t*."

"They won't give you a date certain?"

"Nothing is certain in this life, George."

"Cabot's wife is not the problem?"

"On my honor, George. Trust me. This has nothing to do with Cabot's wife."

Hawkins certainly had one thing right. Somebody with serious clout had been hard at work behind the scenes. The result could be found in a small story on page B7 of the metro section of the morning's *Washington Post.* Tater knew a thing or two about police departments and newspapers, and he was impressed. Somebody with serious clout had obviously been at work behind the scenes.

BRAKES BLAMED IN CRASH

Bad brakes were blamed by District police today for a two-car accident Tuesday that seriously injured the wife of a high government official and the child of the other driver.

The brakes apparently failed on the uninspected 1981 Buick driven by Mrs. Violetta Ramos of Suitland, police said, causing her to lurch into the path of oncoming traffic on Wisconsin Avenue as she was leaving the parking lot of a liquor store near Q Street. Police said that Mrs. Ramos entered the United States from El Salvador on a tourist visa that expired two years ago.

Mrs. Ramos's five-year-old son Eduardo continued in serious condition with internal injuries today at Greater Southeast Community Hospital. The driver of the second car, Mrs. Catherine M. Cabot, of McLean, was listed in stable condition at Georgetown University Hospital. Her husband, Franklin S. Cabot, was recently nominated to head the CIA.

Police said their investigation was continuing.

Tater's obvious first step was to contact Patrolman Scully, the investigating officer Tater had met two nights earlier, promise him anonymity, and ask how this amazing reversal of priorities had been achieved. On the night of the accident, Scully had told him an arrest was inevitable as soon as it was clear that Cabot's wife would live. Scully was an approachable man. He had cocked his head in the direction of the tight-lipped young woman standing with arms folded across the hospital waiting room. Had Tater spoken to her? Cabot's niece. She was in the car. Worked in the District. Jennifer Moore. In the phone book.

Tater had been thinking about Ms. Jennifer Moore. Pursuing a story through a man's wife or children was generally dismissed as morally doubtful by reporters, but in this case Tater wondered if it might not be a sound approach. He sensed many fissures in Cabot's home life. Besides, he liked the looks of this young woman. Just how he might find a way to cross her path in a natural way had not yet occurred to him, but it shouldn't be too hard. He'd spot her in a crowd long before she would spot him.

Cherry finished with George Tater's right hand and switched sides, dragging her stool across the tiled floor. Tater opened his eyes and looked around. The other chair was still empty.

He settled back and closed his eyes again as he felt Cherry pick up his left hand in her cool fingers. He had a way of opening himself to a subject in his mind, inviting his unconscious to tell him what was missing, what was in the wrong place, what jarred, what didn't sound right. Something Hawkins said didn't sound right. The FBI. Special inquiry. *On my honor, George.* Why the emphasis? *This has nothing to do with Cabot's wife.*

This.

Tater repeated the sentence in his mind, stressing the first word: *This* . . . has nothing to do with Cabot's wife.

The next question was obvious. So what *did* it have to do with? The more Tater thought about it, the clearer it seemed. The FBI had got hold of something a lot more important than an errant wife.

As Cherry made her way through Tater's left hand, the door opened and Sally Morelli's voice greeted the newcomer. "Good morning, Senator." Tater opened his eyes.

Striding across the room was the meaty, freckled, red-faced figure of the junior senator from Massachusetts, second in seniority on the Senate intelligence oversight committee, a man whom Senator Harrison

Hawkins would be compelled to inform, however reluctantly, when something came up, the notoriously anti-CIA Brian MacLaverty.

"Just a second, Cherry," said Tater. He pulled the lever and brought his chair upright.

"Good morning, Senator," said George Tater. "What's new?"

17

Before Thursday came to an end, Harrison Hawkins would feel the full weight of his years.

When he walked into his office in the morning he was met by Rhoda with a message delivered in a low voice to call Frank Cabot; he'd said it was urgent. Rhoda knew urgent when she heard it and so did Hawkins. He punched in the number himself. Cabot explained the problem without ceremony, but all Hawkins really needed to hear were the words "Aldrich Ames."

"Frank," he said, when Cabot explained just what had turned up in the files, "this has a bad sound to it."

"I know the Bureau is going to make a stink—" Cabot began.

"No," said Hawkins. "Stink doesn't cover it. If the media get hold of this you're going to be in the deepest kind of trouble. You know what I'm talking about: endless questions, delay, personal attack. We've both watched this sort of thing too many times. But it's early days, Frank. You can get out of this with your honor intact. A man with a wife in the hospital . . ."

But Cabot wanted to go ahead; he insisted he was ready for the ordeal and assured Hawkins there was nothing the president had to worry about. "I know that," the senator said sadly.

Frank Cabot was the only man in the federal government who had ever seriously tried to help Hawkins find MIAs. They weren't friends in the usual meaning of the word, but they were Washington friends, political friends, men who did things for each other, kept confidences, gave warnings, were quick to call with congratulations or sympathy. Hawkins owed Cabot, and he prided himself on paying his debts. "If you're sure," he said, "I'll start cranking up the machinery."

"Of course I'm sure," said Cabot. "It's go forward or disappear."

At the top of the chairman's to-do list was a heads-up call to the White House.

"What's the problem?" asked Peter Schleicher without preamble.

"The FBI special inquiry has run into a technical snag," said Hawkins. He explained that it was nothing of substance, a classic glitch, one of those intelligence community squabbles you just had to steel yourself to live through. Seven or eight years back the CIA should have passed on to the FBI a report in which Cabot's name had appeared; it slipped between the cracks; the Bureau was angry and determined to conduct a full-scale inquiry, not only into the original report—which of course would present no problem whatever—but into the Agency's failure to forward the report in the first place.

"Cabot's name in what report?" asked Schleicher.

"One of the many interviews a few years back the Agency conducted when they were doing damage assessment on the Ames case."

"Wait a minute," said Schleicher. "You mean Ames brought up Cabot's name?"

"Apparently he did."

A considerable silence followed.

"Peter," Hawkins said, "I know what you're thinking. But we've just got to face facts. There is no way in this life that I can curtail the pissing match heading our way if we don't get together and handle this right. The Bureau doesn't answer to me, but it's possible that if you were to call the Bureau in the president's name—"

But Schleicher wasn't falling for that. He cut Hawkins off. In a voice flat with anger he said, "You told us Cabot would present no problem for your committee."

"Peter," Hawkins said, "my committee has no problem with this. We have complete confidence in Frank Cabot. I'm just telling you that without the FBI report there can be no hearing next week. As I see it, the question before us is how to explain the delay."

"Ames!" said Schleicher. He was furious. "Cabot told us he had nothing to do with the Ames case."

"He didn't. Ames just mentioned his name; that's it. Ask Cabot. Ask the Bureau. But we need a plausible public reason for delay. Your job is to get the Bureau to keep its mouth shut. We can contain this, but you've got to help me."

They argued it back and forth. It was obvious no word of Ames could be allowed to attach itself to the delay. After a while Schleicher calmed down and said he'd call back with a plan. No goodbye.

Hawkins had reached cruising speed now, and he put in a call to Special

Agent Philip Durkin of the Washington field office of the FBI. Hawkins had spoken to Durkin only the previous Saturday, an hour after the announcement of Cabot's nomination by the president. Very helpful man, in Hawkins's view, very forthcoming. Hawkins had assured Special Agent Durkin that he knew Cabot well and he could assure Durkin the nominee had been polygraphed, along with every other official high and low at the CIA, following the infamous debacle with Aldrich Ames. There were no blank pages, no unturned rocks in Cabot's history, nothing to give the FBI pause. Hawkins was sure everybody else who knew Cabot would say the same. If the Bureau could provide a summary of its inquiry for the eyes of senators only by Friday—Hawkins knew this was asking a great deal—he could schedule hearings for the following week. Special Agent Durkin had said he believed he could comply with the senator's request. How long ago that seemed now.

"Phil," said Hawkins, "I'm calling to let you know about something I expect will soon be crossing your desk if it hasn't already. I know this is something you'll need to take into consideration. I've just learned that the CIC out at the Agency was making a routine file check yesterday—"

"Senator," interrupted Durkin, "I am apprised of this matter. We were informed by the Agency yesterday evening. Naturally we will need to look into this carefully, and of course it will affect our timetable."

"I know this gives you one more base to touch—" Hawkins began.

Durkin interrupted. "We have a task force that deals with Ames material," he said. "They'll need to know precisely what Ames said, they'll want to know what prompted the CIC file check now, and of course they'll want to know why the report was not circulated at the time."

"Of course."

"It goes without saying that the Agency is not always open and forthcoming about sensitive matters like breaking every rule in the book."

"I have some influence with the CIA," Hawkins said. "You are going to have their full cooperation."

"Obviously tomorrow is out of the question."

"Obviously."

"You understand I can make no promise as to how long this is going to take?"

"I understand."

"I'll keep you informed of our progress," said Durkin. Hawkins couldn't have reasonably hoped for more, but he had—not for himself but for his friend.

. . .

It came as no surprise when Brian MacLaverty, reached by telephone, insisted on coming up immediately in person to argue the whole thing through. The exchange did not go well.

"I don't agree with this at all, Harry," MacLaverty said. "Cabot was a piss-poor analyst. Now he's got some kind of counterintelligence cover-up in his record, and the Bureau knows about it. This guy is a liability to the country."

"That's not fair—" Hawkins began.

"You can't bottle this up. I don't care what you and Schleicher dream up. Ames put the finger on Cabot, and the Agency buried it. The Bureau's going to tell everybody in town. You can't make this go away."

"They should have passed it on, that's true," said Hawkins, "but—"

"Harry. One word of this in the papers and Cabot will be hung out to dry. We're all going to look like idiots. The man was lying to us."

"He wasn't lying," Hawkins said, his voice rising. "Ames simply mentioned his name; he was just making trouble."

"I don't believe it. You don't even know what's at the bottom of this, do you?"

"I'm expecting a full report."

"He didn't tell you? Listen to yourself. You can't just say 'national security' and move on. He's not going to slide through this with a smile and a slap on the back. Tell the truth—do you know what Ames said?"

"Cabot's writing a letter to the committee," said Hawkins. "It will be in there."

"A letter!" MacLaverty barked with laughter. "You're dreaming. The Bureau is going to have a field day. The media's going to be all over this. They're going to drag it out one piece at a time. You know what this is like—death by a thousand cuts."

"It won't come to that. You're overreacting. The Agency failed to touch every base. That's all."

"Stop kidding yourself. Ames pointed a finger at Cabot, and the boy wonder sat on it!"

"Brian. I won't have you shouting in my office."

MacLaverty's face was red and Hawkins was breathing heavily. Both men made a conscious effort to calm down.

After a moment MacLaverty said, "This nomination is up to its ass in trouble, and it's only five days old."

"This nomination is going forward," said Hawkins.

"You're the chairman," said MacLaverty. "You can stick with it as long as you like. But don't expect me to lie down for it. And don't look at me when the pissing starts."

"I'm not looking for someone to blame."

"You will be. Cabot is going to put this committee through hell, and the crazy thing is, he's going to get the worst beating of all. Why are you pushing Cabot into this?"

"I'm not pushing. I told him he could call it quits. But he wants his chance."

"We have our differences," said MacLaverty, "but I'm your friend, Harry. Here's my advice: Call the president and tell him to pull the plug. You'll be saving everybody a lot of pain. That's all I've got to say. I'm getting out of here until I cool off. If you come to your senses you can find me at Morelli's. I'm going to get a haircut."

With MacLaverty's departure the hard part had been over. Hawkins had telephoned the other members of the select committee, telling each of them not one word more, if he could help it, than the member had a right or needed to know. They all understood the problem was not trivial but agreed with Hawkins's decision to go forward.

Every afternoon following his return from lunch, Senator Harrison Hawkins removed his shoes, stretched out on the butter-soft leather couch in his office, and took a thirty-minute nap. Today he felt he needed it more than ever. The door was closed, his aides were instructed not to open it for anything short of fire or the person of the president, and the phone did not ring. Hawkins loosened his tie, undid the third button on his shirt, and slipped the fingers of his right hand in over his heart. Sometimes after lunch, especially on days when he threw caution aside at the Cosmos Club and had deviled beef bones, crisp with the succulent fat his doctor had assured him was a cholesterol time bomb, Hawkins felt a kind of jittery, squeezing sensation play over his chest, like a breeze rippling the surface of a country pond. Lately, he was pretty sure his heart had begun to miss the occasional beat. Sometimes it had an extra beat. It didn't feel dangerous but it didn't feel right.

"Oh, Harry," said his wife, Lydia, "you're going to bury us all."

That irritated him. For one thing, he prided himself on concealing his fears. Worse, she treated his worry like a joke. Wondering how much time you had, thinking you might die suddenly between one sentence and the next, was no joke.

"When I'm gone," Lydia said, "you can find a brand-new wife and be young all over again."

That irritated Hawkins even more. He'd been married to Lydia for nearly fifty years. She understood him. When they had dinner at home she always made sure they had a dessert he liked. When he snored at night she poked him and told him to roll over, and that made him feel safe. It was Lydia who rousted him from bed the morning of his heart attack and drove him to the hospital. Lydia always understood what was on young Harry's mind, and she knew who had to be invited to their parties, and she knew when he needed a new tie and picked it. Lydia held his hand when he cried at funerals, weddings, and ceremonies of farewell. Hawkins disliked thinking about his own death but feared just as much the awful possibility that Lydia might die first and leave him alone.

"I don't want to be young all over again," he pouted.

Besides, a younger woman, one of those buxom Georgia girls who always seemed to be working in his office down home, might be too much for him. For decades Hawkins and the rest of the silver-haired solons had laughed about "the Rockefeller syndrome"—sudden death in the arms of a young lover. That was before Hawkins knew how tricky hearts really were. He liked watching those leggy girls in their summer dresses and he loved impressing them with tales, all more or less true, of the great times he had lived through and the great men he had known. But Hawkins didn't want to turn the clock back. He didn't want a second life. He didn't want to find himself in bed with some flat-bellied tennis-playing girl in her twenties. The thought frightened him.

But content as he was to grow old gracefully, hair turning silky, laugh lines deepening, Hawkins still felt his work was unfinished. His secret ambition was to accomplish one truly notable thing before he called it a day. He hoped that inner serenity and sticking to his diet would give him a few more years. The danger was that he loved ice cream, and needling from guys like Brian MacLaverty pushed him into the red zone. Hawkins often felt for the pulse in his neck and fingered his chest for the first tingling, squeezing, fluttering signs of coronary shutdown because he feared time was short and a severe accountant, drawing up the final balance sheet, would say his long public career had not added up to much. One or two well-crafted pieces of legislation. A few extra years of operation for military bases picked by the Pentagon for closure. A new federal mail-sorting facility outside Savannah. Two sentences of eloquent sorrow on national television after the assassination of John F. Kennedy.

Hawkins had squinted and sweltered in the hot television lights of hundreds of press conferences. He'd questioned numberless witnesses at hearings, given thousands of speeches, whispered over voting strategy, put a finger on the scale for or against platoons of men who aspired to become president. There had even been talk once of the number-two spot on the ticket with Walter Mondale. Of course Hawkins disparaged the job of VP, but he had nonetheless basked in the glow of national attention for a week or two, until the name-recognition polls said think again. Whenever Hawkins totted it all up, the hard answer he gave himself was always the same. He had nothing to be ashamed of, but he wasn't going into the history books.

But even at this late hour in his political life, Hawkins believed, there was still one thing he might do which could win him a place in the folklore of America, and that one redeeming thing was to perform the miracle of Lazarus—to bring home a man his country and family had given up for dead.

Hawkins had taken up the MIA cause two elections back when a redneck Republican went after him for being weak on defense in the seventies. Hawkins *had* been weak on defense in the seventies, and the race was a damned close-run thing. But beating the drum for MIAs forced him to meet their families, and their faith was contagious. To himself Hawkins admitted he had more than stretched the law in keeping young Harry out of the Vietnam war. This added the goad of guilt.

For the last dozen years Hawkins had listened to every story of a white man glimpsed in the streets of Hanoi or the rice fields of the Red River delta. Not all of these stories sounded crazy. Things were confused in that part of the world. An assistant to an assistant to Henry Kissinger during the Paris peace talks once confessed to Hawkins privately that the Nixon administration was morally certain it had recovered every living POW *captured in Vietnam.* Hawkins pressed. The assistant to the assistant explained that Laos had been beyond their reach; there were some sticky issues in the final political settlement of the war; they had done their best, but as a purely practical matter . . . But the assistant to the assistant would go only so far; he told Hawkins solemnly that he would shoot himself before he would repeat any of this under oath in an open hearing.

Hawkins knew the odds as well as anyone, but he longed for a miracle. To those closest to him, even to Lydia, Hawkins pretended to believe that too much time had passed, the MIAs were all dead. But privately he harbored a secret hope.

. . .

"It's all set," Schleicher said in midafternoon. "The president is going to ask Cabot to chair a special study of nuclear terrorism before the Brussels conference. He's asking you to postpone the hearings for a week or two, and he apologizes to the committee for the inconvenience."

"I like it," said Hawkins. "Will the president say something at the White House? Should I be there?"

"He wants to play this down—say what he has to say, answer a few questions. He's already scheduled to make a drop-in at the British embassy, so he's decided to do it there. The Brits are going to join in the special study. Presidents never say anything important on foreign soil so nobody will be expecting anything; the press won't be out in force. You'll get an official letter in the morning."

Hawkins thought it might work. He liked the explanation; it sounded plausible, it made no mention of the FBI, and it contained not a hint of a whisper of the name of Aldrich Ames. But he knew there was a wild card—the media. "Ames is the kiss of death," Schleicher had said. "One word of that and it's batten down the hatches."

Hawkins ran a tight ship. When something leaked from his committee he raised holy hell. But the committee had a dozen members, Hawkins had informed them all, and Brian MacLaverty detested Cabot down to the way he parted his hair. He'd leak Ames's name if he thought he could get away with it, so Hawkins dropped in on MacLaverty at the end of the day to discuss the leak question. MacLaverty listened politely as Hawkins listed the names of those who knew what was going on, stressed his warnings to each, and said Schleicher had promised the president would back up the effort with a personal call to the head of the FBI.

"Have I overlooked anything, do you think?" Hawkins asked MacLaverty. "Anybody who needs a special warning?"

"No," said MacLaverty, "you sound like you've done a very thorough job. But this remark by the president at the British embassy tonight—you think nobody's going to notice?"

"I expect it'll find its way into the paper."

"No, Harry, it's going to be a bombshell. The word's out. The networks, CNN, George Tater—they all know about it, and they're all going to be there. No way they're going to brush it off as routine."

"I didn't tell them."

"Harry, when the story is big enough, even God leaks."

"God better watch his step on this one," said Hawkins. At the door he paused and said, "Nice haircut, Brian."

18

"I can draft the letter any way you want it," Leo Weissberg was saying in Frank Cabot's office that Thursday afternoon, at roughly the hour Senator Hawkins was taking his daily nap. "But I don't think we can leave out Golenpolsky. He's the reason we've got a problem."

"Let's see if we can't find a way," Cabot replied. "I am extremely reluctant to explain Golenpolsky to Hawkins, and if you'll bear with me you'll see why."

Frank Cabot was taking this one step at a time. He had called Hawkins to tell him the FBI was up in arms. He had spoken with Peter Schleicher to say the sin was purely one of omission. He had conferred over a lunch of tuna-fish sandwiches with Otis Jones in the latter's office and agreed that the less said about Otis the better. He had asked Jane to make an appointment for an initial interview the following morning with Special Agent Philip Durkin of the FBI's Washington field office. He had called Jenny to ask if she would be free to accompany him to a reception that evening at the British embassy before visiting Kitty at the hospital. He had summoned Brad Cameron to express his extreme irritation with the way he and what's-her-name had royally screwed up. And he had set aside forty minutes in the middle of a busy afternoon to work out the details of whatever he planned to tell the Bureau and the Committee with his chief assistant Leo Weissberg, who had watched DCIs come and go and had nurtured a profound feel for how much of the truth a man in trouble was going to be required to spill.

"You've got to explain why the Agency sat on the report at the time," said Weissberg. "And you've got to put their minds to rest about Ames. So we've got to include some version of what Ames told the debriefers and some explanation of why you went to Moscow back in nineteen seventy-eight. If you don't need Golenpolsky, okay."

Leo Weissberg had been around a long time and had pulled many a CIA official back from the brink of public disaster. He had a law degree from New York University, but it wasn't legal advice he excelled at, it was the rare ability of a man who has spent his life on the inside to maintain a gut feeling for what will fly on the outside. William Casey had once too often ignored Weissberg's sound advice; Robert Gates had listened, had survived, had eventually been confirmed as DCI, and had invented a new position for Weissberg in the congressional liaison office. It had an official name but nobody used it; when Weissberg's special services were required, people in trouble said they were calling the fire department. "Jane," Cabot had asked that morning, "can you track down the fire chief for me?"

When the fire chief said he saw problems, Cabot responded.

"I think this is doable," he said. "We'll start with Ames. Ralph Sommers was running the CIC at the time, and Sy Osgood skipped a grade or two and personally took it to Sommers and said, 'We've got a problem. Ames has told us this story.' "

"Which was?" asked Weissberg.

"I'll get back to that. So Sommers said, 'Don't write anything up. There's bound to be some innocent explanation. Let me check this out. We've got enough trouble.' It was a perfectly reasonable thing to do. You don't turn the Agency upside down if you don't have to. I mean for God's sake we're talking about the DDI. Sommers must have been sick to his stomach. I don't see how anyone can make an uproar about the way he handled it."

"Okay," said Leo. "It's not kosher but it's reasonable. We can live with that."

"Sommers goes to Alastair Woolcott, same day. He says, 'Mr. Director, we've got a problem.' Tells him what Ames said. Woolcott says, 'Ralph, this is just another case of Ames causing trouble. I'm not going to allow this. I'm going to ask Cabot about this personally. If I am not totally and completely satisfied by his explanation, we will conduct a no-holds-barred investigation and let the chips fall where they may. But first I'm going to give Cabot a chance to explain himself. You go back downstairs. I'll let you know before close of business today.'

"Woolcott will testify to this. Technically you're supposed to write it up, consult the Attorney General, and so on, but Woolcott will say he looked into it, made his decision not to disseminate the report, and that was that. Of course, the FBI will protest that's not according to regs, but no one's going to second-guess Woolcott on this."

"The Agency broke the rules," said Weissberg. "Not you."

"Exactly."

"So burying the report offers no cause for refusing to confirm."

"Exactly."

"Okay," said Weissberg. "That sounds like Woolcott to me. Now, what did Ames say."

"This wasn't yesterday," said Cabot. "Give me two minutes to rifle the memory banks."

At certain moments Frank Cabot had the ability to withdraw entirely into his own mind, where he felt he could see all the separate elements of a problem, almost as if they formed a stack of books waiting to be sorted and shelved. The pieces all had to connect, and in his mind, without moving or speaking, Cabot would start putting each piece in its proper place. It might take a minute, it might take twenty. He looked like a man listening to distant music, head cocked to one side in thought. Everybody who had ever worked for Frank Cabot had seen him thus and had learned patience. When he had a solution to his liking, he would return to the here and now as if no more than a bare moment had passed, lay out his solution to the problem, and accept comment and suggestion utterly without pride. But you had to let him sort it out on his own first; you couldn't skip a step or hurry the process. Leo Weissberg had watched Cabot do this many times over the years, whether he was writing up sensitive estimates on Soviet missile programs during the 1970s, or preparing testimony for Congress during the many investigations of the mid-1980s, or just deciding how to tell a man he was fired.

While Cabot pondered, Weissberg went out for coffee. By the time he returned with two mugs Cabot was ready. "Okay, Leo, I think what I told Woolcott is a good place to begin. He calls me in. 'Frank,' he says, 'Osgood was debriefing Ames today downtown in the federal detention center, and Ames told him he heard something from one of his Russian handlers—I think it was during one of the meetings in Rome. He says back in the mid-seventies you met secretly with an officer of the KGB in Moscow.

" 'Frank,' Woolcott tells me, 'before we write this up and circulate it to the Office of Security and the Soviet Russia Division and the FBI, we'd like to know what this is all about so perhaps we can avoid a bucket of trouble we don't need.' "

"Okay," said Weissberg. "I'm with you."

"I told Woolcott substantially the following. I didn't put it down in a memo at the time and neither did Woolcott. But this is what I told him and he'll confirm it before the committee.

"I said, 'Alastair, I went to check out a report from a friendly service that required very sensitive handling. I didn't dream this up on my own. It was a request from the White House that sent me. I would just as soon not identify the source of this report but it was an officer of the Mossad. This came at a delicate moment in the battle over the SALT treaty, and the White House wanted to move cautiously because we had good reason to fear this report would completely wreck the climate of trust we needed for the Senate to ratify that treaty.' I told Woolcott, and I am telling you, that the Mossad had learned—from Golenpolsky—the Russians were holding an American prisoner in the Gulag."

"An American?" said Weissberg. "What kind of American?"

"An army sergeant who was listed as missing in Vietnam—Laos, actually, but he wasn't supposed to be in Laos so the official records said Vietnam."

"Whoa," said Weissberg. He looked stunned.

"You see my concern," said Cabot.

"I do see your concern. Was it true? What happened to him?"

"That's what I went to Moscow to find out. I learned that it *was* true but he had died in a typhus outbreak and his body had been cremated. This promised nothing but trouble. So it was decided to say nothing."

"You told Woolcott all this?"

"Yes, and he did just what I would do or you would do. He goes down to the CIC and tells Sommers, 'Ralph, I'm not going to let Ames blacken the name of this Agency any further. This is on my head; it's my call. This trip to Moscow was on legitimate government business and it wasn't written up for sound and sufficient reason. So I don't want it to leave the building.' So they wrote up a report that left out the details—everything I'm telling you now—and they buried it in the CIC and put a block on all file references to Golenpolsky."

"That's what Rashevsky pried open."

"Exactly," said Cabot. "Once Rashevsky knew the Golenpolsky file was flagged to Ames, she dragged the rest out of her friends at the CIC. They got an attack of the jitters and decided the time had come to tell the FBI. There was nothing I could have done at that point, and I wouldn't have tried."

"It all makes sense to me," said Weissberg. "It's hard to see how it could have been handled differently. But God knows how Hawkins will take it."

"I'd like to avoid that."

"But how?" asked Weissberg. "Golenpolsky and the MIA are the heart of it."

"Think about it," said Cabot. "If we mention the MIA we have to say what happened to him. And we have to admit nothing was said to his family. And we have to say who sent me to Moscow and who decided to keep it secret."

"And that was?"

"I already told you. The highest authority in the land. Who would not appreciate having his name dragged into this."

"What a mess," said Weissberg. "So we plead national security."

"I think that's the way to go," said Cabot. "We say we got a report from a friendly service to whom we have sworn anonymity. And I was sent to Moscow to check it out, no further action was taken, and my superiors—not me—decided to make no official record. Woolcott was satisfied that Ames was only telling us something we already knew and that was that."

"I'll write it up," said Weissberg, "but everybody's going to have the same question: Check out what? I want to suggest something, Frank. I think you ought to tell Hawkins personally. Don't run the risk of his finding out from somebody else."

"That's good advice, Leo. I appreciate it."

An hour later Weissberg returned with a draft of a letter. Cabot read it carefully. "That's perfect," he said, when he was done. "No one can craft a letter like you. Let's stamp TOP SECRET all over it and see what happens. Now there's one other thing I wish you'd take care of."

"What's that?"

"The Rashevsky woman. It's time she retired. I don't want a big noise about it. I just want her out of the house."

"She *is* retired, Frank. She's been on contract for years."

"Well, can't we just cancel it?"

"Rashevsky has a lot of friends. People are going to make a fuss if you just kick her out."

"Then send her someplace far away. Cameron doesn't really know his way around; she's the one who makes him dangerous. Send her across the ocean. Give her temporary duty in Australia. It doesn't matter where. Just make sure she's not at the main gate Monday morning. If we get her out of the equation I'll breathe easier."

"I'll handle it," said Weissberg. "But that still leaves one problem."

"What's that?"

"Ames. What does Ames know? What happens if somebody like MacLaverty decides to call Ames as a witness?"

"Don't worry about Ames," said Cabot. "Ames knew I went to Moscow, and he knew it had something to do with Golenpolsky. But there's no way he could know the rest of it. Ames is not a problem."

"If he's not a problem," said Weissberg, "why have we been worrying how to handle him all afternoon?"

19

As soon as they were in the car Thursday evening, Jenny asked about Aunt Kitty.

"Everything hurts," said Frank Cabot, "but she's going to be all right. The docs went over it all with me this morning. Nothing's broken, she's completely oriented, and she can wiggle all her fingers and toes. She's banged up, she had a concussion, she cracked both collarbones, but all that stuff we were afraid of—we can quit worrying about that."

He didn't say what they'd been worrying about, he never did. Jenny had been worrying Kitty would never wake up, would never walk again, would stop being the Aunt Kitty who always knew what was going on in Jenny's life.

They were creeping out Massachusetts Avenue. People with umbrellas were bent forward into the driving sleet along the sidewalks, waiting at corners, making their way through puddles and piles of slush. The car appeared to be an utterly ordinary sedan but it was unnaturally quiet inside, the ride was smooth, the seats were plush, the tint of the windows gave the world outside a cast of beige-gray.

Most of the people Jenny knew in Washington were recent arrivals, a couple of years out of college or law school or graduate school, come to seek their fortunes. They were serious and hardworking, full of hope that great things were possible—and a little dazzled by the concentration of conspicuous money, famous faces, and power. Jenny took all that as a matter of course, like others who had grown up in Washington political and government families. Her home town was Baltimore, where her father taught French literature and art, but Washington was more than a second home. She'd been living here since she was fifteen, when she left boarding school abruptly only two weeks before Christmas. A girl down the hall at boarding school had said she saw Jenny steal $120 from a wallet in the top bureau drawer of a third girl. The headmaster, a man with thick white hair carefully brushed, had called Jenny into his office, told her of the charge, and explained it could be resolved if Jenny were mature enough to confess her mistake, return the money, and apologize.

"I can't return the money," Jenny said, trembling. "I didn't take it."

Her father was on a sabbatical year in Paris, working on a revised edition of his great book on the rose window in the cathedral at Chartres; her mother had gone too, of course, and both parents had told her to stop making a fuss about a few words of apology, if that's all it would take; stay where you are and do what you have to do. It was Aunt Kitty who said, "Honey, if you think you've gotta go, get on the train and come live with us." So Jenny did.

"I'm glad you were free," Uncle Frank was saying in the seat beside her. "I dislike walking into a big reception alone, and I don't like going with those scrubbed young fellows from the Agency. They're so attentive, they never make jokes, and when it's over they don't seem to have noticed anything."

"They're probably scared of you," said Jenny.

"Am I that forbidding?"

"No, but you're at the top of the ladder and they're at the bottom. How hard do you try to put them at ease?"

"Probably not hard enough."

"In that case," said Jenny, "maybe they don't really know what you want, and maybe that makes them nervous."

"You're a sensible girl," said Cabot.

Jenny's friends, working as young reporters and congressional staffers, bustling about town for think tanks, lobbying groups, and foundations of every stripe, were all pressing toward the centers of power and influence like salmon fighting their way upriver in spawning season. Her friend Meg from Indiana, who had spent four years with Jenny at Bryn Mawr and was now working in the international department of a bank downtown, was starstruck by Jenny's uncle when he was nominated to head the CIA. Meg was smart and she was rising fast—two promotions in two years—but she had never known anyone at the center of power, routinely photographed, cited in the newspaper, given thirty seconds on the evening news. To recent arrivals, Meg included, such prominence added up to famous. Jenny had been going around Washington with Uncle Frank long enough to know that CIA directors could hardly be called famous unless they were in the worst kind of trouble, but Meg was right in one sense—Uncle Frank was about to get what he admired most in this world: the respect that comes with position. Of course he already had that; Jenny felt it unmistakably whenever she entered a public room with him. But he was about to get a whole lot more.

"There's another reason I was glad you're free," Uncle Frank was saying. "I'd like your help about something."

"My help?"

"It's awkward, and I probably shouldn't say anything about it. But if you don't mind?"

"Of course not."

"I've got a problem with your young man, Brad. Now don't worry—he hasn't done anything wrong and I think the world of him—but he has made a small misstep, and I'm not quite sure how to get him to see it."

"He's made a mistake?"

"It's not exactly a mistake, it's a question of judgment. He was doing some routine research with one of our counterintelligence people—Jenny?"

"Yes?"

"I'm not about to tell you a lot of highly classified info here, but it *is* confidential and you need to exercise discretion."

"You're being awfully mysterious, Uncle Frank."

Jenny was concerned but she was amused, too. The Uncle Frank she had known since childhood asked questions—for the most part good ones that didn't crowd children or force them to describe the progress of their studies in school. But he wasn't a storyteller and he wasn't the sort of man a child might comfortably interrogate. There was a wall up where his work was concerned. In the three years she had lived with Frank and Kitty while she finished high school in Washington, Jenny had never heard Frank talk about the CIA.

"Your young man," Uncle Frank was saying, "is hot on the trail of an old report of an American prisoner, and that is exactly as it should be. But it sometimes happens in this business that a routine matter touches upon a highly sensitive matter, and that is the case here. The problem is that Brad and his guide, who is an old hand in this game and ought to have known better, poked their way into files that were clearly marked NO ENTRY."

"Well, can't somebody just tell him to stop?" asked Jenny.

"Of course, and we have," said Cabot. "But it's my sense he's being a little headstrong. I don't want to jump down his throat. I just want somebody he trusts to tell him to let this go. Does he confide in you?"

"He tells me how he feels about things."

"I mean"—Cabot tried again—"does he actually tell you anything about his work? Some men do, some don't."

"Very roughly, I guess. He doesn't go into detail."

"He hasn't mentioned this?"

"I don't know what *this* is."

"Of course," said Cabot. "Well, here it is with the bark off."

By this point Jenny understood that her uncle was genuinely worried and concerned.

"Brad is trying to find out something about a Russian whose name was once mentioned during a debriefing or confession of a rather famous American spy. I also had occasion to refer to that Russian, so my name and the spy's name got into the same file. This is just one of those strange turns in a business where everything is written down and squirreled away somewhere.

"Now I want you to understand something. There is no big secret here. But every time someone asks about that Russian, the name of the American spy comes up, and his name has the capacity to get the Congress and the FBI and the media very, very excited. I don't want to burden you with a lot of detail, I just want you to understand that Brad is in a position where he could, entirely without intending to, create one hell of a lot of trouble—for me personally."

"Has he already done it?" Jenny asked. She didn't clearly understand what Brad had done, but she knew her uncle felt threatened. She had never heard a note of apprehension from him that even came close to matching it.

"He has got things stirring, yes, and he's being just a little bit stubborn. But I would say nothing's out of control, and it might all blow over anyway. But if you felt comfortable about it—"

"Of course."

"I really would appreciate your just telling him to *let Golenpolsky alone* till this confirmation process has run its course. I know how he feels about you. You won't have to explain any further—if you could just say that."

"I'll tell him," said Jenny. "I'll call him tonight as soon as I get home. I can't believe he hasn't taken the hint already."

"I really appreciate this," said Cabot.

Jenny assured her uncle there was nothing she wouldn't do for him or Kitty, and Cabot sighed with what sounded like genuine relief. He had always seemed completely collected and in charge of his feelings, and it was disturbing to Jenny to realize that he actually felt threatened.

"Things are going to be fine," Uncle Frank said. "I'm sure a word from you will be more than enough."

Jenny had never told Brad the boarding school story but was furious at him all the same for not knowing how she felt about Kitty and Frank. She would read Brad the riot act. She was already choosing her words in her mind.

"We can quit worrying," Cabot said. "It's a great relief Kitty's going to slide by on this one, everything has been sorted out with the police, none of the media seem to have latched on to the story. But I can tell you, Jenny darling, I was a little worried there for twenty-four hours."

20

As soon as Jenny entered the brilliantly lit reception hall she picked up the buzz: the president was going to appear any minute. Uncle Frank was scooped up at the door by three or four Brits in dark Savile Row suits, tall lanky figures with red faces, slicked-back gray hair, and the manner of men who often spent the evening in rooms with chandeliers. Uncle Frank introduced her, of course, and they smiled a greeting, but then they quick-marched Uncle Frank across the room to a knot of dark suits and bobbing heads, leaving Jenny in the momentary care of the youngest of the welcoming committee, who identified himself as Jon Aspinwall—plain Jon, no aitch.

"Nobody told us," he said, "that Mr. Cabot would be arriving with his niece. You must be very proud of your uncle. The next Director of Central Intelligence. That puts him right at the center of things, doesn't it? You too."

"Oh, no," said Jenny. "It'll make no difference in *my* life."

"No? I'd have thought it couldn't help but do so. I suppose you heard. Your uncle must have told you. We're expecting the president a bit later on."

"Yes, he told me. So did the doorman and the girl at the cloakroom and the attendant in the powder room."

"Ha-ha," said Jon. "The word does get out. Not every day the British embassy receives a visit from the president. See those fellows over by the bar?" He gestured.

Fit men in gray suits were quietly surveying the room. A thin wire ran from the collar to the ear of each. One of them was whispering something into his fist.

"Checking out the place from top to bottom. We said, 'Look, we're pretty careful ourselves, you know.' I won't tell you what kind of look that got us. What would you like?"

He brought Jenny a glass of Columbia Valley chardonnay and introduced her to a pretty blond girl in a blue satin dress, Annabelle something-something (with a hyphen) who worked in trade statistics, and at that point with many smiles slipped away. Annabelle was full of excited enthusiasm for the brilliant future of Anglo-American cooperation with the help of Uncle Frank.

Jenny recognized many faces but knew none of them. Fresh arrivals didn't often get invited to embassy parties. But plenty of people took an interest in her, men mostly, in the rising middle of government careers. None made much impression on Jenny, who had grown impatient with men who believed none too secretly they were on their irresistible way to the cabinet, the Senate cloakroom, or the partners' lounge of Covington & Burling. Their level of expectation was breathtaking.

Washington was part of it, the occasion was part of it, the fact she was young, thin, and single was part of it, but Jenny wasn't kidding herself; it was Uncle Frank who brought them swarming. People congratulated her as if she'd engineered his career herself, and the fires of excitement burned all the hotter for the imminent arrival of President Norman Anderson. They appeared to take this calmly in stride; each reported Anderson had done or said thus-and-so, as if they had been in very recent communication with someone extremely close to the president, if not the man himself. Jenny heard bits of half a dozen explanations for the president's decision to appear, all plausible, all different. The huge room, bright and noisy, gorgeous with uniforms and expensive dresses, was steadily filling as the minutes passed. Waiters carrying silver trays with champagne and drinks made slow progress through the room. Elbows were jostled, drinks were spilled, ashes were flicked on the polished wood floor. Jenny was carried around the perimeter of the room by a kind of deep current, almost as if she were being handed on like the Olympic flame. She lingered nowhere. Brief conversations seemed each the same: "How pleased you must be. . . . Oh! You must be so proud. . . ." Only one face was a genuine surprise.

"Hugh Diamond!"

"Darling girl! You look quite frantic. I can imagine what you've been through—all these people so happy for your wonderful Uncle Frank."

"I'm his niece, for God's sake. Why are they congratulating *me*?"

"So they can tell people they saw Frank Cabot's niece at the British embassy last night. The alternative is going nowhere and seeing nobody.

It's Washington. Here, the humbler we are, the more we dream of knowing and being known. Don't fret about it."

"What are you doing here? You told me you were never allowed out of your cubicle."

"It's true. I spend my life in a windowless room with a white-noise machine and no phone. But just this once they have let me out. Please don't repeat this. What I am about to divulge is a highly classified national secret. I am working on terrorism with the Brits. Shhh!"

"So what's this all about? Why the president, for goodness' sake?"

"Actually, that is a bit delicate. Ostensibly it's to announce a blue-ribbon crash study of nuclear terrorism to be led by your distinguished uncle and his British counterpart. But in reality . . ." Hugh Diamond rolled his eyes toward the chandelier like a man succumbing to an epileptic fit.

"Hugh!" said Jenny.

"Doesn't Brad tell you anything?"

"He's been avoiding me."

"Darling girl, he's been hunting you like a bloodhound in heat. Slow down and let him catch up. Believe me, he's got a lot to tell you. All this is his doing, in a way. I'd better let him explain it."

"Hugh!"

"The essence is this. They're trying to keep everything supersecret but I've been here before—it's all heading for the papers. Your devoted Brad has contrived to drag a red herring directly under the noses of the FBI, and they are going to investigate the hell out of it before they let Cabot's nomination go forward with a clean bill of health. It's all a great deal of to-do about nothing, but there is no budging the Bureau when its feelings are hurt, and all this—in particular the imminent arrival of the president—is intended to give your uncle something to do for his country while the Bureau checks out the sexual orientation of his teachers in kindergarten. Don't blab this on the street corners."

"How could Brad do all that?"

"It wasn't easy. But I'm just giving you the essence. This isn't the place for the details. Enemy ears are all around us."

"Will you see him in the morning?"

"Unless they shoot him."

"Will you tell him to call me and to keep trying?"

"Darling girl, when he hears that he will weep with joy."

A team of Brits including Jon, all smiles of apology, came to take Hugh Diamond away, and Jenny, momentarily alone, cut through the crowds to the far wall. There the crush had thinned and she found a place beside a long table groaning with masterpieces of the canapé maker's art. Gazing across the room with an absent look she sampled half a dozen pâtés on small white toast rounds. After that she moved to a poached salmon sprinkled with dill and topped it with chunks of South African lobster tail dipped in a light mayonnaise. Across the room, the knot of dark suits and bobbing heads had grown larger. The suits all towered over the small trim figure of her Uncle Frank, but occasionally the wall parted for a moment and she could see him chatting within. Near the group some men were fiddling with a light on a pole. The lobster was incredible.

"Try the langoustine."

Jenny turned.

"It's something about the temperature of the water."

Next to her was a man of cool demeanor who had appeared from nowhere. Faint accent. Southern? Jenny had a vague sense she had seen him before, a common feeling in Washington, where the face hurrying past in the street might belong equally to the waiter at the French place on the corner or the junior senator from Montana.

"You're wondering if we've met."

Jenny blushed. "No, I . . ." She searched for a polite lie.

"Don't worry about it," he said. "Happens all the time. Reporters are standard fare on the talk shows, and if you're addicted to talking heads, sooner or later you're going to see the face of every scribbler in town." He speared a chunk of langoustine and offered the toothpick to Jenny. "I love this stuff. Some weeks I live on this stuff. What's your favorite?"

"I like them all," said Jenny.

"You certainly tried them all. You went down that line of pâtés like a preacher at a church picnic. Hmmmm! Creamy, rich, nice little tang of mustard. Guide me."

"That one then." Jenny pointed. "Plain honest pork—cooked crisp—just enough pepper to give it bite."

The man tried it. "You're right," he said. "I'm going to make a light supper right here. Then I'm going to ask one question if I can get it in. Have you ever seen the press gather around a president?"

"Only on TV."

"Well, come with me when I go up. It's different in the flesh. You'll see. You've got to get right up there in the crush. Then you'll feel it."

"Feel what?"

"The power of the presidency. There's only one other thing in the world like it."

"Sex," said Jenny.

"What makes you say that?"

"I thought it was what you were going to say."

"No," said the man. "Winning. It doesn't matter what it is—just so long as the eyes are all on you."

"You mean prizes?"

"I'm not a prizewinner. But I've won a few battles. That's the kind of winning that sticks with you. Come with me. You'll feel it right here." He slapped his hand on his abdomen.

The men fiddling with the light pole had now been joined by numerous others with additional lights, video cameras, big aluminum boxes, cables, and cable junction boxes. There was a dense forest of equipment all focused on a dais moved in for the purpose. At the front of the dais was a lectern bristling with a thick copse of microphones and wires. The lights were turned on and off, the cameramen and grips stood idly, feasting from little plates of finger food. Fifteen or twenty men and women—some as turned out as movie stars, others scruffy and rumpled—were positioning themselves behind white tapes laid on the floor.

"That's about half the cast of usual suspects," said Jenny's companion, continuing with his light supper. Between remarks on what was good and what to skip, he talked about his fellow journalists. "One of my favorites," he said, pointing. "Richard Kramer. *Time* magazine. Looks like a diplomat. Watch his elbows and feet. He'll ask some big puffball question he'll use in an essay on the mood of America. Next to him"—pointing again—

"Sam Donaldson," said Jenny.

"Right," said her companion. "He's the Quantrill of television."

"Quantrill?"

"Hit-and-run genius of the Civil War. That comes from my southern background."

"I couldn't quite place it," said Jenny.

"Texas southern. It fools people," he said, "but trust me. Where I come from is southern. Over there's another wordsmith—Faith Osborne. Writes a column for the *Post.* I'm kind of surprised to see her here."

"The tall one in red?"

"No, the one next to her. Black hair."

"Very red lipstick."

"Glasses up on forehead."

"Plain leather backpack, no jewelry."

"No jewelry, but she's got a MontBlanc pen."

"You can't see that," said Jenny.

"No, but it's there."

"I take it you know this woman."

"Everybody knows everybody in the media biz."

"I mean really know her," said Jenny.

"No, I don't really know her. We dated for a while but it wasn't meant to be. Uh-oh—when all the lights go on, it can mean only one thing. The prez. Are you coming?"

Jenny went. As they approached the crowd of reporters whose backs appeared to form an unbreachable wall, the man took her by the arm, quite firmly, and brought her with him right into the crowd. She hesitated, but his firmness carried her forward and to her surprise the reporters, men and women alike, glanced at her and then parted very slightly, turning their bodies, so that their progress was almost like passing through a series of turnstiles. She let the man wedge her forward; she was very conscious of his hand on her arm.

In a moment they were deep within the crowd and in another moment they were in the second rank but fully in view of the dais and the door behind it, through which now appeared four or five men striding briskly toward the lectern, tallest among them the instantly recognizable figure of the president: the nose, the dimpled right cheek, the curly salt-and-pepper hair. Jenny had seen him in the flesh only once before. The lights were all on; the brightness was intense, to Jenny it was like being on a movie set. Bodies were pressed in close all around her, and when the first man reached the lectern—Jenny recognized the British ambassador from Style section photos in the *Post*—she felt the crowd close almost like a physical embrace, the people in front holding fast, refusing to be pushed across the white tape on the floor, while those behind strained forward to see and hear. She had to hold herself rigid to keep from being shoved this way or that, and against her firmness bodies molded against hers from all sides; it was like a kind of weird pushing contest.

The ambassador was speaking, little words of welcome, introducing the faces with him: the first minister, Sir John Something of Her Majesty's Government; Uncle Frank, working his way toward the front, the tall commanding figure of President Anderson at his side. Now Anderson stepped to the thicket of microphones. Jenny was struck by his left eye—it was half closed, almost in a conspiratorial wink—which made him look incredibly . . . friendly. In the briefest of glances, he took in all the reporters on all sides and seemed to settle for a moment right on her.

"Thank you, Sir John," he said. "Friends—I have only one brief announcement to make. I need not remind any of you of the long and intimate cooperation of our country and Great Britain on urgent matters of national security throughout the violent century so recently drawn to a close. Tonight marks another small but important chapter in this special relationship in our ongoing effort to free the world of the scourge of terrorism. I am asking my good friend Frank Cabot . . ."

He explained the study Cabot and his counterpart would undertake, said that of course they would be working without ballyhoo and fanfare as befits simple, honest men—this time he really did wink. He thanked his good friend Frank for agreeing to drop everything on such short notice, and he thanked his good friend Senator Hawkins for kindly agreeing to postpone Cabot's confirmation hearings for as long as necessary. Then, drawing gracefully to a close, he invited a few ques—

"*Mr. President! Mr. President! Do you . . . ? Can you . . . ? Have you . . . ? Mr. President! Mr. President!*"

The president's eyes rolled over the throng; he seemed to pick out one drilling voice. "*Mr. President! Are you issuing a warning*"—the rest of the reporters fell silent; the hush was complete; the questioner continued in a normal voice—"a warning to the outlaw nations of the Middle East that you are drawing a line in the sand, sir?"

The president explained that he didn't want to single out . . .

"*Mr. President! Mr. President!*"

The man beside Jenny had a question that he began to formulate in a precise, drilling voice, as if pushing the words like an ice pick through the crowd. The president took another question. Almost before he was finished the man began his question again with exactly the same words, tone, and focus. Again the president nodded elsewhere. A third time the man began his question and this time he simply refused to let go.

"*Mr. President. The threat of nuclear terrorism has been with us for some years . . .*"

The reporters fell silent. Anderson's attention was directed fully toward the man at Jenny's side, and she could sense that every face, every camera, every ear had turned in their direction. It seemed the whole world was watching the president, the man at Jenny's side, and Jenny herself. Her heart was pounding. She stopped breathing. She was terrified that the man was going to make some awful gaffe, lose his train of thought. . . . She uttered a silent prayer for him. His voice returned to normal.

"Have you received—a follow-up question, if I may, Mr. President—have you received intelligence information of some specific new threat?"

The president said no in four ways but as the last words of the last negative died from his lips the man was speaking again.

"Mr. President, in that case why are you putting off the Cabot confirmation hearings? Is there some difficulty with Cabot's confirmation?"

"Not at all. Cabot's the man I want for his job. But we have a major conference scheduled for Brussels next month, as you know, and I thought this investigation by my personal choice for DCI would prepare us well. The story here, if I may make so bold—you'll forgive me, friends?—the story here is that Brussels is not going to be just another talk fest; we are going to unveil a strong new program to combat terrorism wherever it is found. Brussels is going to be the turning point. That's your story."

"I see what you mean," Jenny said when it was over, and the camera lights were out, and the president and his entourage began to work the room. Jenny had retreated to the banquet table with her new friend. Jenny had been around Washington all her life, but this man with one gesture had shown her what made it run. "It's like all eyes are on you, and if he listens to you then the whole world is listening."

"Nobody can beat a president," said the man. "I've seen people try, and the next thing you know they're covering the Department of Agriculture. But you can get their attention, and the attention of a president is a very powerful thing."

"What do you do with it?"

"Well, I'm a reporter. When you get a president paying attention, any story becomes a big story."

"Are you writing about terrorism?"

"No, I'm writing about Cabot."

This Jenny had not expected. "You're writing about Frank Cabot?"

"I'm sorry," the man said. "After you said 'ahhh' back there I thought you more or less knew who I was. I apologize. I shouldn't be such an egotist. I'm George Tater. I've been with *The New York Times* for thirty years. The CIA is my beat." He held out his hand. "And you?"

"Come on," said Jenny. "You know who I am."

"Ma'am," replied George Tater, "as they say in East Texas where I spent my formative years, I sure don't."

21

"You want a hit?" asked Dean.

Russell had settled himself in the oak chair in front of the counter. He had to stretch out his left leg just so. When he was done, the pant leg settled down over the brace that ran from his hip to his ankle and you could see the outline of the metal rods and ratchets that helped him to walk. It was nearly midnight, closing time. Dean had already locked the door.

"I don't smoke pot," said Russell.

"Blows your troubles away. Helps you mellow out."

"I don't want to mellow out," said Russell. "I like to stay focused."

"Don't you ever feel like taking a break?"

"No, I don't," said Russell. "Life's short. I've got an agenda."

"Yeah, what's on the agenda?"

Dean had lied to Lisa Benson. Vodka he could take or leave; pot was the thing that kept him going. He had already sucked down two or three long drags and the moment suddenly stretched out. All the problems of his life floated away: the night clerk job, the DUI hanging over his head, the needling of the therapist, the overdue rent, the departure of his girlfriend (already nearly a year in the past), the aches and pains. A joint really did relieve pain.

Cheryl had blown up one night while Dean was mellowing out, shouting at him, trying to get a response. "Are you just going to sit there with that stupid smile on your face?"

He was too mellow to get mad. One of those long stretched-out moments passed slowly right in the middle of Cheryl's fit, and the next thing he remembered was the slam of the door after what seemed like an hour later. It might really have been an hour. Cheryl went through that door with a suitcase just the way they did in the movies. He tried to think of something to say, but the words were a long, long time in coming. At last he said, Write when you get work! and began to laugh.

But that was the last time he laughed about it. Sometimes when he thought about Cheryl he was sad, but most of the time it made him angry. Sad or angry it made no difference. He never spoke to her again. Loss, sorrow, and pain, that was life. They fuck you over and then you die.

"First on my list," Russell was saying, "is to penetrate that arrogance and that complacency and permanently introduce into their lives an element of fear."

"Whose lives do you mean?"

"The lives of the people who run this country. The president. The senators who shake down big business for *campaign* contributions. The Pentagon. The CIA. All those people who got their own kids into the National Guard and sent the high school dropouts to Vietnam. They never heard of your friend from Accokeek. He's just another one of the two thousand and whatever dumb fucks who are missing and presumed dead. Frank Cabot says the CIA leaves no stone unturned in its tireless search. The United States has a moral obligation. Bull-fucking-shit! Guys like him—nothing ever touches them."

To Dean, Russell's speech seemed to be coming from the moon. He was feeling too mellow to get mad.

"I'm going to tell you something not everybody knows," Russell said. "Can you keep your mouth shut?"

Dean gave himself a small shake and tried to look awake.

"You aren't going to read this in *The Washington Post* or *The New York Times.* You want to know what happened to the MIAs? Listen up.

"When the war ended, Nixon and Kissinger made a secret deal to give the North Vietnamese billions of dollars in aid after the prisoners came home; it's all in the government's secret papers. But then they kept the money—billions and billions of dollars, enough to make hundreds of people rich. We stopped the bombing; the POWs in North Vietnam came home. But Charlie wouldn't release the MIAs because they didn't get the money, and the government said, What MIAs? Those men are all dead in the jungle somewhere.'

"That's it. Money is the secret. The money promised in the Paris accords was all transferred to numbered accounts in Switzerland and offshore banks in the Caribbean. Very, very few people knew about this. Once the POWs were out the money was frozen. Not one dollar ever got to Hanoi. Not one MIA has ever been found and released. No money, no MIAs. It's that simple. That's the reason your buddy Dyer is rotting in a bamboo cage in Laos somewhere. This is fact I'm telling you. The government thinks we'll never find out."

Dean was having a tough time keeping all this straight. He wanted to say, Christ, Russell, can't it wait? His leg was hurting. His groin. That black sergeant used to call it the *groan* area. Very gently Dean touched the lump. Last spring it was the size of a pea. Then it was the size of a grape. Now it was the size of a walnut. The docs would love to get their hands on Dean and start pumping their poisons into him. No fucking way. Dean had read up, and he had stopped eating all animal products. He was taking 1,000 IUs of vitamin E and drinking two quarts of bottled water daily. Once he had cleaned the toxins out of his system, he would be okay. The lump would go away. These things don't work overnight, but the lump was actually beginning to feel a little smaller. The marijuana helped. When he smoked the pain went away, pretty much. Almost entirely.

"They think no one is on to them and no one can touch them," said Russell. "What they need is a good dose of fear. To understand that even someone on the inside is vulnerable—someone like the honorable Frank Cabot, or Senator Harrison Hawkins, or the chairman of the Joint Chiefs of Staff. If we hit somebody like that, the rest would *identify.*"

"How are you going to do that all by yourself?" Dean asked.

"I'm not going to do it by myself. That group in Michigan I told you about—those are serious people."

But Dean had turned away. He was trying to get up.

A cold blast came from the front door. Curly-haired Niko in an overcoat slammed the door behind him and marched across the room, fanning his hand in front of his face.

"Cutter," he said, "are you smoking dope in my store? Are you out of your mind? Who the hell is this?"

22

The receptionist at the Earth Defense Trust Friday morning said Jenny was in a meeting so Brad called her home phone, got the answering machine, suggested dinner, said he'd call back. There was no way he could explain where he was and what he was doing. "I miss you," he said, and hung up.

Eight sharp, Myrna's note had read. *Records.*

Brad glanced at the clock—10:15 a.m. He watched the pale, motionless man at the front desk. Wisps of hair crossed his pate. He was writing in some kind of ledger. When Brad had opened the door into Records a few minutes before eight the man had given him the thinnest of cold little smiles.

Brad was irritated, not worried. Myrna probably had some hot lead and had gone off without him. He was popping with exasperation. He'd been wrestling with this all night, and the more he thought about it the clearer it became: there could be only one possible reason why Aldrich Ames and his Russian handler had been talking about Lev Golenpolsky back in 1985—something to do with the American in the Gulag. He was the key. It was the Ames connection that had everybody in an uproar, but that was all political bullshit, a bureaucratic turf war; nobody thought for a minute Cabot had a security problem. It was the American who mattered; Brad was sure of it. If he could just talk this through with Myrna. . . .

But the morning passed and Myrna did not come. Brad called upstairs four or five times, but each time he got her voice mail. "This is Myrna Rashevksy. I need to know"—pause—"so leave a message." Brad quit leaving a message after the third call. After a while he stopped fretting and began to think.

There was no way Security or the Counterintelligence Center was going to let him start browsing the Ames files. He could forget that. Same went for casual chatter with the CI people, who probably had orders to shoot him on sight. Cabot's personal history was obviously off limits. Brad didn't know any Israelis who might tell him about the Avraham Lipskys, father and son. James Angleton was dead. Terry Tyler had shrugged and held out his open hands; everything he knew was on the table.

So who else might know? Tyler had reported to Larry Winter, the Director for Operations back in 1978. But Myrna said Winter was no easy touch and Myrna probably knew. Winter had reported to Admiral Stansfield Turner, Jimmy Carter's Director of Central Intelligence, but that door could hardly be called open. What was Brad supposed to say? "Hello, Admiral, this is the new kid out at the Agency that everybody's mad at; if you've got a minute, I think I've found a way to drag you into the Ames case"?

And Lev Golenpolsky. Brad wasn't sure how old Golenpolsky was when he got out of Russia, but nothing he'd heard suggested a decrepit old man. Golenpolsky was probably alive and well in Israel.

Brad rolled that thought around in his mind for a spell: Golenpolsky, alive and well in Israel.

What was it the guy in the operations course said down at the Farm? At any given moment, 80 percent of the people in the developed world are in a room with a telephone.

Odds were, Golenpolsky had a telephone. He was probably in the phone book. Was it possible Brad could just . . . call him up?

Now Brad *really* wanted to talk to Myrna. He was panicked by the enormity of what he was proposing to do. What awful chain of trouble might he unloose with an unauthorized, out-of-channels telephone call to a onetime source for a theoretically friendly but notoriously prickly intelligence service? One thing Brad had fully grasped: The next Director of Central Intelligence did not want this to happen.

The pale man at the front desk scratched in his ledger.

Maybe, thought Brad, he'd just put one tentative toe in the water: try directory assistance, see if Golenpolsky was really listed, then decide what to do. Surely that couldn't hurt.

Jenny finally answered the phone in late morning. "Dinner's out," she said, cutting him off in mid-greeting. "I don't care how you treat me—"

Brad wasn't expecting this. "Wait," he began.

"No, you wait. What the hell are you doing to Uncle Frank? He told me you've been stirring up serious trouble, and I'm mad as hell."

"Let me explain—"

"No, you listen. I don't care what you think you're doing, this is causing him trouble and I want you to stop. Frank and Kitty are as important to me as my own parents."

"Of course, Jenny, I know that."

"Well, quit this stupid project of yours. Wait till the confirmation is over. Uncle Frank was very upset. He actually asked me to see if I had any influence with you and could urge you to stick to channels and follow orders like you're supposed to. If you care about me—"

"Of course I care about you."

"Then drop it," said Jenny. "Promise. Swear to me. If I mean anything to you."

"You mean the world to me," said Brad.

"All right," said Jenny. "You've promised. I'm trusting you."

Brad did not have the courage to clear up just what he was willing or unwilling to do, and Jenny gave him no time.

"We'll talk in a day or two," she said.

. . .

"I can't believe I'm hearing this," said Hugh Diamond. "What you're describing is a failure of the clandestine mentality. You're an embarrassment to the profession.

"Brad—you've got to think black. Secret agents of the CIA don't call people up and ask what's going on. That's what newspaper reporters do. Secret agents recruit assets, tap phones, plant bugs, bribe housemaids and doormen, listen from the next bar stool, pretend to be somebody else, ask friendly services. When all else fails, they study the files."

Hugh Diamond's office was small, just big enough for a desk, two chairs, the obligatory safe for classified materials, a chest-high bookcase along one wall, floor-to-ceiling shelves on the other. Most Agency offices were crammed with books bristling with little colored sticky notes, House and Senate hearing transcripts, thick sheafs of photocopied texts of foreign broadcasts, budget documents, multiple drafts of reports—the great churning river of paper that poured daily from the copying machines of the Central Intelligence Agency. "Paper is our most important product," Hugh often said.

But while Hugh had a solid reputation as the Agency's most facile reports writer in a generation and was constantly in demand for emergency scribbling on whatever subject was for the moment hot in the corridors of the White House, his office was as neat as his person. His bow ties were bright and snug, his suits would not have been out of place in the boardroom of a great bank, a crystal vase on his desk bloomed with a single perfect flower, changed daily. Hugh's hair always had a just-out-of-the-shower look, his face beamed, his eyes behind his round tortoiseshell glasses were wide with pleasure. By the light of candles in an expensive restaurant, Hugh looked half his forty years. In the surgical glare of CIA fluorescents you could see that this was a man who would match you drink for drink and was never one to call an end to the evening.

"You are such an innocent," Hugh would say, when Brad asked the sort of questions only Brad would ask. "How could anyone fail to love so dewy a rose!"

Hugh was a decade and some older than Brad. He had a firm place in the world of the CIA, was valued for his talents, was liked for his humor, and was respected for the keenness of his instincts about what would fly and what would never get out the door. In recent years it had been understood by all that Hugh was gay, which in the not-too-distant past had been an absolute disqualifier for a career with the Agency. But Hugh had quietly argued that he was impossible to blackmail, he was discreet, and he would be compelled to go to court if the Agency tried to fire him. It took a special ruling by the DCI at the time to save Hugh's clearance, but he got it and his job had been secure ever since.

Brad could never quite remember how he'd first met Hugh. They were on different floors, working in different shops, but one day Brad realized he was having lunch with Hugh once or twice a week, then they were talking on the phone, and after a while they met for drinks, dinner, perhaps a movie or concert.

"We need idealists and dreamers like you," said Hugh, "to leaven the cynics and the hustlers in our frowsty old intelligence bordello."

When Brad wondered if the Senate liaison job was important or a dead end, it was Hugh Diamond who explained to him the facts of life. "In this town," he began portentously, "hell is to go unnoticed, and heaven is to be patted on the head by a man who works for a man who works for the president. Brad, you've got a dream job."

When Brad made his awful gaffe and started to call everybody in Washington about his discovery of an honest-to-God MIA, Hugh talked him down, said it was okay, advised him to go around personally to everyone he'd blitzed to make his apology. "They were all young once," he said. "They won't be hard on you. How could anyone not love someone so innocent?"

But Brad was not so innocent he failed to get the picture. When Hugh Diamond used the word *love* he meant the word *love.* Hugh had no illusions about his chances with Brad, who was already volubly in love with Jenny the day Hugh met him, but he watched out for him. By the end of Brad's first year he realized that Hugh was the one person in the CIA he really trusted.

"I know how agents behave," Brad conceded now. "It sounded crazy to me too, at first. But I thought, you know, We're missing what's important here. You say the word *Ames* and everybody turns pale."

"Sure," said Hugh. "Like when the doc says, 'You don't have flu, you have cancer.' "

"But Ames doesn't really have anything to do with this. Golenpolsky told us he'd seen an American in the Gulag. That's what this is about. So did anybody look into it? Was Golenpolsky telling the truth? Do we care?"

"So you got out the phone book . . ."

"Not exactly," said Brad.

First he argued it back and forth in his mind, trying to decide what was the right thing; then he dialed Myrna's extension one last time; finally he decided he couldn't live with himself if he didn't check at the very least whether Golenpolsky was only a phone call away. But not, he reasoned, from his desk or any other phone in the building. Brad didn't really know what Security could or couldn't do, and he wasn't sure how much they knew or cared about what he was up to. But he damn well knew the whole subject of Golenpolsky was now fraught with trouble, so he packed up his gray file boxes, checked them with the pale man at the front desk in Records, and left the building. On the George Washington Parkway heading back to town, he decided on one further step of caution. He didn't want to be paranoid, but it was nevertheless at least conceivable that his own phone at home was being monitored. So he decided to use the pay phone at a convenience store.

"Smart move," said Hugh. "Sneaky. You're getting the hang of it."

The store was empty. He started punching numbers.

It was so easy it was scary.

He dialed the international operator, got the Israeli country code and the Tel Aviv city code, and direct-dialed information. When somebody answered in Hebrew, Brad simply asked in English for the home phone number in Tel Aviv of Lev Golenpolsky. The woman said she had no such name in Tel Aviv, but there was an L. V. Golenpolsky in Jerusalem. Brad said that was it. She gave him the number. It took less than two minutes.

"I can guess the rest," said Hugh.

"What choice did I have?" asked Brad. "Either I was an ass-kissing careerist opportunist afraid to do my job or I was going to call the guy up."

"That's exactly how I would put it," said Hugh. "Only a slime ball would think about his career first."

"So I called him up."

"And?"

"He must have been sitting by the phone. He picked up on the first ring."

The voice was raw, harsh, confident, like the voice of a man who had smoked for years, had much on his mind, was in a hurry. "Shalom," he said.

"Mr. Golenpolsky? Lev Golenpolsky?"

"Who is this, please?" said the voice in English.

"I apologize, sir," said Brad. "I'm in Washington. I'm looking for a man named Lev Golenpolsky, a Russian who left—"

"Who is this, please?"

"I'm sorry. My name is Bradford Cameron. I'm—ah, an analyst here in Washington, with—uh, the government. I—uh . . ."—he sighed.—"I'm sorry. I'm with the Central Intelligence Agency. I realize this is a little irregular—"

"What is this about?"

"I apologize for calling you out of the blue without warning like this, but I've run into a problem, and I think you may be able to help. . . ."

Brad let his voice trail off, hoping Golenpolsky would break in to help out, but no help came. Brad was on his own. What the hell, he decided, shoot the works.

"It's my job to track down American POWs and MIAs, and I have discovered in the files that back in nineteen seventy-seven you told a debriefing officer for the Mossad that you had met an American in a special detention wing of the camp at Akmolinsk but our files don't record the details of your report and it occurred to me that the best thing I could do under the circumstances would be to go directly to the source. That would be you, sir."

A longish silence followed.

"Mr. Golenpolsky?"

"I can see you are a young man," said the voice, not unfriendly. "I appreciate your frustration. But if you want to speak to me about this, you must proceed through channels."

"Channels?"

"Of course channels. I should not have to explain this to someone in the business. Go to your liaison office. They know how to put a question to a friendly service."

"Mr. Golenpolsky?"

"Please," said the voice. "Channels." Brad heard the click of disconnect, like a sound from a distant planet.

"So," said Hugh. "You break every rule in the book and your reward is nothing."

"Not quite nothing," said Brad. "What he said was, 'If you want to speak to *me*.' That means I got the right guy. It's Golenpolsky. And he said, 'Go to your liaison office.' From that I conclude he's gone to work for the Mossad. So I'm getting somewhere. . . . There's just one problem," he added thoughtfully.

"There's dozens," said Hugh. "Which one is troubling you?"

"Jenny. She's going to be furious."

"Can you blame her?" asked Hugh.

"She thinks I promised to drop it."

"She thinks?"

"I didn't say I wouldn't promise, so, you know, she thinks I did."

"You're in trouble, fella," said Hugh.

"Very interesting," said Myrna, when Brad finally got her on the phone that evening. "But I'm sorry, I can't stay here and keep you out of trouble. My old friend Leo Weissberg tells me the acting director has been favorably impressed by my work and has offered me an important foreign post. I fly to Tel Aviv at dawn."

23

By midnight Friday, Brad was sure he'd left his passport in Maine. He could almost see it in his mind's eye, in the top drawer of the old school desk in his old room at the end of the hall. His Boston Latin diploma was in the same drawer, along with his diploma from Williams, some letters from old girlfriends, his first driver's license, his father's will, the letters exchanged by Uncle Max and John Bross at the Agency the summer Uncle Max took him on a three-day trip to Washington when Brad was in high school. This was something Uncle Max had long been wanting to do. He had known Bross since Groton days, but for some reason they always addressed each other by last name.

Dear Bross, Uncle Max had written. *You will see John in the boy. He has the same directness.*

Dear Phelps, Bross had replied. *I'd welcome a chance to meet John's son. Make sure to bring him by.*

Brad did go to see him, wearing his best dark suit on a hot day in July, and it was the twenty minutes in Bross's office downtown, not Uncle Max's prodding over the years, that convinced him to make his career in the world of secret intelligence. Brad didn't know what sort of clout Bross had at the Agency. Uncle Max said he had been in at the beginning and had seen it all, but what did that mean? Bross had an old man's translucent skin and freckled hands and he was already weak with his final illness. But there was authority in his voice, and he looked directly into the boy's eyes as he spoke.

"Max hopes you'll join us when you've finished college," Bross had said. "But there's something about this business you need to think about—it takes much and gives little. It treated your father badly, through no fault of his own. It happens all the time in this town. You're involved in something that gets pumped up by the newspapers, and for two days you're the most famous man in America. But in this business that generally ends a career. It certainly ended your father's. The papers were full of spy stories back then. A lot of good men got caught up. If you join us someday, I'll tell you all about it."

Bross treated Brad like a man. Perhaps he already understood he would get no other chance. He issued an invitation, but it came with a warning. "If you join us down here," Bross said, "you will be modestly paid and you will have to put up with a great deal of crap from yahoos. You will make some very close friends. You will learn how to read the newspaper. You will come to understand why some things are secret and how hard it can be to keep them secret. There will be moments when you will find it damned hard to keep your peace. There will be days when you will earn your pay in sweat and blood and you'll think no one has noticed. When you do get noticed, about half the time you will be praised or blamed for the wrong things.

"But one thing I can guarantee you," said Bross. "You won't be bored, and you will have a meaningful life."

By that point the teenage boy's lips had gently parted, his blink rate had dropped to nothing, and he would have followed John Bross barefoot into the desert.

For an hour Brad had ransacked the apartment, looking for his passport in every drawer, under every pile of clothes, behind the books on the shelf. He stopped in the center of the bedroom, clenched his fist, and called himself an idiot. Slowly the conviction built that after returning from Quebec the previous summer he'd stopped in Maine to see his mother, spent a couple of nights in his old room, took the passport from his jacket pocket, and placed it in the desk drawer on top of Uncle Max's letter. It was crazy but he must have done it. Brad could almost see it lying there, in the dark drawer of the desk in the dark house, while the February wind howled outside the windows and the frigid waves crashed on the rocks in the cove below the house. Without that passport Brad was trapped. It was almost as if Uncle Max were holding it back, and the odd thing was, if Uncle Max had known what was going on he'd have burned that passport before turning it over. Brad wondered what Bross would have said: Keep your peace, or Today you earn your pay. He'd met Bross only once; he wasn't sure.

Brad knew he couldn't put this off. He'd looked everywhere. The goddamned passport must be in Maine. He dialed Myrna's number and asked if there was any way he could get through Israeli customs without a passport.

"Are you out of your mind?" she inquired.

In that case, Brad said, it was no go. He couldn't find his passport, and the last place left to look was in Blue Hill, Maine—no way he could get there and back to New York in time to catch the plane.

"Please," said Myrna. "A smart boy like you? A secret agent? Lose your passport? I doubt it."

"I didn't lose it. I left it in Maine."

"Same difference," said Myrna, "but I don't think so. I've seen this a million times. The last-minute glitch. I'm sorry, I forgot my pen, how can I take notes? You'll have to parachute into France without me. Happens all the time.

"Now be attentive. Here's what to do. Finish packing. Then clean up. Put everything where it's supposed to go. I mean everything—dirty socks, trash, all that stuff on your bureau, all those secret papers you aren't supposed to take home. Get that apartment ready for the Inspector General. Don't worry, trust me, your passport's there and you'll find it. You've got all night."

So it proved. He put his socks in the drawer. He put the telephone book under the telephone in the kitchen. He put his sneakers in the closet next to the cardboard box filled with paperback spy novels. He put all the old newspapers into the bin by the back door. He threw the junk mail away and put the bills on his desk. He put the stub from his last paycheck into the desk drawer with his tax stuff. Next to it was his birth certificate. Under the birth certificate was his passport. He dialed Myrna. "Don't ask," he said. They arranged to meet at the gate at Kennedy Airport the next day.

"Security may have watchers," said Myrna.

"What?"

"It sounds crazy, but they know the seventh floor wants me on that plane, and they're going to make sure I go. They won't be looking for you, though, so keep your eyes open and don't run up to give me a hug."

Brad promised caution but he thought Myrna was deliberately exaggerating. He had never heard of anyone being followed by security. Why would they think they had to do that?

But Myrna was right about one thing. With the passport in his hand he began to feel sick about telling Jenny. They had parted on the phone with a tentative date for tomorrow—Saturday night—and now he wasn't just breaking the date, he was breaking his promise and proposing God knows what sort of trouble for the man she loved like a father. But he couldn't call her now.

Brad's bag was packed. His apartment was neater than it had been in months. He was too keyed up to sleep. He got himself a bottle of stout, popped the cap, pulled down a copy of an old Le Carré novel Hugh Diamond had been telling him to read, and took a seat at the table by the window. Winter had settled in outside, cold and still. Brad opened *The Honourable Schoolboy.* If he wanted the true feel of the business in the glory days, Hugh said, this was the book. But Brad was in no mood to read. He knew he was crossing the Rubicon this time.

Joining Myrna on the flight to Israel had seemed such a natural thing to do, he said yes before he really thought about it. But now he wondered if anyone besides Myrna thought he was doing a reasonable thing.

What his father would have done, Brad had no idea. His mother always told him to keep out of trouble. Uncle Max, if Brad had asked, would have told him to stay put, let the men with the responsibility decide. Hugh made jokes, but within them all was a counsel of caution. He had little doubt about Jenny's response. Where Frank Cabot was concerned she was like a guard dog. No one was telling Brad he had to do this.

Brad flicked off the desk light. Then he crossed the room and turned off the overhead light. He could get in bed but he hated to lie there when he couldn't sleep. He fetched a second stout and resumed his vigil by the window. The slush had frozen. Most of the cars parked along the street were covered with spatter and snowed in tight. Occasionally a car or a cab passed down the street. Once a couple walked by arm in arm, a little unsteadily.

Rule one was stick to channels, learn to take no for an answer. The whole damned agency was built on no. Almost every door had NO written on it. Almost every document had NO stamped at the top. Down the computer search paths, NO lurked behind the password to every file. The answer to idle questions was always NO. The job of the young intelligence officer was to stick to the narrow path of YES for which he was cleared and ignore the universe of NO. The system loved perfectionists and workaholics, people who gave a hundred and ten percent and people who always had an answer.

But the system had no tolerance for people who went around testing doors and limits and thumbed their noses at security with the mingled scorn and contempt for rules displayed by Myrna Rashevsky. Brad marveled that she was still around. If Brad had learned anything in two years, it was to expect bells and whistles when you stepped out of channels. At the first hint of rebellion, the system started to issue threats—nothing melodramatic, no cars with failing brakes or exploding telephones or island prisons from which no one returned. You might get away for a while with failing to do what you were told to do, but very little slack was cut for those who ever did what they were told *not* to do, and none if they did it twice. If Brad didn't return from Israel with the golden fleece, his career as a secret intelligence officer was over—and maybe even if he did. Cabot had made it unmistakably clear he wanted Brad to stick to his knitting and drop forthwith all interest in the ancient history surrounding Lev Golenpolsky. His only hope was to find an actual American POW/MIA. Even a dead one would do.

Myrna was right. In one corner of his heart Brad wished to God that passport was in Maine.

In the darkness of the room, the blue-green numerals on his clock radio slowly ticked away the quarter hours of the night. Each time Brad reached the end of his chain of thought he found the same irresistible conclusion: It was the right thing to do, but he was going to catch holy hell.

But then, when the clock approached the hour the writer Scott Fitzgerald had called the midnight of the soul, just as he felt himself imperceptibly lean in the direction of listening to the inner voices pleading caution and doing the smart thing for once—at just that moment Brad witnessed a small lesson in the ABCs of clandestine tradecraft, physical surveillance, maintaining a stakeout. Myrna was right again. He was amazed. Their mistakes were elementary. They could have been lifted from a lesson plan at Camp Peary. Don't park directly in front of the home of your target. Don't start the car engine at three o'clock in the morning to get the heater running. Don't light a cigarette, don't reach over to light your buddy's on the same match, don't sit there puffing, don't crack the window and flick the butts out into the street.

Brad watched in disbelief. "What in God's name," he asked himself, "are those security guys so worried about?" That settled the question once and for all. If they cared that much, he was going.

His mind at rest, Brad got into bed and slept till first light. The watchers were still out front when he awoke at last. He drank half a quart of orange juice, swung up his shoulder bag, locked the door behind him, and headed down the back stairs. He was pretty sure the watchers didn't know about the back alley, and when he emerged no one was in sight.

24

"I gotta get comfortable," said Myrna.

Brad stood in the aisle, sucking in his hindquarters to let people pass, while Myrna got herself settled. She couldn't reach the overhead bins, so Brad fetched down two pillows and two blankets. She placed the pillows next to the window. She took a great sheaf of newspapers out of her string bag and stuffed them into the seat pocket. With them she squeezed in a liter bottle of Evian water.

"If you don't want to catch anything," she said, "you gotta keep hydrated. You're too young to know how to travel, so I brought water for you too."

She pulled a second bottle from her string bag and put it into Brad's seat pocket.

"Magazines," she said. She crammed them in with her newspapers.

"Walkman," she said. That went onto the pillows.

She twiddled the overhead knob to turn the air flow on full and then pointed it down on the top of her head. She settled herself into her seat, wiggling her bottom down into a cavity. She hiked up her dress so it didn't pull in back.

"Pills," she said. From the string bag came a plastic bottle. She shook two into her hand, swallowed them with a swig of Evian. "One melatonin and one echinacea," she said. "Helps me relax."

Finally from her string bag she took a soft puffy thing that looked like a stuffed animal. She placed it on the floor, removed her shoes, put them in the string bag, and handed it to Brad for stowing overhead. When she put her feet onto the puffy thing, a faint hum could be heard and Myrna sank back with a sigh.

"What is that?" said Brad, as he settled into the seat beside her.

"Twinkle-Toes," said Myrna. "It vibrates your feet. Two D batteries will last me to Tel Aviv. Now tell me your adventures."

Brad described his quiet departure, down the back stairs, through the garden, and into the alley, and his slow cautious walk down the line of fences to Nineteenth Street, where he had turned left toward Dupont Circle. He was pretty sure he'd crossed the street without being noticed; he could see the watchers' car parked opposite his front door with a wisp of water vapor rising in the cold air from the exhaust. At the circle he caught a cab to the back door of the Mayflower, crossed briskly through the lobby to a second cab out front, and proceeded to National Airport. He was certain nobody had been waiting at La Guardia or had noted his departure for Kennedy.

"Just a minute," said Myrna. "When I take off I like to think of my family—all those people who cared about me." She put her head back, closed her eyes, took Brad's hand. "You don't mind?"

"I don't mind."

"Sweet Aunt Tilly. Misha. Cousin Samuel and his Trudy and little Solomon. . . ." She murmured a long list of names, sometimes repeating herself, as the pilot taxied the plane down the runway, turned into the wind, and revved the engines for takeoff. When they were airborne at last and heading out to sea, Myrna said, "I wonder how they'd feel about Israel. We weren't religious, my family. Part of the year in Poland, part of the year in Berlin—German, Polish, and Yiddish I spoke when I was three. I miss them."

Without thinking, Brad asked, "They're all gone?"

"My cousin Rachel we're going to stay with. I got out, but I was the only one of my immediate family. We're talking about Jews in Poland, you know."

"I'm sorry," said Brad. "I wasn't thinking."

"It's okay. It's hard to remember all the time. A single woman like me needs a family so she doesn't dry up and blow away. I cherish what I've got. You've got family?"

"Not a big one. My mother and Uncle Max."

"You got a Max? I had a Max, my father's younger brother, first Rashevsky in the history of the world to get a university degree. University of Krakow. Musical theory. Music was a big thing in my family. . . . No brothers? No sisters? Just you and your mother? What happened to your father?"

Brad had developed a technique for imparting this information one bit at a time. The language never changed. When Brad was ten, his father had a heart attack on his way to work. He was on the train, and after it pulled into South Station the conductor walked through and found him. He looked like he might be sleeping. No one had noticed a thing. Brad was in school.

"Ohhhh!"

"Uncle Max was the one who came to tell me."

"Poor boy, to lose your father so young. It must have been hard."

It was hard. All the rest of the time, in boarding school or camp, Brad lived in a kind of low-intensity nagging terror that another day would come when he would find Uncle Max waiting for him in somebody's office. He disliked thinking about that day, but what struck him now was Myrna's voice and the tears that welled up in her eyes. "It's all right, Myrna, I got along okay."

"Your mother never remarried?"

"Three times," said Brad. "She's very good at finding husbands. One lived in California, one in Dallas, and the current one is in Palm Beach."

"You lived in all those places?"

As Brad explained that he had visited all those places but lived, if you were going to be frank about it, in a succession of boarding schools, a look of severe disapproval gradually suffused Myrna's face. Her lips narrowed and her eyes were cold. "Well," she huffed, "she didn't know what she had."

"Don't think that way. She calls, she writes, she used to send me five-pound boxes of cookies. I loved my school."

"And Uncle Max?"

"Uncle Max is the one who got me into college and got me into the Agency."

By the time Myrna had extracted these basic facts, the crew was serving breakfast. "That's why I like to sit in front," she said. "You get served first, you get off first, you get the pick of the magazines, you get to see who's sitting in first class."

After the breakfast trays were cleared away, Myrna hauled out her sheaf of newspapers, handed Brad *The Washington Post,* and opened *The New York Times* for herself. For a moment she was motionless, scanning. Then she said, "Oh-oh, we got trouble."

Brad glanced over at a three-column story above the fold. The headline read:

FBI PROBE HITS CIA CHIEF;
HEARINGS FACE "LONG DELAY"

"What have they got?" asked Brad.

"They've got *long, perhaps indefinite delay,* blah-blah-blah, *hearings postponed . . . unexpected snag in routine FBI background investigation. . . . Senator Hawkins insists nomination still on track* . . . blah-blah. That's it. The special study's got nothing to do with it. FBI won't provide a firm date for delivering the SPIN, so the hearings are in limbo. That's what they've got."

"It's not so bad," said Brad. "What do you think?"

"It's only the first day," said Myrna. "Start pulling on that FBI thread, and pretty soon you get to *us*."

"Who'd tell him?"

"I don't know," said Myrna. "But this reporter has a way."

"Who did the story?"

"That *tzaddik* George Tater," said Myrna.

Brad read Tater's story two or three times during the flight, but it was only much later—after they had landed at eight in the morning Israeli time, cleared customs, and spent the day getting introduced and being shown around—that he began to think there was something odd about Tater's story. It was after dinner, and they were sitting on the porch of Rachel's house near Ashdod, south of Tel Aviv. A faint light came from the kitchen window. The subject was the price of eggs. Myrna's cousin Rachel ran the farm with the help of a son; her husband had died a few years ago but he left the fruit trees in good condition, Rachel was in wiry good health, the price of eggs held steady, and they could sell all their grapefruit to the European market in midwinter.

Rachel's son and granddaughter stopped by the house to say good night. He was thin like his mother, friendly, appraising. He didn't sound at all like Brad's idea of a farmer. The girl was dark-haired, in her twenties.

It was pleasant on the porch, quiet but for the occasional car passing on the road out front, the air calm but a bit cool. To Brad and Myrna it felt like May in Washington, but Rachel put on a sweater. After a moment she pushed the sleeves back up to her elbows. When she raised her wineglass Brad noticed on the pale skin of her inner forearm a little string of purplish letters or numbers. He knew what they were. Myrna had filled him in on the way down from the airport.

"Rachel celebrated her sixteenth birthday in Birkenau, poor thing. It was a family of ten that got crowded onto the trucks, but only Rachel saw the end of the war. We don't talk about family. We don't talk about the war. I'm all she's got from the old days."

Sitting on the little porch in the dark, looking at the trees in the yard, listening to the murmur of the two women discussing bad backs and Rachel's granddaughter, just out of medical school, and the politics of the Arab boy who helped with the henhouse, Brad's mind began to wander. Tomorrow they were going to call Myrna's old buddy in the Mossad, Shabtai; he was retired but he was still working; he was out of the loop but he knew everything; he let nothing slip but he never said no. Shabtai was perhaps just the guy to put in a good word with Lev Golenpolsky. Myrna couldn't hear enough about Shulamith, the granddaughter. She'd spend the next four years in the army, but she didn't have to go till spring. Rachel was glad for the help.

Brad's mind wandered back to what George Tater had written about the delay in Frank Cabot's confirmation hearings. There was no hint in Tater's story of Russia, Israel, Golenpolsky, the CIC, or Aldrich Ames—none of that, not a whisper, just FBI go-slow on the background investigation. Brad had argued Tater was a long way from having the story. "*Boychik*," Myrna had warned on the plane, "don't be so sure. That *parech* is a pro. He knows how to play out a story. The FBI got him on the front page; maybe he saved something for tomorrow. I can tell you one thing. He's after Frank Cabot, and you can bet your *tochis* that Cabot is going to stay up tonight thinking about it."

What struck Brad, thinking about it himself, was the way Tater spun out one fact into a major story. There was column after column inside the paper about Cabot's career, the Senate intelligence committee, the problems presidents had getting their nominees confirmed, the hidden hand of the old boy network, all the troubles of the CIA in recent years. And then, in a couple of paragraphs way down at the end, just sort of tacked on, a brief account of Kitty's accident on Tuesday. And there they were, three sentences that began to pick at Brad's mind:

> Cabot, notoriously hard-working in a town of workaholics, has not taken a vacation with his family in six years. . . .
>
> Mrs. Cabot, a talented painter who once studied with Josef Albers. . . .
>
> Her niece, Jennifer Moore, was in the passenger seat but escaped injury. Witnesses questioned by the police said Mrs. Cabot had failed to buckle her seat belt but Miss Moore had just fastened hers when the collision occurred.

End of story. What bothered Brad was . . .

"I'm beat," Myrna was saying.

"Do you mind a pullout bed?" Rachel was asking him.

What bothered Brad was . . .

"That's fine," he said. They went inside, got the bed ready, put things away, fixed a time for rising, used the bathroom seriatim, said good night, closed doors, turned out the lights.

What bothered Brad—lying on his back in the dark, listening to the hum of the refrigerator, to the padding of Myrna's slippered feet in the next room—what bothered Brad was . . .

It was so *intimate.*

25

"Forget the Greek," said Russell.

They were sitting in the window booth of the coffee shop on Fifth Street. Flat gray light poured in over the Formica tabletop. Dean had just repeated that he was going to get that sonofabitchin' Greek.

"If you want to make a difference," said Russell, "let's cross the line. Let's strike a little fear into the hearts of the powers that be."

It was midmorning. Russell tapped his finger on the front page of *The New York Times* lying on the Formica. "Listen to this idiot from Georgia:

" '*I can assure you that Frank Cabot's nomination is still on track.*'

"Harrison Hawkins. Distinguished chairman of the Senate intelligence committee. He's the one supposed to keep the CIA honest.

"*Senator Hawkins is widely respected on both sides of the aisle for his decades of support for the families of MIAs.*

"This is the man," said Russell, tapping his finger. "Forget the Greek."

Dean Cutter was staring into his empty mug. He wavered between anger and tears. He was trying to brace himself to catch the eye of the waitress, who had already refilled his mug twice. The second time she had given him a long frosty look before coming over. Dean was feeling exhausted and horribly depressed and a little queasy. Kind of sandpapery. Hollow. His groin hurt. The Greek had fired him.

"This is the man," said Russell, "who appointed himself champion of the MIAs. He has not done the job. It is time the people removed him."

"Remove?"

"With an act of righteous anger."

"You mean, like—"

"Call it a fatal wound, to be followed by a statement to the media."

Dean was not surprised. Russell had been kind of sidling up to this for days. He'd been dropping little hints about the group in Michigan, big plans; the government didn't listen to anyone it didn't fear. That was Russell's big thing: fear. Dean wasn't about to say anything that made him sound afraid.

"Why pick Hawkins?" he asked. "If you want to go out in a blaze of glory why not the president?"

"Presidents are hard to reach," said Russell. "This is about making a statement, not committing suicide."

"Then why not Cabot? He's the one going to be running the goddam Agency."

"Nobody has ever heard of Cabot," said Russell. "They'd think we were some leftist anti-American bullshit group mad at the CIA."

"I still don't understand why Hawkins," said Dean. "He's just the geezer they haul out on Memorial Day."

"That's it," said Russell. "He has a face people know. According to this guy Tater"—Russell tapped his finger on the *Times*—"the president is counting on Hawkins to get Cabot confirmed. He's going to be on the front page of the newspaper for as long as it takes. He's forever on the tube talking about the tragic fate of our MIAs. How many people you think ever heard of the chairman of the Joint Chiefs of Staff or the director of the CIA? Hawkins is Mr. Missing-in-Action. Do you see what I'm saying?"

"Yeah," said Dean. "It's like killing the anchorman on CBS. They'll think we're crazy."

"No," said Russell. "They'll think we're serious."

Why not? thought Dean.

For days he had felt himself slipping. The video store job had barely paid enough to cover his rent. His car, so-called, had a hundred and ten thousand miles on it and two flat tires, and he wasn't even legally allowed to drive it. He hurt so much some days he could hardly walk. Not even the dope seemed to do it for him anymore.

Over the past five or six months when he was feeling the red devils stirring inside, Dean would sometimes drive over to Alexandria and park across the street from the dry cleaning place where his former girlfriend worked. He'd watch Cheryl through the big plate-glass window. He never caught her eye except just one time, but he was sure she knew it was him. In the beginning he had been dumb enough to hope she might come out and cross the street to his car and say, We made a mistake, let's give it another chance.

Think again. An Alexandria cop showed up, who pulled him out of the car and asked him a lot of questions and then informed him that stalking was a crime and the next time the cop found Dean hanging around the dry cleaner's he was going to place him under arrest and make sure he spent a night in a jail cell with some black guys who didn't like white guys.

That was the one time Dean caught Cheryl looking through the plate-glass window right at him. She watched the whole thing. It made him want to hurt her. After that he drove by slowly and gave her a hard stare. There wasn't much satisfaction in it, but at least he had the pleasure of knowing she was mad or scared.

Then one day a few weeks back she was gone. At first Dean thought maybe she was sick, but she was gone. He built up his nerve and went into the place and asked where was Cheryl, and the woman that ran the place said, "You seriously think she left a forwarding address so you could go on bothering her?"

Dean was so angry he was ready to vault the counter and smash her face, but at that moment a very big guy in a white sleeveless undershirt emerged from the steamy interior with a baseball bat and Dean left.

All his life Dean had felt he didn't get the credit he deserved. His mother, his teachers, most of the kids he knew, his girlfriends after a month or two, everybody who had given him orders in the army—they all treated him like an asshole fuckup. Once or twice in his fury Dean had beaten the living crap out of somebody, and on twice as many occasions he had gotten the living crap beaten out of him. Somehow he wasn't very good at spotting who was really tough. He bought guns because they made him feel strong and dangerous, but he had never shot anybody, not even in the Gulf. He told everybody he'd seen a lot of action in the desert before the poison gas episode, but it wasn't true. He'd been in the Gulf, that was true, but nothing went right. Dean didn't like to think about it.

All his life Dean had wanted somebody to see what was really special about him, but right now there were only two people even half paying attention: Russell, the ex-marine, who gave him a cool, appraising look sometimes as if he thought Dean might have it in him, and the therapist, Lisa Benson, who was at least willing to remain after the end of the Wednesday sessions to let Dean ask a question or two.

The therapist was kind of cute. She had a lot of curly brown hair and wore slacks that cupped the rounds of her ass. Dean liked her slim little body and tried to imagine what her breasts were like. After the second session he lingered to ask if she knew of any program to help a guy like him understand the reasons behind his drinking. He was angling for an opportunity to tell her more about his life and see if he could pluck her heart strings a little.

"We're very solution-focused," said Lisa Benson. "My advice to you is quit drinking. Go to AA. Get sober. Don't waste a lot of time trying to figure out why you started drinking in the first place."

She was gathering up her stuff. End of question-and-answer. Dean didn't kid himself. It was never going to happen.

So why not?

Whenever somebody got on the news for shooting up a post office or a school, Dean read everything he could find about it. *This small town is asking itself tonight how could this happen? What drove those two high school students to commit an act of such senseless violence?* If you killed enough people, everybody wanted to know what made you tick. If you suffered in silence, they didn't give a flying fuck. It was that simple.

So why not?

"Well, maybe Hawkins doesn't go everywhere surrounded by Secret Service agents," said Dean, "but how are you going to get close enough to shoot him? All those government buildings have got guards. How are you going to get into the Senate with a gun? How are you going to get into Hawkins's office? How are you going to get out again?"

"I know how to do all that," said Russell. "But it won't be necessary. Hawkins doesn't spend all his time in the Senate. We just need to know his routine and then arrange to meet him someplace nobody is expecting us."

"You're going to call his office, I suppose, and get his plans for the week."

"I don't need to. There was a story in the Style section of the *Post* a couple of days ago. A piece about the president's barber, Salvatore Morelli. He's cut the hair of every president since Lyndon Johnson."

"So?"

"For presidents, Morelli goes to the White House. But he has a shop, second floor of the Mayflower Hotel. Select clientele of the rich and famous, everybody who's anybody."

"Okay."

"Including Senator Harrison Hawkins. Five mornings a week he's there for a shave. Leaves at a couple of minutes of eight by the side entrance. That wasn't in the story. I've been down to check it out. Trust me. Every morning—a couple of minutes of eight."

Dean was thoughtful. "You're serious," he said.

"You never met anybody so serious," said Russell. "Forget the Greek. It's Hawkins you want to be thinking about."

26

Myrna's instructions to Brad were explicit. Dial, wait till someone picked up, listen for two or three seconds—if it was Shabtai, he would say nothing—then deliver Myrna's message. Brad did as instructed. The phone rang five times before the pickup. He half expected an answering machine but what he heard was breathing at the other end, the rasp of someone older, heavier, probably a smoker. No word of query or greeting. Just a wheezing inhale-exhale. Brad counted slowly to three and said, "This is an American friend. You can expect a call from M on the other number."

He hung up and looked at Myrna as if to say, Well?

"People in this business," said Myrna, "they pick up habits, little ways of doing things, little precautions. My friend Shabtai says he likes to know who he's talking to. It keeps him out of trouble."

Myrna was wearing a pink housecoat, drinking a mug of tea.

"Rachel," she called, "show Brad the chicken house. I'll just be a minute."

So Brad followed Rachel out across the yard, leaving Myrna to pad around the room in her slippers, waiting to call.

The chicken house was a long shed with a metal roof, blinding in the morning sun. Inside were rows of wooden nesting boxes, out back a large fenced yard. Chickens came and went at will, clucking and squawking like villagers filling the streets on a festival day. They seemed quite interested by Rachel's approach. It was all very sociable, very companionable. In the yard a dark-haired teenager wearing black bell-bottom trousers and a T-shirt was filling watering cans. He worked in no great hurry and stared openly at Brad. Working beside him was Rachel's granddaughter, who smiled and said hello in the frank, direct way Brad was already beginning to think of as distinctly Israeli. She wore khaki shorts and a white sleeveless shirt open at the throat—a sunburned, golden sort of girl. She smiled hello but made no effort to hold Brad in conversation, so he followed Rachel into the chicken house. In one hand Rachel was carrying a wire basket, filling it with eggs from the laying boxes. As she reached in beneath the hens he thought they gave her a hurt look.

"Myrna says you've been here since the war."

"Since nineteen forty-eight," said Rachel. "I got off the boat in Haifa the day the Arabs invaded. The first thing I heard in Israel was air-raid sirens."

"Do you know Myrna's friend Shabtai? Was he here then?"

"Sure I know him. He and his wife used to come often for dinner. He was born here," said Rachel.

"Myrna's your cousin?"

"A distant cousin. We were neighbors in Warsaw. Then came the war."

"And you've always been friends," said Brad.

"More than friends. I can see it already with you. When Myrna takes an interest in somebody she holds on tight."

"She hardly knows me."

"Oh, she knows you," said Rachel. "She thinks you're a man who will stand up for what's right."

Brad was both pleased and embarrassed. "I don't know about that," he said. "I'd hate to disappoint her."

"She told me about it last night—the man in prison in Russia," said Rachel. "Don't forget him. That's all you have to do."

Rocks, heat, and sandy glare had always been Brad's idea of Israel, but the drive up through the hills to Jerusalem on Monday afternoon was pleasantly wooded part of the way and almost parklike in places where rusted old tanks and guns marked sites of the fighting in the first Arab-Israeli war.

"A lot of this stuff," Myrna said, gesturing out the window at ancient armaments, "was paid for in Newark and Brooklyn, and the people who handled the money and found the tanks and guns, they knew the men who built the CIA. You ask me who they were working for—they were working for the United States, for Israel, and for the Jews in the DP camps in Europe. It was all mixed up.

"I'm telling you this," Myrna said, "so you'll understand my old friend Shabtai. He goes back to those days. The only one he's never worked for is himself."

Brad caught only occasional glimpses of the antique glory of Jerusalem as Myrna circled up into the hills just west of the city, finally turning onto a tree-lined street of houses and yards with the look of California. At the end of the street Myrna parked in front of a fence, got out, and opened the gate. Immediately a slow weak barking issued from a wooden doghouse halfway up to the house, followed by the dog itself, a round white tube with a gray muzzle and a deliberate pace on legs splayed to either side. Its bark was like the fitful turning of a car engine with a dying battery: *uurrr-ruff! uurrr-ruff!*

"He's blind," said the man who opened the front door to the house, "and he's only got half his teeth, but he thinks it's his job to protect me from thieves and assassins." His English was perfect but delivered with the heavy gutturals of Hebrew. Brad liked the way he said "thieves and assassins."

Brad couldn't get a good look at the man until they were seated in a living room with a score of paintings large and small on the walls. The house itself was substantial and cool, rising and falling between levels, cluttered with books and papers. At either end of steps leading up into the kitchen were two huge clay pots that appeared to have been recovered after a couple of millennia beneath the sea. But it was the view from the large window facing north and west that caught Brad's breath. He was startled to discover that the house looked over a panorama of the city, with the golden hemisphere of the Dome of the Rock shimmering in the sun in the center.

"When I wonder what it's all about," Shabtai said, noticing Brad's gaze, "I look out the window and there it is. Of course, the Palestinians do the same thing. So . . . coffee?"

Finally he took a seat himself, and Brad saw a thick man of middle height with a generous nose and mouth. Short gray hair rising stiff as badger bristles covered his head, and his skin was dark with sun and weather. Altogether Shabtai presented as impressive and intimidating an appearance as any man Brad had ever seen. He had the tranquil look of someone who not only knew what was coming next but what would follow after that, and again after *that.*

"So," he said. "The CIA comes yet again looking for a Jewish door into Russia." It was not a question.

"Please," said Myrna. "Not that."

"But it's true."

"And how often did you come knocking on the American door? Whose diplomatic pouch carried your mail to Moscow?"

"And who ran the cleaning staff at the Frunze Military Academy? Yes? And who knew the cousin of the shorthand reporter for the Politburo?"

"*Bubkes,*" said Myrna. "Who opened the gates for Soviet Jewry? Half Israel speaks Russian now."

"Not so many," said Shabtai. "Maybe ten, twenty percent. Not everybody thanks you, but I do. So tell me what you're looking for."

"It's Brad who's looking," said Myrna.

"Okay," said Shabtai. "Let Brad tell."

Brad wasn't quite sure which end of the matter to approach first. "There's a Russian living here in Jerusalem," he said, "a man who came in the mid-seventies, a former prisoner from one of the camps in the Urals—"

"Sure," said Shabtai. "I've known him for years. Lev Golenpolsky."

Brad was stunned. He'd been trying to decide whether to mention the name right away or circle around to it. "How did you know?" he blurted.

"How did I know? You called him on the telephone, remember? Two days later you're in Israel. How could I not know?"

"I'm just surprised. I was expecting to have to explain everything."

"Not everything," said Shabtai, "just what you want to ask him, who wants the information, why you're out of channels, why you're traveling with Myrna, and especially"—he pointed a finger into the palm of his hand as he ticked off his points—"can a man who telephones a secret intelligence officer with a friendly service, identifies himself on an open line without any security, makes open reference to a clandestine contact twenty years in the past—"

"All right, all right," said Myrna.

"Can such a man be trusted with secret information if we decide to share it with you? *That's* what I want to know."

"I'm not sure where to begin," said Brad.

"Begin with the thing every intelligence officer always wants to know first," said Shabtai. "Who are you working for?"

Answering that initial question to Shabtai's satisfaction took Brad the better part of an hour, and the rest went no quicker. Shabtai spared no pains. He explored every nuance of what Brad said. By early afternoon, when he abruptly proposed they take a break and perhaps seek some lunch at a place on Ben Yehuda, Brad had not only accounted for his brief career in very substantial detail but had delivered what amounted to a full-scale briefing on the Washington politics of the POW/MIA issue, with a history of his step-by-step progress toward learning the name of Lev Golenpolsky. When Brad started to explain just who had granted him access to the DDO operational files Shabtai interrupted. "I know Joe Flint. When he was stationed here we spent a lot of time together. Very able man. Very ambitious man."

Myrna spoke up. "He's still ambitious. A lot of people in the DDO thought Joe would be Anderson's choice for the next DCI."

"Perhaps Joe thought so too," said Shabtai.

"Joe Flint?" said Brad.

"Sure," said Myrna. "He's got a lot of friends in Congress. And he's a neighbor of Peter Schleicher in Bethesda."

"Who?" said Brad.

"The White House chief of staff," said Myrna.

"I don't understand," said Brad.

Myrna explained. "Schleicher is an influential man. He's known President Anderson for many years. He raises funds. He has lots of friends in the business community."

"Especially among the oil companies," said Shabtai.

"Exactly," said Myrna. "And Joe, of course, knows a lot about the Middle East."

"And about the Arabs," said Shabtai.

"And about the oil business," said Myrna.

"I don't understand," said Brad.

"Don't worry," said Shabtai. "Myrna can tell you all about it later. So my friend Joe Flint made available the operational files. I remember him as a very tight-fisted man when it came to paper. I suppose he must have wanted very much to be helpful. And in these files you came across a report of the visit by Avi the elder."

"I hadn't gotten to Avi yet," said Brad.

"No, but you said somebody passed on a report to the late James Angleton, whose name all Israelis know, at least in our business. And of course I know Avi and his son. This is a very small country, and the business we are in is even smaller. So naturally I also know that Avi and Jim Angleton were always great friends, ever since their days together in Italy. And besides, I had plenty of time before you came to ask some questions and look into the files myself."

Shabtai spread both hands out, palm upward. "There are no secrets here," he said.

With that Brad quit worrying about what to say. Shabtai seemed to know everything anyway. But at the same time Brad remembered his instructions on dealing with the Senate intelligence committee—answer the question you are asked and stop. He volunteered nothing about anything else Shabtai might have found interesting. He stuck to what he knew about Golenpolsky and what he thought Golenpolsky might know.

"That was all twenty years ago," Shabtai said. "Even if it was true, it doesn't seem possible this American could still be alive."

"Probably not," said Brad. "But I'm hoping Golenpolsky will at least help me with the name."

"His name won't bring him back."

"Not alive, perhaps. . . ."

"Dead, what good is he? You could be stirring up a lot of trouble."

"That's not my purpose," said Brad.

"Maybe not. But you are doing it anyway. Golenpolsky doesn't want his name in the paper, and we wouldn't like that either. Better to say a prayer and move on."

"Just a minute," said Brad.

"It's war; he's dead; let that be the end of it."

"You don't know he's dead," said Brad.

"Well," said Shabtai.

"His family wants to know what happened. Does Israel walk away from its dead?"

"No, you're right," said Shabtai. "What you say is just." He placed his hand on Brad's arm and turned to Myrna. "This young man doesn't give up easily. All right. Maybe Golenpolsky can help. I'll see what can be done."

At dinner that Monday night they were five; Rachel's son and granddaughter Shulamith joined them and lingered afterward over wine. "They know what I do," Myrna had said, "and they'll guess about you. Don't worry about it. We'll tell them we're here looking for a Russian émigré from twenty years ago and that's it. People understand secrets in Israel. They won't try to pry anything out of you."

Sitting on the porch later, the company slowly dwindled. First Rachel's son went off to write a report; in addition to running the farm he managed a regional fruit cooperative that was preparing to negotiate a contract with an Italian importer. Then Myrna said it felt like the middle of the day but she knew it was the middle of the night. Rachel followed a moment later, saying there was something she wanted to ask Myrna.

That left Shulamith, sitting in a wicker chair with her legs crossed, and Brad—who had much to think about but not so much he failed to notice just how attractive this girl was, with her short brown hair and full lips, and the skin where her breasts met in the vee of her blouse like the golden color of olive oil. Brad found himself thinking that in physical type Shulamith was just exactly the sort of young woman the blond, slender, milk-colored Jennifer Moore was not. He wasn't trying to follow that thought in any particular direction, just noting quietly to himself that physically they were about as different as two women could be.

"You met Shabtai," she said. "What did you think of him?"

"He seemed to know everything about me."

"Of course, that's his business. I've known him since I was a child. Grandmother always invited Shabtai and his wife for dinner whenever Myrna was here. He used to help me with my homework in English. Did he show you the city?"

"He took us to a wonderful place for lunch. On a terrace on Ben Yehuda."

"That's the street where terrorists like to set their bombs. Shabtai always takes Americans there to feel the life in the city. So they'll know why Israel will never give up Jerusalem."

"Never is a long time," said Brad.

"That's why we say never. A lot of things we'll do," said Shulamith, "but that one never. If you have some free time, maybe I can show you Israel too. Places I love."

"I suppose Israelis never leave this country."

"Oh, no, that's wrong; we all leave. I can't wait to leave. After the army I'd like to do a residency in the States. I could never leave Israel forever, but I might live someplace else. It depends."

"Depends on what?"

"Life. Love. If there's another war."

"Do you remember the last one—the Gulf War?"

"Of course. I was a teenager. I was scared we'd be bombed, but we didn't see anything here. Shabtai has seen all the wars."

"He said the same thing at lunch. He said that's why he can't retire. I don't think I could work for the same organization for fifty years and still go to bed thinking about it every night."

"Naturally," said Shulamith. "It depends who you're working for."

That's what Shabtai had wanted to know: Who was he working for? Brad thought about this later. It was his last thought as he drifted off to sleep, not the young woman who had gone to her bed in the house across the road.

It had seemed such a simple question at first. Who are you working for? Brad thought he could answer in a sentence or two, but Shabtai wasn't easily satisfied. He wasn't trying to be difficult but to be clear, to be exact, to understand who would have access to the information Brad obtained. Brad tried to answer, but gradually, as Shabtai pared away the obvious and the trivial, Brad began to see that he was not really working for the U.S. government, nor was he working for the Central Intelligence Agency. The DDO was only his temporary home in the CIA table of organization and his immediate bosses—Randy Short, Joe Flint, Frank Cabot, even President Norman Anderson—were just names in the chain of command. Hawkins and the Senate intelligence committee had claims on his loyalty, but they weren't the answer. No law or regulation required him to put the families of MIAs before all else. It was a sense of obligation that had brought Brad to Israel. Maybe the word was conscience.

Shabtai had walked him through it, and by the end of an hour the answer to Shabtai's question was clear and unmistakable. Sometime over the last week, Brad had begun to work for himself.

27

"Go!" said Myrna. "There's nothing doing here. Shabtai says the wheels are still grinding, and he'll let us know about Golenpolsky later. I'm going to do my nails and take Rachel to lunch; we'll pick up the *Trib* on the way back. Go! You're in Israel. See a little of the country. Are you crazy? Shula offers to show you the sights and you want to sit around a chicken farm? What's the matter with you?

"We can't push Shabtai on this. It'll take as long as it takes. He'll call some people, they'll call some people, maybe they'll look up a few files. You don't have to sit around here worrying, I know what they'll say. They'll say Sure, why not, it's ancient history, it can't hurt. Besides, it's not like we're reporters, planning to tell the world.

"When Shabtai has something to tell us he'll tell us. You want to spend your day watching me do my nails in front of the TV? Go see some ruins, sit on a beach, tell Shula to take you to the squid place; she'll know where I mean. You think you hate squid—just wait! Nice terrace overlooking the sea. Nobody in a hurry. There's a path down a cliff to a little beach—I'm too old now but it's very nice there. Take the day. Come back when the sun goes down. We'll read the *Trib* then, check the Internet, see what that *parech* George Tater is digging up. Maybe it's a one-day story. Maybe nobody will tell him anything."

But somebody was telling Tater plenty. When Brad got out of the car in the early dusk Tuesday evening he found Myrna sitting on the porch with the *Trib* spread across her lap and worry on her face. "Bad news," she said, as Brad made his way across the yard. "He's got the Russian angle, says the FBI is looking into an unreported meeting with an officer in the KGB. Hawkins says it's all a formality, maybe technically it should have been reported—here, you read it." She looked up. "You kids have a good time?"

"We had a fabulous lunch at the squid place," said Brad.

"We talked about life," said Shula.

"We explored the beach," said Brad.

"We watched the sun go down," said Shula.

"Sounds nice," said Myrna. Then she told Brad that Shabtai had set up a meeting with Golenpolsky first thing tomorrow morning in Ma'ale, one of the new settlements just outside Jerusalem. It hadn't been easy. Somebody didn't want this meeting to happen. Shabtai didn't say who, but Myrna guessed somebody in the prime minister's office, not Mossad, somebody worried about Washington.

"The big question," said Myrna, "is who's talking to Tater?"

At that point Shula said she'd leave them to their work, and for the next hour Brad and Myrna analyzed every detail of Tater's recent stories. Any one of half a dozen sources could have filled him in. Tater might be talking to Hawkins or someone on his committee, the White House, the FBI, the CIA's Office of Security or the Counterintelligence Center. He could even be talking to Frank Cabot himself. Tater was describing a classic Washington turf war. Cabot had stepped on someone's bureaucratic toes, and in the intelligence community the most sensitive toes belonged to the FBI. "A source familiar with the investigation" told Tater that no one was suggesting Cabot was a security risk. "That's Tater quoting himself,"

Myrna said. "He wants to make sure nobody thinks he's calling Cabot a spy. That really would crash in flames."

But somebody was sure as hell talking. Myrna's best guess was somebody Tater *hadn't* quoted in the story—which meant not the committee and not the CIA. But it was only a guess. The bad news was, Tater had the core of the problem: Cabot's unreported meeting with the Russian. Every other part of the story was tied to that. He could walk the cat back in two or three different directions, all bad for Cabot, and one—the one that brought Golenpolsky into the picture—would be fatal to Brad's hopes of becoming director someday. "Just kidding," Myrna said.

Brad wondered if they should call somebody at home and ask where the Langley rumor mill thought Tater was heading?

"Who have you got in mind?" asked Myrna.

"My friend Hugh Diamond."

"Does he know where you are?"

"I was afraid to tell him."

"How about Jenny?"

"I was twice as afraid to tell her. Nobody knows I'm here, unless the security guys have figured it out."

"Shabtai says no frantic calls from Washington so my guess is, Not yet. Does Jenny know about Golenpolsky?"

"Yes, I told her about my meeting with Tyler. I thought I was about to find an MIA."

"Does she know about the snag with Aldrich Ames?"

"Cabot told her about that."

"Does she know how all that ties up with his confirmation?"

"She gave me holy hell for putting him on the spot, so I guess she does."

"So she basically knows everything except where you are. Does she know George Tater?"

"I don't think so. She's never mentioned him. Come on, Myrna—Jenny's furious at me for digging this up. She's not going to tell some newspaper reporter about it."

"Maybe," said Myrna. "But she's one of the few who knows what's going on. That puts her on the bigot list. This is how we do our job, so I say no calls. Sit tight. Rule one in the intelligence business: When people don't know what you're doing, they can't stop you. So we'll let Tater do his job, and we'll do ours. Maybe we'll get there first."

"Has Tater got some reason for going after Cabot?" Brad asked. "Why's he pushing this so hard?"

"It's not Cabot," said Myrna. "It's the Agency. He never passes up an opportunity to put us on the rack. Somehow he never got his teeth into the Ames case, thank God. Maybe he thinks Cabot is giving him a second chance. It's personal. George Tater hates spooks. There's two theories. One, he was a young reporter in Saigon during the war. He had a girlfriend famous in all Saigon for her beauty. Daughter of a humble schoolteacher in the delta. Naturally she was working for the VC."

The year was 1970. Not having been born yet, Brad would not know what was going on in the delta in 1970. Had he ever heard of the infamous Phoenix program? Multiply whatever he knew by two. There was a war on, the CIA's bright idea of the month was a program to identify and then neutralize (don't ask) Vietcong cadres, which included spies, which included the beautiful Alice Nguyen, who was George Tater's live-in girlfriend.

Unfortunately, the South Vietnamese intelligence units attached to the Phoenix program in the delta during one of Alice's visits home had not been fully briefed on CIA policy against the use of physical coercion during interrogation. The South Vietnamese counterparts did not actually kill Alice. She managed to escape, or maybe they just dumped her out the back of a jeep. At any rate, she got back to Saigon somehow. There she killed herself—in George Tater's apartment, where he found her.

"That's one theory," said Myrna.

"The CIA did that?"

"Well, people the CIA paid, anyhow. Theory number two, have you ever met or seen Tater?"

"No," said Brad.

"Acne," said Myrna. "The scars remain but people say you had to know Tater in high school—the Godzilla of Tyler, Texas. His face was pitted like the surface of the moon, all red bumps and white pustules. The young George Tater was not popular with girls."

"That doesn't make sense," said Brad.

"It makes sense to me," said Myrna. "He hates everybody and wants to get even with the world."

"And that's why he's after Frank Cabot?"

"Sure. You know Cabot. Skin like a slick peach, pink as a baby's bottom," said Myrna. "Teacher's pet. Eagle Scout. Seven hundreds on both SATs. First in his class. Boss's favorite. Youngest DCI since Robert Gates. Everybody likes Frank Cabot. Nobody has anything bad to say about him."

"You make it sound like junior high school. I don't buy it. I go with theory one. At least that would explain why he goes after the CIA."

"So does theory two. Think about it. The heartbreak of acne kept Tater on the outside. So in this world who's the deepest inside? What's the hardest circle to break into? Where is the line between inside and outside sharpest?"

"Sorry," said Brad. "I'm sticking with theory one."

"That's why there's two theories," said Myrna.

Going down the long hill the next day, from Jerusalem toward the Dead Sea, then turning onto the side road that wound back up to Ma'ale, Shabtai explained the ground rules. "Golenpolsky works for us, refugee affairs; he handles questions that arise about people coming from Russia. That's all you need to know."

"What he means," said Myrna, "is they're worried about Russian spies and Golenpolsky is a spotter."

"Please," said Shabtai. "What I mean is that what you're interested in has nothing to do with what he's doing now, all right?"

"We don't want to make trouble," said Myrna.

"No tape recorder. You can take notes. He'll tell you all about the camp and about getting out and coming to Israel. But I should warn you, so you're not disappointed, he doesn't know too much about the way his story got to America and what happened to it there. All he knows is he talked to somebody, then he talked to somebody else, and from time to time that somebody else came back to ask a couple of questions."

"Avi the elder?" asked Myrna.

"Yes, Golenpolsky and Lipsky got to be good friends. He still knows the son."

"But Lipsky never told him about Angleton and all that?"

"To tell the truth, I don't know how much Lipsky told him; I'm not sure how much Lipsky knew himself. You know how it is—you pass something on, they say thank you, maybe you never hear about it again. But I can tell you, Golenpolsky took an interest in this matter. He pushed us hard to do something; it was back and forth for a year or so. Just how it played out I don't know. Maybe I'll learn something too," said Shabtai.

"But remember—this is for your information only. Golenpolsky doesn't testify before Congress. He doesn't go on TV. He doesn't talk to reporters. And he doesn't go to Washington or take a polygraph or get debriefed by the FBI."

"That's not what I want," said Brad.

"It's what everybody else wants that I worry about."

"Well, you don't have to worry about me," said Brad. "What I want isn't complicated. Golenpolsky said he met an American prisoner in Akmolinsk. I want to know the man's name, rank, and serial number."

"Last rule," said Shabtai, stopping the car. "I say when the interview's over. Agreed?"

"Agreed," said Brad.

"*Nu?*" said Myrna.

Lev Golenpolsky, a small man with expressive eyebrows, lived in a house crowded with relatives that had a great view of the Jerusalem skyline from a small back terrace. A wife served coffee. An aged mother watched TV in the next room. A cousin passed two or three times through the kitchen where they sat, as Golenpolsky explained—in English as good as Shabtai's, but even more heavily accented—that he was not the only Jewish boy from Odessa who got kicked out of the university after he applied for an exit visa to go to Israel, and he was not the only one who couldn't find a job, and he was not the only one who bought jeans from sailors in the port and sold them on the black market and used the money to buy vodka. Actually, there was quite a little group. Somebody would lose the toss of a coin and get the job of standing in line to buy half-liter bottles of the cheap vodka with the gold foil caps. Then they would go into a park through the tall grass—in the Soviet Union of the early 1970s they had not yet invented the lawn mower—to some dark and secluded corner where they would smoke the cheap Russian cigarettes called *papirossi* and knock back the vodka, while discussing the miseries of sharing a single kitchen and bathroom with parents and grandparents or the glories of the music of John Lennon and Mick Jagger, or how many black-market dollars it might take to bribe a sailor to let a couple of guys into the hold of one of the ancient, rusty freighters making the crossing to Turkey.

The answer, Golenpolsky learned one hot June evening in 1973, was three hundred American dollars. A new face provided the figure, a fellow who had showed up with one of the regulars a couple of weeks earlier, a little older than the rest of them, not a big fan of the Beatles or the Rolling Stones but full of sympathy for the plight of young Soviet Jews who wanted to make *aliyah.* That should have been the tip-off right there. Golenpolsky and his friends weren't dreaming of Israel. They wanted to go to Hollywood. Young and foolish could not begin to describe the depth of Golenpolsky's innocence, and to say he was surprised, even stunned, barely hinted at the depth of his shock a few nights later when two black Volgas roared up to the dock where the freighter waited and disgorged half a dozen burly men in shiny suits who relieved Golenpolsky and a friend of their black-market dollars, took them into custody, and beat them senseless.

Much later, aching in every part of his body, Golenpolsky awoke in a windowless cell. With him was one of those pudgy Russian-peasant types with a nose like a beet and a hairline that reached almost to his eyebrows. A very friendly but inquisitive fellow. Golenpolsky thanked God he was not so dumb those bastards could fool him the same way twice. Over the long months of interrogation, threats, promises, and occasional beatings, Golenpolsky shared nothing more compromising with his cellmate than the complaint that his soup, in addition to being cold, had not enough potato in it.

Golenpolsky had been charged with violating sections of the Soviet Criminal Code defining conspiracy, sedition, and subversion (that is, trying to flee to the West), aggravated by additional charges of black marketeering, slander of the Soviet State, parasitism, hooliganism, and public drunkenness. Perhaps twelve years in a labor camp followed by ten of internal exile would teach him the error of his ways.

On the other hand, it was suggested by the investigating officers, Golenpolsky might spare himself these hardships by cooperating with the organs, by confessing his contacts with the Zionist secret services, and by agreeing to insinuate himself into the circle of a leading Jewish refusenik known to be working for the CIA. Golenpolsky's answer to this invitation might be translated into English as fuck you and the sow who is your mother.

That ended the four-month fact-finding phase of Golenpolsky's case. The trial phase lasted ten minutes, including the minute during which Golenpolsky's lawyer pleaded for leniency by the court on the grounds that his client was a drunken university dropout of weak moral character and suspect family origin. The sentence was twelve and ten, as predicted.

Golenpolsky lingered over this part of his story because Brad, to Golenpolsky's amazement, seemed to be hearing it for the first time. No one else in Golenpolsky's experience had ever been the least bit surprised by his story or had shown a tenth of the interest. "I can't believe it," Brad said more than once. "For wanting to leave? For asking to leave? For buying and selling a pair of jeans? Twelve *years*?"

Golenpolsky said that Brad's indignation was very welcome to him and reinforced his conviction that a sense of justice is inherent in man.

So at the age of twenty, weighing sixty-two kilograms (down from seventy-seven), with twenty-six teeth (down from thirty), and having suffered partial loss of hearing in his right ear, Golenpolsky left Odessa in the back of a truck chained to six other prisoners, all sentenced to long terms to be served in the labor camp at Akmolinsk, which at least was not in Siberia, for which they were all genuinely grateful. Golenpolsky had completed two years toward a degree in chemical engineering, so they assigned him to work in the kitchen. There for two years he mopped floors and scrubbed the huge steel pots used to cook soup, if cook was the right word and if you could call it soup.

Akmolinsk was not hard to describe. Hot in the summer and cold in the winter. The trees you could count on one hand. Everything was a long way from everything else: the wooden barracks; the central administration building; the work area; the garden tended by older prisoners; the block of punishment cells, a relic of czarist times; the infirmary, with a fading red cross painted on its roof, a relic of World War Two; and farthest off of all—a brutal trudge on winter nights—the special annex surrounded by its own fence. Year in and year out in this dismal place, the principal subjects of conversation were food first, tobacco second, and vodka third. Vodka could be obtained. You paid with tobacco. Tobacco could also be obtained. You paid with sex. One look at who was paying convinced Golenpolsky to give up drinking forever. The camp was organized around a factory that made shovels. This was not a sophisticated industrial enterprise. Much of the work was done with hammers and anvils, and partial loss of hearing in one ear could be described as ideal preparation for a decade as a *zek* in the shovel factory at Akmolinsk.

But having brought himself to a condition in life that could well be described as barely worth living, Golenpolsky managed to make things worse. After two years of mopping and scrubbing he was promoted to delivery boy. His new job was to transport big pots of soup and sacks of bread in a wheelbarrow to the infirmary and to the block of punishment cells, from both of which prisoners were often carried out feet first. The guards in the punishment block were under the command of a man named Myakov, who was always dressed neatly with his boots and his belt shined and his cap at the correct angle.

The very first day, Captain Myakov called Golenpolsky over to his desk and questioned him.

"What is your name?"

Golenpolsky knew the routine. "Captain, my name is Lev Vasilievich Golenpolsky, *sir*!"

"What is your sentence?"

"Captain, my sentence is twelve years at hard labor to be followed by ten years of internal exile, *sir*!"

"What is your crime?"

"Captain, my crime is section eight, paragraphs two, three, and four, conspiracy to violate border controls, *sir*!"

Captain Myakov addressed him with a look of shrewd appraisal. "Golenpolsky," he said, "the men in these punishment cells are not allowed to ask questions of anyone except me or the sergeant of the guard. If they try to ask you questions, I want you to report them to me. Under no circumstances are you to answer their questions or to bid them good day or to converse with them in any way about any matter. Do you understand?"

"Captain, I understand you, *sir*!"

When Golenpolsky brought them their bowls of soup, the prisoners frequently did try to ask him questions. What they mostly wanted to know was what day it was, but occasionally they asked other questions—for example, whether his health was good, if the soup had any meat in it, if an answer had been received to letters sent to General Secretary Leonid Brezhnev, if it were true that Czar Nicholas had been observed riding a white steed through Red Square, if Myakov were a man or a beast, if Golenpolsky would inform the prisoner's wife that he had died with her name on his lips, if it was true that the Jewish cooks spit in the soup, if there was an end to suffering this side of the grave, if Golenpolsky could obtain American cigarettes, if God's mercy might not also be sought by political prisoners, if it was true a general amnesty had been declared, if Golenpolsky thought there would be meat in the soup on the anniversary of the October Revolution, if Golenpolsky had a sweetheart, and if Golenpolsky had a tongue.

For the first few weeks Golenpolsky listened, said nothing, and reported the questions to Captain Myakov, who would open the ledger book on his desk, flip the pages, and make a mark. The sergeant of the guard explained to Golenpolsky that for each mark a prisoner's sentence in the punishment cells was extended by one day. Golenpolsky soon quit reporting the questions. But he feared that the cells were bugged so he thought about the questions of the prisoners but did not answer them.

One day near the end of the third year of Golenpolsky's sentence, Captain Myakov stopped him on his rounds for a little chat. Did he think the prisoner in number two was beginning to go mad? Had he noticed that the sergeant of the guard occasionally smelled of vodka? Had he received the new felt boots Myakov had ordered? Would some new gloves be of use? Did he happen to know English?

"Without thinking," Golenpolsky said, "I told him no. I don't know what prompted me. It was just as likely there would be some special job with special privileges for somebody who *did* speak English—but I said no."

"But your English is practically perfect," said Brad. "How could they fail to know you spoke English?"

"It wasn't perfect then. I wanted to be a chemist, so I taught myself a little English to read scientific journals. The truth was I could hardly speak two words. That all came later. I learned it from the prisoner in the special annex."

"The prisoner in the special annex," said Brad.

"There was only one," said Golenpolsky. "Myakov needed someone to take over the food detail, and he wanted to be sure I couldn't understand anything the prisoner said. He was right to worry because the first day I showed up with food the prisoner said, 'My name is Jason Dyer. I am a sergeant in the United States Army. I need your help to contact the American embassy.'

"And I said, 'Are you crazy? How can I do that? I am a prisoner too.' "

28

For nearly two years Brad had been dreaming of a moment just like this one. After all the fake photos, false leads, dead ends, and reports of MIAs that led nowhere, Brad was listening at last to a reliable witness with firsthand knowledge describe an American soldier who was not dead or part of a scam or a figment of some illiterate peasant's imagination but an honest-to-God American soldier, carried on the roster as missing in action, praying he had not been forgotten and longing to go home.

It was late in the day approaching dark, that Wednesday, February 27. A winter evening was settling over the hills surrounding Jerusalem, and the city lights twinkled on the horizon. They had covered an amazing stretch of history. Brad had listened for hours, hardly moving, to Golenpolsky's astonishing story of what he had learned during the two years he spent as the other prisoner in the special annex at Akmolinsk. One week Golenpolsky had been making the long trudge with food to the special annex morning and night, and the next he was locked up in the same cell.

He could not honestly claim it came as a surprise. Captain Myakov had warned him: Don't talk to the prisoners. Golenpolsky's mistake was thinking that because the Kazakh guards who played dominoes in the front room smiled when he gave them cigarettes and offered a nip of vodka in return, they liked him. They probably did like him. But at the end of his third week of delivering food twice a day to the special annex, one of the Kazakh guards reported him all the same to Myakov, who said, "I thought you Jews were supposed to be smart."

There was no delay or ceremony about what happened next. Manacles were promptly welded around Golenpolsky's ankles, and he was locked in with the American. When their bread and soup was brought the next day by another prisoner, a fellow parasite, hooligan, and black marketeer with whom Golenpolsky had shared a bottle of vodka once or twice in Odessa, Golenpolsky asked him, "How long is my sentence in here?"

The man said nothing and did not even look Golenpolsky in the eye, but shortly after he went away Myakov appeared. "Do you never learn?" Myakov asked.

"How long is my sentence?" Golenpolsky asked.

"You know the camp regulations," said Myakov. "You are not to speak to the man who brings your food. If you do you will receive only bread and water."

"How long is my sentence?" Golenpolsky asked.

"You do not have a sentence," Myakov said. "You have been placed in administrative detention."

"How long does it last?"

"It lasts until you are released."

"But how long is that likely to be?"

"Frankly," said Myakov, who was not such a bad fellow really, "I do not think you will be released until *he* is gone"—he pointed to the American—"and they are never going to let him go. How can they let him go? Officially, he does not exist."

Myakov departed, leaving Golenpolsky standing in the room with the manacles heavy on his ankles, thinking that now, truly, he had got himself into the kind of trouble his grandmother had been predicting ever since he started meeting his friends in the parks of Odessa. The American did not know Russian, but he had understood. He shrugged, smiled, and said, "Tough luck, buddy."

The food was no worse in the special annex than in the rest of the prison. The Kazakh guards spoke little Russian, so there was no temptation to try to converse with them. The two prisoners were given free run of the yard in back, since there was no danger they would try to escape. The fence was a tall one, with razor wire coiled along the top, and beyond it, surrounding the entire camp, was a second fence with watchtowers at the corners. Stretching out in all directions from the fence were several hundred miles of wilderness with few roads or villages—not exactly a promising highway to freedom for a young man with fifteen kilos of chain joining his ankles and an American with one leg and a homemade crutch.

So there was nothing to do but talk. Golenpolsky's story of how he got to Akmolinsk was simple enough; Brad had already heard it. But how U.S. Army Sergeant Jason Dyer got to Akmolinsk took a great deal of telling.

It began with the loss of his leg. Deep inside Laos on a reconnaissance mission in 1970, Dyer had been wounded by a booby trap and left—at his own insistence—by the rest of his unit, which had gone for help. What happened to them he did not know. No one ever came for him, but his captors never claimed the others had been killed, either, and it was Dyer's experience during the time he spent in the hands of the North Vietnamese People's Army that Major Duc never wasted an opportunity to explain to him how hopeless his prospects were. If the NVA had killed Dyer's men, Duc would have told him so in detail and proved it with the men's ears or perhaps even their heads. So Dyer figured his men probably got away, they probably begged to take part in a rescue mission, and the brass probably told them No way, José.

The loss of his leg was just the luck of war. An exploding grenade, part of a booby trap, had peppered Dyer's right leg between the hip and the knee with twenty or thirty pieces of shrapnel. Dyer was lucky he hadn't been killed outright, but his captors didn't think much of the wound. After wrapping him in a few lengths of dirty cloth bandage they made him walk anyway. They allowed him to cut a crutch from a tree limb—he had it still—but every step pulled his wounds open, and one by one they became infected, turning first an angry red, then purple, then black. The bandages and what remained of his trouser leg were soon soaked with yellow pus and blood. Flies and other insects swarmed over the wounds, and the whole leg began to stink worse than the cat that died under the kitchen porch one July when Dyer had been a kid.

His captors didn't seem to give a damn whether he lived or died, and after a few days of too much pain and too little water Dyer didn't care much himself. The leg quit hurting—it did not strike him as an encouraging sign—and then he developed a fever, he lost his voice, his lips cracked with thirst, his vision blurred, and at last he fell beside the trail too weak to rise. He thought he told the bastards he only regretted he would not live to piss on their graves, but probably he only dreamed it; he doubted he could have spoken by that time. The last thing he remembered was something that never happened—the voice of his sister Stacy calling his name, which made Dyer think it must be okay; if his sister was there he must be at home.

Dyer did not remember what happened next, one of his Russian debriefers told him about it later. Instead of shooting him or leaving him for the ants or the tigers, whichever came first, the NVA carried him up the trail in a litter to one of the drop-off points for North Vietnamese trucks carrying supplies along the Ho Chi Minh Trail. There he was loaded with some NVA wounded and trucked to a jungle hospital farther north, where his leg was amputated just below the hip.

Why they bothered he had no idea. But when Dyer finally opened his eyes there were a couple of friendly Red Cross volunteers in his tent who were collecting information for a Red Cross roster of American prisoners of war so their families could be contacted and the process begun of prisoner exchange and repatriation. Dyer might claim the excuse of his weakened condition combined with the hope of the desperate, but he was nevertheless deeply ashamed to confess he had bought this line of horse crap and told the Russians pretty much everything they wanted to know. But when they began to press for the names of the civilians in sunglasses who showed up occasionally at fire stations in the boondocks, Dyer realized he had been had.

In truth these Russians knew more about the cross-border operations run jointly by the Special Forces and the CIA than Dyer did, and once the Russians understood that Dyer had never even been in the Agency's regional base in Pleiku, much less the station in Saigon, they quit trying to pump him for information. But the one who spoke English best, a colonel named Ivan, continued to visit Dyer during his long recovery to practice his English, listen to stories about stock-car racing at Virginia speedways, and complain about the utter lack of humor of the officer corps of the North Vietnamese People's Army.

Now came a part that was a little bit sensitive. Golenpolsky preferred that Brad not take notes concerning this matter. To understand how Dyer came to Akmolinsk it was necessary to know what happened at the end of the American war in Vietnam, but at the same time the facts of his situation raised certain questions of potential difficulty for the sergeant, as Brad would readily understand. Golenpolsky had also extracted many promises of delicacy and understanding from Avraham Lipsky, who had promised to make the Americans understand the difficulties of Dyer's position when he passed Golenpolsky's report along in America.

Golenpolsky wanted Brad also to understand that a common language and what amounted to a common fate, condemned to endless lonely months in a strange country as pawns in a war that meant nothing to them, created a bond of human sympathy between Dyer and his friend Ivan, the Russian colonel. It was the Russian who had arranged for Dyer's medical treatment and saved his life. For two years they had lived side by side in a succession of Laotian villages. Dyer was free to come and go because it was obvious no one-legged man could escape through the jungle. At the same time, he was a great help in dealing with the other American prisoners occasionally brought to these camps for interrogation by the Russians. Dyer said the Pathet Lao were pretty rough with their American prisoners, mostly downed fliers but also some Army Special Forces men much like Dyer himself and even one man in civilian clothes whose claim that he worked for the Agency for International Development was highly doubtful. The other Americans were at risk of escape and were kept in bamboo cages or chained to posts. More than once Dyer saved them from beatings by the NVA; he brought them water and extra food, changed their bandages, told them not to lose hope, memorized their names and serial numbers—as they memorized his—so the fates of those who died or simply disappeared might be known when the war at last came to an end. But it had to be remembered and understood that while Dyer in no way collaborated with the NVA, or assisted the Russians in their work, or by any other word or deed compromised his loyalty to the United States, during the two years of his captivity in Laos his friendship deepened with several of the Russians, and especially with Colonel Ivan, who saved Dyer's life for a second time in January 1973.

In the bustling transshipment point near Houamuang in northern Laos, where trucks and North Vietnamese soldiers frequently passed on their way south, the first sign of the impending peace agreement between the United States and North Vietnam was an abrupt change in the status of all American prisoners. Dyer told Golenpolsky there were about a dozen—it was hard to be sure; the number changed frequently as new prisoners arrived and others died or were trucked into North Vietnam. But suddenly with loud shouts a group of Laotian officers arrived one morning with a guard detail who said the Americans were no longer prisoners of the North Vietnamese but of the Communist Pathet Lao. Dyer, who had been filling a water jug nearby, watched unnoticed. One of the officers spoke a rudimentary broken sort of English, not much more than shouted words, demanding name, rank, and serial number of the prisoners. When the answer was not quick or clear enough, he shouted all the louder and beat the prisoners vigorously with a wooden stick.

Dyer slipped away and sought refuge in the house of the Russians, where Colonel Ivan told him it would be better if he stayed out of sight for a day or two until it was clear what was coming next. But the very next day word spread like wildfire through the camp: the Americans had made peace with Hanoi, the bombing had halted, the POWs would all be released. As soon as Dyer heard the news he wanted to tell the prisoners in the cages that they would be going home; Ivan insisted on going with him. As they crossed the camp they heard angry yelling and came upon the Americans trotting into the jungle with Laotian guards all around them, urging them down the trail and shouting all the while. Some of the men were wounded and had to be carried by others. All were thin and weak and after long periods of cramped inactivity struggled to maintain a slow shambling shuffle as the guards shouted and beat them with sticks. From a distance Dyer and Colonel Ivan watched the group disappear. A few agonizing minutes later came the sound of automatic weapons fire—rapid bursts of scores of rounds and then a slow string of methodical single shots, perhaps a dozen, before silence returned.

There was no mystery; Dyer knew all the men had been killed. Still hidden by the Russians, he learned the reason a few days later. It was a matter of bookkeeping. The prisoners had not been reported to the American negotiators, there was not time to get them to Hanoi for the exchange, so the North Vietnamese officially turned them over to the Pathet Lao and the Pathet Lao promptly disposed of the problem.

Here Brad interrupted for one of the very few times during Golenpolsky's long narrative. "Did Dyer tell you any of the names?" he asked.

"Oh, he told them all to me, and dozens of others too. Dozens and dozens. But you must remember, this was almost twenty years ago. I have forgotten. I told all this when I first came here, all the names I could remember, and my friend Avi assured me he had passed my report on to Washington. But I don't remember them all now—just a few: Dombrowski, Fleming, Jarvis . . . those he knew well. He often talked about them. I'm sorry I don't have the first names."

Major Anthony Dombrowski, United States Air Force, 31, of Bloomington, Indiana; F-16 shot down over northern Laos 29

November 1972, parachute seen to open. Search and Rescue aircraft spotted Dombrowski as he was taken prisoner by NVA soldiers; photographs showed him being marched off. Hanoi authorities reported no prisoner of that name under their control.

"Dombrowski's name I know," said Brad. "The others sound familiar. Dombrowski is still listed as missing in action. His parents write every year for information. Now I'll have something to tell them."

"But not how you know," said Shabtai. "This is part of our understanding."

"I won't tell them how I know," said Brad.

Golenpolski continued.

Motivated by their two years of friendship, the Russian colonel smuggled Dyer to Luang Prabang and accompanied him on a flight to Moscow. But there Ivan's authority suddenly evaporated. It was clear the Moscow authorities were furious with the colonel. Dyer was promptly placed in a detention cell in Butyrka prison and he heard nothing further from Ivan, then or later. By this time Dyer knew something about jailors, and it was obvious that they did not know what to do with him. Weeks passed. No one came to ask questions; the guards apparently knew no English and in any event told him nothing. For the first time in his life Dyer was utterly alone. It was winter, the cell was damp and frigid, there was barely room for a cot and a bucket for his waste, the lights were always on, his single blanket was thin. When he looked at the damp concrete walls on all sides of him he grew panicky. He kept his eyes closed or stared at the floor.

Dyer realized he could not live long in this place, nor did he want to. One day he began to weep, with heavy racking sobs and pouring tears. The guards came and shouted for him to be quiet. There was a tiny window in the door to his cell. Dyer put his mouth to the window and screamed out in a high-pitched, insane wail, "I'm an American! I want to speak to the embassy! If you won't let me go, kill me! Kill me!" Somehow this shouting relieved Dyer's agony and he kept it up—for hours, then again the next day, and the day after that.

Later, Dyer reasoned that this cry of despair had proved a strangely brilliant maneuver. The words he shouted were of course in English; they echoed down the corridors deep into the surrounding prison block. In a day or two at most, everybody in or passing through the prison was going to know that in the Butyrka the KGB was holding an uncontrolled English-speaking prisoner begging for death. Naturally they would wonder why. The KGB was smart enough to know that dozens, scores, maybe hundreds of people all wondering the same thing were pretty soon going to find out. This presented the Russians with a problem they were strangely incapable of resolving. The obvious choices were to let him go or to kill him, but neither answered to the facts of the case. Golenpolsky confirmed to Dyer that he had reasoned it out correctly: Since Dyer had broken no law of the Soviet Union there were no grounds for detaining him, much less executing him. But they could not surrender him to the American authorities without confirming that Russian intelligence officers had been questioning American prisoners of war in Laos, which of course they had always denied. Dyer had never been legally admitted to the Soviet Union and could not therefore be legally expelled to his country of origin, which was Laos, which in any event would have been sure to shrug in bland refusal since it, too, had no official record of Dyer's existence. The best solution, the authorities evidently reasoned, was to do nothing—that is, to remove Dyer to a distant location where none might guess his nationality and leave him there until he died of natural causes or somebody got a better idea. In his transfer papers he was identified only by the Russian word for unknown, with instructions appended to the camp commandant of Akmolinsk that the prisoner was to be held until he provided proof of lawful entry into the Soviet Union.

"Perhaps," said Shabtai, "this is enough for one day. It is nearly dark—"

"You told all this to Avraham Lipsky?" asked Brad.

"Yes, all this."

"And did he ever tell you what came of it?"

"Not Lipsky, an American."

"An American?"

"Sure, one of your people; he was in the station here. I had been pressing, you know. I wanted to know if my friend had been rescued. I was very concerned for him. I called Lipsky, and the American came—"

"The American."

"—came to my house. He said they had checked with Moscow. Yes, there was such a man—of course I knew that; I lived with him for two years!—but he was dead. He died of typhus and his body had been cremated. There were no personal effects. That was the end of it."

"This American—"

"Enough!" said Shabtai, getting abruptly to his feet. "We stop here."

"Who was this American?"

"You have accepted the rules, Mr. Cameron. For now the interview is over. Another day perhaps we can continue."

"You know we're going to find out who this American is," said Myrna.

"Maybe," said Shabtai. "But not before I find out myself."

29

"Babylonian captivity," Myrna called it. Stuck fast, but with nothing to complain about. Assured again by Shabtai that another interview with Golenpolsky would soon be arranged, she seemed quite content with Rachel and a book. Brad, however, was sharply restless. He wanted to finish up his MIA inquiry and get back to Washington and Jenny to sort things out if he could. He had promised Myrna not to let Jenny know where he was but then suddenly, late that Wednesday night, Brad discovered he was no longer away without leave. His boss, Randy Short, had telephoned from Washington to say he had been formally given a TDY slot in the Tel Aviv station while he continued his discussions with Golenpolsky.

"How did you know where to find me?" Brad had asked. There was a small sick doubt in his mind that Jenny knew somehow and had betrayed him.

"We're in the intelligence business," said Randy, with obvious pleasure.

"No, really."

"Two and two," said Randy. "When you didn't show up Monday we figured you might have flown the coop with Rashevsky, and sure enough. But don't worry, it's okay. You've got interest at the highest levels now. The seventh floor wants no stone unturned. The thinking in the head shed is that Golenpolsky could be only the tip of the iceberg. Maybe other émigrés know about American prisoners in the Gulag. Your assignment is to check it out. But we don't want a lot of gossip about this in the station. So sit tight till we set it up. We'll be in touch."

Myrna agreed there was no longer any reason to keep quiet, so Brad had e-mailed Jenny at length to explain everything. Her quick reply was brief and sounded final:

> Do you have any idea how much trouble you've caused here? You promised to stop. I'll never trust you again.

"She's angry," said Myrna. "Today it's over, but you can't predict about tomorrow."

Brad had been miserable all evening, angry throughout a sleepless night, tired the following morning. The household seemed to pay no attention. At the breakfast table Thursday Myrna spun a new theory about Tater's source—maybe somebody who had worked for Delaney. Rachel inquired what they might like for dinner. Shulamith suggested a drive to a nearby archaeological site. In the car, suddenly freed from guilt by Jenny's curt rejection, Brad admitted to himself it wasn't exactly easy to keep his eyes on the sights instead of Shulamith's bare suntanned legs.

When they got back, Myrna was waiting with Tater's latest story, downloaded from the Internet. The reporter was methodically filling in the background. It was like watching an army prepare for an attack, bringing up the troops, positioning the big guns. Cabot's confirmation was effectively stalled while the FBI completed an investigation, the exact focus of which apparently continued to elude the reporter. It was difficult to say for sure; Tater often sounded as if he knew more than he had chosen to write. But in the meantime, waiting for the Bureau to complete its work, he explored the politics of the nomination.

The president who nominated Frank Cabot had a reputation as vaguely liberal. A lawyer, in his youth he had been active with Amnesty International; as a congressman he often spoke out on human rights, focusing especially on the abuses of right-wing regimes in Latin America; even as governor of Wisconsin he traveled frequently on humanitarian missions. "No man," claimed the aging Republican senator with the pompadour who ran against him eighteen months back, "has ever been photographed beside more prisoners, domestic and foreign, than Governor Anderson. What's this man running for—chief warden?"

The line always got a laugh, but laugh lines do not win elections and Anderson ended the Republican senator's career with a crushing defeat in November. Anderson's first DCI, a man he inherited, was Patrick Delaney, but the chemistry between them, Tater reported, was not good. (*"Oy!"* said Myrna. "Delaney was an oilman. Old Senator Pompadour got all the oil money. What's the matter with this Tater? He ought to know that.") After the inauguration, Tater wrote, Delaney was rarely invited to White House briefings. A year went by before Delaney called in the reporters. (Myrna explained that Tater had not been among them; he was banished for revealing some Agency secret that was supposed to be really secret.)

Delaney said what men in his situation always say: He was getting older, he wanted to spend more time with his family, it was time for a change, there were plenty of able career intelligence officers for the president to choose among. There was no mention of what everyone knew: Anderson had given him the boot. Insiders found it no surprise, Tater wrote, when, after a few weeks of conspicuous search among the celebrated names of American public life, Anderson picked somebody from the analytical side of the house who had been there all the time. Anderson had none of that 1970s George McGovern tut-tut dislike for secret operations. What he opposed was not the plain fact of interference in the domestic affairs of sovereign nations but the traditional operational ethos of old covert hands like Joseph Flint, who would work with anybody, so long as they knew how to keep the secrets and never expected to get something for nothing. Police regimes in Latin America; the oil sheikhs of the Persian Gulf, each with his own *mukhabarat;* one-man states like Singapore—Flint calmly accepted them all and made no secret of his contempt for the American goo-goos who were always shaking a finger at the rest of the world for ignoring the First Amendment.

Cabot represented something different. Bland, immaculate, soft-spoken, and well-fed, as Tater reported (and Myrna confirmed), Cabot belied appearance. He was just the man you'd want to preach human rights at Harvard on Monday, while organizing a coup d'état against some uppity Third World president-for-life the following morning.

"So who does the president want to overthrow?" asked Brad, unconvinced.

"Read Tater's list," said Myrna. "The death-squad governments south of the border, the corrupt oil sheikhdoms, offshore banking regimes . . . people who flout the law and put democrats in jail."

"Anderson wants Cabot to go after all of them?"

"He wants a man who's willing. Flint would put up a quiet, stubborn fuss: that's not our job, we can work with this crowd, the next bunch could be a lot worse—the usual spiel."

"So Cabot's the cowboy," said Brad, "and Flint's for keeping hands off. It's funny—I'd have figured them just the other way around."

"That is so often the case," said Myrna.

An hour later Brad found himself trying to explain his interest in Golenpolsky to Shulamith, who had offered to give him lunch. Myrna and Rachel had gone to Tel Aviv; Shulamith's father was helping a neighbor repair an irrigation system; the Arab boy had the day off. Brad kept Shulamith company in the kitchen. He liked watching her move about in her brisk way. Agency regs forbade him from telling Shulamith anything about Golenpolsky and the rest, but much had changed in the last ten days. Knowing Shulamith could be trusted, he personally granted her a top secret clearance, and spoke to her freely.

"I have the feeling," he said, "that I'm missing something important. I mean I know roughly what Tater's looking for, I think I know why Shabtai is taking his time about setting up another interview, and I know for damn sure the story about the American in the Gulag is going to be a nine-day wonder until it's obvious it's just one more damned case of the POW who wasn't, but . . ."

Shulamith was washing lettuce for a salad. A double window above the sink looked out on a terrace of red bricks behind the house. It was bordered by big terra-cotta pots filled with flowers. Beyond was an orchard of grapefruit trees with the sun pouring brilliantly down through their branches. A light wind rippled the brown grass in the dry field beyond the trees.

"What I can't understand is my boss in Washington. I thought I was going to get fired when I told him I was here. Last week everybody was mad at me for poking my nose where it didn't belong. I was doing the same thing I always did, trying to track down reports of POWs, but when I found something they told me to keep quiet and back off."

Brad was sitting on the counter watching Shulamith's hands wash the lettuce, the water on her skin. He had to admit he loved her color, a kind of gold with a bloom of pink from the sun. She was wearing sandals, her usual khaki shorts, a sleeveless white blouse. No makeup. No jewelry.

"Now suddenly Golenpolsky is priority number one. I'm to stay right here until I can download everything he knows. It doesn't make sense. Why the switch?"

"Maybe it's not what Golenpolsky knows that worries them," said Shulamith. "Maybe it's something they're afraid you'll find in Washington."

"Like what?"

"I don't know. But something like this happened to me at a clinic where I volunteered in Tel Aviv during medical school. One day I was checking the blood supply, and I discovered that a lot of blood was being thrown away. So I asked why. They told me it was for administrative reasons, don't worry about it. But that didn't make sense, so I began to ask my professors."

Shulamith opened the refrigerator and dropped down onto her haunches to pull a bottle of white wine from the back of the bottom shelf. Her shorts pulled tight against her thighs. Brad had to admit he loved not only the color of her but the sleek roundness of her legs and arms as well. The palm of his hand seemed alive; he could almost feel the exact degree of the cool softness of the skin of her thigh against his hand. This combination of image and sensation popped into his mind without warning from nowhere. He could not believe he was thinking this.

"So a couple of days later the doctor in charge of the floor asked me to go to the hospital in Lod. The blood-drawing unit was getting complaints from the Arab community there. So I went and there was a problem: There were no Arab nurses, and none of the Israelis could speak Arabic. So I spent a few months moving people around and trying to smooth things over."

She took a large salad bowl down from a shelf and began to break up the lettuce into the bowl. Her fingers were long and slender, and she broke each stalk delicately, pausing frequently to look at Brad as she talked.

"Later," said Shulamith, "I learned what happened. The real problem was at the clinic. They were throwing away all the blood drawn from the Falasha—the black Jews from Ethiopia. Some of them were HIV positive, but instead of testing the blood, the way they were supposed to, they just drew it and threw it away. They didn't want me to find out. So they switched my internship to Lod."

"Just to get you out of the way?"

"Yes, but it didn't work. I kept calling up my professors, and eventually one of them told me what was going on."

"Did they threaten you?"

"Not openly. But the head of the clinic could tell the medical people what to do. He gave me a lecture about the records they send to the army and obeying orders and what the good jobs in the army were and what the awful jobs were. But I thought, Really, how bad could it be? It's still the army, you're still a doctor."

While she talked Shulamith put a long loaf of crusty bread into a basket, placed cold chicken breasts on a plate, poured each of them a glass of white wine. It was cool and sharp and Brad felt its slow bite rising into his brain.

"It's not so different, what happened to you and me," said Shulamith. "But now they're telling you everything's okay?"

"Yes, but it's not. Everything has come to a stop. Shabtai says Golenpolsky must go to Europe on business, but I don't believe it. I tell myself to be patient, it's all about Cabot's confirmation; once that's over, things will start moving again."

"No," said Shula. She was washing her hands in the sink. Brad was sitting on a counter next to her. Her elbow brushed his leg. "It's about the man in the Gulag."

"But he's dead," said Brad.

"He's dead," she conceded. "But you should trust your feelings. He's the one who matters. He's the one they're worried about."

Sometimes Brad had an adolescent's unruly smile, so intense he would begin to blush. Then suddenly his face might turn serious, furrowed with concentration—the way he had looked as Shulamith prepared lunch. But when she told him to trust his feelings he smiled and blushed. "How can you trust feelings?" he said. "You never know where they're going."

"That's why you have to trust them," said Shula. She was shaking the water from her hands. "There's a towel behind you."

Brad turned and found the towel. Shulamith stepped directly in front of him, drawing close to the counter where he sat, and held both hands palm up in front of him. She had a warm rich smell that settled the matter. He folded her hands into the towel, leaned forward—it was only a few inches—and placed his lips on hers, which opened to meet his. No thoughts troubled him. It was quite a while before they proceeded with lunch.

"He's that close," said Myrna, from where she was sitting with Brad on the porch after dinner. She'd been ransacking the Internet. "The FBI wants to know why the Agency didn't pass on a report of Cabot's meeting with a Russian intelligence officer. They learn about it a week ago when 'someone' tries to get into a protected file. So Tater has just about got it. I think he's playing with Cabot now. A couple of days more, maybe in the Sunday paper, he leads with Ames, and Cabot is in the fight of his life. What do you think?"

Brad was standing by the railing, looking out into the darkness. "I don't think he's worried about Ames. I think it's the American in the Gulag. I think Shula's right: I should trust my feelings about this. If we want to know what Golenpolsky's got to tell us, we need to go ask him. I'm tired of waiting for the phone to ring."

"Whoa!" said Myrna. "What's got into you?"

"I want to know who told Golenpolsky the American was dead."

"Naturally," said Myrna.

"And I want to know how he knew."

"You're getting the hang of it," said Myrna.

30

Shabtai and Myrna chattered away during the forty-minute drive from Jerusalem to the airport. Brad sat in the back seat gazing out the window at the warm, hazy sky hanging over the Mediterranean. He felt sad and anxious, without knowing why. If he had any sense he'd be worrying plenty about his reception back at Langley. He broke all the rules when he left the States and now he was doing it again.

"We faxed your TDY papers to the station," Randy Short had told him on Wednesday. "Your orders are to show up at the embassy beginning next week. When you get there ask for Chuck Halliday, he's the chief of station. He's going to help you make a thorough check of the émigré community, and that's all he knows about what you're doing. All that stuff you were poking into here—you don't talk about that. We'll let you know when the assignment is over. Do I make myself clear?"

Only too clear. Brad was safely out of town and his bosses wanted him to stay there until they had everything nailed down tight.

On the phone Brad had agreed, but within minutes he began to tick off the reasons why he needed to be in Washington. By the end of the weekend he told Myrna he had made up his mind. He had learned what he came for; he had to go home—tomorrow.

"It's late," said Myrna. "Everything's closed. Maybe our friend can help."

"Yes," said Shabtai, when Myrna called, "but not first class on El Al."

Brad's new readiness to ignore orders represented quite a change. As recently as a month ago he'd grow tense when his boss looked at him, he felt a little sick when he handed in a report, and he lived in terror of making another awful gaffe, like his announcement to the world that a dike worker in black pajamas was really an American POW. He'd spent the last two years trying to understand the rules of the game so he could follow them, and his diligence had paid off. He'd learned the rules but now, sitting in the backseat of Shabtai's Toyota on the way to Lod on Monday, he was breaking the second stay-put order in ten days and it didn't worry him a bit. Something in him—whatever it was that made all his grade-school teachers call him the best little boy in the world, made him a straight arrow in high school, and kept him at his desk studying on Saturday nights in college—some fear, probably, that no one would like him, that he'd drop the ball, that his mother would die, whatever. It had snapped. "You don't need to explain it," Shulamith had said. "I understand you have to go back. This was just . . ." She hesitated.

"Something I'll never forget," said Brad. He was going to say more, but she placed a finger gently across his lips to silence him. He kissed the finger. She lay naked beside him on the bed in her room, rosy as a peach. They were resting and they needed a rest. Brad wanted to tell her everything he felt, which was a hundred contradictory things, but Shulamith had touched his lips and shaken her head. There was a light film of sweat across her belly. . . .

Now, at the thought of the pucker of flesh around Shulamith's belly button, a small sound, halfway between a bleat and a moan, escaped Brad's throat.

"What?" said Myrna from the front seat of the Toyota, turning around.

"We turn off here," said Shabtai. They passed a sign in Hebrew and English that read BEN GURION INTERNATIONAL AIRPORT. A moment later he turned again, at another sign in Hebrew and English. CARGO AREA, it said. RESTRICTED ACCESS.

Shabtai slowed as he approached the gate, lowered his window, and flipped open a little identification wallet. Two Israeli soldiers in olive green waved him through. "It works like this," said Shabtai. "We ship cargo by air all over the world. To California we send wine from Mount Carmel. It's not very good wine but it's from Mount Carmel. To New York in February we send grapefruit.

"Behind the cabin in the plane is the cargo bay. Usually there's a little room left over and people can travel there. Of course there's no food service, no toilets, and no windows, but that's no hardship. The cargo area has its own passport control officer. He'll stamp your passports in the usual way, but while he works for immigration he also works for us. He doesn't ask questions, and he doesn't tell people who's coming and who's going.

"If you left from the main terminal on KLM or El Al, your friends at the embassy would know about it before the plane reached Cyprus. They have access to all the passenger manifests; we know it but we don't make a fuss. It's an understanding. But here they write your names down in a log, and at the end of the day they put the log in a briefcase and somebody drives it to the immigration office. It doesn't go into a computer; it doesn't get transmitted over a telephone line; nobody speaks your name on a cell phone or a walkie-talkie. This isn't for spies, it's for things that need . . . a little extra security. We know who's coming and going, but your Chuck Halliday doesn't."

It was a long speech for Shabtai. He stopped between sentences to wheeze heavily, catching his breath.

"At the other end in New York, roughly the same. The American passport officer there doesn't get all the watch lists. It's an understanding we have. Of course next morning you're in the computer but you're also in the country. That's the point. Not to be noticed. Things go more smoothly in this world when no one is paying attention. . . . No, no, you don't have to thank me. For an old friend like Myrna I'm happy to do it. We've known each other thirty years. What wouldn't I do for Myrna?

"And you," he said to Brad. "I'm not sure I understand what's so urgent you get back, but you seem to know what you're doing. Maybe it's the right thing; I don't judge. I've spent time in a camp—not in Russia, here in Palestine, under the British. I know what it is to wonder if you'll ever get out. Maybe you can help someone, I don't know. But Myrna asks, that's enough for me."

"No food, no toilets, no windows," said Myrna. "Anything else we ought to know?"

"You'll be traveling with ten thousand kilos of grapefruit," said Shabtai. "They keep the cargo bay at ten degrees Celsius. That's why I told you to dress warm."

Cold didn't begin to describe it. They wrapped themselves in blankets provided by the crew but shivered anyhow. Brad could hear the faint vibrating hum from Myrna's stocking feet on the woolly Twinkle-Toes. Half a dozen seats lined the fuselage wall on each side, but they were alone in the cargo bay. Overhead lights cast a pale yellow beam on their laps.

Once they were airborne, the door to the cabin opened and a crew member stuck his head out and asked, "Everything okay?"

"Everything okay," they said.

The door closed and locked with an audible *snick.*

"Such a quiet, thoughtful boy," said Myrna. "All the way in from Jerusalem. What were you thinking about so hard?"

"George Tater," Brad lied.

"Not Golenpolsky?"

"Him too." Brad was lying again.

"Not our nice stay with Rachel and her family in Yavne?"

"Of course," said Brad, telling the truth at last.

"That was some trick you pulled Saturday," said Myrna. "All day I thought you were off seeing the sights with Shulamith. Then I get a call from my old friend and he is very angry and he tells me where you've been and he tells me he thought we had an agreement and he tells me they are going to be very unhappy in Jaffa Street—he tells me a lot. I say nothing. What can I say?"

"I'm sorry," said Brad.

"You aren't sorry a bit," said Myrna, "and I don't blame you. That was pretty good, what you did. Now what?"

"Now what?" Brad repeated. "I guess the first thing we do is go knock on Joe Flint's door."

"Let's think about that," said Myrna.

So they thought about it for an hour. Brad described for the third time the drive with Shulamith to Ma'ale, twenty minutes east of Jerusalem on the steep, winding road down to the Dead Sea. But this time he put in all the details—they had ten hours to kill before they landed.

Shulamith had had no trouble with the guards at the gate to the town, and finding Golenpolsky's house wasn't hard. The Russians all lived on the western slope, looking out over the Jerusalem skyline. As soon as they came to the dead-end road, Brad recognized where he was. Beyond the parking lot was the row of small houses of Jerusalem stone with tiny front yards. Every one of them was filled with kids' toys, and there were lots of kids around too—infants in carriages and bassinets, toddlers in overalls and sweaters, four- and five-year-olds running and pushing. The mothers and grandmothers sat on metal chairs with puffy plastic seats, watching the kids. It was Shabbes and no one was working.

It was the same at Golenpolsky's house at the end of the street. Three small children stopped to look as Brad and Shulamith opened the gate. A slender black-haired woman smoking a cigarette called out "Lyova!" and a moment later the front door opened. He was obviously surprised to find Brad there but he immediately invited both of them in, made tea, poured it into glasses on the kitchen table, and pushed over a large sugar bowl.

"Shabtai didn't tell me you were coming," said Golenpolsky, when he had been introduced to Shulamith and the tea had been poured. "I was expecting him to call."

"I understand," said Brad. "I shouldn't be here and you shouldn't tell me anything. If you like, I'll say thank you for the tea and leave."

"First tell me what you want," said Golenpolsky.

"I want to know why nothing was done about your report twenty years ago."

"I was angry about that—twenty years ago," said Golenpolsky.

"And now?" asked Brad.

"I am still a little angry," Golenpolsky said. "Maybe what I know can help."

He was a wisp of a man, and he had an odd, appealing way of turning his head this way and that as he spoke, almost as if gesturing with the trace of gray beard that came to a point at his chin.

"I told you already how it began," he said. "We get off the plane at Lod and then we go into a room and fill out forms. A woman asked me lots of questions. She wanted to know how I got out. I said it was simple, in the Soviet Union everything happens by chance. Every year in Akmolinsk I wrote a letter to Brezhnev saying I was unjustly in prison, there was no future for me in Russia, I wanted to emigrate to Israel.

"You may think it's silly but these letters go to Moscow, they go to the Kremlin, they go to office of the Central Committee, and somebody reads them. Every year my letter gets read and it gets put into a special file: Jews wanting to emigrate. Then your Senator Henry Jackson begins to make a fuss about Jews in the Soviet Union. No arms treaty unless the Soviet Union lets the Jews go. The government wants a treaty so they go to the file of Jews seeking to emigrate and they pick a group and all get visas. That simple! So I was in a punishment cell in Akmolinsk, so what? Kremlin says let Golenpolsky go, they let me go.

"The young woman at Lod says it sounds crazy to her but okay. Next I talk to a man who wants to know all about my time in prison. When I mentioned the American he holds up his hand, says wait, he'll be right back. Next man wants to know all about the American. Two days we talk.

"What happens after that I learn later. This is private for you. Please. In Mossad they all know the American is hot news; right away it goes to the office of the prime minister. There they discuss who gets the news: the American chief of station here in Israel? the ambassador? somebody the Israeli ambassador knows in Washington? This is like a big present, and you want to get credit in the right place. Now it happens at that moment there is a little quarrel between the Mossad and the CIA about certain information CIA used to give Israelis but stopped. There was a new director in Washington, I think. Stansfield Turner, I think. Someone says forget the chief of station, forget Turner, let's go to this man Angleton, he is always our friend; he will be grateful and he will open the door for us. This is what I learn later. So Avraham Lipsky went to Washington and he saw Angleton, and then—nothing."

During the two years Golenpolsky spent in the special annex with the American, the men had grown close. Golenpolsky taught the American chess and learned checkers in return. They talked about their lives, their countries, their dreams. Of course, both hoped one day to be free but neither believed it was really possible. The Russians would never admit they had the American and they would never let Golenpolsky go because he knew about it. They had no chance. They would learn to flap their arms and fly before the Russians would ever open the door to let them out. Of that they were certain.

But then one day without advance notice of any kind Captain Myakov showed up at the special annex and told Golenpolsky, "Come with me." That was all. Golenpolsky put on his coat and followed Myakov out, and one week later he was in Israel attending his first class in Hebrew. Of course he was thrilled to be free.

"But one thing made me sad," he said. "I had no chance to say goodbye to my friend. And I was afraid he would think I had been a spy, someone put there to report on him. So every few weeks after I came here I would call up Avi and ask, What news? They were telling me Don't worry, it's going to happen. Then nothing. After a few months I got angry with Avi. Why wasn't anything being done? An American was locked up in the Gulag and nobody seemed to care? What was the matter with these people? I thought, It must be something political, so I told Avi one day, 'Look, these Americans are dragging their feet, they are too timid, someone needs to light a fire under them. You say to them I am going to *Ha'aretz* and tell the whole story and make big trouble.' "

That worked. Only a few days later, Lipsky called to arrange a meeting with Golenpolsky at a café in Tel Aviv. At the appointed hour, Lipsky came up the street, only he was not alone. There was an American with him, a big man with fair hair. Lipsky introduced him only as Ben or Bill, some American first name. He had come especially from Washington. The Americans were very grateful for Golenpolsky's help and they understood his concern, but this was a delicate matter.

"This case has been considered at the very highest level of the American government," the American said.

"He means the White House," said Lipsky.

The American nodded his head. "An officer in my Agency was sent to Moscow, very quietly, completely without publicity, to ask if this report was true. We didn't want the Russians to panic the way they did with

Raoul Wallenberg—'We never heard of this man' and next thing he suffers heart failure!

"Our officer had a friend in the KGB, someone he'd met in the course of his official work. They were both serious professionals, but they trusted each other too. They met in Moscow; it was quite natural. Our man promised there would be no publicity, but Washington had obtained certain information and had reason to believe an American POW had somehow been incarcerated in a camp under the control of the KGB; was this true and, if true, how could they arrange his release completely without embarrassment to the Soviet Union?"

One week later the answer came back. The KGB man said it was true but the American had died. There had been an outbreak of typhus in the camp, more than a hundred prisoners died, and their bodies were burned. Among them was the body of Sergeant Dyer.

"Did you believe this story?" asked Brad.

"Yes. Prisoners died in the camp all the time, and they often burned the bodies. I was very sorry but I believed him. I thanked God it hadn't been me."

"Lipsky never told you the big American's real name?"

"No. I never asked. I understood the rules. But you know how things work. One year it's a big secret; three years later he comes back as chief of station in Tel Aviv and everybody knows his name. They tell me he has a very important job now. My friend Avraham Lipsky always said he would be director some day."

Golenpolsky didn't need to speak the name. Brad had known immediately who it was: the Deputy Director for Operations of the Central Intelligence Agency, Joseph Flint.

"So Cabot went to Moscow, met with Kondrashov, and got the bad news," said Myrna. "In fact, the news couldn't be worse. Not only our man is dead but now we know the Russians have been lying and we've promised to say nothing. If the news gets out the Russians are furious, Congress goes crazy, the SALT treaty is out the window, it's back to the Cold War, and the president looks like an idiot."

"So nothing is put down on paper," said Brad.

"Exactly right," said Myrna. "The only problem is Golenpolsky, so Flint is sent to Israel to keep him quiet."

"Why Flint?"

"He's a known quantity. Avi trusts him, so Golenpolsky does too. Back in Washington maybe six people know what happened and all sigh for relief. But for some reason in the eighties the Russians tell Aldrich Ames about the meeting, why I don't know, and ten years later he tells his debriefers in Langley."

"I don't get it," said Brad. "Why would they tell Ames?"

"We'll come back to that. The debriefers sound the alarm, but the supergrades powwow and shut them up with some *mishegoss.*"

"I don't get it. Why not tell the truth? Security isn't going to blab it to the *Post.*"

"We'll come back to that. The problem now—"

"Is Cabot knew the Russians had an American POW but said nothing all these years."

"Exactly right," said Myrna.

"And it comes out now because I start nosing around."

"Exactly right."

"And what gets me started is a report in old DDO files—"

"Right."

"Put under my nose by the said Joseph Flint—"

"Right."

"Who is not-so-secretly hoping to end Cabot's chance to be confirmed as DCI."

"*Absolutely* exactly right. There's just one question you haven't asked," said Myrna. "Did I know what Flint was up to when he let you into the files?"

"Did you know what Flint was up to?"

"He would never explain himself to somebody like me. But I did wonder why he sent me down to help you out."

"Why?" asked Brad.

"To help you find your way around," said Myrna.

"And it worked," said Brad. "That leaves me one question. Why would the Russians tell Ames?"

"That's a mystery."

"Should we worry about it?"

"What good would it do?" asked Myrna.

Right now, she said, all they had to do was keep quiet about the fate of Sergeant Dyer until after the confirmation. Cabot would find a way to make the FBI happy, the hearings would go forward, the names of Golenpolsky and Ames would never come up, and Cabot would get the votes he needed. If Brad and Myrna kept their mouths shut for a few weeks, Flint would be taking early retirement.

Brad hated to wait but was willing. "Nobody knows Dyer's name," he said, "except you, me, and Golenpolsky, right?"

"And Shabtai," said Myrna. "But Shabtai we can trust."

"I thought you said you can't trust anybody in this business."

"You're right," said Myrna, "I did say that."

While Brad and Myrna were debating how long it would take Senator Hawkins to bring the hearings to a close and schedule a vote on the Senate floor, Shabtai was ascending by elevator to the third floor of a wing of the U.S. embassy in Tel Aviv. There he was met by a middle-aged woman wearing a photo ID who greeted him by name and then preceded him down the hall and through double doors marked SERVICE AREA. At the end of another corridor they entered through a second set of double doors marked DEPARTMENT OF AGRICULTURE, passed the desk of a receptionist with an exchange of smiles, crossed a second room with three desks where young men in shirtsleeves clicked on keyboards, and at last entered a large well-lit corner office with numerous photographs on the wall of American figures, well known in certain Washington circles, shaking hands with a beaming man in a bow tie looking at the camera. Scrawled more or less legibly on every photograph was some wordy expression of gratitude for the indispensable help and support of the writer's good friend and valued colleague, Chuck Halliday.

Halliday himself rose beaming from his desk to greet Shabtai, but over the next hour the broad smile gradually faded as he listened to Shabtai's account of the assistance rendered by the Mossad to the young intelligence officer on temporary duty from Langley. The prime minister's office was glad to offer the Mossad's help in this affair, Shabtai told Halliday, but owing to the possibly sensitive nature of the inquiry, and because it had been the subject of previous exchanges conducted in a somewhat informal manner twenty years earlier, the prime minister's chief intelligence advisor felt it would be only right to submit a complete written report of the entire episode, from Golenpolsky's first report of meeting an American prisoner of war in a Russian labor camp—

"An American POW?" said Halliday in pained amazement. No trace of a smile remained now. He looked stricken. "I thought Cameron was interviewing émigrés."

"It's all here," said Shabtai. He leaned forward and placed a manila envelope on the desk in front of Halliday. Speaking frankly, he went on, the prime minister's office of course fully understood that Franklin Cabot's role in this affair—

"Cabot? What's Cabot got to do with this?" Halliday was beginning to be angry.

"Chuck," said Shabtai, "read the report. I'm in no hurry. Then you'll know what is what and we'll do what we can to help."

While Halliday read the report, Shabtai smoked a cigarette. He closed his eyes. When Halliday finished he said, "Where are they now—Cameron and his friend?"

"I'm not quite sure," said Shabtai, with the look of a man trying to be helpful. "I saw them earlier in the week. I know they were staying with a friend in Yavne, near Ashdod. I can't tell you what their precise plans are." He shrugged his shoulders. "You're a friendly service. You wouldn't like it if we followed your people around. But if you want us to check into it—"

Halliday said he would be very grateful.

31

Dean Cutter stood near the corner of De Sales and 17th, blowing on his hands, pink and raw from the cold, and looking up De Sales toward the side entrance of the Mayflower Hotel. It was Tuesday, March 5. Dean's heart was pounding in his chest. He knew he could turn and walk away. But Russell was keeping watch inside the hotel. "I'm depending on you," he'd said, and that held Dean where he was. Dean was afraid but he wanted to do this. For once in his life he wanted to do something people couldn't ignore. He was praying for the moment when it was over and he'd meet up with Russell and they'd get drunk and talk about how they'd pulled it off and sit in front of the tube watching official Washington go crazy.

"Why do *I* have to do it?" Dean had asked, when they first started to plan seriously. "Why not you?"

Russell stood up and swung his leg back and forth. The ratcheting sound of the joint was loud. "You've seen me walk," he said. "How far do you think I'd get?"

He had a point.

They'd gone through the drill the morning before. Everything happened exactly as Russell said. The black Lincoln pulled up by the hotel doors at seven-thirty. Out stepped the tall figure of Senator Hawkins, bundled into a heavy coat with a high collar of brown fur. He disappeared into the hotel. Not quite half an hour later he came back out, face pink and clean-shaven, strode briskly around to the passenger side of the car, where his driver was waiting with the door open, and got in. That coat looked thick enough to stop bullets.

"He's from Georgia," said Russell. "He's probably freezing to death up here. Just aim for the trunk of the body—below the shoulder, above the belt, as close to the center as you can make it. Those bullets will tear him up."

Russell had prepared the bullets himself. Dean would use the Beretta .380. The clip carried six rounds plus one in the chamber. All Dean had to do was ease the hammer back while the gun was still in his pocket. There would be almost no sound.

"What we want," said Russell, "is a big messy wound. The shock will kill him even if you don't hit his heart or an artery."

He was sitting at Dean's kitchen table, the bullets lined up in front of him.

"Where'd you learn all this?"

"This isn't rocket science," said Russell. "Everyone knows this stuff."

Russell was working with a Swiss Army knife. He had opened the awl, placed the point on the tip of the bullet, and slowly twisted it in. It dug out a cone-shaped hollow in the soft lead.

"If you were trying to hit anything at a distance," said Russell, "this little trick would make it impossible. Close up it doesn't matter."

He liked to talk while he worked.

"When the bullet hits something, it expands in unpredictable ways," he said. "It'll probably travel six or eight inches through Hawkins's body. It might do a one-eighty in there. It might carry a piece of that coat as big as a fifty-cent piece right into his chest. If you fire three times you're bound to hit him once."

"Trust me," said Dean. "At that range, if I shoot three times I'll hit him three times."

"Once will probably do it. Three will be better. That'll leave three for any heroes who try to stop you."

Dean had dreamt that night about shooting his way free, but he wasn't feeling so confident right now. His hands were numb with the cold. He could hardly move his fingers. He was afraid, and he hadn't decided what to do.

The whole time Russell had been planning out loud, Dean had been thinking maybe he would and maybe he wouldn't. If he didn't he'd say, "I thought I saw a cop car coming up the street" or something. He liked planning it out. He liked thinking about the aftermath—all those talking heads on the tube, the newspaper headlines, Dean laughing somewhere, thinking, Nobody has a clue. But once that gun came out of his pocket he'd be in deep shit and he knew it. He didn't kid himself about that.

They'd worked out a simple plan. Three shots. Gun back into the pocket. Cross the street, turn the corner onto Connecticut, keep walking and don't look back. It would happen so quickly no one would have time to act.

"They'll be rubbing their eyes," Russell said. "Then you'll be around the corner and out of sight. The psychology of the sudden blow is what makes it work," Russell went on. "Nobody wants to chase a man with a gun. So they make excuses, they're not sure it was really you, they hesitate, you're gone. If you ran they might chase you, but if you walk. . . . Do you see what I'm saying?"

Dean did see. He believed the plan would work. He could pull the trigger and he could walk away. What frightened him was crossing the line. Once the gun came out the old life was over. He had no love for the old life, but a new outlaw life was going to be hard—right up against it, trouble on every side.

He blew on his hands; he imagined the minute hand of the clock approaching eight; he watched people marching by in their winter coats at the end of De Sales. Every time the hotel door opened, Dean's heart jumped. Russell was inside. When he came out it meant the senator was just behind him. Dean would start walking briskly up the street. Fifteen or twenty steps. He'd reach the car, the driver would be opening the door, Dean's hand would close around the gun in his pocket. . . . Maybe he would do it, and maybe he wouldn't.

The turning point had come Sunday morning while they were watching Hawkins on *Meet the Press.* Dean had been expecting more of the same, but that wasn't the way things went. The moderator, Walter Moss, who opened the show, went right to it and never backed off.

> Moss: Senator, we're all thinking the same thing. For those viewers who haven't heard the news, let me say that this morning's *New York Times* has a story that raises serious doubts about Frank Cabot's chances of being confirmed as the next director of the Central Intelligence Agency.

HAWKINS: That is putting it too strongly. The facts are not all in.

MOSS: Raises doubts, then. I don't think I'm exaggerating. This is quite a story, Senator.

HAWKINS: Let's not jump to conclusions. We've been around this town a long time, Walter. We've seen many a sensational story fade away to nothing.

MOSS: This one doesn't sound like a fader to me. Let me explain for our viewers. George Tater of *The New York Times* says that Frank Cabot, President Anderson's choice to run the CIA, went to Moscow in 1978 to ask if it was true that an American prisoner of war, left behind in Vietnam, was being held in a Soviet prison. We've heard much about the FBI's interest in Cabot's trip to Moscow over the last ten days, but this is the first we've heard about an American POW. That is your field of special interest, is it not, Senator?

HAWKINS: I have done everything I could for Americans still listed as missing in action in Vietnam. That is true.

MOSS: The *Times* claims there was such a prisoner, that Cabot failed to bring him home, and that no official report was ever made of his discovery.

HAWKINS: Tater is not infallible. Neither the White House nor the CIA has yet issued any statement. We don't know what happened. It's still early days on this one, Walter.

MOSS: But if Tater has got this right—and let's assume so for the moment—what would be your response?

HAWKINS: I would want to know all the facts.

MOSS: We'll stipulate these are the facts.

HAWKINS: I won't stipulate any such thing. This is all hypothetical. What if this? What if that? My response, Walter, is that this story raises questions that must be seriously considered, and I don't want to go beyond that. I will wait until I have had a chance to speak to Frank Cabot myself. I have known him for many years, I trust him completely, I admire his abilities. I will not play games with the reputation of a man who has served his country long and well.

MOSS: You have known him for many years?

HAWKINS: Years and years. We have spent many, many hours together since I took over the Select Committee on Intelligence.

MOSS: Did you know Cabot in 1978?

HAWKINS: No. He was a young analyst in the Agency then. I met him later, when he spent a couple of years on the National Security Council staff.

Moss: I remember the question of MIAs in Russia came up some years back. Do you remember that?

Hawkins: Of course. Somebody claimed to have found a list in Soviet files, I forget the details—but that story was absolutely false. It was exactly the sort of one-day story I'm talking about: big sensation, completely wrong. I'm sure you remember how that turned out.

Moss: Yes, I do. But let me ask you this, Senator: Did Frank Cabot tell you then, or at any other time, that he had gone to Moscow to check out a report of an American prisoner?

Hawkins: There was nothing in the paper about that, nothing at all.

Moss: Did he tell you?

Hawkins: I never put such a question to him. I had no reason to.

Moss: Did he tell you?

Hawkins: I don't see your point. It wasn't an issue. George Tater has only just published this report.

Moss: You have known Frank Cabot for years. You like him, you admire him, and you trust him. Did he ever tell you that he had gone to Moscow to check out a report of an American prisoner?

Hawkins: No. No, he never told me that.

"You see my point," said Russell. "Hawkins is the man we want."

"Cabot's the one who left him," said Dean.

"Yeah. But Hawkins is the face people know."

"Mr. Cutter," Lisa Benson said at the last meeting. "Have you got a minute?"

She hadn't done that before. She was wearing a satin blouse open at the neck. Dean liked that little flash of white-rose skin. He was feeling powerful—it was the talk with Russell about killing Hawkins. *If you only knew who I really am,* he was thinking.

The others filed out.

"Sit down. I want to talk about the group for a minute. And specifically what you owe the others."

Dean couldn't quite follow what she was getting at. He was staring at her breasts.

"You've got to be honest with the group," she said.

"I'm being honest," Dean protested. "I'm doing the work. I'm not just sitting here. I told them about some of the toughest stuff I've ever been through."

"Mr. Cutter, stop there. You need to understand something. You're in the system: all the traffic charges, a drunk-and-disorderly from way back, and then there's the VA files. They keep very extensive files at the VA."

"Those are confidential," said Dean. Now he wasn't feeling powerful at all.

"When you signed up for this course you released those files to the group facilitator, which is me; that was all explained to you. I'll show you the paper if you like."

"You can just look into any file you want?"

"Yes, I can. You were in the Gulf; I checked it out after the group's first meeting. But there wasn't any chemical weapons depot or any smoke cloud."

"I told you they were trying to hide all that," said Dean.

"You suffered an asthma attack the day you arrived in Saudi Arabia. You spent two nights in the hospital there. You were flown back to Texas and you were given a medical discharge—for asthma. I've read the files."

Dean was looking at the floor.

"You aren't the first man to rewrite history to explain why you've got a problem with alcohol. This is how denial works. First you deny there's a problem at all; then you deny the problem is really yours. The group can help you deal with this. But you've got to be honest with them."

"You mean tell them I made it all up?"

"Put yourself in their place. How do you think they'd feel if they found out three months from now?"

"I don't give a fuck how they'd feel."

"That's something you need to work on," said Lisa Benson.

Maybe he would and maybe he wouldn't.

Dean unzipped his jacket and slipped his hands inside, hugging them in his armpits. Up the street a steady exhaust of watery vapor emerged from the tailpipe of the senator's long black car. Dean looked at his watch. One minute past eight. What was keeping him?

As Dean stamped his feet and paced back and forth in the cold February gloom, he heard a siren coming up the street from a long way behind him—a faint wail blocks away but approaching steadily, the siren warbling through its long cycle, rising and falling as it approached. Then suddenly it passed Dean and roared up behind the senator's car. Men in white scrambled out.

What the hell?

Dean started forward, hand in his pocket and thumb on the hammer of the Beretta.

The doors of the hotel burst open and Russell stiff-legged it out in the rush of a crowd—the hotel doorman in his uniform, a bunch of men, people walking backward. They spread to clear a path as the men in white snapped a stretcher on wheels up into shape and hurried it into the hotel. Dean eased the hammer back in the pocket of his coat. He was expecting the heavy-coated senator in the crowd any second. Maybe all the confusion would make it easier.

People seemed to be appearing from nowhere. The lights on the ambulance flashed. The crowd gathering around the door was craning to peer inside.

Suddenly the hotel door opened again and a white coat backed out, pulling the now-loaded stretcher. A second white coat pushed from behind. Dean could see a man lying on the stretcher—a blanket was over him, he had gray hair, one hand held a hat perched on his chest, and the other was frantically tapping his breastbone.

It only took a moment. The white hair, the long lean body, the lantern jaw and bushy eyebrows—it was Hawkins lying there. The doors to the ambulance were flung open. Dean was in the street, only two strides away. He pulled the gun from his pocket, pointed it, was beginning to squeeze the trigger—thinking: Yes, he was going to do it—at the very instant that the crowd began to surge forward, the men in white started to lift the body, someone shouted. . . .

Dean fired. There was no time for a second or third shot. It was the best he could do. He put the gun back in his pocket and turned to cross the street, ignoring the shouts behind him.

One shot, straight to the heart, Dean thought. Then he was around the corner on Connecticut, where no one thought twice of the striding man with the look of triumph.

32

"Has Tater got a new story?" Cabot asked on the phone. It was twenty minutes before nine on Tuesday morning, March 5, and he could feel Tater breathing down his neck.

"No," said Weissberg, "it's Hawkins. I'll be right there."

What Cabot immediately feared and half expected was a report of a news conference scheduled by the senator from Georgia. It would be short. It would stick to a few bald facts. It would be final.

This fear had been growing for the nearly two full days that Frank Cabot had been trying to chase down Harrison Hawkins. Even before *Meet the Press* concluded Sunday morning, he asked his secretary to dial the cell phone in Hawkins's car and left a message with the driver. He called both of Hawkins's offices and his homes in Maryland and Georgia, but the senator had picked up none of his phones, responded to none of Cabot's messages, left no word with his staff or friends. The closest Cabot got was the flat voice of the senator's wife, Lydia, who answered on the first ring when Cabot tried the unlisted line in Chevy Chase.

They were not close. Hawkins and Cabot had often lunched together, or shared a drink in the senator's office at the end of the day, or schmoozed on the phone beyond the call of business, but Senator and Mrs. Hawkins had never dined with Mr. and Mrs. Cabot. Indeed, Kitty had never met either one of them, and Cabot had run into Lydia only once or twice over the years. But while they were hardly friends they had always been friendly, as if the relationship might quickly grow intimate under altered circumstances, so Cabot knew things were in a bad way as soon as the frigid voice of Lydia Hawkins on the phone explained that the senator was out and she was not sure when he would return.

"I will tell him you called," she said. And that was that. No word of friendly greeting, no reassurance of any kind, not even goodbye.

During the first awful minutes on Sunday, watching Hawkins sparring with Walter Moss on the television screen, Cabot had assumed he would get a chance to tell Harry his side of the story. But as the hours went by without any direct personal word, Cabot concluded the worst. Hawkins was too hurt and angry for explanations. He was going to pull the plug. He was going to tell the press corps he could no longer support Cabot, would vote against his confirmation, and would tell the president the time had come to pick another man. By dark on Sunday evening, Cabot had decided to call Otis Jones. They had agreed on the day of Cabot's nomination that for the time being the less they saw of each other the better, but Cabot knew his hope for confirmation was now in free fall, he needed serious help, and Otis Jones commanded more kinds of help than any other man in town. They arranged to meet, and Cabot went upstairs to dress for the evening.

For the previous two weeks it had been Cabot's custom every evening about six to visit Georgetown University Hospital and have dinner with Kitty. Whatever she got, he got: boneless, skinless, saltless chicken breast; whitefish in white sauce; linguine with steamed vegetables. Salt and pepper could do only so much. Kitty still wore a neck brace to hold her head in place, but the bruises and scabs were almost gone, she had little difficulty in getting to the bathroom, she was getting no special medication, and she might easily have been sent home. No one ever explained Kitty's prolonged stay in the hospital in so many words, but the doctors, the nurses, a few friends, Cabot and his niece, Jenny, and of course Kitty herself all knew the reason. In the hospital there was no smoking and no drinking. Catherine Cabot was drying out.

When Cabot got up to Kitty's room, he found Jenny sitting by the bed reading the Sunday papers while Kitty did the crossword. Cabot was relieved. Kitty's tongue could be sharp when they were alone together, and Agency etiquette did not extend to wives, or at least not to his. He allowed himself to hope for a quiet family hour before going on to see Jones.

Kisses all around. "What do you hear from the boys?" he asked.

"The usual," said Kitty. "Am I listening to the doctors? Am I getting enough to eat? Do I want them to come down for a visit? Frank, when do the hearings begin?"

"I wish I knew," said Cabot. "What's for dinner?"

"Chicken broth," said Kitty. "Macaroni. Boiled carrots. Iceberg lettuce salad. Jell-O."

"Jell-O again?" said Cabot.

"Of course Jell-O," said Kitty. "If you want real food, get me out of here."

"How are you, Jenny? Keeping busy?"

"I'm okay."

"I understand your young man is away."

"Uncle Frank, he's not my young man. Brad works for you."

"He did once. Now I'm not so sure. He walked off from his desk here in Washington without by-your-leave, so we gave him a job in Israel and told him to stay put. Maybe you've heard from him."

"No," said Jenny. "Just that he's there."

"I thought you two were serious. Have you broken up?"

"I gave him hell for stirring up all this trouble, and I guess that put a chill on things. Aunt Kitty knows the gory details. You can ask her later."

"I never thought Brad was cut out for this intelligence business," said Kitty, "and the last couple of weeks. . . ." She hesitated.

"Tend to confirm it," said Cabot.

"You'll have to ask him," said Jenny. "I can't tell you what he's thinking."

"Uncle Frank has other things on his mind at the moment, dear," Kitty said. "He's got George Tater breathing down his neck. He's feeling like the fox at a fox hunt. This might be the moment for Uncle Frank to make a career change."

"It's too late for that," said Cabot. He sounded weary, as if he'd explained this over and over again. In a sense he had. Every night since Tater's first story, Cabot had rehearsed some version of this speech as he fell asleep, getting ready for the moment when all bets were on the table and he had to show his cards.

"The Agency's done nothing wrong," he said, "but if I withdrew now it would really open the floodgates. Tater has played this like Toscanini. If I tried to skip out the back door, everybody would want to know where the body was, an investigation would get going, we'd have to haul records and witnesses up to the Hill, and every time we tried to hold back some inconsequential piece of paper there'd be a chorus yelling cover-up."

"So tell 'em and be done with it," said Kitty.

"Tell them what?"

"The truth. You're the one who knows the truth."

"The truth about what? You've read Tater's stories. Have you been following this, Jenny? Do you think Tater really knows what he's going after?"

"No," said Kitty. "You tell us. What are you afraid Tater is going after?"

"Tater doesn't worry me," Cabot said. "It's a dozen senators with fire in their eye and the power of subpoena. Tater is pushing all their buttons: Russians, Israelis, a secret meeting in Moscow, an American in the Gulag."

"Well, what about that American in the Gulag?" said Kitty. "I'm curious about him myself."

"We were too late. He was dead. I had the word of a man I trust on it."

"So it's all just—"

"Another complicated story that goes nowhere. You could take testimony on this for a week and what would you have at the end? Somebody sending somebody else to check out a rumor. The secret isn't what I was sent to do, it's who sent me. That's why the whole story wasn't on page twenty-eight of *The New York Times* long ago."

"Okay. Who sent you?"

Kitty was looking at Cabot over the rim of her glasses, which were resting on the tip of her nose. With her head held erect by the neck brace, she looked as stern as a third grade schoolteacher. Jenny was equally rapt.

Cabot decided to tell them. Kitty's question would soon be on everybody's lips and he would soon have to answer it if he hoped to get out of this in one piece.

"The White House," said Cabot. "My marching orders came from Jimmy Carter."

"President Carter *personally*?" asked Kitty.

"No, but it was President Carter who was issuing orders."

"I see the problem," said Kitty. "Some of those senators would love to put an ex-president on the hot seat."

"Especially that ex-president," said Cabot. "They'd forgive Reagan. But Carter?"

"Forgive what?" said Jenny. "I don't understand."

"Failing to rescue an American from the Gulag."

"But you said it was too late; he was dead."

"It *was* too late. But who's going to listen? Once a senate committee begins dragging out the details, they never stop."

"It doesn't sound good," said Kitty.

"It's a nightmare," said Cabot. "But I can't just go into the hearing room and say, I did it all on my own hook. They wouldn't believe it, and before I knew it they'd have me up on perjury charges."

"So you *have* to tell the truth," said Kitty.

"Yes," said Cabot. "I'm trapped. It's a bitter way to end an honorable career of telling lies for my country."

"That's what I love about you," said Kitty. "You've got a sense of humor. And you're such a feisty little guy."

Cabot blushed.

At that point a nurse swung open the door with their dinner trays and Jenny said her goodbyes. "She seems out of sorts," Cabot said, as Jenny's footsteps died away down the hall.

"She's confused in the love department," said Kitty. "I gather some new man has appeared on the scene."

What worried Cabot now, two days later, sitting in the big office so recently vacated by Patrick Delaney and waiting impatiently for Weissberg's arrival, was Hawkins's appetite for battle. If that was gone, MacLaverty would take over and drive the inquiry with unanswerable questions: "Is it true, Mr. Cabot . . . ? Do you deny, Mr. Cabot . . . ? Are you trying to insinuate, Mr. Cabot . . . ?" The one thing Cabot could never survive would be a long battle and weeks of headlines. In this town, he knew, trouble sticks. President Anderson wouldn't think twice about getting rid of him just to end the trouble, once it was clear that was the price. He was probably thinking about it already, egged on by the malignant Peter Schleicher.

Cabot knew he'd never ranked high on Schleicher's A-list. It was nothing personal. Schleicher simply wanted someone who understood that politics came first. From the beginning he'd urged the president to pick somebody like George Shultz, some solid well-connected guy who'd made a fortune in microchips or the construction of airports or pipelines in the oil states. Schleicher was the sort of guy who liked to rub things in. Every morning when Anderson arrived at his desk in the Oval Office, Cabot was certain the president would find a copy of the *Times* with a big red circle around Tater's latest story—a daily reminder that Anderson's choice was turning into a tar baby. At some point, probably soon, Anderson would say to Schleicher, "I don't know, Peter, is it time to rethink?"

Cabot had no illusions about what would happen next. He'd get a call from some old friend, someone he'd known for years, someone he trusted completely. They'd meet for a drink. A little small talk, praise for the brave fight Cabot was putting up in the hearings. "I'm speaking strictly as your friend," he'd say. "Anderson has no idea I'm doing this; he'll stand by you till hell freezes over; you know how loyal the president is. But, Frank, I want you to consider—is this pissing match good for the country?"

Hard to answer yes to that one.

All the way up Massachusetts Avenue, after leaving Kitty on Sunday evening, sitting in the back of the Agency car, Cabot had wondered how long it would take Carter's name to reach Tater's keen ears. Cabot had never before named him in this context, not even twenty-some years ago when Otis Jones had passed on the president's instructions. In the career of an American intelligence officer two things have sacred power—secrets and the wishes of presidents. And very often a president's wish was to remain unheard and unseen. Young as Cabot had been at the time, no one had to tell him he was to carry his knowledge to the grave. Otis Jones had never said anything of the kind. It was the tone of his voice, the grave hush, the careful words conveying the wishes of the unnamed person who was not present but alone had the authority even to have such a wish.

But the more he thought about it, the surer Cabot became that his best hope now lay in muddying the waters—finding somebody else for Tater to go after. Yes, Cabot would confess, when the time came, it was wrong of me to keep secret the name and fate of an American POW. But what else could he have done? Junior intelligence analysts do not defy the wishes of presidents. They do what they are told.

Feeling alone but resolute, Cabot arrived at the big apartment building on Massachusetts Avenue, where he found Otis Jones sitting in the small dark room he called his study. It was not books that lined the shelves but birds from Alabama and Tennessee, shot and stuffed by Jones's father as a boy. There were dozens, ranging in size from hummingbirds to owls. Servants dusted them weekly and their feathers still shone. One or two of the birds in Jones's study had since become extinct.

Jones was bundled into a thick blue-velvet bathrobe with a gray scarf around his neck. He explained that he had a head cold but he looked far worse—weary and slow in movement, gray and drawn, with watery eyes, pink jowls, wattle hanging loose. The skin of his hands looked translucent over the big knuckles. Jones was deep into his eighties, but Cabot had never seen him look his age as much as he did tonight.

He might be frail but his appetites remained. "I held off till you got here," said Jones. He asked the houseboy, Emilio, for two fingers of the old Macallan in a snifter, and Cabot said he would have the same. The drinks came in a few moments. The Filipino padded out on slippered feet and shut the door behind him.

They chatted for a moment, like old friends. Jones wanted to know about Kitty's progress, the condition of the roads—had the doorman salted the walkway?—Cabot's spirits. Then he got down to business.

"Who's talking to Tater?"

Cabot confessed he did not know. The Office of Security was looking into it but so far had come across no marked information—something only X or Y or Z could possibly have known. What Tater had printed could have come from the FBI, from someone on the staff of the Senate intelligence committee, or from Hawkins, at least in theory.

"No one else knows?"

"Lots of people are aware of pieces of it, but there's no way to tell which of them is talking. I'm guessing it's the FBI; they're furious. But the Bureau knows about Aldrich Ames, and so far Tater hasn't published word one about that."

"Hawkins holding fast?"

"He was last week. He told me he'd spoken to the president and not to worry. I haven't talked to him today. He's not answering his phone or returning my calls. My guess is he's upset and angry about the MIA angle. But that was long before his watch. It never came up, so there was nothing to tell. He'll be hurt but I'm hoping he'll accept what I say—that I checked it out but came up empty."

Jones grunted. He was thinking. He reached up to stroke the tailfeathers of some kind of game bird with a long bill. Cabot knew nothing about birds.

"Where does that leave us?" Jones asked.

"At the mercy of the Bureau. We need to get those hearings going. We need to make a little news and put Tater on the defensive."

"Well, how long can the Bureau drag this out?"

"As long as they like. The Bureau can't complete the report for Hawkins until they talk to me, and they won't schedule an interview with me until they're satisfied they've seen all the paper the Agency has collected. They could easily keep this going for another week or two."

"Anderson won't call up the director and say chop-chop?"

"Ken Watts is ready to retire. He's hard to push."

"Things were easier when Hoover was still alive," said Jones. "He knew when to cut and when to deal the cards. But Watts—weren't his people from Tennessee? Turpentine business? Paper pulp? I'm thinking Tullahoma."

"He made his name in California," said Cabot. "Last white chief of the LAPD."

"I'm talking about his people. Something tells me his daddy was a lawyer and judge down around Shelbyville or Tullahoma. Watts is an old name around there. There's a big Watts sawmill in Shelbyville. Maybe I can do you some good there."

They talked on, weighing this and that. Jones knew something about everybody: the old money Hawkins acquired along with his wife, MacLaverty and his backers in Boston real estate circles, Schleicher's ties to the oil business, even George Tater's first wife, who had never remarried and now earned a six-figure salary on Wall Street. Cabot was just beginning to wonder where this was going when Jones said, "Any sign Tater knows about your father?"

"My father?" Cabot's heart skipped a beat.

"All that trouble with the Griggs Bank in Cleveland," said Jones.

Cabot was stunned. He hadn't heard the Griggs Bank named since his childhood, when his father and the bank's president narrowly escaped prosecution for bribing a public official. It had ended his father's career and wrecked his life.

"Why would that come up?" Cabot asked.

"Tater's digging into your past. You can't tell what he'll find."

Jones might have been discussing something in the paper, but the message was clear: Cabot had better stick to the story.

"Tater's been out front on this from day one," Jones went on. "Where's everybody else?"

"Tater's got the source," said Cabot. He was angry but he was trapped. He betrayed nothing.

"What does the source have? That's the question, isn't it?"

"Ames delivered the basic who, what, and when. I think that's all they know."

"They haven't dragged anything out of you in-house?"

"No, Otis."

"My name's never come up?"

"So far as I know, only you and I and one other person really know what happened here. Maybe two."

"Two?"

"The peanut farmer and my friend in Russia."

"The Russian," said Jones. "Is he still around?"

"I don't know, but it's not likely. He was involved in the coup in 'ninety-one and spent some time in jail. Then he was a business consultant for a while. We talked maybe five or six years ago. But he had terrible emphysema, he carried an oxygen bottle wherever he went, and he couldn't quit smoking. He said goodbye the last time we talked, as if he didn't expect to be around much longer."

"But he could be alive."

"He could be. I wouldn't worry about it."

"But he knows and he could be alive."

"It's conceivable. But he's not our problem. Trust me on this, Otis."

"They're going to ask what happened. What are you going to say?"

"I'll say I went, I asked, I was told I was too late."

"They're going to want to know who sent you."

"I've been thinking about this," said Cabot. "I think the time has come to say the White House wanted it handled this way."

"No," said Jones. "If you say it came from the president, the next name is mine."

"But everybody knows I went to ask about a POW," said Cabot. "They'll never quit till they know why I didn't write it up. The answer is I was under orders. It has the additional merit of being true. It's awkward, I admit, but once the president confirms the story they'll stop asking questions."

"That is dead wrong," said Jones. "They'll go after the president instead of you, and the president is bigger quarry. It will be ten times worse. No, we've got to find somebody else—somebody safely dead who can no longer be subpoenaed to testify. Who was the DDO back then? Larry Winter? Why can't you say Winter was telling you what to do."

"Not Winter," said Cabot. "Winter's out."

"What's wrong with Winter?"

"Winter hated my guts, Otis. We got into a major pissing match about Soviet missile guidance—I wanted to know the identity of some asset who was feeding them a lot of crap, and Winter said not in a million years. In the end Turner himself told Winter to give me what I wanted, and after that he never even looked my way in the hall. No way would Winter give this sort of job to me."

"He's been dead ten years, Frank."

"He may be dead but he's not forgotten. I'm telling you this was the talk of the Agency. If I tried to tell the Senate that Larry Winter sent me to Russia, all sorts of people would know I was lying and one of them would go to MacLaverty. Winter is out. We need somebody else."

"Well," asked Jones, "who else is dead?"

"Jack Maury, head of the Soviet Russia Division. He had the right job at least. Drexel Godfrey. George Carver. How about Larry Houston?"

"Houston didn't have it in him to fudge on his income taxes," said Jones. "He'd have littered the files with memos. Maury never had that kind of weight. Nobody would believe Godfrey or Carver. They're not the right sort of people and they weren't in the right place. What we want is somebody outside the chain of command—an old boy, known to all the insiders, the kind of man you'd trust to break the rules when it mattered. We need a name that makes everybody say, Yeah, him, okay, that I believe."

He was tapping his finger against his pursed lips, thinking hard.

"Did you know John Bross?" Jones asked finally.

"I did know Bross," said Cabot. "I was attached to the transition committee in nineteen eighty and we spent quite a lot of time together. I liked Bross."

"We all liked Bross," said Jones. "If you testify that John Bross came to you, stressed the importance of secrecy and discretion, told you what we knew, and asked you to check it out, people would accept that."

"It's roughly what actually happened," said Cabot.

"Roughly, yes. Can you hold up your right hand and look them in the eye and tell them that?"

"Sure," said Cabot. "Terry Tyler told Larry Winter, Winter told John Bross, Bross told me. Who else Bross was talking to I don't know. It could have been Turner, it could have been the president, or he could have just taken this on himself. I was still a GS-Fourteen on the analytical side. I never would have questioned a man like Bross."

"And he told you not to write it up."

"Right. I told him what I learned and that was the last I heard of it."

"I'm comfortable with that," said Otis Jones. "That keeps the president's name out of it."

Cabot was not at all comfortable about that, but he said nothing.

When Leo Weissberg at last arrived in Cabot's office Tuesday morning, he wasted no time in delivering the bad news. Cabot heard him out patiently, asking only one or two clarifying questions. The senator's office said he had suffered a heart attack at Sally Morelli's, he had been alive when the ambulance left the Mayflower, and one of his staffers was heading for the hospital.

But there was one more thing, Weissberg said. It made no sense. While they were loading Hawkins into the ambulance, some nut case stepped out of the crowd and shot one of the medics.

"Did they catch the shooter?"

"Not yet. This all happened just a few minutes ago."

When Cabot knew all Weissberg had to tell he said, "Leo, I want somebody over there in the waiting room. Any word on Hawkins's condition, I want to hear it."

"Of course."

"One other thing, Leo. You remember our conversation the other day? I said we had to keep the president's name out of it."

"I remember."

"Do you think that's possible?" asked Cabot.

"Frank," said Weissberg, "what do you think?"

"I think they'll keep after me until they drag it out."

"You haven't been listening to my advice," said Weissberg, "but my advice is—call the man from Plains and tell him what's coming his way."

"I'm beginning to agree with you," said Cabot.

33

"A reporter is only as good as his sources," George Tater liked to say. It was his way of being modest, waving off praise when he had nailed someone's feet to the floor. The real secret of his success, Tater also sometimes said (late at night, after drinks), was his competitive spirit. Other reporters wanted to get bylines and front-page stories; they wanted to win awards and be invited to give speeches; they wanted to be treated as equals and called by their first names when major players were shmoozing off the record. Not many people understood how Tater felt about his work, but his editor at the *Times*, Morrie Bloom, was one of them. "Tater's like a junkyard dog," said Bloom. "He doesn't want to be patted on the head or given a bone. He wants to kill rats." This was not a side of his character Tater revealed to his new young friend of twelve days' time, Jennifer Moore.

But at the same time Tater took sources seriously and it was his rule to trust a source only when he understood the real reason—the fundamental bedrock reason—why a source was willing to talk to him. Self-interest was of course the big one, but the emotions sometimes played a role. In Tater's experience these generally fell into a narrow range between the desire to impress and the hope of inflicting an injury. Sometimes a talker's motive was obvious, sometimes not.

The round-faced senator from Massachusetts, for example, the florid Brian MacLaverty, spoke of Franklin S. Cabot in tones of bitter contempt. "He's spineless," MacLaverty said. "He'll suck up to the White House, and he'll bend over for the Pentagon." MacLaverty didn't like the way Cabot looked or the way he talked, he disliked Cabot's English tailoring and the perforated toes of his Church's shoes, and he gave a wicked imitation of the way Cabot folded his hands on the table in Senate hearings, like a choirboy at prayer. Above all, MacLaverty detested Cabot's way of pausing after a troublesome question and then saying, with a look of mild surprise, "Pardon?"

MacLaverty was vigorous in listing Cabot's failings as a man and a public servant, but it didn't take long for George Tater to spot the deeper thread: MacLaverty had been instructed to block Frank Cabot any way he could by some longtime campaign contributors who did not trust Cabot when it came to the Middle East. When people took a position on the Middle East it usually involved one of two things, oil or Israel. In MacLaverty's case, Tater decided, the mix was about 30 percent oil and 70 percent Israel. MacLaverty had collected a lot of money from people who thought Cabot was going to help Anderson upset the applecart in the oil states and even more money from lobbying groups who believed Cabot was hostile to Israel. Tater guessed the sore point was the old one: intelligence sharing. Israel wanted stuff they didn't think Cabot would give them. Ergo: stop him before he gets started. MacLaverty's reason for talking to Tater was the most common and trustworthy of all: he was being paid, it was his job.

Tater's most important sources after MacLaverty were two special agents of the FBI who knew nothing about Israel and cared less. One of them, Kenneth Holmes of Lawrence, Kansas, had been a U.S. Army judge advocate general's lawyer in Saigon when Tater spent time there on a story in the early 1970s. They became, and remained, friends. Holmes told Tater things because he liked him and wanted to be helpful and was smart enough to know when it was okay and when it was a firing offense. Lucky happenstance assigned Holmes to the FBI working group checking out Cabot, and the director of the Bureau, Ken Watts, did not mind, Holmes knew, if the occasional leak helped to ruin Cabot's day. Holmes's partner, Matthew Curran, a lawyer from Fordham University, was one of those innocents who imagined he was only adding a few details to stories Tater had already smoked out on his own.

Lots of other people had been talking to Tater as well—Senate staffers, serving CIA officers, paper shufflers at the Pentagon, major players behind the scenes at the Pentagon, some Harvard professors who had previously been at the Pentagon, the director of the arms control program at MIT who hoped to go to the Pentagon, a retired officer of the KGB now teaching intelligence ethics at Johns Hopkins University, the president's National Security Advisor on deep background, two former directors of Central Intelligence, who rather liked Cabot but in all candor never thought he would go the distance, a member of the President's Council of

Economic Advisors who specialized in the Persian Gulf, a Defense Intelligence Agency analyst who had resigned nearly twenty years earlier in a spat over Soviet missile accuracy, a former senior officer in the Iranian Savak who was now a consultant to American oil companies doing business in Russia, a Saudi businessman who gave lavish and frequent parties in Washington, several old counterintelligence hands who reported that Cabot did not know the first thing about internal security, several retired chiefs of station in countries of the former Eastern Bloc who said Cabot did not know the first thing about recruiting agents in the field, a former director of the former Czechoslovakia's Hlavni Sprava Rozvedky now selling Czech machine tools from an office in Baltimore, and a dozen friends, golf partners, and relatives of Cabot himself, including, to George Tater's continuing amazement, the nominee's bright, too-confident niece.

Tater had seen fifteen or twenty people since first catching the scent of Frank Cabot, and he had talked on the phone to maybe twenty more. Scores of other names scribbled in Tater's notebook were waiting their turn. All had their reasons for talking; most transparently wanted something in return, including Jenny Moore, who believed it might make some kind of practical difference if George Tater understood that Jenny's uncle was a good man, hard-working, devoted to his country, simple in his habits, fair in his actions, willing to take a hit personally rather than betray a confidence. Tater said nothing to encourage Jenny's faith that she was doing her uncle some good. He simply listened, and when it became necessary, after his stories began to appear in the *Times* and after their relationship had taken a further predictable turn, he frankly explained to Jenny some basic facts of journalistic life: namely, that a delay in a confirmation hearing so the FBI could reopen its original investigation was a dramatic event, requiring explanation, and Tater was only doing his job—trying to figure out what was going on. "You can't tell me because you don't know," he told her correctly. "The difference between us is, I really want to know, and when I do know I'm going to tell everybody."

"You judge too harshly," she said.

"I try not to judge at all," Tater said. "I lay out the facts and let other people judge."

Jenny knew this didn't cover it, but Tater held up his hands and said, "I'm not trying to do the man harm. I'm trying to cover a story." Tater knew how to look and sound like a man completely without guile. So Jenny let it go.

. . .

The real surprise was that Jenny Moore seemed to take to him. She gave no sign of knowing her uncle thought Tater was dangerous as a snake. He puzzled over it suspiciously later. Was she pulling the same trick on him he'd tried on her, the I-declare-I-never-would-have-guessed routine? Tater decided she was too young for such a deep stratagem. He was careful to make no fuss over her relationship to Cabot. It was a fact, like living near Dupont Circle or driving a Volvo.

Jenny had turned down his proposal for dinner the night they met at the British embassy, but the next day she called him up and suggested a new dim sum place on H Street in Chinatown.

As soon as he heard her voice on the answering machine, he picked up and said, "I just walked in."

"Don't give me that bullshit," she said. "You're screening your calls like every other egomaniac in town."

He dropped the denial immediately. "You're right," he said. "But you I want to talk to."

"Because I'm the niece of the next director."

"Come on," he said. "What do nieces know? It's Chinese food I want to talk about."

They met, they ate, they talked. Tater didn't think Jenny was flattered; she'd been around Washington too much for that. But Tater had a way of approaching women, and with her it worked. If she asked about his work, or his opinions, or his views of people and events, he would answer, but he never volunteered. He never lectured; he asked her lots of questions. Above all, he listened to the answers and remembered what she said—the names of her friends, where she worked, what she felt about the illegal traffic in animals and animal parts that occupied her working day. Over their first weekend, although they ate together twice and went for a long walk in the cold on Sunday, he spoke no word and made no gesture that could be interpreted as a sexual advance. At dinner Tuesday night he said, "Is it okay if I put you in a cab? I've got to get back; there's somebody I want to see on *Nightline*." When Jenny asked who, Tater said it was a recent Iraqi defector thought to know something about the mental health of Saddam Hussein. Jenny said that sounded interesting. Twenty minutes later they were drinking beers in front of Tater's tube. They settled toward each other on the couch, there was a fumble or two as *Nightline* ended, but when he kissed her she kissed him back and things thereafter unfolded in the usual urgent way.

Writing about the favored uncle of a woman he was sleeping with was an iffy proposition at best and Tater said so. Jenny said she could handle it.

The riskiness of the whole thing appealed to Tater, but it was also true that it had been many years since he had been in bed with a woman still ripe with the bloom of her twenties. For her part, Jenny wanted to know what made Tater tick. Within a week they were pretty deeply involved with each other.

But that didn't stop Jenny from giving him hell for a story about Uncle Frank's close scrape with the special prosecutor during the Iran-Contra affair, another bit of ancient history to her. Tater said, "It's not me dragging it in, Jenny, it's what Special Counsel Walsh wrote in his report. He did everything but point his finger at your uncle in the town square. I can't ignore what's in the public record."

Jenny accepted that. Tater deliberately wrote his stories as strings of facts. The doings described had all been secret and were about things that aroused strong feelings, but Tater made no charges and assigned no blame. He made sure to stick a couple of humanizing details into his stories that he knew Jenny would like: the silver trophy Uncle Frank won on his high school debating team (lifted from his Fremont Park high school yearbook); Aunt Kitty's work with Josef Albers (taken from the *Times* notice of their marriage thirty-four years earlier). When he started digging up the stuff about the FBI and the trip to Russia, he made damned sure she knew he wasn't getting that from her. Jenny was curious about Tater's way of pursuing a story: how he found things out, what his editors wanted to know, why he put some facts high in the stories and others near the end. Once or twice she asked specifically how he had learned something, and he either told her or invented a plausible lie. He knew his luck couldn't hold forever; at some point he would print something about Cabot she couldn't tolerate and he didn't want her marching angrily out of his life with the names of all his best sources. The fact they shared a bed was one of those things, Tater told himself, both simple and mysterious—why he wanted to keep it going was as simple as the appeal of a cold beer on a hot day; what was in it for her was as mysterious as deep space. Tater was not vain. It did not occur to him that what she got out of it was him. He guessed pure adventure was the draw. But that was okay. Take what's on offer and don't look back, that was George Tater's philosophy.

It was Tater's experience that in every really good story there came a moment of crisis when he couldn't see his way forward, nobody was telling him anything new, the target had shored up the wall of denial and seemed to be sitting pretty. Tater had come to such a moment now in his pursuit of Franklin S. Cabot. Morrie Bloom at the *Times* had been after him to push the story forward. Tater respected his editor. He always took Bloom's calls. But Tater at the moment didn't know how to give Bloom what he wanted. Tater still had one arrow in his quiver—the name of Aldrich Ames—but he sensed the moment to launch it was not yet right. Ames would get everybody's attention, but this wasn't really an Ames story. It wasn't about espionage; nobody thought Cabot was a spy; he hadn't been covering up for Ames or for the bungling sleuths who let Ames sell secrets to the Russians for nearly ten years. Ames was going to come into it—Tater was certain of that—but the story wasn't about him.

When Tater sensed he had reached the crisis point in a story he forced himself to put away his Rolodex and quit answering his phone, to dump all newspapers into the trash and shove all loose paper on the surface of his desk into a cardboard box. In short, he stopped where he was. He locked the door. He took off his shoes and put on his sheepskin slippers. He poured himself a big glass of mineral water. He walked over to the window and looked down on the slushy gray streets of Washington. Then he began a slow, relentless circle around the room—past the bookcase, past the locked door, past the glory wall of framed front pages with stories he had worked on. What Tater picked for framing wasn't his byline but pictures of the men he had beaten back into a corner, their faces distorted with the agony of resigning, withdrawing, conceding, and confessing. Cabinet secretaries, a general, a lawyer once close to Richard Nixon, a man nominated to become ambassador to the Court of St. James's—they had all lied about something, concealed something, tried to sneak by with something. Many, many powerful men in Washington over two decades had felt the sting of George Tater's attention, but the framed front pages on his wall recorded the final or near-final public moments of men Tater might fairly be said to have destroyed.

Now, making his rounds, face knotted in thought, sometimes punching the palm of his left hand with the fist of his right, Tater did not glance at this record of past victories. On he paced, trying to pick up the thread of Cabot's story like a Daniel Boone in the wilderness following the blood spoor of a wounded enemy. He would keep on pacing—ignoring the blinking light of his answering machine, letting his e-mail and faxes pile up, refusing to acknowledge the occasional pounding on his door from some irritated colleague down the hall. They knew damned well Tater was in there, but he would give no sign until he had the figure of Franklin Cabot once again clearly in his crosshairs.

. . .

Tater had already collected bushels of facts, and his stories of the past two weeks had given off the ripe scent of the hidden, the sinister, and the corrupt. But Cabot, restless as he was at the delay in his confirmation hearings, seemed confident and untroubled. Only three days earlier, accosted by reporters as he left the White House following a routine meeting of the National Security Council, Cabot lingered at curbside, snug in his camel's-hair coat, to tell the cameras and microphones he had no reason to believe Senator Hawkins would not convene his confirmation hearings within the next week or ten days as promised.

"I don't want to comment in detail until that time," Cabot said, with what seemed to Tater, watching the exchange later on television, a distinct trace of amusement, "but I will say that your colleague George Tater seems to be devoting a great deal of energy and effort to a very small episode. To read his stories you'd think he was on the trail of a war crime, but really—you've all read his stories, you tell me—what is he so excited about? As near as I can see, Mr. Tater's principal complaint is that the government of the time somehow neglected to tell *him*."

Cabot delivered the line nicely—cheerful, polite, condescending. It brought a big laugh from the reporters and camera crews; the whole ten-second bite, with the laughter that followed, was used by Dan Rather and Tom Brokaw on the Friday evening news; and the clip played repeatedly throughout the weekend. Walter Moss had showed it yet again at the beginning of *Meet the Press* on Sunday morning. Tater knew goddam well that his latest story about the MIA angle was going to turn up the heat, but at the same time he realized he had not yet placed his finger on the tender spot that meant the man could be brought down. Tater's stories were filled with phrases like "Congress was never told" and Cabot "secretly traveled to Russia" and claims that Tater's report of an MIA in the Gulag "is here revealed for the first time." But he had to do better than that.

All Tater knew for sure was that something about an MIA kept everybody quiet back in 1978, and the episode was still sensitive when Aldrich Ames told his debriefers about it in 1994. Cabot and his bosses must have known they were inviting the wrath of the Bureau by keeping quiet. Why did they risk it?

Tater was pretty sure MacLaverty had told him everything he knew. They'd met twice following their chance encounter in the barber chairs at Salvatore Morelli's, and they had talked almost daily on the phone since, but MacLaverty had been repeating himself for the last few days. They were plowing the same field. The special agents of the FBI had given Tater a somewhat richer and more detailed version of MacLaverty's story, but Tater was pretty sure MacLaverty and the agents were ultimately drawing from the same source—whatever the FBI was now dragging out of the CIA's Office of Security. Cabot's niece, Jenny, was no help on that. She said the whole mess was the fault of an officer who was pushing the MIA angle. Tater's ears pricked up. He was causing all the trouble but said he was just doing his job.

"Like me," said Tater.

"Exactly," said Jenny. "Why can't you two just drop it?"

"I don't know about him," said Tater, "but I can't drop it till I know what happened."

It didn't take long to get the picture. There was something between Jenny and this young man, or had been. She seemed in doubt just where things stood herself. His name and phone number were something Tater wanted but he said nothing. When the fruit is ripe, he sometimes said, it will fall into your lap.

The next step came to Tater as it always did. Look where you haven't looked yet. In Sunday's story he had written that the report of the MIA came from Israel, a fact he had been told by his friend Holmes in the FBI. Holmes said he did not know the name of the Israeli who had passed the story to Angleton, but Tater had met a few officers in the Mossad over the years. In his experience they all knew everything; he knew damned well they were paying attention to the Cabot nomination, so he quit pacing and started to work the phone. Monday turned up nothing, Tuesday he got lucky. He found a senior officer attached to the Israeli trade mission in his Washington office, a man named Pinchas Shani.

"Hey, Pinchas, George Tater here. We met a couple of years back. I was doing a where-is-he-now story on Pollard. We talked. Maybe you remember."

"I'm sorry," came the voice. "I don't remember. But it's a good subject for a story. You Americans are very unforgiving about Pollard. Life in prison is a long time for one mistake."

"It was a big mistake. But maybe down the road we can raise that question again. Right now I have something else on my mind. I need a little help. Have I caught you at a busy time?"

Tater laid it out, knowing of course that no Israeli intelligence officer would have failed to note a major intelligence story unfolding day by day in the *Times.* Tater started to explain what he'd like to know on background: the man who spoke to Angleton, the source of the POW story—

"Wait, Mr. Tater, please. I know nothing about all this. I can't help you at all. I haven't been reading these stories. I don't know these names. It sounds very interesting and I wish you luck, but I have nothing to tell you."

But twenty minutes later, when the call-waiting tone interrupted Tater in another conversation that was going nowhere, he excused himself and switched. "We talked a moment ago," came the voice of Pinchas. Tater could hear the *whoosh* of cars in the background. "If you're free we might meet . . ." He named a coffee place on upper Wisconsin. Tater said he would be there—he checked his watch—was ten-forty-five okay? It was.

The coffee shop had a nice southern exposure; even on a gray day the place was bright and welcoming. Half a dozen people were sitting here and there. Tater spotted a copy of *The New York Times* held up by someone in the rear—both pages spread out wide, concealing the reader. Who else? Tater made his way to the booth and slid in.

"Coffee, darling?" asked an Irish voice.

"And a corn muffin," said Tater. "Lightly toasted. No butter."

Pinchas Shani folded his paper. "Nice to see you again," he said without apology. "Maybe I can help you a little. If you were to raise the question of Pollard's release in a few months, I would be very grateful. But I can only speak on background."

"Of course," said Tater.

"Of course" wasn't enough for Shani. He pinned Tater down tight: no attribution to Shani, no reference to the embassy or Israel, no hints to the knowing. "I understand," said Tater. "You can trust me."

Then the Israeli told him the story of the one-legged American in the Gulag, of Golenpolsky, of Avraham Lipsky, and of the repeated inquiries pressed by Israel on Golenpolsky's behalf, until an answer was finally conveyed in late 1978 that the American had died during an outbreak of typhus and his body had been burned.

"Who did the asking?"

"First we sent Lipsky," said the Israeli. "But after that it was our chief officer here in Washington, Amichai Gazit. Golenpolsky was very upset—he was worried about his friend; nothing seemed to be happening. He would complain to the people in Jerusalem, they would call Gazit, he would go to Langley to talk to Winter."

"Larry Winter? The DDO?"

"Yes. But if you want to know the whole story: what Gazit said to Winter, how many visits and when, the answer you Americans finally sent back to Golenpolsky—"

"Sure."

"—who else was involved on the American side," Shani said. "That is quite important. It's all in the report. But I have not seen the report."

"What report is that?"

"The report that was delivered to your chief of station in Tel Aviv—yesterday I think. The Dyer report. It has all the details. It was handed to Chuck Halliday. Do you know him? Your chief of station in Tel Aviv. He was briefed fully. We're not trying to cause trouble, you know, but it's always a delicate matter when a president is involved."

"Not this president?" said Tater. It was a question.

"Not yet," said Shani. "But if you want to look into this more deeply, I would say the CIA is your place to look. The Near East Division. Halliday would have sent the report electronically after checking first with the ambassador. Yarrow will be dealing with it today, I should think, perhaps just about now. You know Bud Yarrow—very efficient, very correct. He will go straight to Tommy Johnson, or to his deputy if Johnson is out of town. But of course, he's not out of town, he got back from Beirut on Friday. So Johnson will have the report very soon, I am sure, and of course once he reads it and sees what it is—well, he'll take it directly to Joseph Flint, won't he?"

"I imagine he will," said George Tater.

"And Joe Flint will want to be sure this report is not lost or mislaid. Where do you think he'll take it first?"

"By rights," said Tater, "it ought to go directly to Frank Cabot."

"Cabot, you think?" asked Shani. "Not Senator Hawkins? Not his assistant, Morse? Well, you understand these things better than I do, George. Trade's my field. I'm just trying to keep your American doors open to Israeli fruits and flowers."

He put down a bill and rose. He put on his green overcoat of loden wool.

"Give me a call when you want to talk about Pollard."

Driving back downtown, George Tater flicked on the car radio for the news:

> . . . have no word yet on the senator's condition.
>
> In a bizarre footnote, police report that while medics were putting the senator into the back of the ambulance, a crazed young man ran

> up out of the crowd with a pistol and shot one of the medics in the hip. Bystanders then helped put the senator and the wounded medic into the ambulance. The shooter disappeared around the corner, and police say they are asking for the public's help. We'll keep you posted.
>
> In other local news . . .

But Tater was barely listening. Another nut-case shooting. He was thinking about the words of Pinchas Shani. "The Dyer report," Shani had said.

Tater felt the door opening.

34

Throughout the nine- or ten-minute race across Washington to Georgetown University Hospital, Harrison Hawkins, strapped to the gurney in the back of the ambulance, kept his eyes open, looking first at the ceiling of the swaying vehicle, then over to the shocked and frightened face of the medic beside him and back to the ceiling again. Hawkins was sure he was about to die; his whole chest seemed to be strapped tight with rubber bands, his left elbow hurt worse than bursitis, he felt hot and nauseated, and his brow was clammy with cold sweat. The awful thought came to him that the last thing he would see in this life would be the ceiling of the ambulance, plain white metal with rows of rivets. And the last face he would see in this life would be the medic's.

A flicker of hope would touch Hawkins—new drugs, eat right, cut out the ice cream—but then he would see the awful look on the medic's face. The young man's body was shaking; his face was pale. Hawkins was grateful for this outpouring of sympathy, but at the same time it terrifed him; he knew with a deep, implacable certainty that he would die, right now, strapped to the gurney, with so much of his life unlived, so many of his dreams unfilled. He thought of Lydia; he thought of young Harry; he thought of the cool breeze that came off the water as he sat on his porch on summer afternoons gazing out at Georgia's inland waterway. The medic was holding Hawkins's wrist. "You're going to be okay," he said. But he sounded tense, frightened. Hawkins was deeply moved. He tried to prepare himself for the darkness.

But Hawkins did not die.

The ambulance made a couple of sharp, lurching turns and pulled to a halt. The doors were thrown open. Some men in white coats hauled out the gurney while others—Hawkins was startled to see—picked up a second medic who appeared to have been taking a nap on the floor of the ambulance. Hawkins was confused.

But what happened next was familiar and reassuring. He'd been through a heart attack before; the drill was the same. With every passing minute of continued life, Hawkins allowed his hopes to rise. His gurney was wheeled into a room, where a doctor asked him how he felt. "Terrible," Hawkins rasped.

"How much does it hurt?"

"A lot."

"Open your mouth," said the doctor. He was young but he seemed to know what he was doing. He popped a tiny pill under the senator's tongue. Hawkins felt the sharp little reassuring bite of nitroglycerine. "On a scale of one to ten," said the doctor. "How much does it hurt."

"Maybe . . . eight. And a half."

Hawkins sighed. There was a kind of buzzing in his ears. He closed his eyes. He let himself be poked and prodded by the doctor and his helpers. His shirtsleeves were pulled up. A needle went into his arm. Hawkins answered questions and waited for things to work. He took a little nap, and when his eyes opened again Lydia was standing beside his bed. There were tubes running everywhere. Lydia was holding his hand, and he was conscious of how warm her hand was. She smiled at him and put a finger to her lips, and Harrison Hawkins, anchored to this earth by his wife's reassuring grasp, felt he might live yet a little longer.

Hawkins slept for most of a day. Lydia's face was there whenever he awoke. Young Harry, already middle-aged, came and stayed and told his father not to worry, he had everything under control down home. Hawkins knew there was something he ought to ask his son, but he let it wait. When he awoke next he sensed it was morning outside, and he was pretty sure it was Wednesday.

Lydia was there. Young Harry was there. The round face of his secretary, Rhoda, popped in. The young doctor was there. A nurse was there.

Sounds of people came in from the hall. Around the middle of that second day two things happened: Hawkins felt hungry—famished!—and everybody stopped talking in low serious voices.

"Can't I get some real food?" Hawkins asked.

"No, you cannot," said Lydia.

"Give it a day or two," said the doctor.

When the doctor returned that evening, Hawkins asked, "How long do I have to stay in here?"

"I'd recommend another few days," said the doctor.

"And then we're going home to Savannah," said Lydia.

"Well, not for too long," said Hawkins. "I've got a hearing to conduct. Things can't wait forever."

Neither Lydia nor the doctor spoke.

"All right," said Hawkins. "I'll give it a week. But then I've gotta get back at it."

Lydia went to the door. "Wade? You better come in here."

"Wade's here?" said Hawkins. Suddenly he was frightened again.

The big bulk of Wade Tilton, M.D., entered the room, followed by young Harry and the faithful Rhoda Pratt. Wade was not wearing his white coat, but he looked every inch the doctor. Now there was a row of somber, determined faces lined up in front of Hawkins: his wife of nearly fifty years, the old friend who had doctored him for twenty, the secretary who knew things even his wife did not, his son, Harry, and the handsome young heart doctor the nurses all called Jerry. Hawkins shrank back deep into the bed.

"Harry," said Wade Tilton, "pay attention. Dr. Zimmerman here is a heart specialist of renown. While you have been goofing off here in bed, he has been studying EKG charts and checking out your blood chemistry and going through those old stress tests and angiogram X-rays, and I have flown up here to tell you that Dr. Zimmerman and I are in complete agreement that you are a goddamned lucky man. Pay attention, Harry. You have been spared by a miracle. But if you don't listen to what this highly skilled expert tells you, and if you don't follow his directions like sacred writ, you might just as well wave goodbye this minute. Because if there's a next time, all of us here will be gathering by the riverside to mourn your passing."

The deep silence and solemn expressions of the people lined up before him left no room for doubt. In that moment, Harrison Hawkins confessed to himself with an odd feeling he didn't quite recognize—part sorrow, part relief—that his hour upon the stage had come to an end.

. . .

On Thursday morning, however, feeling weak but otherwise okay, the senator rallied and began to scheme for a reprieve. Arguing that talking to old friends was good for him, Hawkins insisted he could not creep out of town without a single word to the good people who had depended on him for so many years. With Lydia, his friend Wade, and the heart specialist he negotiated a deal—twenty minutes on the phone and two visitors each day.

Not counting his wife, his doctor, or his son.

Or his secretary.

Or his chief staff assistant, Grafton Morse.

Lydia put her foot down. If Morse came through that door he was a visitor, and he counted as a visitor, or the whole deal was off and they were leaving for Savannah *this afternoon.* "Make your choice, Harrison Hawkins!"

The first call came from the president, late Thursday morning, 11:20 to 11:31 a.m.

"Harry—Norman Anderson here. Phyllis and I are thinking about you. We're praying for your recovery. You're a vital man, Harry, a great American. Your country needs you. I need you. So you do what those docs tell you. You listen to that sweet wife of yours. You take care of yourself, take it easy. What are they saying, a week? Two? Then come back like a new man."

"Mr. President," Hawkins said, "they tell me no more work. I don't think I can come back."

"Hmm. Hmm. That's a real setback. That means Mac. I don't like that. Do you think Mac can do the job? I know he doesn't have much good to say about Frank Cabot. Will Mac listen to me and do what's right for the country?"

"Mr. President," Hawkins said, "Mac hates Cabot's guts."

"Yeah. Yeah. That's not good. I don't want to tire you out. You deserve a rest. Is there anything I can give Mac that he wants, you think? Post office named after his father? Signed photo? Job for his son? What's his price?"

"Everybody likes a new post office," said Hawkins, "but the problem is the oil guys. And the Israeli lobby. They agree on Cabot."

"The Israeli lobby? That's a new one. What do they care?"

"Delaney gave them satellite photos. They know Cabot won't."

"Israeli, huh? Hmm. What do you think? The oil guys, and now the friends of Israel. And that damned Tater is on to something, God knows what. Do you know what that's all about, Harry? That's your area, MIAs. Is that serious?"

"It could be. The MIA thing. You wouldn't believe the mail I get on that."

"Tater's an artist at this; every day he's got something. What do you think? Should I pull the plug? Find somebody else? Or can I get Mac in a corner somewhere, maybe give Israel a little something, tell the oil guys not to worry?"

"There's still Tater."

"You're right. You're right. I don't know what I'll do without you, Harry. You bring me back to reality. Washington won't be the same. Do you think you might have a little talk with Cabot—tell him I'd put my hand in the fire for him, but this isn't good for the country?"

"You might give it another week."

"You think Tater's run his course? Shot his bolt? I see what you mean. A little more time, avoid the painful duty. I see what you mean. You've done a wonderful job here, Harry. Your country's grateful. You take care now."

Hawkins was astonished by how tired the conversation left him. He closed his eyes and slept for an hour.

Thursday afternoon, call from Grafton Morse, 2:06 to 2:14 p.m.

"Everyone's very concerned, Senator. We're getting lots of calls and mail, place is filling up with flowers, fruit baskets, all sorts of gifts—"

"Send 'em all a note, Graf, you know the sort of thing—so touched, thanks so much, I draw strength from your kind et cetera."

"Mac's in and out every two minutes: How's Hawkins doing? Hawkins going to be back soon? Anything I can do for Hawkins?"

"I'll bet. Listen, Graf, when you get off the phone, ask Mac to come see me tonight, all right? Around seven. We eat at five here. Then I watch some news. Seven-fifteen would be perfect. Anything else?"

"The governor's been calling. Best wishes, speedy recovery, blah-blah. Wants to know exactly what the docs are saying. I told him yes, you had a heart attack. But nothing else is clear yet. I didn't know which way you wanted to go."

"Let him stew. Get any flowers from Wendell Dorsey?"

"Nice note, actually. He's not a bad guy. He knows damned well the governor's never going to give him an interim appointment."

"Have you talked to Cabot?"

"His man Leo Weissberg called two or three times. Says Cabot doesn't want to make a pest of himself but he's feeling a bit hung out to dry."

"Serve him right," said Hawkins.

"Harry," said Lydia. She was pointing at her watch.

Hawkins put his hand over the phone. "One minute," he said. "I promise." Then, into the phone: "Graf, tell Cabot no visit. Tell him to call me tonight." Lydia shook her head no. "Tell him to call me tomorrow morning. Around nine or so. After I've had a chance to read the *Times*. Say that. Tell him you don't know a thing. I'm alive and that's all you know."

"You two talk," said Lydia at seven-fifteen that evening, after opening the door for Senator MacLaverty. "I'm going to walk up and down the corridor for a while and stretch my legs. Brian—just ten or fifteen minutes, okay? This stubborn Georgian has had a heart attack, but he doesn't like to admit it."

"I promise, Lydia," MacLaverty said. He hung his coat on the hook on the back of the door and popped his hat on the coat. He pulled a chair up beside the senator's bed. "Harry," he said, "you look awful but you look okay. I'm relieved. I brought you something." He opened a paper bag and took out two large plastic spoons and a pint of ice cream. "Chocolate cookie dough," he said. "I don't know about you, but I love this stuff."

"Oh, Brian. Let me at it."

MacLaverty opened the pint of ice cream and drew his chair up close, and the two men ate in silence for a moment, dipping into the pint container, first one, then the other.

"Grafton tells me you're coming back but that's bullshit, isn't it? I recognize that look on Lydia's face. She's gonna haul your ass back home."

"And you probably asked the doctor a few questions too, I imagine."

"I did," said MacLaverty. "And the nurse. And when she wasn't looking I peeked at the chart. You probably didn't know it, but I was premed before I switched to law. Couldn't stand the blood."

"How's it look?"

"You're a lucky man."

They ate in silence for a moment. "God, this is good," said Hawkins.

"I'm going to be fair to him," MacLaverty said. "I'm not going to go after him for screwing up those old estimates about Russia. Or the invasion of Kuwait. I know how you feel about that. We gotta let people make mistakes."

"If you want them to take a chance," Hawkins said. "Stick their necks out. Otherwise—nobody will dare do anything."

"I'm going to let that alone," MacLaverty said. "For you, Harry. You've been fair and decent to me, and I appreciate it."

"Thanks."

"But this Russian thing. What Tater's dragging up. I'm going to get to the bottom of that. There's something I don't like there, and I'm not going to let it go. I just want to let you know."

"Brian," said Hawkins, "I want to tell you two things. That was the best damn ice cream I think I ever ate in my life. Thank you."

"You're welcome."

"And if Frank Cabot left an American POW to rot in the Gulag," Hawkins continued, "I want you to squeeze his balls until he dies of the agony."

"I thought you might feel that way," said MacLaverty.

35

The two men in Jenny's recent life differed in every way but one: they were both obsessed with work. At lunch early Wednesday afternoon, while Senator Hawkins dozed in a hospital bed, Jenny had tried to explain and thereby justify the fact of Tater to her friend Meg as they sat near the window at an Italian place just above Dupont Circle. They'd been telling each other everything since tenth grade and Meg was not shy about speaking up when she thought Jenny was headed for trouble.

Brad (whom Meg liked) had always been all nervous apology whenever he had to confess that work had come in the way of some plan he had made with Jenny. George Tater was blunt and direct about that, and he was the same way about everything else—including sex.

"Whoa," said Meg. "Say that again."

"I know, I know," said Jenny. "It sounds crazy. I'm working up to it."

The point was that Tater listened; he never lectured, like so many Washington know-it-alls; he made no excuses about the place of work in his life. It came first. It came only.

Meg was eating linguine with mussels and drinking soda water. The word *sex* had captured her attention. The look on her face was one of polite disbelief. Jenny was alarmed by that look and wanted Meg to understand.

What made Tater different, Jenny said, was the way he felt about his work. He didn't just enjoy it.

"Guys with families," he told her the first night they went out, "are crazy to drop everything for a job. I understand that. But I've got no kids, my mom's in a nursing home in Tucson and isn't sure if it's me or my brother visiting her, I've got one niece in Galveston who runs a beauty parlor. But you know—"

This was typical of Tater; he would interrupt himself and completely change the direction of whatever he was saying.

"That's not it. Forget that. It's the work. It's my life."

Jenny was interested and Tater tried to explain. He'd been on the staff of the paper at his Texas college and heard something about a real estate deal, so he called up the president of the college, a man named Blackmer. One of those guys always planning his career two moves ahead. Next stop was the state house. Tater was a kid; his voice was shaking. He told Blackmer he'd learned the college was planning to pay a very high price for a piece of land in which Blackmer had a concealed interest.

"That is not true. Quote me on that," Blackmer had said. "The rest I'm telling you privately, and I suggest you listen closely."

Even if it *was* true, Tater couldn't prove it; no one would believe it, and the bringing of false charges with reckless disregard for the reputation of the institution was grounds for immediate suspension from school pending a full investigation by the board of trustees, over which Blackmer had very considerable influence. "Mr. Tater," he said, putting a fathomless contempt into the utterance of his name, "you are young. I'm going to give you a piece of timely advice. Forget all that crap about Peter Zenger. Don't go after people who are bigger than you."

It was quite a long story. Parts of it were funny. Tater loved the hunt, that was certainly clear. But the feeling at the core of the story was anger. Tater had discovered in himself a gift for anger on an exalted level. All it took was a hint that some guy thought he couldn't be touched. The experience for Blackmer was like walking into an airplane propeller. At the end he was out of a job, and a state judge had sentenced him to a thousand hours of community service.

"It probably has something to do with my childhood," Tater said. "My father had a heavy hand. Who knows. But some guy gives me that fuck-you look and I want to drink his blood."

"Jesus," said Meg. "Are you telling me you're sleeping with a guy who feels that way about your uncle?"

"That's what I thought," said Jenny. "I was grabbing up my stuff, but he said no, in this very reasonable way; he didn't feel that way about Uncle Frank. He kind of liked him."

What Tater had said was, "I think Cabot's a pretty good guy, and if he's done something awful I don't know about it. But this Russian thing is interesting—it's got the smell of Washington. The trick is to find out why it scares people. I'm not out to get your uncle, Jenny."

"So I said, 'Well, you're giving him a helluva lot of trouble.'

"And he said, 'It's not me. The FBI is giving him trouble, and I'm just making sure everybody gets to know about it.' "

That's what made it so tough to argue with him. He wasn't trying to pick a fight, he just explained the way things looked to him. Work was one thing, dinner with Jenny was another; that's the way he saw it.

"What is it," asked Meg, "the thrill of danger? The older man thing? Bored with the Boy Scout?"

"I'm not sure," said Jenny. "For about a minute I thought maybe I could help Uncle Frank somehow."

"Which is insane."

"I know. I can't make it sound smart. It was something about that first night at the British embassy. I've started listening to the way people talk about Tater, like he's some kind of force of nature. It's true. One minute I'm eating salmon caviar on toast rounds, and the next I'm two feet from President Anderson while Tater is shooting questions at him. And the president was really paying attention. It was—"

"Kind of sexy," said Meg.

"Definitely sexy. It had its effect. It started something going."

"You know this can only end one way."

"I know."

"In some kind of awful disaster."

"I know."

"There is *no* future with a guy like Tater."

"I know."

"You're being totally unfair to Brad."

"Hold on. I'm not worrying about Brad. He's the one who caused all this trouble; I'm never going to forgive him for that. He knows how I feel about Frank and Kitty."

"He was doing his job," said Meg.

"He promised to stop and he broke his promise and I don't want to hear any more about it. It's final. It's over."

"But for Tater it's okay? Do you hear what you're saying?"

"I know, I know," said Jenny.

They drank soda water for a reflective moment.

"Good in bed," mused Meg. "What does that mean?"

"Exactly what you think it means," said Jenny.

"Better than Brad?"

"Brad sometimes treats me like I might break. That's not Tater's style at all."

Meg thought that over. "I could use a little of that," she said.

When he was really working the phones, George Tater wore a cordless headset, a contraption with an earpiece and a small sponge-covered microphone suspended by a gray plastic arm in front of the speaker's mouth, seen on telephone operators, television camera crews, and NASA mission control officers. Tater dialed numbers on a keypad on his desk and then paced about his office, talking into the sponge-covered microphone and, with reluctant informants, accompanying his words with the unrestrained body language of a football coach. It would have been quite a sight, but no one had ever seen it.

Pinchas Shani had mentioned Bud Yarrow and Tommy Johnson the day before and both were in Tater's database—a drawer filled with bits of paper inscribed with names and phone numbers. Yarrow was a Berkeley grad who spoke Farsi and Arabic and had served all over the Middle East. Johnson was one of the many spooks Tater had known in his youth in the Mekong Delta in South Vietnam where young men from good schools—Johnson confessed to being one of them—had learned, by watching their South Vietnamese counterparts, how to wire up a hand-cranked telephone to a man's testicles.

Tater was shocked by the confession, but he kept quiet. Johnson was a decent stand-up guy. His life had been darkened by personal tragedy: a son that died, a marriage that failed. If you had the heart of a story Johnson would tell you the rest, and sometimes he'd tell you something just because he thought you ought to know.

Tater didn't know Yarrow as well. They'd talked once or twice. Just before the Gulf War, with Yarrow's help, Tater had done a series on Saddam Hussein's atomic bomb. Yarrow thought everybody in Washington had their heads in the sand on this one, and he told Tater a very useful thing—the name of an Iraqi physicist who had defected in Germany. With the Iraqi's name Tater had dragged quite a lot out of the Pentagon, and that opened doors on the NSC and so on, culminating in a mini-war of press releases and headlines and, the following spring, yet another Pulitzer Prize that George Tater never received. He was a little bitter about this. But Yarrow told him he had handled the story exactly right, so Tater knew both men would help if they could.

Before he went after them, he wanted to know roughly what they thought of Cabot as DCI—good for the Agency, bad for the Near East Division; good for the wizards of technical collection who kept track of the terrorists, bad for the political operators who thought there was real promise to get something going in the Gulf—whatever. Everybody had some sort of stake in the game; precisely what it was didn't matter. Just so Tater knew roughly what was in it for Yarrow and Johnson before he started wheedling for a peek at the Dyer report.

Tater began with an old hand, long retired, Henry Stieber, a heavy, comfortable guy now but a real Cold Warrior in his youth who had run operations against the Soviets from Berlin in the fifties and sixties, tracked international arms sales in the seventies, held hands in Kuwait and Bahrein in the eighties, and now made a comfortable living providing investment counsel and unlisted telephone numbers to rich Arabs from a small office in a large building on M Street.

"Hey, Henry," he said when Stieber's secretary put him through. "George Tater."

"I don't know anything about the Russian thing," said Stieber. "I never met Frank Cabot. Maybe once. I don't know any of the CI guys or the people from the Bureau. I've never been to Israel. I never had anything to do with MIAs or POWs. I don't know Hawkins or MacLaverty. I definitely never met the president. And I have no opinions about intelligence targets in the new century. Have I left anything out?"

"Heh-heh," said George Tater. "How you doing, Henry?"

"Too much time in airports," said Stieber. "I miss that good French place in Alexandria. My doctor won't let me eat white sauce. I've lost two umbrellas in the last week. Otherwise I can't complain. I know you're fine. I know you're all over town, ruining everybody's day. Same old Tater."

"I need a little help, Henry."

"Sell Exxon. Buy Texaco."

"No, I'm serious. I know you're reading me. The FBI is giving Cabot a hard time and they're sharing it with me. That's under control. But I'm missing something: what the troops think about Cabot. He spent his whole life in the Agency. I mean, are they for this guy or what?"

"He's too brushed and powdered for my taste, if that's what you want to know."

"Me too. But how about your old shop? What do you hear? Is there anything at stake in this for NE?"

"Well, Flint wanted the job pretty badly. Of course you know that. He's very tight with the Israelis. A lot of people thought Flint had a good shot at it."

"How about Tommy Johnson?"

"Call him up," said Stieber. "Ask him."

"I'm planning to," said Tater, "but you know how it is. I'd like to know where I am before I get him on the phone."

"Usual rules," said Stieber. "You found this under a rock. Tommy served under Flint in Laos. There's no question they're close."

"And Bud Yarrow?"

"Same only different. Flint has given Yarrow his two best jobs. He put both of them in Near East to keep an eye on things. If Flint was DCI they would move up, there's no doubt about that. So you gotta figure they're for him."

"And Chuck Halliday. What sort of guy is he?"

"You've got hold of something, haven't you?"

"I don't know yet."

"Halliday's a good, competent, steady-as-she-goes line officer. The kind that makes no enemies and keeps his friends."

"What would he do with a hot potato?"

"Hand it on to the next guy in line as fast as he could. I'm beginning to get the picture. Halliday has learned something about this MIA Russian deal, am I right?"

"I think you're right," said Tater.

"So do you want to try me with what you know or say goodbye?"

"I don't know much. I'm informed that a report was recently dropped on Halliday's desk in Tel Aviv and is now making its way up the chain of command at Langley. 'The Dyer report.' "

"Uh-huh," said Stieber. "Dyer is not a name I recognize. Does it mean anything to you?"

"Not yet."

"Was this an American told you about it?"

"No."

"Well, I'd say two things. One, Cabot is not going to be happy about whatever's in that report."

"Yeah."

"And two—forgive me for being obvious—Dyer certainly isn't an

Israeli name. And it isn't a Russian name. If you were asking me, I'd say Dyer was an American name. Have you checked it against the MIA files?"

"Henry," said George Tater, "next time we meet, I will wash your feet."

"How about the seafood stew at 1789?" said Henry Stieber.

Without looking up, Randy Short said, "Take a seat." He made no gesture, offered no greeting, but went on writing with a loudly scratching fountain pen on a sheet of letterhead foolscap.

The office was good-sized, with a window looking out over the woods of Langley, but it was also incredibly cluttered—books stacked on the floor, cardboard boxes of documents, shelves overflowing with folders, reports, old newspapers, green Government Printing Office tomes of Senate hearings. In front of Short's desk was a single gray-metal straight-backed government-issue chair. Teetering atop it was a pile of loose papers.

Brad picked up the stack carefully and placed it gently on the floor near the window. He patted the top few layers together with his hands and then sat down on the chair and watched the bald pate of his boss as he bent over his writing.

Brad felt curiously calm. He knew what was coming. Making his way down the hall Wednesday afternoon in response to Short's summons, past all the open doors where guys gave him the embarrassed smile you give a man on his way to the executioner, Brad realized he had lost his fear of this man. Short was a problem to be circumvented. Brad needed time to finish what he was doing. After that he'd worry about things like life and career.

But one thing did have Brad's stomach in knots—he was practically ill with physical desire at the thought of Shulamith, and he thought of her constantly. He had no idea how he'd gotten himself into this mess. Was Jenny still even part of his life? Could he ever explain to her what had happened? Did she care? Did he care? He used to think of her in a loving way. Now the thought of her made him angry, argumentative.

Finally Short put down his pen. He held up the sheet of paper and read it. Then he looked at Brad.

"Do you know what this is?" he asked.

"No, sir."

"This is a Request for a Special Performance Review and Recommendation for Summary Dismissal of Bradford Cameron. Do you know how many of these I have written in twenty-two years of working for the Central Intelligence Agency?"

"No, sir."

"Two. This is the second. Do you know what happened to the first?"

"No, sir."

"It was forwarded to the Deputy Director of Operations, who was then John McMahon. He convened a performance review board. The subject was invited to justify his actions if he could. The board voted to dismiss with prejudice. Are you familiar with that phrase?"

"No, sir."

"It means the subject will never again work for any branch of the U.S. government. There will be no severance pay. There will be no adjustment for accumulated leave time. There will be no little office party with white wine in plastic cups to say farewell. Do you know how much time the previous subject was given to clear out his desk and vacate the premises?"

"No, sir."

"None! His identity card was stripped from him where he stood. He was escorted from the building in broad daylight by armed guards. His personal belongings were returned to him in a cardboard box at the main gate. Do you know what I am going to do with this request?"

He held up the single sheet of foolscap.

"No, sir."

"I am placing it in this drawer." Short slid open the central drawer of his desk. "It is going to be right there on top. And if you break another regulation, if you fail to appear for work, if you speak to a reporter, if it is learned that you have seen or conversed with Myrna Rashevsky, if you so much as look insubordinate . . . I am going to take out this request and hand-deliver it to Joe Flint."

"Yes, sir."

"Are you having trouble understanding what I am telling you? Is this sinking in? You don't seem to be taking any of this very seriously, Cameron."

"No, sir. I am, sir. I'm very upset and concerned."

"All right. Listen up. As of yesterday you are relieved of all duties with regard to MIAs and POWs. You are being reassigned to the Freedom of Information Office, where you will serve as a fact checker on classification review. Harriet has got the names and particulars. Stop by her desk on the way out. If you keep your nose clean for ten years we may forget this sorry episode."

Brad was pretty sure he understood what Short had in mind—keep Brad on his good behavior for a week or two, until Cabot had been confirmed, then fire his ass.

"Sir?"

"What is it?"

"Sir, I don't think I can just walk away from this job."

"Oh, you don't?"

"No, sir, there are a lot of loose ends. I've signed out files from half a dozen different departments of the government. I've got all sorts of correspondence on my desk—authorized correspondence with people outside the Agency and even outside the government. I've got twenty unanswered calls on my voice mail. I've promised reports on routine matters to a bunch of different people: Hawkins's office, the Pentagon, the State Department. If I just walk away from my desk, a lot of people are going to start calling up wanting to know what's going on. I think it would be a whole lot quieter, sir, if you would just let me have some time to clean up the loose ends."

"How long?"

"There's quite a lot to do, sir. I suggest two weeks."

"No way. You get this cleaned up by close of business Friday, and on Monday report to classification review. Tell everybody you're moving on, routine reassignment, somebody will be taking over soon. Listen to me, Brad. Loose ends only—no more poking around. Is that clear? Do I have your word on that?"

"My desk will be clean, sir. You've got my word."

"You going to be free later on tonight?" Tater asked. He was pacing his office, speaking into the sponge-covered microphone.

"What about earlier?" asked Jenny from her office.

"Earlier I have to go see a guy. He doesn't like to talk while he's at work."

"I suppose he's a source."

"In my life everybody's a source," said Tater. "Except you."

"What does that make me?"

"Special."

"Give me a break," said Jenny. "What do you mean, special?"

"I mean I want to see you. I've been wanting to see you all day."

"Oh, yeah? How come?"

"Because you're beautiful and wild."

"Why do I listen to you?" said Jenny. "What time?"

Tater set a late hour and suggested an Irish place with mahogany booths downtown. Houlihan's. Nobody ever went there.

. . .

There were certain small vices that always made Jenny depressed—buying two of anything because she couldn't choose between them, eating dessert when she was alone, purchasing a book she wasn't sure she would read, going to Elizabeth Arden for a facial in the middle of the week, and everything to do with George Tater.

She hung up the phone with a bleak feeling that she had to bring this to an end. She liked verbal sparring with Tater, she liked the way he explained the world, and she liked him in bed. But at the same time she was sick at the thought of trying to explain him; even Kitty, who understood everything, would think she was crazy. Meg was right. This thing with Tater was wrong and Jenny was going to end it. But not over the phone. That was for cowards. Maybe at dinner. Or maybe in the morning.

Over the next few hours, one eye on the clock, waiting for Tater to ring her bell, Jenny worked out quite a nice little speech: firm but warm, not angry, not plaintive, something beginning *George, this isn't your fault, it's nothing you've written, but I'm sorry. . . .*

Then bury the whole affair so deep no one else would ever know.

"It's a good thing you weren't working for the Russians," said Bud Yarrow. They were standing in his kitchen in Falls Church, drinking scotch. "How the hell did you know we got that report today? I'm not even going to try to deny it."

"I can't tell you that," said George Tater.

"You expect *me* to tell *you* things."

"Somebody on the sending end."

Yarrow thought that over. He was roughly Tater's age, in good shape, a runner. He wore round glasses with gray steel rims. The house was filled with stuff he'd picked up all over the Middle East. "The Israelis," said Yarrow.

Tater made a noise. "I'm told," said Tater, watching Yarrow's face calmly, "the Dyer report lays out the background of Cabot's meeting in Russia."

"I didn't read it," said Yarrow.

"Why not?"

"*This* is why not. If I'd read it you'd try to wheedle it out of me. The Senate would want to know all about it. Maybe before it's all over some special prosecutor would accuse me of lying about it. I don't need that. I'm a patient man. I can wait to read it in the *Times.*"

"You must have read the cover sheet."

"I read the cover sheet."

"What did it say?"

"Just the usual stuff. It had a date, it was from somebody, it was to somebody, it had a title, there were some routing codes."

"Let me just try this on you. If I'm wrong, tell me and we'll leave it at that? Okay?"

"Okay."

"The date was late last week, maybe Friday or Saturday." Tater paused very briefly, just a beat. Yarrow made no sound. "The sender was Yakov Kotler, director of the Mossad. It was addressed to Franklin S. Cabot, acting director of the CIA. And the subject was an Israeli report in nineteen seventy-seven of an American prisoner of war in a Soviet prison camp. Identified as Sergeant Jason Dyer of the United States Army."

"Not bad," said Yarrow. "But you got one thing wrong. There were two addressees."

"Cabot and . . ."

"William Chambers. Legislative counsel."

"Christ," said George Tater. "They weren't leaving anything to chance, were they?"

"Mike, I want you to bring this young man a stand-up martini. Bombay gin. Not too dry. About this much vermouth." Myrna held her thumb and forefinger about a quarter of an inch apart. "Two pearl onions. No plastic sword. Stick the glass in the freezer while you're shaking it up. You know how to do it, Mike. Me, I'll have a glass of white wine."

They were sitting in their regular booth, Brad facing the door. Mike shuffled off.

"Don't you want one?" asked Brad.

"Are you kidding? If I drink one of those I won't make sense for a week. I'm getting to be an old lady. But you, that's different. Sometimes you need to blow out the tubes. A martini, it's like electroshock therapy. You're feeling *krenk.* Nothing goes right. So stop fighting it for a night. Take a martini. Take two. But!"

Myrna held up her hand like a traffic cop.

"Caution. Two's it. And never at lunch. This used to be a big martini-drinking town. Those guys are long gone. You know who taught me how to make a martini? Allen Dulles. It's true. Allen Dulles.

"Cheer up. I'll tell you a story. This was years and years ago. A dear friend of mine was in some kind of security trouble. Sylvia Press. I doubt you heard of her. She was like my big sister when I first came to work. I didn't have much family here, you know that. We were in temp buildings then, down by the Reflecting Pool. I was only twenty but I read Polish, I read Russian, I read German and French. Sylvia was the one showed me around, taught me how to read a file. A pretty girl, nice curly black hair, nice smile. Single. But during the war she had a boyfriend, he was in the Party, they went to Mexico; then later somebody read a cable—a huge *mishegoss.* They pulled all her cases, gave her a job reading newspapers. Long, long sessions down in security. 'We're trying to help you, Sylvia. Tell us everything. Trust us.' But they wouldn't tell her what the trouble was.

"After maybe a year of this, just endless questions, questions, they said, 'We can't help, Sylvia, you're not telling us what we need to know; we've got no choice.' This whole time she never told anybody a thing. But finally she told me and I was angry, I was so angry. I went to see Allen Dulles. I was ready to make a big fuss. He asked me to his home. He said, 'Myrna, I want to show you how to make a martini.'

"It's like I just told Mike, only different; I improved it. That *meshuggener* Dulles thought vermouth ruined the martini. Vermouth makes the martini.

"Dulles's wife was there but she disappeared. Very beautiful home. He measured, he stirred, he poured. We held up our glasses. We took a sip. 'The first sip,' says Dulles, 'that's what it's all about. Ho, ho, ho!' Then he said, 'Myrna, I've followed this case closely. Nobody thinks Sylvia is a spy. But she went to Mexico with her boyfriend; that is a fact. And the boyfriend is a secret member of the Party; that is a fact. What I'm going to tell you now must not be repeated to your friend. Do I have your word on that?'

"What could I say? I said yes.

" 'We know these things because the code breakers have read a cable from the KGB resident in New York City to Moscow Center. This is not guesswork. This is fact. Of course the FBI had to be brought in. Here's the choice we have. One, tell Sylvia she's cleared, go back to work. Then the FBI sneaks the cable to Joe McCarthy and we read headlines about Reds in the CIA. Result: the Russians find out we're reading their cables.

" 'Or two, we let Sylvia go, do everything we can for her, help her find a job. And go on reading the cables, and catch some real spies.'

"Then he says to me, 'Myrna, I'm not going to ask what you would do. That wouldn't be fair. She is your friend and you would stand by her through anything. I'm going to tell you what I've decided. Myrna'—very serious, like I was an important person—'you're young, I want you to trust me on this. We'll do everything we can for Sylvia. I give you my word on that. But I've got no choice.'

"This is the director of the CIA; I'm just a clerk in counterintelligence. I did what he asked: I trusted him. I kept my mouth shut. What happened? One, they did nothing for Sylvia—no recommendation, no severance, no job, only a whispering campaign that wrecked her life. Two, the Russians knew all about those cables we were reading. Three, McCarthy went after us anyway.

"Why am I telling you this story? I had a point but it's gone. My brain's like a sieve. So you've really had a day. Short is sending you to Siberia. You're confused in the love department. Tell me about it."

"I haven't got the report anymore, and if I did I wouldn't give it to you," Tommy Johnson said. He'd picked up Tater in town and driven out to Hains Point, where they could park and talk. "But I can tell you there are only two things in it that really matter. One is that Cabot went to Moscow twice. The report doesn't say why and I don't know either. But there were two trips about a week apart."

"I think I know why," said Tater. "Whatever they told him the first time wasn't covered by his instructions."

"It makes sense," said Johnson. "The second thing is that the Israelis were told the president had been informed."

"So the instructions, ultimately, had to be his," said Tater.

"I would think so," said Johnson.

"What happens now, do you think?" asked Tater.

"I think Joe Flint has done his duty and passed on copies of this report to Cabot and the legislative counsel."

"Who else knows about it?"

"Officially, nobody. But I can tell you twenty people knew the report was in-house the first day, and I can tell you the routing slip was pretty extensive. Anything to do with MIAs goes to four or five different desks at Langley, starting with the Special Assistant to the Director for POW/MIA affairs, who is still in charge for the rest of the week."

"Still?"

"He's out of there. He's going to be walking the halls until he gets the picture and quits. Cabot would have had him up on charges except he's dating Cabot's niece, I hear. He's the one who dragged all this up."

"Can you fill me in on that?" asked Tater.

Tommy Johnson could.

When he was done, Tater had a final question. "It's not just Flint," said Tater. "The whole DDO seems to be turning against Cabot. I thought they'd back a career guy."

"It's the MIA angle. People think Cabot somehow fucked up and left an MIA to rot. People don't like that."

"Fucked up how?"

"Nobody knows," said Johnson. "Maybe you can find out."

Tater picked up Jenny a little before ten. He had one thing on his mind—explain what he was going to be putting into a story tomorrow or the next day in a way she'd forgive. It wasn't going to be easy. He was really digging, and this new stuff was going to turn up the temperature on Uncle Frank to new levels of agony.

"I don't understand," said Jenny in the cab. "How did you know the name of the prisoner?"

"That wasn't hard. Somebody told me about a Dyer report and another guy says Hey, come on, Dyer has to be the prisoner. I must be getting old or I would have figured it out myself. So I called up the MIA office in the Pentagon and asked them to fax me the sheet on Dyer. The guy got back to me and said, 'Harold or Jason?' I asked for both. One's from California, one's from Maryland. But the Maryland guy was a high school dropout, he was in the Special Forces, he'd been to ranger school and jump school, he'd won a marathon at Fort Gordon, Georgia. There was a big hole in his service history, which I figure means black operations in Vietnam. He sounded like the kind of guy who might turn up alive in a Russian prison. So I tried his name on one of the people I saw tonight and then I used it as a pry bar with the other."

"It's a good story, isn't it?" said Jenny.

"Yes, it is," said Tater.

The cab pulled up by the curb and Tater paid. On the sidewalk he stopped Jenny with his hand. "I know this is hard on you," he said. "I wish you weren't part of this. But I can't just walk away from it."

"Why not?" she said. Tater didn't like the sound of that. He touched her cheek, kissed her gently, then turned her face into the blue light from the sign over the door reading HOULIHAN'S. With a finger Tater touched Jenny's lips. "I'm making a mess of your mouth," he said.

"How about my life?" said Jenny.

"I regret that," said Tater.

"I'm doing everything wrong," said Brad. "Two weeks ago I was trying to figure out how to get Jenny to marry me. Now she won't talk to me, and if she did I wouldn't know what to say."

"My advice," said Myrna. "Shut up till you know what you want."

"I want too many things," said Brad. "I want a chance to explain things to Jenny. I want to spend a year in Jerusalem. I want to do something that makes a difference with my life. I want somebody to tell me why everything is secret. I want to know who's telling George Tater all that stuff. I want to know what Cabot is hiding. I want to tell Randy Short I don't give a damn what he does with his Request for Dismissal. I want—oh, God, I don't know!

"I guess I want that second martini."

Tater was holding the door for Jenny when she placed a hand on his arm. Something had caught her eye. Tater couldn't see what. Through the half-open door the place looked practically empty. But Jenny said, "It's late. Let's go back to your place."

"What I used to want," said Brad, "was to take good news to the mother of some long-lost boy in Vietnam. I didn't kid myself but I used to daydream about it. Now they've given me two days to clean up loose ends."

"What sort of loose ends?" asked Myrna.

"There's only one that matters. Don't you think Dyer's family has a right to know we found their son—twenty years ago? In Russia?"

"Didn't anybody ever tell you about channels?"

"If I don't tell them," said Brad, "who will?"

36

By midmorning on Thursday, March 7, it was clear to Frank Cabot that support for his confirmation as the next Director of Central Intelligence was rapidly evaporating. With everyone who asked him, Cabot argued that George Tater hadn't laid a serious glove on him yet, but argument was futile. Two weeks of front-page stories by a reporter whose specialty was the exposure of secrets and the destruction of careers—it didn't take a prophet to see which way this was headed. Cabot had noted a change in the voices and faces he encountered during the daily round. At committee meetings, lunches, and receptions; in the lobbies of hotels, the reading rooms of clubs, the corridors of Congress or the Pentagon—wherever he went the congratulations had turned hollow. No one lingered to chat. The phone was ringing only for urgent business. He didn't have to turn down ten invitations to get home at a decent hour in the evening. The real tip-off would have been his reception at the White House, source of the only support that made a difference, but for many days now Frank Cabot had not been to the White House.

Twice in one week Cabot had been called by a White House secretary to say a meeting had been canceled. First was a routine session of the National Security Council where no news about Iraq was the principal item on the agenda. Cabot told himself it didn't matter. But then, this morning, less than an hour before Cabot had been scheduled to get in an Agency car for the trip downtown, his secretary buzzed him to say the White House had canceled again. Called off this time was a long-planned, full-dress, principals-only policy meeting on covert support for the Iraqi opposition.

"Did they give a reason?"

"They just said it had been postponed."

"Did they set a new date?"

"They'll let me know."

Jane had been around; she knew this was bad news. Cabot could hear it in her voice.

Irritated and concerned in about equal measure, Cabot had asked his secretary to get Peter Schleicher on the phone and he sighed with relief when Schleicher called back only four or five minutes later.

"Peter. What's up?" Cabot had asked. "I've got six guys ready to go on safari here. The van's loaded with vuegraphs and blue binders. We've been planning this for weeks. This was at the top of the president's want list. I don't understand."

"Don't concern yourself, Frank," said Schleicher. "The president told me to assure you that this is still his absolutely number-one foreign policy priority."

"So?"

"He feels his thinking is maturing. This is a big step. He wants to go over this again with a couple of people whose judgment he values and trusts."

"Peter—that's supposed to be us."

"It *is* you, Frank. But it's not only you. Tell your people to stand by. We're going to set a new date. Trust me."

Cabot hated the way Schleicher ended a conversation: "Trust me." *Click.* But he also knew Anderson was a moody, cautious, changeable man, subject to sudden squalls of second thoughts. He tried to tell himself it didn't mean anything, but he knew the rumor mill wouldn't agree. Word would be spreading through the building like blood in water. Six guys scheduled to make a presentation at the White House—a big deal in any bureaucrat's life, source of power and pride—had been told to stand down. They would inform their bosses. The bosses would exchange looks with their aides. Within fifteen minutes forty or fifty people would know. By lunchtime the word would reach hundreds. Cabot had seen it before. On the great exchange where shares in reputations were traded daily, Frank Cabot's stock was on the verge of free fall.

The word was out—there was no hiding it. People were shoving it in his face. Everybody in town knew Hawkins was out of the picture, and everybody knew MacLaverty hated Cabot's guts. With Tater on one side and MacLaverty on the other, Cabot was truly between a rock and a hard place. The chilling effect of Hawkins's heart attack was only too obvious Thursday morning, while Jane was tracking down Schleicher. The president was sending him a message. *I know this is rough on you, Frank. I'll understand if you've had enough.*

For another few days, maybe even for as long as a week, Cabot could ignore the cold shoulder, the brush-off, the phone calls that went unreturned, the insult of abruptly canceled meetings. But very soon an envoy would come knocking on his door who could not be turned away, some intimate of both men to say that Cabot had the president's undying gratitude and loyalty, but the country needed to move on. Cabot wondered which of his numerous "friends" was being groomed to play Judas.

In the brief time remaining to him, Cabot needed to move heaven and earth to get George Tater off his back, strike some sort of deal with MacLaverty, get those hearings going, and orchestrate a grand march-past of supporters, admirers, and influential friends to dazzle and impress the grim line of senators on the dais who would hold the power of confirmation.

But the look on Weissberg's face, when he arrived a few moments later, made it only too clear he knew the boss was in trouble.

"Hawkins is stable," said Weissberg. "We've got a new problem, Frank."

"Old problems aren't enough?" Cabot was ashamed to hear the plaint in his voice; he prided himself on never betraying self-pity. "Go ahead," he said. "What is it?"

"I found this on my desk this morning." He handed a thin sheaf of paper to Cabot. "It's a report of some kind from Israel."

"Israel?"

"From Yakov Kotler. Addressed to you and to Chambers."

"Bill Chambers? The legislative counsel? Why haven't I seen this?"

"I don't know. Yours must be coming by slow mail. The Israelis have decided to jump in with both feet and Flint is helping them do it. I've never seen anything like it."

Cabot was staring at the paper in his hand. The title sheet read:

FOR: Franklin S. Cabot, Deputy Director of Central Intelligence
William Chambers, Legislative Counsel, CIA
FROM: Yakov Kotler, Assistant to the Prime Minister
DATE: Sunday, 3 March, 9:20 p .m. GMT
SUBJECT: "THE DYER REPORT": WHAT ISRAEL KNEW

Information concerning presence of American MIA/POW [Sgt. Jason Dyer, United States Army] in Soviet Prison Camp [Akmolinsk, Kazakhstan] and Report of Same to U.S. Intelligence Authorities, Washington DC, July 1977.

He read through the page twice, then flipped open the report. The first paragraph began: "In view of recent inquiries by U.S. intelligence officials in Israel concerning the fate . . ."

Weissberg said, "One of their guys handed it to Chuck Halliday Monday. It's addressed to you but Halliday sent it to Flint. The 'recent inquiries' came from Brad Cameron and Myrna Rashevsky. I'm sorry about that, Frank. You said get her out of town, and I didn't think—"

"Don't worry about it. We should have talked it through. It's my fault. What's the bottom line?"

"Trouble," said Weissberg. "The problem has two sides, what's in the report and who has it. The short answer"—Weissberg was delivering the news as he always did, calmly, one point at a time—"is the report says we fucked up, and there are copies all over the building."

"Fucked up how?" Cabot asked.

"Failed to act despite timely warning from Israel that the Russians were holding an American POW," Weissberg told him. "It says you made two trips to Russia a week apart. Is that correct, Frank? Did you make two trips?"

"That's correct."

"We didn't put that in the letter to Hawkins," said Weissberg. "We should expect questions there. The report goes on that only after many requests for information were the Israelis finally told that the president—"

"How did they know that?"

Weissberg paused. "I don't know, Frank. But it's in there. The president was told that Dyer had died of typhus and his body had been burned. This information was conveyed to the office of the prime minister in early nineteen seventy-eight by the deputy chief of Near East at the time, who was Joe Flint."

"Joe Flint," said Cabot. "Who also made all the copies of this report. These are not neutral facts. I am beginning to get the picture here."

"That was the end of it. But—"

"But."

"Let me read it to you." Weissberg flipped pages, found the paragraph.

> "The government of Israel then arranged a meeting between Mr. Flint of the CIA and Lev Golenpolsky, who had conveyed the original report of Dyer's imprisonment at Akmolinsk, in order to reassure Mr. Golenpolsky that his report had been taken seriously. Mr. Flint told Mr. Golenpolsky that in the months following his departure from Russia the American prisoner had died of typhus and nothing more was to be hoped. Golenpolsky was satisfied by what he was told and made no further threats to speak to the press. Subsequently he accepted employment with the Jewish resettlement office of the Mossad, by which he is still employed.
>
> "Several years later [April nineteen eighty-six] Israel came into possession of transcripts of conversations concerning the fate of the American prisoner which indicated that the American envoy sent to inquire about the prisoner Dyer was initially told by his Russian counterpart that the prisoner was alive. These transcripts were summarized in a report to the office of the prime minister, where it was decided that no other government would be informed of their contents. The sole copy of the transcript obtained by Israel was destroyed at that time. No further details concerning this matter are available to the government of Israel.

"There's another pretty serious problem, Frank. Do you have any idea what conversations they're talking about? Do we have these transcripts in a file somewhere? They say you were told Dyer was alive. That's a material fact."

"I understand that."

"He was alive one week and dead the next, and we said let's forget it? This is going to be hard to explain."

"I know it looks bad," Cabot said. "I don't know what to say. I'm trying to recall just what did happen."

"Did you tell Hawkins privately what really happened? Because this is going to be in his hands one way or another pretty damned soon."

"I never seemed to find time to tell him."

"I think now's the time," said Weissberg.

There was a long moment of silence. Cabot had swiveled around in his chair toward the window to avoid meeting Weissberg's eyes. Weissberg had not complained or reproached him, but Cabot knew what he must be thinking. Cabot had been feeding him the story in bits and pieces because he was hoping—stupidly, that was now obvious—to sit on the worst of it, and of course Weissberg was beginning to understand why Cabot had been holding back. An emotion like grief entered Cabot's heart. But at last he gathered himself and started to speak. "Let's attack . . ." His voice cracked. He began again, getting it this time.

"Let's attack the back end first," he said. He swiveled around and looked Weissberg full in the face. "This document contains classified information that cannot be generally released. It's clear we're going to have to provide the Senate with some version of what's here, but before that happens I want every copy in the building to be retrieved, and if any copies have left the building I want them recalled and picked up by courier *now*, immediately."

"Are you sure about this?" asked Weissberg. "Recalling paper is like ringing a bell."

"I know that. But I don't want people thinking I'm about to lie down. And I want to see Joe Flint in this office Monday at one for lunch. But tell him now. I'd like him to sweat a little. And I want to see Pinchas Shani here this afternoon to explain this extraordinary and completely unacceptable intervention by Israel into the domestic politics of this country. I want you to call him, Leo, and I want you to make him understand as I know you can that if he does not cooperate with me fully—"

Cabot was really getting up to speed now. The queasy horror and shame had been banished. Cold and righteous anger had entered his voice; he sounded like a man fully ready to order exemplary executions.

"If Shani does not cooperate with me fully I am going to do everything in my power to guarantee it will be a cold day in hell before Israel can ever again count on the United States for any assistance of any kind in any matter relating to our intelligence gathering."

Speaking without interruption, Cabot outlined a comprehensive program for stopping up every crevice of the CIA through which news of the Dyer report might leak, for crushing Israel's effort to sink his nomination, and for regaining control of the proper interpretation of the emerging story that was threatening his confirmation. While Leo was carrying out these preliminary steps, Cabot himself would write up a full and accurate version of this long-ago episode, which at heart was simply one more tragic story of an American MIA who had, when you understood what had really happened, died following capture by the enemies of his country. There had been good and ample reason not to trumpet the news at the time, but secrecy then hid nothing shameful now. On the contrary, once the full story could safely and responsibly be made known, the feeling of all Americans would be pride.

Cabot was done. He had said what he had to say for now.

"You're a fighter, Frank," said Weissberg on the way out. "I'll do what I can."

But after the door closed, Cabot remained quiet in his chair, desperately trying to think what new angle might offer a way out of this mess. His brave words couldn't change what the Israelis had actually written, and no amount of sanitation before delivering the report to the Senate could completely disguise the central facts. Leo knew. Everybody who saw the report would know.

The big thing was out. Cabot had been told Dyer was alive. He had promised Weissberg to come up with a story explaining what happened next, and now he had to do it. Silence about a man found dead he could survive. But silence about an American soldier, illegally imprisoned in the Soviet Union years after the end of the war in Vietnam, still alive when the United States first learned he was there—silence about that, Cabot knew, would never be forgiven.

He needed a story as big as Texas, and he needed it before the day was over.

37

"I can't believe what I'm hearing," said Hugh Diamond, sitting at the far table near the end window in the open cafeteria early Friday afternoon. The lunch crowd had pretty much thinned out to nothing—a couple of guys reading newspapers over a last cup of coffee, two women whispering, kitchen staff in dirty white jackets clearing tables. Brad Cameron was poking with his fork at a piece of celery left from his tuna salad.

"What else can I do?" he asked. "I checked it out. He's got a sister still living in Accokeek. Don't you think she has a right to know?"

"Oh, absolutely," said Hugh. His eyes looked huge behind his round glasses. "But not now."

"What's wrong with now?"

"It'll kill you now. You can still patch things up if you just back off."

"Come on, Hugh. I'm out of a job and Jenny won't even talk to me. I don't think it matters what I do now."

"Of course it matters. Jenny's just being difficult. I know her type; she wants a little drama in her life before settling down, but you're the perfect guy for her." He waved away all romantic problems with a flick of his hand. "Everybody stubs his toe in this business, don't worry about it. Randy Short can still make your career."

"Randy's going to fire me."

"Randy thinks the world of you," said Hugh. "He moved you out of the hot spot, that's all. But this latest scheme, this latest . . . *brainstorm.*" His hands went up in disbelief. "Brad, you need further instruction before you take your final vows. Old secrets are like old dynamite. They can blow up in your hands. We don't spill them idly."

"Hugh," said Brad, "the fate of an MIA is not supposed to be a secret."

"Maybe, but the fate of this one is. That's a fact. Two weeks ago nobody knew what had happened to your MIA. Then you found out. Now maybe a hundred people know, and it's spreading fast. The big question is, When is it going to break to the surface? Who cares if his sister finds out this month or next month?

"But to Cabot it makes all the difference in the world. This MIA thing is just what MacLaverty is looking for. If you want to do Mac a favor, call up the sister and invite George Tater to listen in."

Brad pushed himself upright in his chair. "I don't buy it, Hugh," he said. "They already know about the MIA. What difference does a name make?"

"All the difference. The name comes with a high school photo, buddies who knew him back when, a sister on *Good Morning America* and *Larry King Live.* MacLaverty will be all over this story. He's going to want every detail. He's going to ask things Cabot can't answer. We're going to see beads of sweat on his brow. The whole country is going to watch him twist and squirm on CNN. Two weeks of that makes anybody look like a war criminal. It isn't fair."

"Maybe not," said Brad, "but waiting doesn't feel right. I've only had one job in this outfit: Try and find out what happened to the boys who got left behind in Vietnam. Leave no stone unturned. But when I actually find one everybody tells me to stop, shut up, and sit tight. I don't like it."

"Nobody likes it. But it's part of the job. We all have to keep secrets we wish we could tell. There's fifty people in the building right now who are popping with a big one."

Brad's eyebrows went up.

"Same one you've got," said Hugh. "The Israelis delivered a report on your MIA to our man in Tel Aviv and somebody in Flint's office—guess who—made multiple copies for everybody who might conceivably have a need to know. Leo Weissberg has been walking the corridors all day trying to retrieve the copies and put the toothpaste back in the tube."

"Have you got a copy?"

"I do."

"Can I see it?"

"Will you keep quiet until the hearings are over?"

"I can't promise that, Hugh."

"Best effort will do. Is it a deal?"

"It's a deal," said Brad.

Hugh drew a sheaf of paper, folded in half the long way, from the inner pocket of his blue blazer. "I think you know most of it already," he said. "But there's one small detail that may be new to you. Page seven, last couple of paragraphs."

. . .

It was past three by the time Brad got back to his desk. He closed the door behind him and dropped the document Hugh had given him in the center of his desk. Another layer of the onion was about to be peeled back. He looked around the tiny office space cluttered with paper collected over the previous years. There were two pictures on his wall: Jenny on a horse a couple of years back, looking confident and beautiful, and Brad's grandmother, sitting on the porch of her childhood summer home in Blue Hill, Maine. Spending four weeks every summer in Blue Hill was what Brad's grandmother valued most in this world. After Brad's father died and his mother started crisscrossing the country looking for rich husbands, Blue Hill quickly became the place Brad called home.

He loved the house, built of logs now black with age, filled with family memorabilia collected over three lifetimes, shelves full of books going back to the 1880s, pictures in birch-bark frames, closets full of fishing gear, wicker furniture on the porch. He loved hiking among the dark wind-wracked spruces along the shoreline. There was always an uncle or aunt around and a houseful of cousins. The older ones taught him how to paddle a canoe, how to bait a crab trap, how to inhale a cigarette. In time he taught the younger ones. In college he started to worry about the place. He read a book called *The Dying of the Trees* that said the great forests of the Northeast were being destroyed by acid rain from the industrial Midwest. Once he'd read the book he began to see it—the dead pines like snags all along the high stretches of the Appalachian Trail. Brad had walked most of its length in Maine and he had seen the trees dying. He joined a couple of wilderness groups, but his concern stopped there. Prompted by his father's example and Uncle Max's urging, he took a different route. But when Washington and the Agency were too much with him, he thought about that spine of mountains and trees running from Georgia to Maine and wondered if it was really true. Were the trees dying up there while he was searching through old files? He had half a mind to say the hell with it, sweep everything on his desk into the burn bag, and take off to look for himself.

But what he did after a moment's reverie was to open the document Hugh had given him. He pressed it flat on the surface of the desk and read the title page. When he saw the name of the chief of the Mossad he thought, My God. They aren't fooling around. He looked at the date and time and calculated backward; the report must have been drafted, completed, and dispatched late on Brad's last night in Israel.

He remembered Hugh's remark—something new on page seven. He flicked pages till he got there. He read the sentence three times:

. . . the American envoy sent to inquire about the prisoner Dyer was initially told by his Russian counterpart that the prisoner was alive.

It was hard to take in. The fact was like a blow. Dyer had been alive in July 1977 and Cabot knew it! Seven years after he was captured. Four years after the United States pulled out of Vietnam. Two years after the fall of Saigon. Brad knew the MIA files backwards and forwards. In all that ocean of paper on over two thousand missing men there was not a single confirmed report of a positive sighting of a living MIA after 1975. None. Zip.

But in 1977 the Israelis told the Americans about a live MIA. They knew his name, and they knew where he was. They gave the CIA something Brad had only dreamed about.

Brad could not yet give a name to what he felt at that moment. He left his office, left the building, and took the shuttle bus downtown with half a dozen other men and women in suits, carrying briefcases, betraying nothing.

That night, Brad lay awake in the dark from midnight until two or later, wondering if he had completely lost the ability to know what he wanted. Hugh thought Jenny still cared about him, and that made Brad wonder if they might still get together and begin again. He had no hope things could ever work out with Shulamith. Now that he was back in Washington, about to switch jobs, feeling lonely in the halls and cafeteria because people always seemed to be looking the other way, Brad felt Jenny's absence keenly. She had been such a big part of his life, and now nothing occupied that place. He understood why Jenny wanted to protect her uncle; he wanted her to understand why he couldn't turn his back on the man in Russia. Understanding, he felt, would be enough. Maybe they could go on from there. So on Saturday morning, March 9, nervous but determined to move forward, he dialed Jenny's number. When she answered he said he'd been thinking about her, he wanted to see her, and he wondered if she was free for dinner.

"I'm sorry," she said. "I'm meeting someone."

Her voice was far from warm. Brad felt his hopes plummet.

"How about coffee? Or a walk?"

"All right," she said. "Franklin Park in half an hour."

Brad's spirits lifted slightly; he knew that was one of Jenny's favorite spots in the city. She arrived a few minutes after he did, hurrying across 14th Street in a gray wool overcoat and a red scarf. Even bundled as she was, the sight of her brought a small sweet burst of affection; the complicated feelings of anger and hurt seemed to fade. But the look on her face was not welcoming, and her first words were angry.

"I don't know why I agreed to come," she said. They walked beneath the bare trees. "If you could see what this is doing to Aunt Kitty."

"I know," said Brad. "I'm sorry about that."

"You don't know, and sorry is no help. She's done nothing to deserve this."

"I don't want to hurt Kitty or Frank," Brad said. "I had no idea any of this was connected to him. All I knew was I found an MIA."

"You found a piece of paper. You could have just put it in a drawer and waited."

"No, this wasn't just a piece of paper. This was a man; he existed; we knew about him. I couldn't just ignore that."

"He was dead. Why did you have to be in such a hurry?"

But of course Brad now knew the MIA wasn't dead. He forced himself to stop, wait, think. "This isn't what I wanted to talk about," he said. "I wanted to tell you how I feel about you. I don't want things to end this way."

"How can I forget what you've done? Don't you know what Kitty and Frank mean to me? He tries to say things will be all right in the end, but I know it's not true. I can see it. He'll never get over this."

"Wait a second," said Brad. "Maybe I opened the door, but after that everything took off on its own. You're not being fair. I didn't call in the FBI. I didn't tell all that stuff to the guy at the *Times*. I have no control over the Senate. That committee isn't angry about anything *I* did."

"It's what *he* did, right?" said Jenny, really angry now. "You think Frank did something awful, don't you?"

"Jenny, I don't know exactly what he did. It's hidden in a file somewhere."

"But you think there's something there, don't you? Well, tell me what you think it was. Go ahead! What did he do that was so wrong?"

Brad wanted to slide around her question but the words wouldn't come. His mouth was open but he couldn't speak. He was angry enough to want to tell her, but he couldn't bear to form the words. He said nothing, but the look on his face must have conveyed all the anger and anguish he felt, and maybe even something of the harsh moral judgment that lay behind it.

"I don't want to hear it," said Jenny, putting her hands up. "I don't care what he did. He means the world to Kitty—I don't give a damn about the rest."

. . .

An hour after parting with Jenny in a manner that seemed utterly final, Brad met Myrna for coffee. He didn't want to go home, but he didn't know what to do next.

He told Myrna about the report from Israel. She was amazed the Israelis would do such a thing. Shabtai ought to have known better; Cabot would be furious, and if he got confirmed he would have plenty of ways to get even. But her interest in Dyer was weak.

"Maybe he was alive," said Myrna. "Maybe Cabot didn't handle it exactly right. But I don't want to give that *putz* Joe Flint the satisfaction. Let's sit tight."

Brad didn't argue; Myrna was on Hugh's side on this question. But Brad wanted to understand what had happened. "The Israelis got some sort of transcripts about Dyer in April nineteen eighty-six," he said. "Why then?"

"I don't know. It could be anything." Myrna wasn't interested.

"Who else would know about this?"

"Cabot, of course. The Russians. Whoever was telling Cabot what to do. I hear Cabot says it was John Bross."

"Why would Bross be involved?"

"He handled a lot of sticky things," said Myrna. "Anyway it's going around."

"I can't ask him," said Brad. "That leaves Cabot and the Russians."

"Good luck," said Myrna.

But Brad was thinking hard. "Well, the Russians told Aldrich Ames," he said. "Maybe it's all in a report somewhere."

"That's an idea," said Myrna. "Why don't you file a FOIA request."

"It's not a joke," said Brad. "The man was alive."

Myrna put her hand on his. "That makes it sad," she said. "It doesn't make it urgent."

He thought about it Sunday afternoon during the hours he spent in sweats, running along the towpath beside the Chesapeake and Ohio Canal. The footing was terrible but the running helped him think, and with every step he grew more convinced that Myrna was wrong. The truth would not wait, and the Russians were key. What came to him first as a preposterous notion gradually blossomed into a practical plan as he lay sleepless again Sunday night, thinking miserably that he had already screwed things up so completely it no longer mattered what he did.

The secret of intelligence, they told the new boys at Camp Peary, is knowing where to look and who to ask. As a new boy, he decided, he had grasped the precept. Deciding to act was by far the hardest part; the rest was straightforward. He knew the drill for setting up a conference at the Federal Correctional Center in Allenwood, Pennsylvania. Myrna had been up there two or three times with CI questions and had explained it all when Ames's name first came up. Brad had a simple plan, really. The Russians told Ames; Ames told his debriefers at the CIA; maybe Ames would tell him.

It was just crazy enough to work.

38

Frank Cabot had a theory about food: a man's defenses were down when he was eating a good meal. A glass of wine helped but it was food that really did the work, especially if someone else had planned the meal so every course was a small surprise and delight. Eating soothed rancor—that was the heart of Cabot's theory. It's hard to be angry at someone who's feeding you. When you're eating you have to listen, the digestive system drains blood from the head, a full stomach makes a man drowsy, to break bread with another is an ancient sign of trust and friendship, eating stirs old memories of childhood, mother, the breast. Cabot liked to feed a man before he delivered bad news or introduced a delicate subject or issued a warning.

So Cabot had spent ten minutes on the phone with the Agency chef who planned meals for the seventh floor, ordering a four-course luncheon for two to be served in his private dining room on Monday at 1 p.m. What he wanted was an overfed, drowsy Joe Flint eager to make peace and return to his office. Cabot liked being one jump ahead.

"Sorry I'm late," said Flint brusquely, as he entered the director's small dining room at ten past one. "Nothing for me," he said, as the waiter was placing the smoked salmon before him.

The waiter hesitated.

"I've already eaten," said Flint. "I had a sandwich at my desk. What's up, Frank?"

Joe Flint was a square block of a man, as wide at the hips as he was at the shoulders; short legs; thick, meaty hands with tufts of silvery hair on the first joint of the fingers. His cheekbones were wide, mouth wide but lips thin, bunches of muscle where the jaw turned, skin pink and glowing. His hair was thick, a silvery blond, cut short in a crew cut. He wore bifocals without rims, just squares of cut glass with stems attached at either side by a single gold rivet. The taste that chose a gray checked jacket and knit tie had been fixed as a teenager in the first term of President Dwight David Eisenhower. The mind and the style had been fixed at the same time. To face Joe Flint was like facing a granite wall.

Cabot held up his hand and turned his head to the waiter. "Thanks, John, I'll have mine later." Then he turned his attention to the granite wall.

"Have you been asked to testify at the hearing?" he asked.

"Yes," said Flint.

"What do you intend to say?"

"I intend to make myself available to answer questions."

"What will you say in your opening statement?"

"I will say that I have worked with you for thirty years, that we have had our disagreements, and that I would be happy to answer any questions the senators might care to put to me."

"And at the top of this list of disagreements?"

"You know them as well as I do," said Flint. "We argued about the Russians for ten years."

"And of course as things turned out you were right."

"The paper backs me up."

"You wouldn't call those honest disagreements?"

"Of course they were honest. The point is you were consistently wrong."

It was Flint as Cabot had always known him: brusque, direct, giving nothing away, implacable. "I take it," said Cabot, "that you read the report from Israel before distributing it throughout the building?"

"Of course," said Flint.

"There are a couple of things I'd like to know," said Cabot. "Who sent you to inform the Israelis?"

"Larry Winter."

"Who told you the president had been brought in?"

"It was common knowledge at the time," said Flint. On comfortable ground he grew expansive. "In the Russia shop alone, half a dozen people knew what was going on. Near East knew. Security knew. People in

Winter's office knew. I suppose they were telling you it was super hush-hush, but Frank, if you'd spent any time in the DDO you'd know you can't keep people from talking about a hot subject like an MIA in the Gulag. A lot hung on that story. The president was fighting with the Senate about ratifying a SALT treaty. The hard-liners were saying you can't trust the Russians. The whole thing was designed for the rumor mill."

"And you knew the prisoner was alive when we first got the report?"

"No," said Flint. "I did not. But it was not exactly secret that Lipsky's report was bounced upstairs until it reached Otis Jones in the White House, and it was no secret Jones was giving you your marching orders. Frank, did you think a middle-level officer from the analytical side of the house could fly to Moscow and meet with an officer in the KGB and nobody would hear about it? If we hadn't known you were on White House business you'd have been arrested, for Christ's sake."

"Well, let me tell you something," said Cabot. "I have no idea what transcripts the Israelis are talking about, but the fact is I was told the MIA had died of typhus. And I know the Agency solemnly assured the president his name would never come up in this matter. And I know that certain sensitive aspects of this episode are still not generally known, even to you. And I've got an obligation to make sure they stay secret."

"Naturally," said Flint. "But I'm going to be under oath in there. If I'm asked a direct question, I'm going to give a direct answer."

"Anything you know from immediate personal knowledge," said Cabot, "you're free to say. But I don't want to hear you expanding into what might have been going on, or what people were speculating at the time, or what the rumors were hinting—"

"You're not a new boy," said Flint. "A Senate committee can ask any damn question it has a mind to. If you don't want the committee looking under rocks, you've got to cut a deal with MacLaverty."

"MacLaverty won't deal."

"You want my advice?"

"I doubt it," said Cabot.

"Bow out. This is only going to get worse. George Tater is after your scalp, MacLaverty is lining up a parade of hostile witnesses, from what I hear the White House isn't answering the phone, your chief defender had a heart attack, your wife is in the hospital, your niece is sleeping with the enemy—there's too much against you, Frank."

Cabot was shocked. It took him a moment to respond. "Brad Cameron is young and inexperienced and too eager to do the right thing," he said, anger rising, "but he's not the enemy."

"I'm not talking about Cameron," said Flint.

"Who are you talking about?"

"My knowledge isn't firsthand," said Flint. "Ask around."

For as long as he could remember, certainly throughout the thirty-odd years he had spent in the Central Intelligence Agency, Cabot had always been confident he knew what to expect. Sometimes he was modestly surprised—things weren't as good or as bad as he had hoped or feared. Sometimes he was flat out wrong, professionally—about the accuracy of Soviet missiles or where Mikhail Sergeyevich Gorbachev was leading the Soviet Union. But in the last thirty years no person in Cabot's personal orbit had ever surprised him fundamentally. His father drank after dinner and his mother always served mashed sweet potatoes on Thanksgiving; his wife loved him and at Christmas gave him novels he would never get around to; his secretary, Jane, cried when he gave her flowers on her birthday; Leo Weissberg would never buy a new suit and would go the final mile for him; Otis Jones added up restaurant checks; Harrison Hawkins never turned down dessert; presidents don't like to be told no, they don't like surprises, and they hate fights they didn't pick. All those Washington friends who had gently drifted out of reach in the last couple of weeks came as no surprise; they had arrived with good fortune and disappeared at bad. Cabot thought he understood his world pretty well.

But Joe Flint's flat claim that Jenny was sleeping with the enemy stunned him—so completely that he wasn't even sure he knew what Flint meant. Cabot did not enjoy thinking about the sexual lives of people close to him, but that didn't explain his surprise. He would have been hard put to name somebody steadier, more consistent, or truer to self than his niece. The Jenny he knew was lively, cheerful, a reader of newspapers, confident in her own opinions, impatient with theory or ideology, addicted to regular physical exercise, a careful, even picky eater with a weakness for finger food at weddings and fancy parties, loyal to her family, devoted to her Aunt Kitty, a stylish young woman, comfortable in society, but someone whose life was swinging like a compass needle toward husband, home, and children.

Sleeping with the enemy? Cabot found it hard to believe, but he knew Joe Flint. The man never spoke for effect.

Cabot called Leo Weissberg, asked if he was free, and said there were several things on his mind. While he waited he called Kitty at the hospital. "Are you all right?" he asked.

"Of course I'm all right. What's the matter? Has something happened?"

"I don't know," said Cabot.

Weissberg showed up a few minutes later. "I haven't had lunch," Cabot said. "Have you eaten?"

"I'll sit with you," said Weissberg. They went into the director's dining room and took seats at the round mahogany table.

"Sure you won't have anything? A glass of wine?"

"A glass of wine?"

"Why not?"

"I've known you for thirty years," said Weissberg, "and I've never seen a glass of wine in your hand unless you were planning to drink a toast."

"So let's drink a toast." The waiter poured for both of them.

"To old friends," said Cabot.

"*L'chaim,*" said Weissberg.

Cabot asked about the floating copies of the Dyer report.

"I think there were thirty-six in all," said Weissberg. "I've got physical possession of thirty-five. Tommy Johnson said he'd taken his home but will bring it in tomorrow."

"That stuff isn't supposed to leave the building," said Cabot. "Johnson knows that."

"It's only stamped CONFIDENTIAL," said Weissberg. "But I can't guarantee anything. That report has been all over the building. Anybody could have copied it."

"Well, at least we made the effort. How's Hawkins?"

"I spoke to Grafton Morse just after noon. The docs say it was a serious heart attack but he's stable now. They'll move him out of the ICU tonight or tomorrow. But there's no way he can go back to work for at least a month. I wrote down a lot of notes about left ventricles, if you want the details. But Morse told me something strange."

Weissberg explained that the FBI had sent someone to Hawkins's office with a warning. The crazy guy who shot the medic? Maybe he wasn't crazy. According to the Bureau, a few minutes after the first bulletin about Hawkins went out over the radio a newspaper in Detroit got a call claiming credit for Hawkins's "assassination." The caller said the killing was a "wake-up call for America."

"Why would anybody want to shoot Hawkins?" asked Cabot.

"The caller said he was speaking for something called the Brotherhood of Ruby Ridge—you remember that? Site of a shootout between the FBI and some kook who didn't want to pay his taxes? Something to do with Vietnam and abandoning MIAs. It's all very confused.

"So I called the Bureau, and they confirmed what Morse told me. They said they had no information about the Brotherhood, but Michigan is full of right-wing militia types who are angry about everything under the sun. The agent I talked to said there's a theory out there that the MIAs were supposed to be ransomed by the U.S. government but Nixon stole the money—something like that."

Cabot shook his head. "Where do they get these crazy ideas?" he asked.

"The Bureau thinks the shooter must have been trying to kill Hawkins, and the guys in Michigan probably figured he'd done it when they heard Hawkins was being taken to the hospital. I can't explain it any better than that. But the Bureau says we should take this seriously and you ought to be aware that you may be a target as well."

"Some cretin thinks I helped Nixon steal the ransom money?"

"No," said Weissberg. "Some group is mad about MIAs and may have tried to kill Hawkins. Your name has been much in the news in connection with an MIA case. You could be a target. You should be aware of this, that's all."

"I suppose you've passed this on to security."

"Of course."

"They're going to assign me a bodyguard, I suppose?"

"Two. They're in the outer office now, talking to Jane."

"I don't know if bodyguards are what I need," said Cabot. "Joe Flint told me something this afternoon. I want you to ask around about it. Can you do that for me?"

Weissberg said, "Of course, Frank."

It was the answer Cabot had expected. Weissberg always said of course. Cabot knew he could count on Weissberg absolutely.

"I don't know quite how to put this," said Cabot.

At the hospital, they said their hellos. Kitty told him both boys had called, and she filled him in on their news. The moment approached for Cabot to speak his mind, but he hesitated. While he searched for words, Kitty picked at her dinner. He loved to watch his wife while she was paying attention to something else. Kitty's hair was almost completely white, wrinkles had appeared by the corners of her mouth, her face had lost the gentle contours of youth and begun to take on the topography of age. Her body had thickened, too, and there was always a kind of question in her eyes—about what, Cabot rarely knew. But she paid attention, she thought about things, and Cabot trusted her judgment.

At last Cabot said, "I heard something disturbing today."

Kitty listened while he explained. "How do they know?"

"I'm not sure," said Cabot. "But when I asked Leo he said he didn't have to ask around, he knew the answer. Jenny is spending time with George Tater."

"Spending time? That doesn't mean sleeping with him."

"Leo says she's spent the night at his apartment at least three times in the last two weeks. Obviously we didn't have anybody actually in the apartment, but I'm afraid she's been seen kissing him, holding his hand, biting his ear."

"Biting his ear?"

"Biting, nibbling. Security has been keeping pretty close tabs on Tater, as a favor to me, I guess. They're not really supposed to do that. But somebody's leaking classified material to Tater and I'm given quite a lot of leeway to protect the Agency's sources and methods, so it's not strictly illegal."

"You think Jenny has been telling things to George Tater?" asked Kitty.

"I don't know what to think. It looks that way. He certainly seems to know things that I know she knows."

"When you're young," said Kitty, "sometimes you make big mistakes."

Cabot was drinking tea. He wasn't hungry because he had eaten his lunch in midafternoon. Two glasses of a pretty good French white and too much lunch had left Cabot all but ready for bed. But what weighed him down in the hospital chair talking to Kitty was a kind of helpless sadness and confusion. He had been furiously trying to plug leaks in the Agency, only to discover the problem was very likely in his own family.

"The big question," said Cabot, "is how much does she know?"

"Not much from me," said Kitty. "I can't tell her what you're afraid of because I don't know. I've been watching you sweat this out for two weeks, but I don't really know what has you worried. Do you want to tell me?"

Cabot lifted his eyes and looked his wife full in the face. This time he knew what her question was. Did he have it in him to tell the truth?

Cabot might have said no, he didn't want to tell her; he was afraid to tell her; he was ashamed to tell her. That would have been as much of the truth as Kitty expected or wanted. But people with secrets do not like to concede that they even exist. So Cabot told his wife what he planned to tell the Senate.

"It's painful, not criminal," he said. "The prisoner had been alive until shortly before I went to Moscow. So his death at just that moment would have raised a lot of emotional and divisive questions. The president told us to keep quiet about the whole episode, but he didn't want the order laid at his door. That's the bottom line. When you know that you know everything."

"God," said Kitty, "that *is* a mess. Is it going to come out now?"

"There's no way I can stop it."

"Do you want me to speak to Jenny?"

"I don't think I could do it," said Cabot.

39

The moral center of George Tater's day—the one thing he never missed short of a genuine emergency—was the 10 a .m. call from Morrie Bloom on the national desk in New York. A million ordinary citizens, thousands of government officials, hundreds of fellow journalists, scores of people who hated him, and two or three close personal friends routinely read Tater's stories in *The New York Times,* but the single individual whose opinion he valued most was Morrie Bloom.

Bloom was no pushover. He remembered the days when New York had half a dozen daily papers, he had rewritten copy for reporters whose names were legend, he had edited many an earthshaking story, and he did not give praise lightly. If Bloom had a weakness it was for good writing—and George Tater, Bloom often said, especially to Tater, couldn't get a job writing catalog copy for Sears, Roebuck. "So I never learned grammar," Tater protested.

"It's not your grammar," said Morrie Bloom. "It's your writing." And then he made a drawn-out noise, beginning with a guttural sound of infinite disgust, learned on the streets of Brooklyn in the days when newsboys still wore flat caps.

But Morrie gave credit where credit was due, and he conceded that Tater was one of the great diggers. "Okay," he'd say, when the reporter pushed a good story another step forward. "Not bad," he'd say, when Tater dug up something that would have made another man's career. "Tough luck," he had said on the three principal occasions when Tater failed to win a Pulitzer Prize even his enemies said he deserved.

"You're flagging," Morrie said at 10 a.m. on Monday morning, March 4, while Frank Cabot, across the river, was discussing the menu for his lunch with Joe Flint. "Enough already about the secret meeting. Where's the story? We've got nothing for the front page. *MacLaverty promises fair hearing. Anderson naps in White House. Cabot mum.* What are we paying you for? I can't justify two-column heads for this dreck. It's time for a four-column."

"Are you done?"

"I am not done, but I'll take a time-out. Talk to me," said Bloom.

"I'm sending you something now. Check your e-mail. Prepare to eat your words. Israel has written up a report about their end and we've got a name: Sergeant Jason Dyer from Accokeek, Maryland. Went missing on the Laotian border in May nineteen seventy. Only MIA ever sighted after January nineteen seventy-three."

"Not bad," said Bloom.

"Not bad?" said Tater. "It's the only genuine MIA story in nearly thirty years. And take note: the Israelis say they learned that the POW was alive—repeat: *alive*—when we first heard about him."

"He's alive now?"

"He was alive then."

"Ah. That's not such a big deal but okay. How did they learn this?"

"Secret transcripts."

"And these would be?"

"I don't have that yet."

They discussed the missing detail for a moment. Should Bloom put somebody on it in Israel, or could Tater get the answer in Washington? Tater said leave it to him. Bloom said he'd give him a day. "Listen, George," he continued, "you've taken a step forward here. But we've still got a so-what problem. I mean, what are we really saying here? Where are you taking this story? You've been gnawing at this for two weeks, and I'm not clear yet if Frank Cabot deserves to get his wrist slapped. I'm going to get you a three-column head for the name and still-alive story, but you've got to get off your bum and learn something."

Tater felt Bloom was being typically unfair. He lined up all the big stories published in English-language newspapers over the last hundred years—the *Titanic,* the October Revolution, "Peace in our time," the atom bomb, the assassination of John F. Kennedy—and awarded Tater's current story, whatever it was, not one ounce of praise or credit more than God himself would have bestowed. In the course of the most routine working week, Tater on the street often encountered fawning praise for his genius, his tenacity, his devotion to the public weal, but it meant less to him than the merest crumb of congratulation from Morrie Bloom. Over the years Tater's tireless effort to dazzle and Bloom's refusal to be impressed had formed a deep bond between the two men. The ten o'clock call was important to both of them.

But it stung to be told he didn't have the story yet. Tater stuck his neck out. "I'm on the track of something big," he said. "We're about to make the great leap, Morrie. This story is going up to a whole new level."

"Do you have it," asked Morrie, "or do you smell it?"

"I smell it," said George Tater.

What George Tater smelled was the old-man scent, part eau de cologne, part bodily decay, of Otis Jones. From the very beginning, Jones had been lurking in the wings of the confirmation story: the man who first noticed Cabot when he was a young analyst, got him a job on the National Security Council, put his thumb on the scale when Cabot was well down on the list of candidates for Deputy Director of Intelligence. On the Hill, Senate staffers told Tater it was Otis Jones who kept SALT—the Strategic Arms Limitation Talks—alive during the Carter years. Old Agency hands told Tater it was Jones who prevented the CIA from being split in two and renamed in the wake of the Church Committee hearings, and he came to the Agency's rescue again in the months following Bill Casey's death from a brain tumor, when the Iran-Contra special prosecutor was trying to crack open the Agency like an overripe cantaloupe. Jones always had his favorites and his enemies, he pushed some careers and sank others. But no one got more nudges forward, more favorable words in the right ears, more doors opened by Otis Jones than Frank Cabot.

There had been lots of men like Jones in Washington over the years—Tommy Corcoran, Clark Clifford, Edward Bennett Williams, Paul Nitze—men of wealth and power with a passion for manipulating policy behind the scenes. Jones was richer than most, older than all, and somehow, despite decades of knowing everybody, still a shadowy figure familiar only to the inner circle of the inner circle. His public appointments had all been deputy-this and assistant-that, but in every case the job he held was where the power lay. He'd been on the boards of many banks, major foundations, and defense contractors, often playing both sides of a narrow street—getting Lockheed a huge contract for navy fighter jets, for example, only a year after leaving the office of Deputy Undersecretary of the Navy.

That was in the bad old days of the 1950s, before the guardians of public virtue had fully wrapped their minds around the concept of conflict of interest. Jones had often slipped out of the room just moments ahead of the phalanx of investigators and accountants who were supposed to keep government honest. Though many reporters had tried, no one had ever laid a glove on Otis Jones—not even George Tater, during the months he spent chipping away at the monumental public reputation of Clark Clifford until it withered in the bright light of a scandal surrounding a failed bank that cost depositors millions while enriching certain Arabs by a similar amount.

One of Tater's private rules was never to sell immunity to one man in return for the skin of another. Prosecutors did it routinely but Tater refrained. When one of the defendants in the Arab bank case tried to buy mercy with a circumstantial story about Otis Jones, Tater made no promises and helped send the man to prison—but not before he extracted a few significant facts, enough to know that Otis Jones, at least once in a long career, had failed to sweep up all traces of a deal in which the money deposited in one of his accounts had not been fully reported to the Internal Revenue Service. With these particulars—the name of a Kuwaiti bank officer, the number of a Swiss bank account, a Xerox copy of the front and back of a certain check—George Tater felt he had a shot at gaining the respectful attention of Otis Jones.

Being a figure of power—knowing people, having a hand in many things, giving occasional advice, making the crucial introduction—is a position from which one can be cast out only by the grave or the penitentiary. Otis Jones had quit working (in any ordinary sense of the term) years back, but he still appeared every day in the downtown offices of the venerable firm of Wells and Kopthorne, where he had a top-floor office with a view of the White House and, rising behind it, the Washington Monument. As a young man just after World War Two, Jones had become a confidant of the elderly Kopthorne, who took an interest in his progress, had tea with him every afternoon, and over the course of a year explained the relationship of money to power in Washington. Then he died.

Now Jones was even older than Kopthorne but, like him, he arrived every morning at ten o'clock in the firm's outer office, where he was met at the elevator doors by his junior partner, Stanley Kiddle, a graduate of the University of Texas Law School, who spent his first decade as a member of the Texas bar trying homicide cases in the office of the Dallas District Attorney. It was said of Kiddle that no other prosecutor in this century had put so many men on death row. Every few months Kiddle flew home to witness an execution. Otis Jones's good friend James Baker had recommended Kiddle, and Jones never failed to thank him when they met.

"Stanley Kiddle is a good man to have on your side of the table," Otis Jones often said.

What made Kiddle such a formidable lawyer? "Lots of good lawyers are intelligent," Jones would explain. "I would never hire one who didn't prepare or wasn't discreet. What Stanley conveys to every opponent is the wisdom of a generous compromise, since the alternative is an extended legal ordeal threatening bankruptcy or prison."

Kiddle was an active partner in Wells and Kopthorne, destined to become seriously rich in time, but the duty he took most seriously, and not only for reasons of self-interest, was the task of making sure Otis Jones was never surprised.

At the top of Kiddle's list on this Tuesday morning were reports of many questions being asked about Jones—especially about the years he spent on the National Security Council in the Carter White House—by the *Times* reporter George Tater.

"He has been asking about you all over town," said Kiddle, "and I am getting calls from people who say he's very interested in the history of your friendship with Frank Cabot."

Kiddle had already passed on what he knew about the Dyer report submitted to the CIA by Israel, of which he had heard several different stories. He reported that Hawkins was gaining strength but would definitely not be returning to chair Cabot's confirmation hearings. He said Peter Schleicher told a friend of a friend that the president "would understand" if "family problems" forced Cabot to abandon the fight. He concluded with a report—he had no way of knowing if it was true—that the CIA's Office of Security believed some kind of relationship, presumably intimate, existed between George Tater and Cabot's niece, Jennifer Moore.

Otis Jones raised his eyebrows as only an old man can, signaling a stirring of thoughts deep within. "How did that bit of news reach us?" he asked.

"Beaufort," said Kiddle, naming the chief of the in-house investigative arm of Wells and Kopthorne, "used to be in the Agency with a fellow named Morrissey, and Morrissey has been intercepting Tater's phone calls."

The eyebrows went up again. "Cabot's bugging him?"

"It's on the up-and-up. He has a court order."

"Can Morrissey get us transcripts?"

"No—but he's willing to give Beaufort a summary of the take."

"And?"

"Tater's developed quite an interest in your meetings with Cabot in nineteen seventy-eight."

"Is there anything in the hot files that could give us trouble on this?"

"Just your office diary, listing calls, meetings, trips to the White House, and so on."

"We'll leave that alone," said Jones. "I doubt Cabot could get rid of every trace of those contacts at the Agency, but so long as they're interpreted correctly it doesn't matter."

"Tater called yesterday and again this morning. You could put him off," said Kiddle, "but if you gave him something he might calm down."

"I like that approach," said Jones. "Will you call him? Tell him to meet me at twelve-ten outside the Renwick Gallery. Will you let the Cosmos know I'll be a little late for lunch? And will you ask Beaufort to come along? I think it would be helpful if he knew who Tater is.

"I think that'll cover it," said Otis Jones.

It was nearly twelve-fifteen, when the black Mercedes with tinted windows eased to the curb in front of the gallery where George Tater stood, holding his gleaming burgundy briefcase. Almost before the car came to a halt, the front passenger door opened and a large man stepped out to open the rear door.

"If you don't mind," said Jones from within, as Tater stooped to enter, "would you give your briefcase to Ollie? It'll be perfectly safe up front with him."

Tater handed it over. The rear of the car was roomy and sealed off by a glass wall from the front.

"We've never met but of course I know a good deal about you, Mr. Tater, and I gather you'd like to know something about me."

"Yes," said Tater.

The car pulled away from the curb.

"Before we talk, I hope you won't mind my asking: Are you wearing a wire?"

"No," said Tater.

"Please," said Jones. He did not wait for an answer. With surprising vigor the old man leaned over and frisked Tater up under his armpits, patted the front of his chest, ran a hand up one leg to his crotch, leaving no corner unexplored, and then smoothed down both of Tater's lapels. It was over in a moment.

"Thank you," said Jones. "It's my hope that we can talk frankly. Everything is off the record: no attribution, no identification, no use of any kind unless agreed otherwise. Is that acceptable to you?"

"You're spry, for an old goat," said Tater.

"I exercise," said Jones, "I eat properly, and I get plenty of rest."

"That's all there is to it?" asked Tater.

"I also recommend a weekly shiatsu session."

"Someone young and beautiful, I trust."

"To me," said Jones, "everyone seems young. I very much doubt my therapist would seem young to you. Would you like her name?"

"Can she do deep-tissue work?" asked Tater.

"She specializes in deep-tissue work," said Jones. From a pocket diary he read off a woman's name and phone number. "Now," he said, "what is it you'd like to know?"

Tater waited a moment, choosing his words. "Frank Cabot," he said, "went to Moscow in July nineteen seventy-eight to check up on an Israeli report of an American POW in the Gulag. I take it you've been reading my stuff on this?"

"Yes."

"This had obvious implications in the fight going on in the Senate at the time: Can we trust the Russians? Is it safe to ratify SALT? and so on. My question—"

"Yes."

"Why was Cabot chosen? You were point man for SALT. You'd known him for years. What was it about Cabot? Was it your friendship?"

"Mr. Tater, it had nothing to do with our friendship."

Tater waited.

"It was a practical matter entirely. Frank Cabot had spent a couple of years in the early seventies in Geneva as a technical advisor to Gerry Smith. There he became friends with a Russian, his counterpart. They spent two years arguing about where to put the commas. You should ask Cabot about this. It's all ancient history now, but you'd be surprised how much those two had to do with reaching an agreement. So it's perfectly simple. Cabot knew somebody with access to information, and he could ask a question without turning it right away into an affair of state."

"How did you know Cabot knew the Russian?"

"Well, as you say—we were friends."

When George Tater was closing in on something, he sometimes held his breath for ten or even fifteen seconds; he didn't want to miss the smallest sound, turn of lip, shifting of glance—anything that, along with the words, constituted an answer. When it came his heart would skip a beat, and it skipped one now. He had just obtained the first big piece of what he wanted to know. Otis Jones had been the dispatching agent for Frank Cabot.

"And the other question," said Tater. "What did you tell the president after Cabot's return—the first time?"

He quit breathing again.

"Well, you already know the outcome of this, Mr. Tater—the sad news of the death of an American POW."

"No," said Tater. "I want to know what you told him after Cabot's *first* trip."

Jones appeared to take a long time to unravel this. At last he said, "I don't think I want to go much further down this road at this time. I feel there's another aspect of the larger story, which—"

"I appreciate that. But this goes to the heart of it. Let me put this another way."

"Mr. Tater—" Jones began.

"Would I be wrong," Tater asked, "if I wrote that 'the sad news of the death of an American POW' was conveyed by you to the president after the *second* trip Cabot made to Moscow?"

"I can't help you there. I am bound by certain promises of confidentiality. Mr. Tater, I want you to consider another aspect of this story."

But Tater wouldn't back off. He felt it was now or never. "Give me a minute," he said. He described the imminence of a large story in the *Times* on the White House involvement in the Cabot/POW story; the central role played by Otis Jones; the crucial fact that the POW was alive at the time of Cabot's first trip. When Jones's eyebrows showed his astonishment at the introduction of this claim, Tater thought, *Yes, yes!* Warming at last to the razor blade concealed within the apple, Tater stated firmly the natural place in such a story for a good deal of background about the Washington career of Otis Jones, including his role in obtaining a charter for the Bank of Credit and Commerce International—

Tater was just getting the words out when Jones raised his fingers in a fluttering gesture of dismay. "Don't," he said softly. "Please, I beg you"—almost whispering—"don't demean yourself. Threats are unworthy of a serious reporter, Mr. Tater. I never give in to threats. And you ought to understand that I respond vigorously to attack. What would your editor,

Mr. Bloom, think if he knew you were sleeping with the niece of a man you are writing about? Please. Let us waste no more breath on this unpleasantness."

Tater's face gave him away. He was angry and caught by surprise.

"I'm trying," said Jones, "to tell you something important about the history of the issue of MIAs. Can you please put aside your previous unfruitful line of inquiry long enough to hear me out on this? I'm asking you a question, Mr. Tater. You are seeking information, and I have some to impart. Will you listen?"

"All right," said Tater.

Tater took no notes, but what he heard over the next eight to ten minutes planted itself firmly in his mind.

"There is a serious unreported story," Jones began, "about the fate of Americans still missing in Southeast Asia when our forces pulled out in January nineteen seventy-three."

It was quite a story. Otis Jones had been in private practice at the time, but he had business dealings and long-standing friendships with certain military figures in the Saigon government. From them and several of their counterparts in Washington, Jones said he had learned that in December 1973 the White House obtained a list of American servicemen, mostly downed pilots with a few Special Forces cadre, held—not missing, held—in Laos and Cambodia. This list came from Hanoi, accompanied by an explanation that while the North Vietnamese authorities had no control over the Khmer Rouge and the Pathet Lao, they were in a position to pass on a proposal for an exchange of those held in return for assistance in rebuilding the war-torn economies of Laos and Cambodia—assistance in the form of cash.

After much haggling over numbers, a deal was struck. It could be found in no piece of government paper, in no secret codicil to the Paris peace accords, in no memorandum of understanding by unofficial observers, but it was a deal all the same. A certain very large sum of money—here things began to go awry, Otis Jones explained—was transferred to Saigon concealed within the larger American aid program. From Saigon, by agreement, the money was to be passed to a bank in Hong Kong that was partly owned by the Chinese government in Beijing. But the money did not go to Hong Kong; in 1975, following the fall of Saigon, the money ended up in the Philippines, whence roughly half of the total soon moved on to California, where it was used to purchase a portfolio of large commercial properties in downtown Los Angeles. The other half went to the Cayman Islands. There it was distributed in certified bank checks made out to cash that were hand-delivered to several former officials of the very highest rank in the Nixon White House.

George Tater listened to this story without speaking. The orderly flow of dates, names, institutions, and relationships had about it a strange sense of the surreal. Otis Jones had a thin atonal voice, a little like a doctor's, concealing a promise of pain and sorrow within a litany of factual details. He spoke in complete sentences; the sentences formed paragraphs; the paragraphs related a story that left its hearer numb. As a reporter, Tater spent his days trying to drag facts out of reluctant informants, facts which, placed in context and carefully explained, might plausibly be interpreted to imply that something had been done or said or agreed which everyone formally involved in the matter heatedly denied. Now Otis Jones was simply telling him the particulars of a Faustian exchange of men for money so dark and cruel even Roman emperors and Stalin's police would have been impressed. All his adult life, George Tater had wondered what really happened behind the last set of doors to the innermost chambers of the world of wealth and power, and now Otis Jones was handing him the key.

As he completed his tale, the old man pulled an envelope from the inside of his jacket pocket and passed it to Tater. The envelope had no return address, and the sheet of paper within was blank except for a list of five names—very very well-known names—and the particulars of five certified checks, not only when they were drawn but where and when they were deposited.

"And how," said Tater at last, "should I describe the source of this information?"

"I suggest you borrow a page from the book of our friend Cabot," said Otis Jones.

"Meaning?"

"Ask everybody in town," said Otis Jones, "and muddy the waters, Mr. Tater. Muddy the waters."

At the end of a long day and a dinner alone, George Tater dropped by his office, tossed his briefcase and coat onto a chair, and threw his notebook on the desk. He had been worrying ever since leaving Otis Jones that afternoon about how to handle the Jenny business. If Jones knew about her, a lot of other people did too—or soon would. Tater did not like thinking what Faith Osborne might have to say about that, possibly in print. He should have been expecting this.

He pressed the play button on his answering machine.

After many familiar voices with news of faint interest came an unknown voice with a message that held him.

"Mr. Tater? I'm sorry to be calling so late. We have never met, but I know something about the story you're working on. I don't think I ought to leave my name; I work for the CIA. Or I did, last I knew. I'll try you again tomorrow."

Tater was pretty sure he knew who this was. Jenny had that right, he thought to himself. This boy doesn't know how to stay out of trouble.

40

When Dean Cutter's money ran out, Russell said, "Don't worry, I've got a few extra bucks." He gave Dean a twenty. A couple of days later he gave him another twenty. Dean was glad to have the money, but he wanted to say goodbye to Russell forever.

Dean said it was his fault, he shouldn't have missed, he was no good at this, and Russell needed to find somebody else. Russell just shrugged and said not to worry. "You gave them a scare," he said. "Believe me. Maybe the newspapers didn't understand what went down but the security people know. They know."

That didn't make Dean feel better; it worried the hell out of him. Secretly he thanked God he had missed and he was looking for a way to convince Russell he had to move on.

"I need a job," he told Russell one morning, after eggs and toast that Russell was paying for. "I've got to get my license back. I've got to get my car running. My life is a wreck."

"You've got a job," said Russell. "With us."

He came by first thing every morning. He brought four or five newspapers to the Metro Diner and paged through them slowly and thoroughly. The day after the shooting he found one paragraph in the *Post* tying the wounded medic to the premature statement in Michigan claiming responsibility for Hawkins's murder. A couple of days later another brief stand-alone story said the FBI still had no explanation for the statement.

"They know there's a connection," said Russell. "They know we're out here."

"I don't feel right," said Dean. "I like to pay my way. I'm flat broke. I'm thinking about leaving Washington altogether."

"Not yet," said Russell. "We're not finished yet. I've got money, don't worry about it." He closed the paper and looked at Dean. "Listen. Let me tell you how the guys in Michigan operate."

Dean made a show of listening attentively. Something about Russell's voice frightened him.

"They trust you," said Russell, "and when they trust somebody they don't want to change. They don't jump from this guy to that guy—they find the right guy, they help him, they give him what he needs. You can trust them; do you see what I'm saying? They're going to take care of you; they're going to help us set things up; next time you won't miss. So quit worrying."

"Let's say I've changed my mind. Let's say I don't want to do this anymore."

"You mean like you're going to the cops? You can't be trusted? You're gonna tell everything you know?"

"No, no, I don't mean that. What are you saying?"

"You're in or you're out. And if you're out you're a danger to the whole organization, do you see what I'm saying? This has nothing to do with me, Dean. I'm your friend. But the guys in Michigan, they're serious. If you tried to quit now . . ." Russell's voice trailed off.

"I'm not trying to quit," said Dean. "I'm just saying I don't know."

"Don't worry. Hawkins was lucky. Frank Cabot won't be so lucky. We'll set it up right."

Frank Cabot, thought Dean to himself. He's probably guarded by guys with Uzis. How the hell am I supposed to get close to Frank Cabot? No way, Dean thought. I'm getting out of this.

But how? He had maybe eight bucks in his pocket.

Doubts and fears assailed Dean Cutter for a week. He remembered what the therapist Lisa Benson said about trouble he couldn't ignore. Well, he'd stepped into it now. Somebody might recognize him. He could be arrested. Russell's friends from Michigan might think he was working for the government.

For a week Dean stuck close to the apartment, slept twelve hours a day, watched television, tried not to think of the gun in his bureau drawer. One week to the day after the shooting, Dean Cutter, down to his last dollar, met Russell at the Metro Diner for breakfast at eight o'clock. Russell came in with the papers under his arm, like he always did.

"You've been feeling useless, isn't that right?" said Russell.

"It's this waiting around," said Dean.

"Like you can't get out of bed in the morning. Like you can't do anything right. Like the bastards will always win, am I right?"

"They *do* always win. That's a fact."

"See? That's defeatism talking. I've been watching you. I understand you. I see the defeat in you. You've forgotten what it's all about."

"I know what it's about."

"Yeah?"

"I'm not a defeatist."

"All right, then. Read this."

He dropped a copy of *The New York Times* onto the countertop, front page up. A three-column headline read:

VIETNAM-ERA MIA DIED IN GULAG
FIVE YEARS AFTER WAR'S END

The first couple of paragraphs pulled up emotions Dean had forgotten: Despite numerous denials over three decades, the Soviet Union had imprisoned American MIAs from the war in Vietnam, and the president's nominee to run the CIA, Frank Cabot, was told authoritatively in Moscow in 1978 that an MIA held for eight years had recently died of typhus.

> Yesterday, the Pentagon's office for POW/MIA affairs confirmed that the MIA who died in the prison camp at Akmolinsk was Sergeant Jason Dyer, U.S. Army, of Accokeek, Maryland. His sister, Stacy Dyer, reached by phone at her home in Accokeek, said her family knew nothing of the circumstances of Mr. Dyer's death until this reporter's call.
>
> Mr. Cabot, whose confirmation hearing is expected to convene next Monday, could not be reached for comment.

"I can't believe it," said Dean Cutter in a faint voice. He was thinking, *Stacy Dyer.*

"I'm not making it up," said Russell. "Are you ready now?"

Still staring at the paper, Dean asked, "Ready for what?"

"To draw blood," said Russell.

41

Winter still gripped the landscape and it was lightly snowing as Brad drove steadily but slowly up through the forested mountains of central Pennsylvania, stuck behind a tractor-trailer much of the way but content to poke along, knowing the man he was going to see had all the time in the world. Two things kept running through Brad's mind as he drove Tuesday morning, and the first was the question of what to expect from convicted traitor Aldrich Ames.

The day before, knowing he was about to enter territory from which there would be no turning back, Brad had done some homework in the Agency's library, pulling down a pile of books on the notorious Ames case of 1994 from the open shelves. It was a sense of the man Brad was looking for, not the details of his crimes and arrest, and he spent most of his time with a book called *Betrayal* by three *New York Times* reporters—a dog-eared volume all but separated from its binding, highlighted, underlined, and marked by many different hands with exclamation points and question marks.

But not lately. Brad was the first reader in more than two years. After a couple of hours of spotty reading, jumping and skipping as the mood prompted him, there emerged in his mind a growing sense of a touchy, frustrated man who had impulsively sacrificed everything for money he would never spend. The first reckless contact with the Russians, the drinking, the sloppy inattention to the most basic rules of operational security—all suggested a man more or less knowingly stepping off the edge of a cliff. That he got away with it for nearly ten years was pure luck. But when the prison doors slammed shut at last they slammed shut for good. There would be no delayed mercy for Aldrich Ames in this world.

Inevitably, Brad had to wonder if he was heading into that kind of trouble himself. He knew the drill for visiting Ames, he had made all the calls, faxed the forms, triggered no suspicions so far as he could tell. But it was no secret the director had great power and wide latitude. Cabot's men, the melon-headed Morrissey and his white-haired assistant, D. Plummer, would find no legal barrier to slapping Brad in cuffs if they caught him at the gates of Allenwood. He did not fear serious jail time but detention, interrogation, summary dismissal, the inevitable whispering campaign, the cloud over the rest of his life—was all that just ahead?

The odd thing was how little the prospect frightened him. Ever since his father died when he was ten, Brad's life had been spent mostly in schools and summer camps, where rules and traditions determined his days. The CIA wasn't much different: school with twice the rules. Now, after years of doing what he was told, he was breaking the rules every day. He dreaded a phone call from his mother—What are you doing? Have you considered how I feel?—but his fears stopped there.

The mind roams on long drives. From the mystery of his own life, Brad's thoughts would shift back to the young man from Accokeek who had died of typhus in a Soviet prison camp. The timing bothered him. Why did he die only a week or two after his country learned he was there? Typhus as a cause of death was perfectly plausible, but why then? The news from Golenpolsky one week, typhus the next. This was a question any reader of spy novels could answer.

So Brad swung between two bleak thoughts during the long snowy drive: the very good chance he would soon be seeking a new career and the solidifying conviction that it wasn't typhus that killed the young man from Accokeek. It was the Russians.

What Brad noticed first was the cock of the head—tossed back and to the right—the stance of a man on the verge of walking out. Which of course Aldrich Ames was not free to do. An impressive number of doors had opened and closed as Brad was drawn into the prison past one guard or checkpoint after another. He stated his purpose, he filled out forms, he signed his name, he surrendered his driver's license and his Agency identity card, he opened his briefcase, he passed through a metal detector, he submitted to a frisk. The first step had been surprisingly easy; knowing the right name and calling in advance the prison official who okayed routine CIA debriefings had opened the succession of doors and brought the pale, gaunt, not very recently shaven figure of Aldrich Ames on schedule into the special visitors' room. Ames wore prison blues and soft black sneakerlike shoes. He flipped a long number-two yellow pencil back and forth with his fingers. He stood, paced, sometimes sat on the edge of a desk. Resistance, displeasure, and impatience marked every gesture. The guards may have passed Brad through, but Ames clearly knew things didn't add up.

"Usually," he said, "someone tells me who's coming and what for. Of course there's always a spin on it. They never say what they want. Scratch an intelligence officer and you scratch a man who thinks he's smarter than you are. Give me a break. I've been there. So who are you? Why are you alone? Why no warning? What are you trying to find out? Why should I talk to you?"

He cocked his head back, waiting for Brad's answer.

Over the span of a second Brad realized there was no way he could pass off his presence as a routine visit from the Office of Security. He needed an explanation Ames would like.

So he told the truth.

"I'm being kicked out as Agency liaison for MIA and POW affairs," Brad said. "But before I go there's one nasty piece of business I'd like to clear up."

"The man in Akmolinsk," said Ames.

Brad was startled.

"Who else?" said Ames. He was smiling, pleased with himself. "It wasn't hard," he continued. "First, it's obvious you're off the reservation. Second, you're looking for MIAs, and Jason Dyer is the only one I know anything about. Third, I know who's running for director, for Christ's sake. He hasn't said word one about this to anyone for twenty years, and he sure as hell isn't going to volunteer it to a new kid like you."

Ames delivered another smile.

"Sorry. Facts is facts. I mean, it's obvious, Mr. Cameron. You're asking me"—he pointed to his heart—"about something they don't want you to know." He shrugged, lifted a hand. "See what I mean? Jason Dyer. Who else? And the bit you'd like to clear up is who wanted him dead."

"I figured out who," said Brad. "The Russians. But why? I don't understand it."

"You sure don't," said Aldrich Ames. "It wasn't the Russians, it was us. *We* wanted him dead."

What Brad remembered later was Ames's malicious satisfaction while he waited for Brad to acknowledge his shocking remark. The anger Brad felt at that moment in the Allenwood visitors' room lingered for many months and never entirely disappeared, despite the fact—he grasped immediately that it *was* a fact—that Aldrich Ames was telling him the truth.

Brad showed nothing of what he felt but merely asked Ames to explain. It was a complicated story, and Ames took his time.

About a year after Ames volunteered to work for the Russians in Washington in 1985, the CIA gave him a routine transfer to the Rome station, where he immediately fell in love with the custom of long lunches in fine restaurants and added a daily liter of good Tuscan red to the better part of a bottle of vodka he consumed before bed each night. Ames didn't thank his prosecutors for it, but it was clear to him that the U.S. government had saved or at least prolonged his life when it confined him to a prison cell. Many times before his arrest he had blacked out or suffered the burning pain of what was one day going to be a ruptured esophagus. But goddamn he missed those Roman lunches! Had Brad ever been to Rome?

Brad had not.

Well, there was a place called Tullio, not far off the Veneto below the American embassy, where the serious lunch crowd began to arrive after two. Embassy folk all said it was too expensive, but of course money was not Ames's problem. He ate a steak at Tullio a couple of times every week and once he even saw his Russian handler there—purely by accident. The trim little man had flown in from Moscow, busied himself at his embassy for a day or two, and purely by chance had picked Tullio for the kind of lunch ordinary Soviets scarcely dreamed about. Ames had met him twice before—once in South America, while visiting his wife's family in Colombia, and once already in Rome. The man he knew then only as Vladimir was not his regular contact in Rome; that was a Soviet embassy officer Ames was allegedly trying to recruit, a man named Aleksei Khrenkov. But Vladimir came all the way from Moscow when something was truly urgent—first in the fall of 1986, to reassure Ames that clever ways had been found to deflect CIA suspicions, if any (which, to Ames's later amazement, there were not), and then a few months later, in the coldest, wettest, darkest heart of the Roman winter when the lights at Tullio burned all the brighter. There Ames's heart had skipped a beat when he noticed Vladimir in his dark French suit enter with an Italian friend; they were seated only a couple of tables away. Graciously, Vladimir insisted that his companion sit facing into the room, looking straight into the slack, panicked features of Ames, while Vladimir settled with his back safely pointed to the best agent he had ever run in a long life of stealing Western secrets. Ames finished his liter, shook his head at the offer of an espresso, paid, and left.

The next day, in an attic room of the Soviet residence across the Tiber, the two men laughed about the incident and Vladimir praised Ames for his extraordinary professional coolness at a tense moment. A generous, loyal, attentive, understanding man; Ames admired him still. But Vlad was an intelligence officer, and he certainly did not announce the object of his many questions about the file to be found among the records of the Soviet Division's counterintelligence staff concerning a certain KGB officer named Mikhail Ivanovich Kondrashov.

"Vlad thought he was smarter than me," Ames said. "I suppose you think you're smarter than me. It's the giveaway sign of an intelligence officer—I know something and you don't."

Right, thought Brad, saying nothing. *Who's the one in jail?*

"I know what you're thinking," Ames said. "Who's the one in jail?"

He threw back his head and laughed.

"Anyway," he resumed, "what Vlad didn't want me to know, among other things, was the identity of the man Kondrashov met in Moscow in nineteen seventy-eight and exactly why Vlad and his friends were curious about it. An American, he said. I had access to all those files. What did they say about the meeting?"

Naturally, off the top of his head Ames did not know. But he promised Vlad he would find out. So Ames and his contact in the Soviet embassy, the man he was allegedly trying to recruit, Aleksei Khrenkov, cooked up a story. Ames went to his boss in Rome, Chief of Station Don Howard, and told him that Khrenkov was willing to go to work for the Americans but he was afraid he'd get caught. He said he'd been told the KGB had an agent in the heart of the CIA, a man sure to betray Khrenkov if Khrenkov ever started feeding them information.

"This is the Agency's chief nightmare," said Ames. "So Howard got excited; we had something hot. A secure line was set up and we started an operation to find the mole in the CIA. It was beautiful, really: I'd go to see Khrenkov, I'd bring back some small piece of information, we'd forward it straight to Langley. Khrenkov had been told a CIA officer had been recruited in Moscow in nineteen seventy-eight. We got the month, then the day."

At first it all came back negative. The Agency checked its travel files: nothing. That was not a good sign. Nothing in the files meant someone had gone to Moscow without authority and without submitting the required report. The Agency did not want to bring the FBI into this, so very cautiously it asked a few friendly services to check travel records—airline manifests, passport controls. Had Brad ever worked on a CI case?

Brad had not.

Well, in that case he would be amazed to learn just how closely intelligence services watch the comings and goings of persons around the world, all of it stored on computer. According to Khrenkov, the American had gone to Moscow from Vienna. That simplified things. He had arrived in July. The possibilities were further narrowed. He had met with a man named Kondrashov.

That did it. The Rome chief of station called Ames into his office and told him the case had been lifted to an altogether new level of operational security. He would be boiled in oil if he so much as *thought* about the case outside the building. Howard was a short, chubby man whose eyes popped when he grew excited. The way they were popping now gave Ames a hint of the hysteria that must have gripped Washington.

"I have it straight from the director's office," said Howard, pacing back and forth and wringing his hands. "We have got to shut this down, everything! You're to break contact with Khrenkov. No explanation. When's the next meet, tomorrow? Oh, my God!" He threw himself into his chair. "They're going crazy in Washington," he said. "How did we let this guy Khrenkov get so close? We've got to shut down this whole line of inquiry. They're talking extreme measures."

Now it was Ames's turn to blanch.

"Extreme measures?"

"Yes. They're wild. They want me to tell the Italians this Khrenkov is smuggling dope—heroin from Afghanistan. Get him thrown out of the country."

"Smuggling heroin?" said Ames.

As Brad watched in silent amazement Ames burst out laughing again, throwing his head back and letting go. His face got red; he rocked back and forth; he began to cough. "Don't you find any of this funny?" he asked Brad. At last he quieted down.

" 'Don,' I said, 'we can handle this. Tell Langley to calm down. Let's think this through.' "

It was obvious. Ames couldn't drop Khrenkov; from the CIA's point of view that would just warn the KGB that they were getting close to pay dirt. Better, he argued, if he went on calmly talking to Khrenkov, tried to get a clearer picture of what the Russians knew, and went back later with some kind of soothing non-answer from the CIA that would put the Russians to sleep.

So that's the way they played it. Howard told Langley to hold their water. Ames went back and forth for a couple of weeks. Finally everybody was satisfied.

"You see what was going on here?" Ames asked Brad. "You spot the problem?"

"The Russians thought Cabot had maybe recruited Kondrashov."

"Right," said Ames. "And that means . . . ?"

"Kondrashov didn't write it up either."

"Exactly right. No official reports on either end. Kondrashov must have been reporting directly to the office of the chairman of the Politburo. You can probably guess the cause of this awful muddle. The best agent the Russians ever had"—the grinning Aldrich Ames gave Brad a knowing wink—"dumped the names of a lot of Russians working for the CIA into the KGB's lap in nineteen eighty-five, April twenty-fifth to be exact. The KGB was horrified and started to examine everybody with a fine-tooth comb. Somehow they discovered the secret meeting between Kondrashov and Cabot way back when and asked me to help figure out what had been going on.

"It's pretty funny when you think about it—the right hand trying to keep tabs on the left hand. It's what keeps the great game going. This is what both sides spent billions on for the last fifty years. This doesn't strike you as funny?"

"Not exactly," said Brad.

"Once the Russians knew what happened," said Ames, "we shut down the operation."

Ames told Langley that Khrenkov was now reassured there was no Russian mole in the CIA, but, alas, he had changed his mind and decided not to defect after all. Langley was satisfied the Russians felt they knew what had happened in nineteen seventy-eight. Vladimir and his colleagues stopped worrying about Kondrashov. Don Howard retired after a distinguished career in the service of his country and left Rome. Everybody was happy.

"There's still something I don't get," said Brad. "What did the CIA tell the Russians about that meeting in nineteen seventy-eight? I mean, one day the KGB thinks Kondrashov is working for the Americans, the next he's clean. What was Langley's story?"

"The same bullshit Cabot is probably telling the Senate this very minute—that we heard there was an American POW in a Russian camp and Cabot was sent to ask Kondrashov if it was true."

"But that's not true?" said Brad.

"It's half true," said Ames. "That's what happened on the first trip."

"And on the second trip?"

"You can't guess?"

"I don't want to guess. I want you to tell me, and then I want to check it out until I know one way or the other for sure."

"I'll tell you," said Aldrich Ames. "And I'll tell you exactly how to check it out. There are files that will back up every word. But who are *you* going to tell?"

42

"*Boychik,*" said Myrna the following morning, Wednesday, March 13, "you're taking too much on yourself. You're forgetting what this business is all about. This isn't personal. It's not you against the world."

"You want me to forget what Ames said?"

"I don't trust Ames," said Myrna.

"Well, what about the Israeli report?"

"They're trying to pick a fight," said Myrna. "I don't trust them either."

They were in a diner in Maryland, a 1950s-vintage chrome and plastic place known for its great eggs. Myrna said to pick someplace they weren't going to run into people, and Brad had been there once with Hugh Diamond, a fanatic about diner food. Brad ordered the mushroom and three-cheese omelet, but by the time the waitress brought it his appetite had gone.

"I can't just sit on this story."

"Why not?" asked Myrna.

"Well, for one thing Tater published Dyer's name yesterday. The media are all going to be scrambling for details. What Ames told me eventually he's going to tell everybody else. It's going to come out anyway. So why is everybody telling me to hide in a corner? Even my mother called last night, and she hardly ever calls. Don't I know I'm ruining my life? What's she going to tell all the blondes in Palm Beach?"

"She's right about ruining your life," said Myrna. "You think it's a big adventure, but it's more like a tornado. You can feel it coming: the air grows still, the sky turns a weird color, dogs prick up their ears, and birds fly around. If you weren't in the middle of it you'd see it too. Things are about to happen."

"I don't think it's a big adventure," said Brad. "I'm thinking about that poor bastard we left in Russia. When I was a kid—"

"When you were a kid has nothing to do with it."

"It explains the way I feel."

"This isn't about feelings," said Myrna.

"Look. Maybe not for you, but it is for me. Listen to me. When my father died I went to the funeral, and the day after—the day after!—my mother enrolled me in the Fessenden School. Grades one through eight. There were six-year-old kids there whose parents lived in Switzerland or Paris."

"I get the picture."

"No, you don't," said Brad. "I was like in shock. My mother said, Don't be silly, you're going to have hundreds of friends. But all I knew was one week I had a home and the next week I didn't. Basically I never lived with my mother again. She'd bring me out for a visit wherever she was, but it was always a visit. The rest of the year it was school or camp, and in between I stayed with Uncle Max. Every holiday Uncle Max came to get me. I've been thinking about that ever since Golenpolsky told us about Dyer. We knew he was there, but nobody went to get him. Myrna, I can't just sit on my hands until the bastard who left him gets confirmed."

"You can."

"Why the hell should I?"

Myrna put down her fork and looked Brad directly in the eye. "I understand how you feel. But I don't care what that schmuck Ames said. There are other issues here."

"Like?"

"Like you don't let Joe Flint sandbag Frank Cabot in a moment of general hysteria with something he did long ago under lawful instruction."

"No matter what it was?"

"No matter what it was," said Myrna. "Somebody knows something about every man appointed to a big job in this town. You want people lining up at George Tater's door every time a little voice whispers in their ear?"

Who are you going to tell? Ames had asked, cocking his head back with a twist of a smile, as if he already knew the answer.

"Maybe sometimes," Brad said, "there's no other way."

There was a moment of silence after Morrissey concluded his briefing, broken only by the faint drumroll of Frank Cabot's fingers on the polished surface of the mahogany desk that he had increasing reason to fear would never be his. Cabot could recognize a noose when he felt one, and he sensed it tightening now.

Leo Weissberg said nothing.

"Can you explain," Cabot asked Morrissey, "how young Lochinvar managed to arrange this?"

"I think he just called up, sir. These debriefings are scheduled by the warden's deputy, and Rashevsky set up a lot of them at one time. She probably told Cameron the drill. All he had to do was say CIA and show his badge at the gate."

"I suppose anybody could call up," said Cabot. "The cleaning lady, say—"

"I don't know about the cleaning lady, sir, I think—" He was stopped by Cabot's frigid stare.

"It's done now," said Cabot. "Do we know what Ames said? Was anyone at the prison listening in?"

"They're not allowed to," said Morrissey. "We send people up there all the time. We've asked Ames about every Agency screwup in the last fifteen years. We don't want a lot of prison guards knowing all that stuff."

"Where is he now?"

"We don't know," said Morrissey. "He's not at his desk." Morrissey looked helpless.

"What about Rashevsky?" asked Cabot. "Is she at home, or is she trotting up to the Hill with young Lochinvar to call upon Senator MacLaverty?"

"We can find out," said Morrissey.

"Well, please do find out—now, before any more damage is done. This Agency is heading for a public battering like we haven't seen since the Ames case broke. It was a miracle we survived that, but frankly I think we're fresh out of miracles. So get those two back under control. I'm not going to tell you how. Just do it."

"Yessir," said Morrissey. He got up and backed toward the door. "We'll do everything we can, sir."

Cabot stared after him.

When the door closed Cabot turned to Weissberg. "This is slipping badly, Leo. I can't seem to get ahead of the story."

"The story is the problem."

"What do you mean?"

"We're all in the dark. You're pretending this isn't happening. I've worked for you for twenty years, and I have never tried to second-guess you or told stories out of school or tried to go over your head. But, Frank—you haven't really explained what's happening here since day one. If you want me to go on running interference, you've got to tell me what I'm likely to find blocking the way."

"Or?"

"Or I can't help. And I doubt if anyone else can either."

Cabot got up and walked to the window. He gazed out for a moment at the dead lawn, the bare trees, a bus pulling up to the stop across from the building's main entrance. At the edge of the woods beyond, Cabot could see a couple of crows fighting over something.

"It's simple at the core," said Cabot, still looking out the window. "But it's full of potential for trouble. I've been holding back because deciding what to say is my problem, not yours." But Cabot knew the moment had come, and without waiting he began to explain.

He said he had no way of knowing whether the Russians were holding an American prisoner in July 1977 or not. It was Otis Jones, speaking for the president, who sent Cabot to Moscow, where his friend Kondrashov said he would find out. A week later Kondrashov told him it was true; the U.S.S.R. had been holding an American prisoner.

"I know the Israeli report says Kondrashov told me he was alive," said Cabot, "but that's not the way I remember it. What I remember is being told he had died of typhus. Once the White House heard that, it was decided to forget the whole thing."

"All right," said Weissberg. "Why not just say that?"

"It's touchy," said Cabot. "Exactly what Jones and the president said to each other I don't know, but Jones told me they were afraid the Russians were lying. Maybe Dyer *hadn't* been killed by typhus. Maybe he had been . . . removed."

"That *is* touchy," said Weissberg.

"How could we know exactly when or how he died? If we said anything the hawks would start shouting, the Soviets would stonewall, the arms race would go into full gear, and the president would be blamed for going to Moscow hat in hand instead of raising holy hell from the beginning."

"Some presidents would have raised hell," said Weissberg.

"Maybe. But what good would it have done? We had no proof, just a story. Why would the Soviets confess? It was a choice of silence or a really ugly little fight. We were trapped, Leo. Dead, he was easy to bury. And as you well know, once you embark on a policy of silence, it's easy to continue."

Standing at the window, watching the edge of the woods seven stories below, Cabot watched a third crow join the other two. They went at each other, then jumped back with wings flapping. Cabot could see now that they were fighting over the remains of a rabbit.

"None of this was easy," Cabot continued. "The White House had to weigh the feelings of the MIA's family against the cost of telling all. Administration policy on arms control was hanging on the decision. Nobody was proud of handling it the way we did."

"It's not pretty," said Weissberg.

"The president didn't want this coming back to haunt him." Cabot turned to look at his friend. "You see why I've been holding back?"

"I do. But you can't sit on it any longer, Frank. You're going to have to tell the Senate what you've told me."

"Maybe," said Cabot. "It depends on what questions they ask."

Kitty was in a chair by the window reading when Jenny arrived. She marked her place with a postcard and closed the book.

"That's a huge book," said Jenny. "What are you reading?"

"*Anna Karenina,*" said Kitty. "A friend told me it was even better than I remembered, and she's right. When I get into a book I like, I want it to go on forever."

They chatted for a moment while Jenny wondered what her aunt wanted to talk about.

"What I wanted to tell you," Kitty began at last, "was something Frank mentioned. He says somebody at the Agency told him you'd been out to dinner with George Tater. I don't know how they find out these things. I don't ask, and if I did ask Frank wouldn't tell me.

"But Jenny darling, if they say something happened it probably did; the Agency has eyes everywhere. So I just want to caution you—assuming they're right. This is a small town, you're the niece of the next director of the CIA if all goes well, and I hate to think what might happen if some of the journalists in this town learned you've been seeing George Tater, since he is, after all, doing everything in his power to destroy Frank's public reputation."

Kitty had dragged out this declaration of concern more than long enough to let Jenny catch her breath.

"They're right," said Jenny, when Kitty paused at last. "I *have* seen Tater and I know it's not smart. You can tell Uncle Frank he doesn't need to worry about it anymore."

They talked about other things for another ten minutes. "You should read this book," Kitty said, when Jenny got up to leave. "It's amazing what trouble people make for themselves."

. . .

Stanley Kiddle knew when to talk and when to keep his peace, and he now sat patiently in the straight-backed leather-covered chair in front of Otis Jones's desk while Jones thoughtfully kissed the tips of his fingers in the manner of a medieval saint at prayer. His full head of brilliant white hair was almost like a halo, but his brow was furrowed and Kiddle knew the old man was not pleased.

Morrissey had called Beaufort in midmorning. Without delay, Beaufort walked down the hall to Kiddle's office to pass on the news, and Kiddle in turn took it to Otis Jones, who listened in silence. "Does Ames know what really happened?" Kiddle asked.

"I think it very likely he does," said Jones. "Enough, at any rate, to make life difficult."

"Who's going to believe Aldrich Ames?" Kiddle asked. "He's got the reputation of a suck-egg dog."

"Americans are quick to think ill of their country," said Jones. "The media have been feeding us horror stories for thirty years. People will believe anything."

"Can we put together a plausible counterstory?" asked Kiddle.

At that point Jones had placed his hands in the position of prayer, kissed the tips of his fingers, and begun to think. . . .

After a time he said, "I haven't been feeling quite right lately. I have no appetite. I don't sleep well. My pulse is weak. Sometimes I feel faint. I don't think this is just the winding down of old age, I think it may be something I shouldn't ignore. . . .

"I think," Otis Jones said, his mind made up, "this would be a good time to check into the Mayo Clinic for a couple of weeks—let the doctors look me over, get some rest. Will you speak to my secretary and take care of it, Stanley? Will you let the partners know? Tell them not to be unduly alarmed; these things happen. Please say I would have spoken to them myself, but I didn't feel quite up to it. Will you field any questions that come up over the next couple of weeks? You know what to say.

"Ask Mary to call the Cosmos and say I won't be in for lunch today. As long as I'm going," said Otis Jones, "I think I'll go this afternoon."

Jenny liked going to the K Street Health Center in the middle of the afternoon. The lunch crowd had moved on, there was no wait for the machines, she didn't see a lot of people she knew, the guys with the wet hair look who came to stare at bodies had gone back to work, and Jenny could settle in for as long as she liked and really work up a sweat. She had a regular routine: Stairmaster, Nautilus for legs and abs, the fly for pecs and the teres muscles just below her shoulder blades. She worked steadily, getting her heart rate up to 120 and then keeping it there until the sudden hot prickly announcement of sweat. She didn't sweat easily. She had to work like hell, but when the sweat came and the endorphins began to crank and her heart was pounding and her back and pectoral muscles were like powerful rubber bands it seemed to Jenny that she could work out forever, keep her body forever, live forever.

When Meg was free she liked to come too, but it wasn't the workout she wanted, it was the hour with her friend. Jenny was a talker, Meg was a listener. Jenny was in condition, Meg was not. They were seated side by side on fly machines, backs straight, forearms up, sweeping the paddles in across the front of the chest and letting them back out—slow and steady at twenty beats a minute. Jenny's muscles took hard form, rippling across her back. Meg's muscles looked like something stirring beneath the bedcovers.

"I can't do this anymore," said Jenny. "Tater, I mean."

"It always sounded complicated to me," said Meg, beginning to breathe heavily.

"First I kidded myself I was just going to explain what a wonderful person my Uncle Frank is."

"He didn't buy that?"

"No, he did buy it. He said he'd always liked Frank, and the funny thing is I believe him. Then I kidded myself I'd never tell him any secrets."

"You don't know any secrets."

"That's what I thought. But then Frank told me something that really *is* secret. At least I haven't read it anywhere."

"A big secret?" Meg was now panting heavily, and her words came out with difficulty.

"Pretty good-sized," said Jenny. "He told me he went to Russia, asked about the American prisoner, and never said anything about it under direct personal instructions from the president."

"And?" panted Meg.

"I thought, I can't tell Tater this. Then I thought, If Tater knows it was for the president, maybe he'll back off Uncle Frank. So I told him."

"And?"

"I just felt sick. I woke up the next morning and I thought, How could I have done that?"

Meg stopped pumping. She was panting heavily. She wiped her brow and her neck with her towel. Jenny began to pump faster, fists clenched, arms up, back and neck tense—pulling the paddles in, letting them out—thirty beats a minute, then forty, then fifty. Meg watched. Jenny's whole body glistened and her muscles stood out in glowing relief—legs, back, arms, neck. The sweat was running, her cheeks glowed pink, then white. Heat seemed to be rising off her.

Finally Jenny stopped, lowered her head, dropped her arms to her sides, and shook them weakly. She was quivering with exhaustion.

"You've told Tater it's over?" asked Meg. "Or you're going to?"

"I'm going to. As soon as I get a chance."

"I never understood Tater," said Meg, "but Brad I kind of like."

"Off limits," said Jenny. "I don't want you taking up with my ex."

"It's my business to know things," said George Tater to the tense voice on the phone. "Your role in this MIA mess is not exactly a secret around town. Of course I know who you are."

"Can we talk?" Brad asked.

"We can," said Tater, "but not this minute. How long will it take you to meet me in front of the Mayflower?"

Tater had played secret agent two or three times over the years and still couldn't say for sure if it had been really necessary. But if young Cameron was right about *his* phone being tapped, the Agency might be listening in on Tater too, and it was Tater's philosophy generally to do what he could to make life tough for the bastards, whoever they might be. So he hailed a cab, picked up Cameron in front of the Mayflower, told the driver to pull over at Dupont Circle, took the Metro to Gallery Place, and then led Brad to the National Portrait Gallery, where they found a spot to talk on the landing of the main staircase with a good view up and down. Attendance was light. With the exception of one class of thirteen-year-old girls crowding up the wide staircase in their white blouses and blue skirts, Tater and Cameron had the place pretty much to themselves.

"I can't say I know much about you as an individual," explained Tater, "but I knew it was somebody in-house digging up the Ames stuff, and I heard your name from two or three people, and they told me about the Israeli angle, and the FBI's interest, and what-have-you. It's tough to hide something, once people start looking in the right place.

"Of course," Tater added, "I'm very happy to talk to you, but, out of curiosity, why do you want to talk to me?"

"I've promised a friend I wouldn't testify at the hearings," said Cameron.

"The friend doesn't care if I tell the world?" Tater asked.

"I only made one promise," said Cameron.

"All right," said Tater. "I won't quibble. What have you got?"

Tater took no notes but just listened carefully. He could see what Jenny liked about this earnest young man who looked so serious and told his story with such evident feeling. It would be easy to make fun of someone so torn about doing the right thing. But Cameron certainly knew the story backwards and forwards; he was practically dictating Tater's piece, if he chose to write it. Tater felt a certain kinship to the youth, whose view of the whole episode closely matched Tater's own.

But at the same time Cameron was a little taller than Tater, his shoulders were broader, he held himself like a man in the peak of physical condition, no acne scars pocked his cheeks, devotion was natural to him, he was as lacking in calculation as a child, and he was visibly twenty years younger. George Tater was listening to a man he knew would win the girl every time, and it irritated him.

"Okay, okay," Tater interrupted. "I get the picture. But how did Ames know all this? You say Cabot left no record, and sure as hell Otis Jones didn't write it up. Who told Ames so he could tell the Russians—and now you?"

Brad explained that once the Russians were satisfied Kondrashov had been telling the truth—that Cabot hadn't been trying to recruit him but had only wanted a quiet back-channels way to check out Golenpolsky's story—the KGB through Vlad in Rome had posed a second question. Did Agency officials in Langley know what Cabot had come to say at the second meeting—as described by Kondrashov?

"They were back and forth on this for quite a while," said Brad. "But in the end it was obvious that everybody on the American side accepted Cabot's version—he was just trying to check out Golenpolsky's story. And when the CIA learned the American was dead, that was the end of it."

"So the Russians knew what happened," said Tater, "but we didn't."

"We didn't and we still don't," said Cameron.

"It's not a pretty story."

"I know, but I can't change that."

"And you want me to print this?"

"I think Dyer's family has a right to know what happened to him."

"Even if it ends Cabot's career?"

"I can't control that," said Cameron.

"Just for argument's sake," said Tater, "why do this? What difference does it make? It was a long time ago, and besides, the wench is dead."

"That's what everybody tells me. But we expect our country to act one way, and if it doesn't, and if we know it doesn't, and if we don't say what we know—it's like we don't care."

"Are you sure you're in the right business?" asked Tater.

"I used to think so."

For a long moment Tater looked at Cameron, whose face was tense and unhappy. It was clear the young man disliked what he was doing. He was breaking every law, regulation, and accepted rule of ethics in the profession of intelligence by telling secrets to an unauthorized person, but even worse—he was leaking the secrets to a reporter. Below that, Tater well knew, no intelligence officer believed it possible to sink. Tater in his career had been on the receiving end of many a leak, but in almost every case the leaker was either under official instruction or had suffered some wound to his self-esteem and was seeking revenge. This young man, it seemed obvious, was prompted by a simple need to tell the truth.

Before him Tater saw two clear choices. He could break the story, destroy Cabot's chance of becoming DCI, and turn Jenny against him forever. Or he could allow young Cameron to do the dirty work.

It took only a moment to decide.

"I don't think I can help you out here," Tater said. "It's a great story, and I'd love to write it. But I can't make all these charges with nothing to back me up. You're the one who talked to Ames and knows the case. So if you want the world to know, I'm afraid you've got only one choice—to march into that hearing room on Monday and raise your right hand."

"I'm not sure what really happened," said Leo Weissberg, "but what I do know doesn't sound good."

"Awful," said Myrna. "I wouldn't let Brad fill in the gory details. But I'm surprised Cabot wouldn't tell *you*. He needs you."

"Oh, he told me a story that was plausible enough," said Weissberg.

They were facing each other across the Formica table of a booth in a coffee shop. As one of her old friends, he had come to warn her to step carefully if she wanted to keep her contract work.

"But Cabot's like a lot of people in this town," Weissberg continued. "He thinks he's got a poker face, but when he's telling you the truth he looks you in the eye, and when he's lying he looks out the window."

Cabot was getting ready to leave for the day when his secretary buzzed to say that Morrissey of Security wanted to see him. The news was not good.

George Tater had been called in midafternoon by someone whose voice was almost certainly that of Bradford Cameron. They arranged to meet in front of the Mayflower, but Security had been instructed by Mr. Weissberg under no circumstances to place Tater under a full-scale watch procedure. So unfortunately Morrissey could not report whether Tater really did meet up with Cameron and what they might have said to each other.

Cabot took this news with him out of the building to the car waiting to drive him to the hospital. He decided things were still manageable. Tater's scoop would get a huge headline in the *Times,* but the second-day story would be weak because there was no one to confirm. He felt the version of events he had cooked up for Weissberg would stand up; it fit most of the facts, it would force Otis Jones to take Cabot's side in any public pissing match, it came under the protective authority of the White House. And who was in a position to say otherwise?

Thus reassured, Cabot greeted Kitty with a kiss and answered her habitual question by saying, "I had a pretty good day really—I think this is all going to work out."

Red meat, cut thick and cooked rare, was George Tater's favorite dish, and the Palm on 19th was his favorite place to get it. When the mood was on him, nothing would satisfy but a Delmonico steak and a bottle of Hermitage ten or twelve years old. Tater's doctor had instructed him to cut back on the meat, and the Hermitage took a big bite out of anyone's pocket money, so Tater did not indulge often—just when he was about to unveil a big story or go to bed with a beautiful woman. On this night, with a carefully written piece on the role of President Jimmy Carter in the Cabot-MIA story scheduled to appear momentarily on the *New York Times* web site and with Jenny Moore seated across the table, fingering the pearl necklace at her creamy throat with one hand and swirling her glass of wine slowly with the other, George Tater felt entitled.

Tater had written this story with great care. He did not state as a fact that the president had done anything one way or the other. He just quoted anonymous CIA sources who said that the White House had been immediately informed about the Israeli report of an American MIA held in Russia; that the meeting with Kondrashov had been requested by the White House, that the White House had been informed of the result, and that the White House had requested the CIA to keep what it knew to itself and to share no information with the Congress or the State Department. These bare facts raised many new questions and left Frank Cabot, the retired president, and the (so far) anonymous Brad Cameron, if he had the courage to go public, to answer them.

"Not bad," said Morrie Bloom, at Tater's summary of what to expect. "That'll thicken the stew."

Tater loved it when his targets had to scramble to explain, but that wasn't what he was thinking about now. He was looking at Jenny with a warm physical desire that had been simmering since his meeting with Cameron in midafternoon, and he was thinking for the first time in many years that this was different. Tater felt something for this lively young woman that was still there in the morning. He wanted to keep her nearby for a while. He didn't spell out his desires to himself any more specifically than that, and he had an uneasy feeling his luck would not hold.

"I've got a friend," Jenny was saying, "who says I'm crazy to be seeing you."

"What do you tell her?"

"I agree."

"But you're here."

"I know. For the moment."

"Well, I can tell you this," said Tater. "I hope the moment lasts."

At that moment Jenny's eyes lifted, and Tater turned to find Faith Osborne coming down the room with Richard Kramer in tow. He cursed silently but said "Hello, Faith" and then introduced Jennifer Moore by name alone and prayed Faith would not pick up on who she was or mention if it she did. "You've been missing from the Style section," said Tater. "What's up?"

Faith looked at Jenny. "He hates my work."

"Not hate," said Tater, also addressing Jenny. "I just take a different approach."

"Right," said Faith. " 'Who's the villain in this picture?' "

"Whereas Faith," said Tater, "wants to know who's the victim?"

"You two have discussed this before," said Jenny.

"I stopped to say thanks," said Faith. "You weren't chasing Dyer's family so I did. He's got a sister still living in Maryland, and I spent a couple of days with her. You can read all about it in the bulldog edition."

"Any hard news?" asked Tater.

"Not unless you call thirty years of agony hard news."

"Well . . ."

"He's right," said Faith to Jenny. "Agony isn't hard news. But it's my kind of story. So"—she turned to Tater—"thanks."

When they were alone again, Tater said, "There have been maybe three serious women in my life. I was married to the first for a year. Faith Osborne was the second." He took a thoughtful taste of wine. "I'm counting on third time lucky," he said.

Jenny seemed elusive through the rest of dinner, and Tater was much relieved when she agreed, after a moment's hesitation, to go home with him. He picked up a copy of the early edition of *The Washington Post* on the way but resisted the temptation to scan the headlines or turn to Faith's story and just dropped the paper on the coffee table in the living room.

When Tater asked what Jenny would like, she said "Nothing." He put his hand on her cheek, then moved to her ear and traced it with a finger. He loved the feel of the place where her hair began. He loved the feel of her skin under his fingers. He loved the way she smelled. "You're a beautiful woman," said Tater, "and I'm a lucky man."

"Luck doesn't explain it," said Jenny.

He kissed her and then began to undress her, slowly, one button at a time. After a moment he felt her fingers on his neck, then her nails running gently down his back. In bed Tater felt the whole wonderful naked length of her against him and murmured with pleasure. Her fingers were cool. Tater wished he were thirty and had all the time in the world. They slipped together and Jenny began to pant. He loved the warmth of her breathing on his ear. He pressed in as deeply as he could, gathered her tightly in his arms, and rolled over onto his back so Jenny would be on top. His fingers gripped deep into her buttocks and she arched her back and cried out—

And then she really cried out. "*Stop!* Oh, God. . . ."

Tater froze. "What's the matter?"

"My back . . . *my back* . . . I've done something to my back. Don't move. Oh, God."

"Your back?"

"I must have pulled a muscle. Help me lie flat."

They separated. Tater eased her down onto her back. "It's in spasm," she said. Her voice was strained. "God, it hurts. I must have done it at the gym, I can't move. Don't touch me. Maybe if I just rest. I'm sorry. . . ."

"It's okay," said Tater. "Let me get you some aspirin. Lie still. Don't move. You can get help in the morning. I have the name of a good shiatsu therapist. She can do miracles with backs."

Jenny groaned. "Can she do deep-tissue work?"

"She specializes in deep-tissue work," said Tater.

Soon Jenny's breathing slowed. Tater got out of bed gently, put on a robe, went into the kitchen, poured himself two fingers of twenty-five-year-old single-malt scotch whisky, and turned to Faith Osborne's story in the *Post.* It was pretty much what Tater expected, a heartrending account of lonely waiting, et cetera.

When he had read through to the end Tater thought to himself, Wrong as usual. There *is* hard news: The sister is ready to testify. Frank Cabot is not going to enjoy that.

In the morning Jenny dressed slowly and carefully. She said yes to orange juice, no to coffee. At the door she said, "George. I can't do this anymore. I wanted to tell you last night."

"I know," said Tater. He looked at the ground, then back at her face. "I'm trying to think of a joke," he said.

43

Dean Cutter was sick of Russell's plan to turn the world upside down. The anger had gone away; he wanted to get his life back on track, and that meant parting company with the ex-marine for good. But Russell was sticking close. Except for the therapy session, he never left Cutter's side, he was sleeping every night on Cutter's couch, and he was a very light sleeper. If Cutter got up for a pee or to get a drink in the night Russell would stir on the couch and say "Hey, man" or "What's up?" just to let Cutter know he was like a cat, hard to sneak by.

So Cutter waited and said little. He listened to Russell work out the details: How they would get the gun into the building, what door Cabot would use to enter and leave the hearing room, where Cutter would stand, where Russell would stand. It was the custom at the end of a hearing for witnesses to pause outside the hearing room and speak to reporters. If it was a big deal the media would be there in strength, lots of television cameras and lights, reporters, people crowding in to listen, noisy as a street fight. Everybody would be paying attention to Frank Cabot, shouting questions at him, trying to take his picture, elbowing for vantage. Nobody would be paying attention to Dean.

"You got any questions about this?" Russell asked.

"No. I'm listening. I think it might work."

"Might work?" said Russell. "This plan is perfect. Tomorrow we start Phase One of Operation Righteous Anger."

Cutter hated that wrath-of-God talk. He was just waiting for his moment to say *Adiós, amigo.*

Phase One was getting the gun inside. Russell disassembled the .380 Beretta. He taped the barrel to the inside of his thigh, right next to one of the steel struts of his leg brace. "I'm taking the risks here," he said. "You watch."

Cutter hoped the guards would nail him but they didn't. The brace set off the alarms, but when the guards patted him down they didn't find the gun barrel taped to his thigh. "Vietnam," said Russell. "Glad to serve my country."

So the guards waved Russell through with the too-big smiles that the sound give the crippled. Inside, Russell led Cutter to the men's room just down the hall from the huge double mahogany doors of the hearing room. While Cutter stood at a urinal near the door, Russell entered a stall, removed the gun barrel, and taped it to the back of a stool. "Two more trips will do it," he said. "Once the gun's inside we're halfway home. Monday we snap it together and get on the evening news."

Cutter made a pretense of enthusiasm. He asked interested questions. "Where did you get the stun grenade? How are you going to time it to go off just after I shoot? How are we going to keep from being blinded?"

Russell had answers for everything. He'd put a lot of thought into this plan. Cutter, however, did not intend to be in the District when the sun came up Monday morning. He was a different man. Shooting that medic seemed to have drained him of two lifetimes' worth of anger. He didn't give a rat's ass if they confirmed Frank Cabot as pope. As soon as he read that story in Tuesday's paper he started thinking about Stacy Dyer. He was pretty sure she would remember him. Back when they were kids—Stacy was a couple of years older—her bike had flipped on a rock and she split her lip on the curb. It was right in front of Dean's house; he saw it and came out with a dish towel and held it to her bleeding lip. He recalled this moment with great clarity. She had placed her hand over his, moaning and rocking with pain. "You're my hero," she said, when she got up. She had a scar after that, a little crooked white line that jagged up from her lip. When she passed him in the halls at school she said, "Hey, hero." Just thinking about Stacy almost brought tears to his eyes.

At group Wednesday night Cutter had said he knew a girl who could change everything in his life, but one of the men said, "Hey, come on, that's the pot talking."

"The pot talking?"

"Yeah," said the guy. "When you're on top of the world it's the pot, and when you want to kill yourself it's the pot."

"Do you think he might have a point?" Lisa Benson had asked.

Hell, no, he did not think that asshole had a point. He knew what he thought and he knew what he felt, and he knew Stacy Dyer was the kind of woman who could make all the difference. So that night after group Cutter found her number in the phone book. He thought about dialing the number as he lay on the bed in the dark, trying to get comfortable. The groin area was acting up, and despite his daily dose of vitamin E and his utter avoidance of animal products of every kind Cutter was pretty sure the plum-sized thing was slightly larger. He wondered if it wasn't maybe time to talk to a doctor about it.

"You smoking dope in there?" called Russell from the living room. He was watching TV.

"You want a hit?" Dean called back.

Russell came to the door. "You should give that up," he said. "You'll get cancer of the testicles."

"What are you saying?"

"I'm saying I know two vets who got cancer of the testicles, and they both smoked dope, all day every day. Dope is death, man."

Cutter's mind was working. His testicles were fine. It was the lump in his groin that was killing him. "Don't talk to me about Mr. C," he said. "I don't let Mr. C in my life."

"Go ahead," said Russell, "kill yourself. Just don't do it before Monday."

Cutter swept all that right out of his mind. He was feeling pretty good. He had had it up to here with Russell. He was going to get his license back, he was going to quit smoking dope, he was leaving the District and going back to Accokeek to hook up with Stacy Dyer. The crazy part of his life was over. He tried to think of the words he would say when she came to the phone.

All these years we've both been thinking about Jason, Cutter would say, and *I've been thinking about you too, Stacy.*

It was true in a way. He'd been involved with plenty of women, but even with Cheryl he often found himself thinking about Stacy, wondering if she had changed.

So he called.

"Who you dialing?" said Russell from the next room.

"I'm calling a friend," said Cutter. "It's my house. It's my phone. Do you mind?

"Stacy Dyer," said Cutter when a voice said hello.

"This is Stacy."

"Hey, it's good to hear your voice. It's Dean."

"Who?"

"Dean." He lowered his voice. "Dean Cutter. I used to live down the street. You remember the time you fell off your bike?"

"What?"

"When you cut your lip? I was there, remember? With the towel? I knew Jason. I've been thinking about you and Jason—what those bastards in the government did. Thinking about you. . . ."

"Why are you whispering? I can't hear you. What about Jason?"

"There's a guy in the next room—he'd kill me if he knew I was talking to you."

"There's a guy what?"

"Russell. He's like—at war with the government. I'm going to be out there. I want to see you."

"What war? The Vietnam war?"

"I've been thinking about you. I want to see you. I'll call again when I'm alone."

But Russell wouldn't leave him alone. He stuck close all day Thursday, and Cutter made up his mind to disappear Friday morning when they went out for breakfast. He'd checked out the diner. There was a back door near the men's room. It would be easy. He had his plans worked out and was ready to get up and start back when Russell suddenly slapped down the paper on the countertop Friday morning and said, "You asshole! Is that who you were calling?"

"What are you talking about?"

"Read this. Tell me this isn't you."

His face was red with anger. His neck seemed to be swelling.

Cutter looked at the paper. The story seemed to cover the whole page. There were two or three photos. He flipped the paper back to the front page, looking for the headline.

"I KNEW THEY WERE HIDING SOMETHING":
MIA'S SISTER TELLS OF 30-YEAR WAIT

"I don't get it," said Cutter. "What's the problem?"

Russell opened the paper again and tapped the page. "There," he said. "That's the problem."

Cutter read.

"I've had floods of calls in the last couple of days," said Ms. Dyer, who has resumed her maiden name. "Old friends, kids I went to school with, the priest who confirmed Jason and me, people from work."

But not all the attention is welcome. Reporters, including this one, have been camping on her doorstep, and some of the phone calls have come from cranks.

"A couple of nights ago I got a call from a weirdo who said the government was trying to kill him," said Ms. Dyer. "He said he was being watched, he knew Jason in the war maybe, the government was watching me, he was whispering. He knew something about Jason.

"I tried to get his name. I thought maybe I knew him. Jason had some friends who were a little wild, you know? Dean something, something Dean. Rusty maybe? I couldn't get it. I certainly never heard of him. He was whispering. He said he'd call back; now I'm afraid to pick up the phone. It was creepy."

"Dean something," said Russell. "Why not call the FBI? Help 'em out. What's the matter with you?"

"We used to be friends. I wanted to talk to her."

"You wanted to talk to her," said Russell. "Let's ask her to meet us on Monday, what do you say? She can be the shooter."

"Okay, okay, you don't have to shout."

"Are you with the program? Because if you're getting cold feet the guys in Michigan are going to want to know. Are you in this, yes or no?"

"I told you I'm in."

"Can we trust you, yes or no?"

"Yes."

"All right," said Russell. "Then let's practice a little elementary security, okay? Till Monday? After that you can go play in traffic. Are you reading me?"

Cutter told Russell not to worry, but he had made up his mind about one thing: He wasn't going into the Senate Building on Monday morning to shoot some man he didn't know. Russell could just find somebody else because Cutter was going to miss that party, he had made up his mind, and one way or another he was going to make Stacy Dyer understand who he was and what he felt about her. All he needed was ten minutes to say what was in his heart.

44

Michael Vose, the assistant majority counsel of the Senate Select Committee on Intelligence, stood just inside the main door at the corner of Constitution and Delaware a few minutes before 8 a.m. on Monday morning, March 18, peering expectantly at all those who entered.

"Thank you so much for coming, Mr. Cameron," he said, stepping forward and taking Brad's hand. "I'm Michael Vose and this is my assistant, Howard Chenery." Beside him was a short man with a moon face, slicked-down hair, and a bow tie.

In a voice of startling depth and richness, the moon-faced man said, "Very pleased to meet you."

"You've seen the *Times*?" Vose asked. "You aren't named, but Tater hints at the testimony. We're mystified. It didn't come from us. We hoped for a complete surprise.

"The senator is waiting for us upstairs," Vose continued. "He has a million things to do before the hearings convene, but he put everything on hold to have a chance to thank you in person for contacting us."

Vose led the way up stairways and down hallways to a small inner room, comfortably appointed, where a man sat on the edge of a couch with four or five newspapers spread out before him on a coffee table.

Brad saw a broad Irish face, inflamed on the cheeks; thick hair turning from strawberry blond to gray, a neck swelling out over a shirt collar, broad shoulders, eyes a kind of smoky blue with a look of triumph. He looked up.

"These reporters," he said with contempt. "Do they even read the newspapers? Have they failed to note Harry Hawkins will not be chairman of these proceedings? Listen to this."

He began to declaim: " 'Despite still unanswered questions about his handling of a controversial MIA case in the nineteen seventies, a majority of the committee likes and trusts Frank Cabot, and his confirmation'—get this!—'his confirmation is virtually assured.' "

He snorted with disgust and got up to shake hands. "Brian MacLaverty," he said. "Very good of you to come. I'd love to spend the morning with you, but I can't stay long. I just want to ask maybe one or two questions, if you don't mind. Mike and Howard will take down the rest.

"May I say one thing first, Mr. Cameron? I admire your integrity in coming forward. Your colleagues all seem to suffer from short-term memory loss: 'If I can't prove it with a piece of paper it didn't happen.' So I'm very, very grateful. It's an inspiration to meet a man who doesn't think twice about putting aside all thoughts of personal loyalty and career advancement because he wants to tell the truth."

Senator MacLaverty's questions, when he finally got to them, seemed almost an afterthought. "Mr. Cameron," he asked, hesitating at the door, "are you currently employed by the CIA? Are you the subject of any disciplinary proceedings? Has your security clearance ever been lifted? Do you have a personal grievance of any kind against Frank Cabot?"

The senator seemed satisfied with Brad's somewhat halting answers. As the door closed behind him, Howard Chenery, the moon-faced assistant, explained to Brad that they needed to prepare for the inevitable questions and placed a tape recorder on the coffee table. For the first time Brad realized that his life was about to change forever.

"Mr. Cameron, if I may," the assistant began. "Have you ever been convicted of a felony in a state or federal court?

"Have you ever been dishonorably discharged from any branch of the United States military?

"Have you ever been audited by the Internal Revenue Service?

"Have you ever been arrested for the use or possession of a controlled substance?

"Have you ever been arrested for driving while under the influence?

"Have you ever been arrested for the commission of a sexual crime?"

The questions stopped at precisely 9:30 a .m., when Howard Vose lifted his eyes from his pad (where he had scribbled seven or eight pages of detailed notes) to check the small room's television set, tuned to the Cable News Network. The screen showed many men in dark suits and a few women in bright dresses taking seats in a large room brilliantly lit with television lights.

"Would you turn CNN up a bit please?" Vose called to the guard. Then he looked at Brad and the moon-faced Chenery. "Let's watch the opening bits of this."

There was much shuffling of papers and adjusting of chairs by the sixteen senators, fifteen of whom were men. In the center of the table, the junior senator from Massachusetts, cheeks pink in the bright lights, flicked the microphone with his middle fingernail, making a loud popping sound. Aides scurried back and forth behind the imposing line of senators, who gazed out into the glare, folded their hands, and composed themselves. MacLaverty turned to the man beside him. His whisper resounded through the hall.

"Is this thing working?"

The camera cut to the witness table directly in front of the dais where the senators sat. Frank Cabot held a pen in one hand and was busy writing on a yellow legal pad as if serenely at work in his own office. He inclined to the right to present his ear to the lips of his assistant, Leo Weissberg, who scratched his nose as he spoke. Brad remembered one of the old boys at the Farm telling a class to beware of lip readers. Obviously, Weissberg had learned the lesson.

On Cabot's left was the CIA's general counsel, the walrus-shaped William Chambers, who had two bulging briefcases leaning against his chair legs and many documents piled neatly on the table in front of him. Clenched in his teeth, like a pirate's knife, Chambers held a mechanical pencil. As he riffled his papers he occasionally made a mark with the pencil and then returned it to his mouth.

The camera ranged the audience around Cabot. Numerous young men in glasses with briefcases in their laps attended older men who carried nothing. Brad recognized many faces from the halls of the Agency, half a dozen from the front pages of newspapers, one or two from standard histories of the CIA, bent and grizzled men who went back to the Agency's glory days, when even well-informed Americans knew nothing about the CIA except its name and the confirmation of a director was a mere morning's work. Cabot had called in an impressive array of national security potentates, a kind of visual endorsement of his high standing in the community of intelligence professionals. Sitting with them in the very first row, side by side, were Cabot's wife, Kitty, in a dark blue silk dress with a matching jacket, and Jenny, in something gray with a white collar. The lights caught the gold in her hair, the pearls at her throat, the dark leather bag in her lap. There was an expression of stress on Jenny's face, Brad noted, and she was sitting funny. Just then Kitty whispered something, Jenny half turned to respond—and froze, wincing. Brad could see she was in pain. But then the camera moved on.

It was odd. For the rest of the morning Brad knew exactly where Jenny was, in the row directly behind her uncle Frank, next to her aunt Kitty. Watching the proceedings he could sense what Jenny was seeing too: her uncle's back, the phalanx of senators on the dais, the bright television lights on either side, the hands of her aunt twisting a white handkerchief in her lap in the next seat. Brad knew the wince was Jenny's back. As long as he'd known her, whenever she was angry or upset she overdid it at the gym, and for the next few days—agony. In the past Brad had kneaded the teres muscle below her left shoulder blade many times. The muscle would bunch up tight as a hempen rope. "Not so hard," Jenny would say. "Not so hard."

Senator MacLaverty flicked the microphone a final time and began to speak.

"It is my privilege—my sad privilege, I have to say—to call to order this first session of hearings . . ."

The scraping of chairs ceased; voices died; the hall fell silent. MacLaverty lowered his voice.

" . . . into the nomination of Franklin S. Cabot to be Director of the Central Intelligence Agency." The senator's preamble spanned several minutes with droning generalities; then the audience noted a change in tone and began to stir. "I want to assure my colleagues," MacLaverty was saying, "that immediately following opening statements this committee will put on the record certain information that I myself learned only in the last forty-eight hours."

With this the stirring in chairs and excited whispers in the hearing room reached audible levels. Several reporters and congressional staffers bustled up the aisles to the doors. Brad watched Weissberg pose a sharp question to Cabot at the witness table, and the television camera clearly picked up Frank Cabot's lips forming his reply. The words were only too obvious; Cabot made no attempt to hide his answer.

"I have no idea."

At last Brad began to sense the enormity of what he had agreed to do.

The door to the inner room where Brad sat opened a few moments later and a tall woman stuck her head in. "Mike? I've got NBC on the line. Can they get a crew into the hearing room now?"

"No way," Vose said. "They can set up during the lunch recess."

A moment later the woman's head returned. "They're not happy."

"Too damned bad," said Vose. "But tell them not to panic. It's the afternoon session they don't want to miss."

. . .

"Mr. Chairman," said Frank Cabot, speaking firmly, "Mr. Vice Chairman, members of the committee, I am pleased to be here today."

By this time Brad was alone in the private sitting room. An assistant had gone away with the empty coffee thermos. First Chenery and then Vose had drifted off midway into an hour of droning remarks by various senators, some pleased to be introducing to the committee their good friend Frank Cabot, others troubled by the many unanswered questions in Cabot's past. But it was all curiously slack; they were wondering what MacLaverty had up his sleeve and were hedging their bets, pro and con alike, in orotund generalities.

Last to rise and leave had been the man from the capitol police, who said he needed the men's room and disappeared. It was then that Brad, finding himself alone, wondered what had happened to the high alert. Nobody in MacLaverty's office really knew a damn thing about him, and here he was unobserved in the private inner sanctum of a restricted area, free to screw with computers or plant bombs. At the Agency, any man who wandered off and left a visitor alone would get a severe reprimand, if not the boot.

For the hundredth time Brad asked himself if he was doing the right thing. It wasn't doubt about the importance of what Aldrich Ames had told him; it made him angry just to think about it. But he wondered what would happen if he got up and left. Would someone be waiting to stop him at the door? Would he be subpoenaed and hauled back?

He looked around the room. The walls were covered with photographs. In most of them Senator Hawkins was shaking the hand, or had his arm around the shoulder, of someone Brad more or less recognized. Hawkins had been young once, that was clear. And it was also clear he could deliver a hundred-watt smile, eat barbecue, clap hands while a fiddler played, wear strange hats, stand on a wooden box and point his finger at the sky, and plant himself within arm's length of presidents, popes, and movie stars. There wasn't even one picture of the junior senator from Massachusetts on the walls, but Brad was sure that wouldn't last long. How quickly things changed. Hawkins held the fate of Frank Cabot in his hands one day and was on his way to oblivion the next. Only a couple of weeks back Brad had been the Agency's boy wonder, his mother was boasting to friends beside some Florida swimming pool, there was a serious woman in his life, and he had a great job, friends who envied his prospects, and confidence in the meaning of the work he was asked to do. Before the sun went down today, all that would be gone.

Brad wondered if Frank Cabot sensed that time was short for him too.

At the witness table shown on the television screen he addressed the senators in a calm, firm voice, rarely glancing at the notes before him. "I welcome these confirmation hearings, Mr. Chairman," he said, looking at Senator MacLaverty with his usual directness, "to address the many issues I know you will raise. That is natural and proper. I will answer your questions as directly and forthrightly as I can. I hope I will still your doubts and win your support.

"I want this job, Senator. Any intelligence professional worth his salt would be thrilled to have an opportunity to shape and guide an institution that does so much for this country.

"I want to tell you a story. I came to this city thirty-five years ago, with a stint in the Air Force behind me, a degree in Russian, an appointment for an interview in a downtown Washington hotel arranged by my Russian teacher, a suit my grandfather left me that I planned to wear to the interview, and the phone number of a girl. I had no idea at the time who was looking me over, but we talked for an hour, and I can tell you, senators, that man in his quiet way led me to the mountaintop. By the time I left I would have followed him barefoot through hell.

"This man's name was John Bross, and we became close friends. Many people in this room knew and respected John Bross. He never had the honor to lead the Central Intelligence Agency, but he had a lot to do with making it what it is today.

"So my first week in Washington I got a job, and I've been working for the same outfit ever since. And when I finished training I called up the girl. We went out, and six months later I put on my grandfather's suit again for our wedding. The job was everything I wanted and so was the girl. She's sitting behind me today."

Cabot turned in his seat to present his wife with a gesture of his hand. She smiled in the bright television lights and nodded slightly. Beside her, Brad noticed, Jenny's eyes were closed and her mouth was grimly set.

"And I want you to know," Cabot continued, turning back to the senators, "that I appear here today also wearing my grandfather's suit."

Unlike the other senators, MacLaverty only smiled faintly, but the room rippled with friendly laughter.

Cabot took hold of his lapel. "Made in Cincinnati, Ohio. Nineteen hundred and two. Good Republican cloth." More laughter.

"Someday, Senator," Cabot said, "I expect to be buried in this suit." There was an artful pause. "I know what some of you must be thinking."

MacLaverty raised a quizzical eyebrow.

"You're thinking," Cabot said, "*Why not today?*"

General laughter.

"But, Senator," Cabot went on, "every story has two sides. And when you've heard mine, I hope you and your colleagues will decide to let me live."

A strange sound seemed to spread through the hearing room, a sound—almost a sigh—of assent: Cabot had struck the right note. No one was really sure, anymore, that MacLaverty could launch a killing blow. Brad was impressed. Jenny's uncle was a fighter.

Cabot spoke for thirty minutes, recounting his career, some of the mistakes he had made, one or two of the things he felt he had got right, his conception of the job he was being asked to perform. Early on he cited the tragic case of Sergeant Jason Dyer, which had been made so much of by the papers. He said he knew he would be asked about that, and when the time came he would give a full and complete answer—grateful for the opportunity at last to express the pain of having come so close to saving the life of a fellow American, only to have him slip away. Cabot wished he could have said something years ago, but when a man gave his promise to keep something quiet he ought to take it seriously. He *had* taken it seriously. When the committee fully understood the whole story, perhaps they would understand why Cabot had held his tongue. But perhaps not. Cabot knew it could go either way. His fate was in their hands. He would trust in their judgment, and he would not complain.

But the story of Jason Dyer could wait another day. Now was the time to tell the committee members what he wanted to do as Director of Central Intelligence, if in their wisdom they voted to entrust him with this awesome job.

Midway in this stream of reassuring words a brief excitement agitated the rear of the hearing room. Brad could hear the sound of a tussle before he could see it; then the camera picked up a crowd of people by the double doors, all trying to get out to see what was happening. "Bernie," came the announcer's voice on the TV, "you're outside—what's going on out there?"

"It's nothing," said the reporter in the corridor outside, speaking into a microphone. "Just somebody trying to get in without a pass. Everything's under control."

The interruption was momentary. Cabot resumed. His defense of himself, never quite identifying the charges outstanding, was smooth, skillful, and surefooted. Brad listened carefully but, so far as he could tell, Frank Cabot never told a single lie.

"Thank you, Mr. Cabot," MacLaverty was saying, when the door to the inner room burst open, startling Brad, and a stream of people poured in: Vose and Chenery in the lead, followed by the guard, various assistants, the tall woman now hugging her folders, and two or three other people Brad hadn't yet seen. There was much excited talk, including expostulation at the shameless effrontery of Frank Cabot's harking back to Pat Nixon's Republican cloth coat.

"Do you want some lunch?" Vose asked Brad. "They'll recess in a minute or two and reconvene at two. Then I'm going to ask Cabot the setup questions."

"Setup?" said Brad.

"Get him on record before he knows what you're going to say. Get him thinking hard about perjury. And then you go on. Probably about three."

"Mike," said the tall woman, sipping a Coke. She had put down her bundle of papers at last. "What was that ruckus at the back of the room?"

"Oh," said Vose, "some retard tried to get through the metal detector carrying an ammunition clip for a pistol."

"Just the clip?" said Brad.

"It wasn't even loaded," said Vose. "He must be a Polish assassin. He brought the clip—but he forgot the pistol."

Everybody laughed.

45

"Don't tell me he's unavailable!" George Tater shouted into the phone. "I don't care if he's in surgery. Go drag him out! Blame it on me. Tell him I'm being unreasonable."

Tater made a snort of disgust and tried to get comfortable in his chair. He looked at his watch and noted the slow ticking of digital seconds. Ninety passed before the familiar voice returned.

"Mr. Tater? He says he doesn't interrupt a front-page conference for anything short of war or the death of a president. But he'll call you back when it's over, and in the meantime, quote, Do something useful, unquote."

"Well, you tell Morrie, quote, This *is* the front page, but that's okay, we'll save it for tomorrow, because who cares if everybody has the goddamned story but *The New York Times*? Unquote. I'll be in my office. Unless I decide to go out for coffee. Or take the day off."

"I'll tell him," said Bloom's assistant, who had passed on similar messages for many years.

Tater thought for a moment. His story that morning had set the stage: committee planned to call Agency witnesses to elaborate upon hitherto unexplained failure to rescue American prisoner, et cetera. Tater hadn't named Cameron, but no one on the inside could fail to see what was coming. What Tater wanted now was a strategy that would carry the story forward to a higher level. Philip Macomber on the *Post* would have the angle on the White House and welcome to it; Tater hated dealing with Peter Schleicher. Otis Jones had gone to ground at the Mayo Clinic, and there would be nothing out of him for the next week except health bulletins.

Israel? No, Tater considered the Israeli angle only a detail.

Weeping sister from Accokeek? No, squared. The Queen of Hearts and Flowers, Faith Osborne, would wring that dry.

Shock and horror from grieving mothers and kids of MIAs? No, cubed. Every paper in the United States would run a piece about the family of the local boy who never came back.

None of the obvious stories held any interest for Tater. What he wanted was something that would help drive a stake through the heart of the villain. Tater knew Cameron was going to lay out the Aldrich Ames story in sensational detail, so everybody would have that. He had watched this process often before; the sudden explosion of a long-hidden secret made everybody crazy until the storm passed. Frank Cabot was finished, that was for sure. Abraham Lincoln couldn't survive what was heading his way. But in Tater's mind Cabot wasn't the real villain. A cold and cynical careerist, possibly guilty of murder, but otherwise not a bad guy. Tater kind of liked him, and he had Jenny's feelings to worry about, too.

No, the villain of the story wasn't going to be Cabot. Whatever Cabot did, he did for somebody else. The villain, Tater decided, ought to be the Agency, the CIA itself. Tater drew up the indictment easily; hell, he had dug up half the charges in the first place. The CIA had grown like some sort of hidden tumor for more than fifty years. Scandals came and went but the Agency survived. Presidents and DCIs promised to open the files, but they remained locked. Governments were toppled, faraway peoples were sacrificed in guerrilla wars, murderers and torturers were on the Agency payroll, drug lords became protected informants, the estimators caved when the White House wanted a new spin, Congress was lied to, reputations were trashed, and maybe—who knew?—people who got seriously in the way quietly disappeared. The CIA had shrugged it all off for more than fifty years.

Pacing his office, trying to see his way forward, throwing a look at CNN on the tube from time to time for a glimpse of poor suffering Jenny—her back was obviously killing her—Tater began to conceive a grand scheme. He thought he knew how this town worked. Once those senators heard young Cameron's story there was going to be high dudgeon, followed by a feeding frenzy. Somebody or something was going to get ripped to pieces. Cabot was first in line, but his corpse would only feed the lust. So this might be just the moment to go after the jugular of the Agency itself, while everybody was in shock over the awful story.

Those who knew and admired or hated George Tater thought he had accomplished just about everything of which a journalist might dream, but Tater himself didn't feel that way. In his view he had failed utterly in two ways—he had never made a pile of money and he had never brought down a giant. He harbored feelings of envy bordering on obsession for Bob Woodward of *The Washington Post*, who had done both. But maybe this Cabot/MIA mess would be just the weapon Tater needed. He wouldn't destroy a president; Tater's ambition was bigger in its way. He wanted to break up the CIA, split it in two, separate the clandestine arm from the estimating branch. The Agency had been fighting that for years but Tater thought it was bound to happen eventually, and he had a feeling Cabot's sins might push the behemoth a little closer to splitting in half if Tater handled things right. Cabot's career was already finished. Let the rest of the media wolf pack rip the body to pieces. Tater was after larger prey.

There was Jenny again in the camera's eye, trying to get comfortable in her seat. Tater did love the way that girl looked. She didn't make a hero out of her uncle, but she stood by him. She wouldn't give a good goddamn what Tater did to the CIA, so long as he showed a little mercy to her Uncle Frank. Maybe, Tater thought, that explained his new strategy. Maybe the simple act of shifting the focus of his attack from Cabot to the Agency was as close as Tater would ever come to telling a woman he cared.

The rest followed easily enough. Jenny herself had told him where the real story was, and Tater well knew that if you want to attack a mighty institution, you need a mighty ally.

He dialed information. "What city and state?" came the voice.

"Plains, Georgia," said George Tater.

"What listing?"

"Jimmy Carter," said George Tater.

Three assistants in ascending order, plain and direct statements to each, and George Tater had the former president on the line.

"I don't like the smell of this," said Frank Cabot. He was sitting beside Leo Weissberg in an Agency car, heading for a downtown restaurant with private rooms where he might get some lunch without being stared at.

"It depends on what Cameron says," Weissberg said. Weissberg had little doubt the young man was going to be MacLaverty's surprise witness. Tater hadn't named him, but who else? Weissberg had only met Cameron once or twice but the impression was generally good—personable and earnest if maybe a little too heart-on-the-sleeve for an intelligence professional. But Cameron was obviously going to be convincing. Of that Weissberg was certain.

"Well, yes and no," said Cabot. "I'm sure Ames told him something lurid. I know Cameron. He's a Boy Scout. He wouldn't break the rules unless he thought God was telling him to go ahead."

"God?"

"Some overriding moral principle."

"Such as?"

"Such as a feeling he knew something about me it would be immoral, in his view, to keep to himself. I tried to tell him it's fatal in this town to take that sort of responsibility on yourself, and I sent God knows how many people to try to tell him the same thing."

"Rashevsky tried," said Weissberg. "She says she did her best, but he's awful stubborn."

"Who'd have guessed it," said Cabot, "from someone so eager to please. I wish personnel could devise some sort of straight-arrow test so we could screen the bastards out."

The car pulled up in front of an Italian restaurant downtown, and they were shown upstairs. Weissberg watched a diner look up as Cabot entered. It was obvious he recognized Cabot but his expression surrendered nothing: no condemnation, but no encouragement either. Cabot was very much on the edge of the precipice. Upstairs in a small room with a large table overlooking the street they ordered San Pellegrino water and veal with spinach in oil and garlic. When the waiter departed, Cabot resumed.

"I don't know what Ames knows or thinks he knows. But I'm pretty goddam sure those senators are going to be shocked and horrified, and we'll have about ten minutes to turn things around if we are going to save this nomination."

It was his skin he was talking about, but Cabot seemed perfectly objective and rational as he reasoned his way forward. Weissberg was impressed by his cool preparation for battle.

"I've been thinking: We need a counter statement that will be the truth, or some part of the truth, depending. But more important—here's my point, Leo—we need a counter *witness.*"

"Besides you," Weissberg said.

"I'll deny it all," said Cabot, "and I'll sound like I mean it. But how far will that get us? Ames told Cameron it happened one way; I say it happened a different way. No. They have a surprise witness, we need a surprise witness."

"Okay," said Weissberg.

"When we finish lunch, I'd like you to do two things, if you would."

"Of course, Frank."

"Do you know Larry Shedd? Bright young fellow in the DO. Did a tour in Switzerland. Speaks French. On the European Desk at the moment."

"I've heard the name. His father was in the Agency in the sixties, I think."

"That's him. Seen a lot of the world for a young man. Will you hunt him up and ask him to meet me in my office this evening, about six? I ought to be back by then, if I can get out of the building at all."

"All right," said Weissberg. "And the second thing?"

"Get Shedd cleared for a trip to Russia. Cash in a few favors, if you need to, and get him a visa. Jane can handle the rest of the details. No fuss. I want him to head out tonight by way of London or Paris—not direct. I want him in Moscow tomorrow as early as possible. Don't tell Shedd any of this. Just say, 'The Director wants to send you out of town for a few days.' I'll fill in the rest."

"What are you cooking up here, Frank?" Weissberg asked.

"We need someone to say it ain't so. I'm wondering if my old friend Mikhail Kondrashov might not be just the right person."

"I thought you said he was dead."

"No, Leo. I said he suffers from emphysema, which is potentially fatal. I don't believe he's actually dead."

It was silk that saved Myrna's life. Her father was a wholesale dealer in fabrics in Warsaw with a partner in Berlin, where he passed two or three months every year, usually in the summer, when school was out. So Myrna as a small girl spent summers in one of the leafy suburbs of Berlin. There was a Jewish day camp not far away where the kids swam and played team sports and learned American Indian crafts from the camp director, who was devoted to Karl May's novels about the old Indian warrior Shatterhand. When Myrna was eight, the summer before the war, she beaded a small silk purse in what she believed was an authentic Indian design. It was one of the very few things she took with her on the journey across Russia to China—that and a red silk dress, which was folded neatly inside a linen sheet and kept in the bottom drawer of her bureau.

She took it out sometimes when she was thinking about her family, and she was thinking about her family now. "In America there is justice," said her father, when Myrna left for the East. She carried with her some money and the address in New Jersey of the cousin of a cousin.

Something about the way the junior senator from Massachusetts said "There are a great many questions to be answered" reminded Myrna of what her father said about American justice. He meant that in America even the powerful had to stand before the bar and answer for their wrongs, and it seemed clear to Myrna that Frank Cabot's long immunity from public questioning was about to end. Myrna had tried to convince Brad Cameron to keep his mouth shut—not for Weissberg's sake, old friend though he was, but for Brad himself. American justice could be a rough thing, and those who turned against powerful bosses rarely got a second chance in Washington. Brad had no idea of the fury that was heading his way. The chance was good he would destroy the hopes of Frank Cabot, but only at the cost of his own.

Myrna lived in the District. She liked street life, and there was plenty up Eighteenth. She had two rooms, a bedroom and a living room/kitchen. The TV was in the bedroom, on top of the bureau, and she watched sitting in bed with a pillow behind her back. Beside her on the bed was the red silk dress. The slender girl who fit that dress was long gone. "In America," said her father, "you will wear this dress to a big family party and you will be the prettiest girl in the room."

He was a businessman, he worked hard, he prospered, he wanted the best for his children, Myrna and her younger brother, Nathan. Others dithered, but Myrna's father made up his mind the day he read in the newspaper that Hitler had reached an agreement with Stalin. "That's it," he said. He sent a telegram to a business contact in Shanghai, he got one in return, and he took Myrna to the railroad station in Warsaw with Levin, a young man from the firm. They arrived in Shanghai the day the war started, more than sixty years ago.

"Our work here will be fair and impartial," said Senator MacLaverty on CNN. Myrna knew what that meant: MacLaverty would take merciless advantage of his power as chairman to control who was allowed to speak, when, and for how long. Myrna was genuinely torn. She knew Cabot was a cold sonofabitch at heart, but he worked for the CIA and he had never done anything he was not asked to do. It was part of the job. Of course that made no difference to Brad. He felt he was standing up for somebody he had sworn to protect, and threats only made him more stubborn. He had none of the intelligence professional's instinct for the subtext of what it was all about—who wanted Cabot in power, who opposed him—the policy issues at stake. Myrna had tried to explain but he didn't get it or didn't care.

She thought Cabot made a pretty good case for himself in his opening statement, which didn't surprise her a bit.

When the hearings recessed for lunch, Myrna went to the kitchen to make tea and toast. She liked strong black tea, the kind the Russians drink. She used a lot of sugar. She buttered the toast generously, making sure to get all the corners, just as her father had always done. "You go," he had said. "I have friends in the silk business in Shanghai, and they will help you get to America."

He did have friends in the silk business, and they did help Myrna to reach America. "We will follow," said her father, "as soon as I can sell the business."

Maybe he suspected it was really goodbye. Nathan was little. Their mother was not well; she did not want to leave her house and her possessions. So maybe it wasn't foolish of her father to stay behind, but only a gamble he lost. What would her father have said, Myrna wondered, if he had been here, watching the confirmation hearings for Franklin S. Cabot and sharing Myrna's lunch of strong tea and toast? Would he, like Myrna, have tried to tell Brad there must have been good reasons for what Cabot did? Would he have said there were larger issues at stake? Would he have told Brad the fate of one man missing in Russia was not the biggest thing in the world? Would he have said, Sit tight, keep your mouth shut, it's nothing to do with you?

"You were lucky," said the woman who answered the door. The name on the tag said Manolele Reed. She was tall, straight-backed, gray-haired, skin a kind of cocoa color. "I had a cancellation about ten minutes before you called last night. Monday is usually a busy day for me. I can see you're in pain. Can you undress okay?"

Jenny said she could. The woman explained the drill. She'd leave the room for a few moments. Jenny should strip, get onto the table face down, pull up the sheet around her, make herself as comfortable as she could, take a few deep cleansing breaths, and forget the rest of her day, the things she had to do. Just put every kind of trouble and concern on the chair with her clothes and leave them there for ninety minutes.

"That'll be hard," said Jenny. "There's a lot going on in my life right now."

"Well, let it go on without you," said the woman, "until four o'clock."

Jenny did as she was told, wincing when the muscle under her left shoulder blade pulled tight. It was difficult getting the sheet up over her back but she finally managed it. She tried not to think of Brad striding down the central aisle of the hearing room to take his place in the glare of lights at the witness table. Just about now, Jenny figured; now or in a few minutes. Uncle Frank and Kitty both told her not to worry, go ahead, they understood, but Jenny felt she was letting them down. Maybe the sight of her there would have changed Brad's mind or softened what he said. But she simply could not sit through another whole session on that creaking wooden chair, and she did not want to listen to whatever Brad had decided he was compelled to say.

The door opened. The woman entered and fiddled with a tape machine. Strange otherwordly music quietly took the place of the cars outside. "How do you pronounce your name?" asked Jenny.

"Man-oh-lay-lay."

"Is it Spanish?"

"It's Hawaiian. We have a long tradition of massage. I've studied shiatsu, but what I do is a little of this and a little of that."

"Well, I need a lot of both," said Jenny. "I pulled a muscle working out, just below the left shoulder blade."

"I can see you have." The woman placed cool hands on either side of Jenny's skull. For a moment she just held Jenny's head, then gently pulled and centered it.

She placed her hands palm down on Jenny's shoulder blades and left them there. "How did you hear about me?"

"From a friend," said Jenny. "He's a reporter. For the *Times.*"

"I don't know any reporters for the *Times.*"

"He got your name from someone he met. A retired lawyer named Jones."

"Otis Jones," said Manolele. "I'm surprised he talks to reporters." She moved her hands slowly down Jenny's back, placed them on the flat of the pelvis, gently pressed. "Would I recognize the name?" she asked.

"Probably," said Jenny. She hesitated a moment, then decided what the hell. "George Tater."

"This muscle right here?" asked Manolele.

"Yes."

"Say his name again."

"George. Tater."

"Is he the only man in your life at the moment?"

"I wish he wasn't in it at all."

"But he is."

"He sure is," said Jenny.

"Well, I would say that this muscle right here tells me you are both happy and not happy about this. And it tells me you had better give your body a rest and quit working out for a while."

She began to explore the muscles under Jenny's shoulder blades with the ends of her fingers, kneading both simultaneously. "Shiatsu," said Manolele, "explores pressure points and deep tissues. Lomilomi is Hawaiian massage, and its purpose is to restore you to your true nature. You have the body of a queen, and I am going to work on these injured muscles with shiatsu and three different oils, and I am going to give you back your queen's body. And while I am doing this," Manolele continued, "I want you to tell me what you admire and love in a man. Not some particular man, George Tater or the other one. But the qualities themselves."

"How do you know there's another one?" Jenny asked.

"Something," said Manolele, "pulled this teres muscle tight as a cello string."

"I don't know where to begin," said Jenny.

"Start with the way a man talks to you."

"Well, first of all," said Jenny, "I don't want to be told things. I want to be asked things."

Jenny talked for twenty minutes and then, in the middle of a thought, fell silent. Manolele started slow and easy but gradually picked up. She used her fingers, her palms, her forearms, her elbows. All Jenny's theories about how to deal with things disappeared from her mind. She almost fell asleep. Then Manolele took Jenny's oil-slippery body in her arms, beginning with the head and shoulders, and passed right down around her back and chest and hips and legs as if Jenny were a fish being squirted through a slippery hand. When she finished, Jenny lay trembling on the table.

"Now you are queen of your body again," said Manolele. "But don't work out for a week."

46

"Not now, Morrie," said George Tater.

He was sitting in his oak tilt-back chair watching Brad Cameron on CNN. He seemed even younger than Tater remembered. A slick of sweat glistened on his upper lip, and the expression on his face kept switching from anxiety to a half smile and back again.

"We'll go into it later," said Tater.

He noted that Jenny was missing from the afternoon session, but Kitty remained impassive in her place. Next to her now was the nominee, Frank Cabot. His face was completely without expression, like a zen master who has transcended mere earthly existence. Tater admired his discipline—no twitching in his seat, no glancing around, no rubbing the sweat of his palms on his pant leg, no sneaking peeks at the now-solid bank of television cameras, no sign whatever that young Cameron's testimony posed any sort of threat to him.

"Watch the tube, Morrie," said George Tater.

His laptop was open on the table in front of him, the screen filled with notes of his morning's work on the telephone. Chenery's deep voice sounded like the voice of divine justice. MacLaverty was as alert and attentive as a judge trying a capital case. One of the senators was stirring furiously in his seat, grabbing his microphone, letting it go, leaning forward, then back. The other senators were conveying shock and horror.

"Let Weaver file the lead story on the hearing," said George Tater. "Run my story as a sidebar. I'm going to send you a lead something like: 'Testimony that the nineteen seventy-eight death of an American prisoner of war in Russia was the direct result of orders from the Oval Office was flatly—no, heatedly—denied today by former President Jimmy Carter and his national security advisor at the time, Zbigniew Brzezinski.' "

"So what else could they say?" asked Morrie Bloom. "We gotta run the denial, but can't you give us some inside poop up top?"

"This *is* the inside poop," said Tater. "These denials are written in blood, Morrie. Something else is going on here. It's not the way it looks."

"I don't know," said Morrie Bloom. "The kid is telling the story of the year, and you say it didn't happen?"

"Something else happened," said George Tater. "Trust me."

CHENERY: Before going further, Mr. Cameron, can you tell us what the reaction of your superiors was to your discoveries about this American prisoner of war?

CAMERON: Well, they weren't happy. As soon as the name of Aldrich Ames came up I was very firmly discouraged from pursuing this inquiry any further. I was given an order, really.

CHENERY: A cease-and-desist order.

CAMERON: Yes, sir. And I felt terrible about disobeying the order because I knew there might be something else involved; I knew there might be other aspects to this case; I knew that intelligence work can be extremely complicated. But I felt I had a personal obligation to pursue this report because it involved an American soldier who had been missing for thirty years. We owed it to him.

CHENERY: That's all very well. Tell us what you learned next.

CAMERON: I'll get to that. But first I want to explain why I stopped doing what I was supposed to do.

CHENERY: You can go into all that later.

CAMERON: No. I want to explain this now. Please bear with me.

CHENERY: Mr. Cameron—

CAMERON: No, sir. I will answer your questions, but I have something I want to explain first.

MACLAVERTY: That's all right, Mr. Chenery. We have plenty of time. You go ahead, young man. Why you did what you did is important, and we want to know about it in all the detail you feel necessary. You felt you had a personal obligation.

CAMERON: I wasn't trying to cause trouble. But I remembered what Senator Hawkins used to say. They didn't ask to be sent to Vietnam. They did it for us. Hell, we made them go. The senator didn't say that, but he said we owed it to them to do everything we could to bring them back or to let their loved ones know what had happened to them. And I thought about this Sergeant Dyer, a young man from Maryland, not far across the District line. He joined the army when he was nineteen. He was sent on secret missions into Laos, he was wounded twice, he was captured by the Pathet Lao, he was taken to Russia. Actually, he was very lucky to get there.

CHENERY: Lucky?

CAMERON: Yes, sir, lucky. When the peace accords were signed back in 1973 a number of American prisoners being held by the Pathet Lao were killed. The only reason Dyer escaped was some Russian broke orders and flew him out. If you think about it, the Russians did more for Dyer than we did. And I just felt I couldn't forget him. He had already been a prisoner for seven years when we first learned about him—and we lost him. It made me sick. The one real MIA I'd found in two years of looking, and we'd lost him. I felt I owed it to him to find out what happened—owed it to somebody. So I guess you could say I sort of quit the Agency. I walked out and went to ask the only person I thought might know the truth.

CHENERY: And that was?

CAMERON: Aldrich Ames.

CHENERY: What did he tell you?

CAMERON: It's a long story.

CHENERY: The bottom line. We'll get the details later.

CAMERON: Well, basically Ames told me the president of the United States wasn't too happy about the discovery of Sergeant Dyer. So he decided to tell the Russians that finding an American prisoner alive in a Soviet camp was going to cause a lot of problems. No prisoner, no problems—that was the way Ames put it. Mr. Cabot agreed to deliver this message. And he did.

CHENERY: The question we must resolve here this afternoon, Mr. Cameron, is how we can be sure that Aldrich Ames really knows what happened. Can you explain to us how this information came to him?

CAMERON: As I said, it's a long story.

CHENERY: We have time. Take as much as you need.

CAMERON: Yes, sir, I'll try to make it clear. A little background. Ames volunteered to the Russians in the spring of 1985. The next year he was transferred to Rome, and there he was handled by two Russian case officers, Aleksei Khrenkov, who was in the KGB *rezidentura* in Rome, and a second man he knew as Vladimir—Vlad—who was based in Moscow but occasionally flew to Italy to meet with Ames. The FBI later concluded this was a man named Vladimir Metchulayev.

In October of 1986, Vlad came to Rome and told Ames they needed his help for a special investigation. At this time the Soviet secret services were going through something of a housecleaning—Ames had already given them a long list of major spies in their ranks being run by the CIA. About a dozen of these people were arrested and executed. What Ames told the Russians came as a terrific shock, so the KGB launched a major in-house investigation to make sure there weren't a lot more spies Ames didn't know about. They went through the whole organization with a fine-tooth comb.

One of these checks turned up evidence of two secret meetings back in July 1977 between a Russian intelligence officer named Mikhail Kondrashov and Frank Cabot. At that time, Mr. Cabot was an analyst in the Directorate of Intelligence specializing in Soviet strategic weapons programs.

Kondrashov told his interrogators this was state business authorized at the highest levels and everything was on the up-and-up but the KGB wasn't so sure; there was nothing in the files to back up his story and nobody in the Kremlin knew anything about it. Kondrashov said of course the files were clean; this was a delicate matter discussed only with very high officials, including the chairman of the KGB, Yuri Andropov, who said he had referred the question to the general secretary, Leonid Brezhnev. What Kondrashov said was plausible, but Andropov and Brezhnev were both dead.

So at the meeting in Rome in 1986, Vlad told Ames they needed his help to sort out Kondrashov's story. Did he really meet with Mr. Cabot to talk about the POW, as Kondrashov said, or had he been recruited by Mr. Cabot to work for the CIA? They worked out a complicated game to get the answer out of the CIA. Basically, Ames asked the CIA why Cabot met with Kondrashov in 1978, and the Agency turned the house upside down to find the answer. It was a very artfully played operation.

It worked like this. Ames told his boss in Rome that his KGB contact, Khrenkov, wanted to work for the Americans but was afraid he'd be betrayed by a KGB spy in the agency headquarters in Langley—a man recruited in Moscow in July 1977. This, of course, was when Mr. Cabot went to see Kondrashov.

Chenery: In effect, Ames and his Russian friends suggested that Mr. Cabot was a spy working for the Russians, is that right? So they got the CIA to explain what the meetings were all about?

Cameron: That's right. The Russians fed details of the Moscow meetings to Ames in Rome in 1986, and he passed them on to the Agency. This rang a lot of bells at first because the Agency had no record of these meetings either—at least not in the usual places. There was quite a lot of concern. The Agency knew something was badly wrong, because the year before we had suddenly lost just about every agent we had in the Soviet Union. A special working group of mole hunters had been set up to look for this spy, but of course it didn't know Ames was the culprit—they didn't catch him for another seven or eight years. He wasn't even a suspect.

CHENERY: Do you mean the special group thought Mr. Cabot was the spy?

CAMERON: For maybe a week they thought he *might* be the spy. Look at it from their point of view. The counterintelligence people had learned about Mr. Cabot's trips to Moscow from the Russians. He never reported the trips according to regulations; there was no immediate explanation of what he had gone to do; the Agency knew *somebody* was feeding information to the KGB; Mr. Cabot had access to that information. So it didn't look good.

CHENERY: Was Mr. Cabot ever confronted with these suspicions?

CAMERON: I don't believe he was.

CHENERY: They didn't tell Mr. Cabot but they told Ames?

CAMERON: No, sir, Ames was never told directly or officially. But the working group sent an analyst named Ted Carlin to Rome, and they gave him a desk there in the office of the chief of station, Don Howard.

CHENERY: Would Mr. Howard know all these details?

CAMERON: He'd know about Carlin's TDY to Rome because he saw him every day, and he certainly knew the reason for it was a sensitive counterintelligence inquiry. But I don't think he was in the loop as things unfolded; it was very tightly held. But of course Ames knew quite a lot because he was working with the Russians, and he had also known Carlin back in Washington. I believe they were pretty good friends.

CHENERY: But why would he tell all this stuff to Ames? You say this was tightly held.

CAMERON: Before Ames went to Rome he was in charge of CI files about Russia. He and Carlin had worked closely together. Ames told me it wasn't hard to explain. Carlin trusted him; they were on the same team.

CHENERY: Does Mr. Carlin still work for the Agency?

CAMERON: Yes, sir, he does.

CHENERY: And Mr. Carlin could confirm this version of events?

CAMERON: Yes, sir, I think he could. I contacted him after I went to see Ames. I just wanted to confirm the general outline of Ames's story; I wasn't sure I should believe him. It wasn't something I really wanted to believe, to tell the truth. On the phone I started to tell Carlin what I'd learned from Ames—just the fact of the inquiry—but he stopped me cold. He said, 'Are you speaking on a secure line?' I said I wasn't but I was just interested in a few very basic facts: the year, was he in Rome, did he work with Ames on a CI case. But he cut me off. He said I was out of line. If I wanted to discuss this with him I needed to go through his boss.

CHENERY: Did you feel he was trying to protect Frank Cabot—keep this story under wraps?

CAMERON: No, sir. Carlin was right. I was breaking rules all over the place. I never would have done it except I felt so much was at stake.

CHENERY: You mean the chance this man would become the next Director of Central Intelligence.

CAMERON: No, sir, I mean the truth about what happened to Sergeant Dyer.

CHENERY: We're going to get to that. But first I want you to finish explaining how Ames came to know about it.

CAMERON: Yes, sir. The Russians told him part of it, and Carlin told him part of it. The Russians told him Kondrashov's version, and Carlin told him what the special group dug up in Washington.

CHENERY: And could you characterize that for us?

CAMERON: The special group received extremely sensitive material obtained by another agency in 1977 that helped to explain what Cabot was doing.

CHENERY: What material was that? [*Long pause*] What material was that, Mr. Cameron?

CAMERON: This is sensitive code-word compartmented information, and I don't think I should go into detail.

CHENERY: Don't go into detail. Just tell us the basic facts.

CAMERON: The basic facts *are* the detail.

MACLAVERTY: You need not concern yourself, Mr. Cameron. What we are asking about was a Justice Department investigation now many years in the past, and I have already cleared this testimony with the attorney general. So you may proceed and answer the question.

CAMERON: Yes, sir. The special group wanted to know the purpose of Mr. Cabot's trip, but it didn't want to confront him until it was pretty sure of the truth. So it confined its search to what Mr. Cabot was doing at the time, who he was seeing, who he was reporting to. And one of those names led to an old CI file from 1977—the year Mr. Cabot went to Moscow. What the group turned up were records of a joint CIA-FBI investigation of the possibility that a member of the White House staff might be insecure.

CHENERY: You mean working for the Russians?

CAMERON: Or leaking things to the newspapers. So the CI people secured the assistance of the NSA—

CHENERY: The National Security Agency?

CAMERON: Yes, sir, the National Security Agency, to monitor communications from certain offices of the White House—the National Security staff and the arms control office. This went on for a number of months. The transcripts of these telephone conversations and, I believe, a number of conversations in the offices themselves—

CHENERY: Do you mean conversations that were monitored by a listening device?

CAMERON: I don't know exactly how it was done.

CHENERY: The National Security Agency was bugging the White House?

CAMERON: I'm not sure which group did what, exactly.

CHENERY: However it was accomplished, these counterintelligence investigators were recording conversations that took place in the White House.

CAMERON: Yes, sir, that is correct.

CHENERY: This is quite a story you're telling us. Proceed.

CAMERON: In 1986 the special group obtained a drawerful of transcripts of these conversations overheard back in 1977, and summaries were forwarded to Carlin in Rome so they could be analyzed in light of what Ames said he was being told by the Russians.

CHENERY: Why were these summaries needed in Rome? Presumably they spoke for themselves.

CAMERON: They recorded what people said, but it was always possible that what they said was wholly or partially false. They needed to be checked against the Russian version of what happened. There was a lot of back-and-forth over several weeks.

CHENERY: Mr. Carlin and Mr. Ames went over it all in great detail.

CAMERON: Yes, they did.

CHENERY: Everything Ames told you was based on what he personally had been told by the Russians, or what he personally knew of tape-recorded conversations between certain officials of the United States government?

Cameron: That's right.

Chenery: One official in the White House and one official in the Central Intelligence Agency, is that right?

Cameron: That's right.

Chenery: Who was that official in the CIA?

Cameron: Frank Cabot.

Chenery: Presently the nominee of President Anderson to become the next Director of Central Intelligence?

Cameron: Yes, sir.

Chenery: And the official in the White House back in 1977, the man who held those overheard conversations with Mr. Cabot, will you tell the committee who that man was?

Cameron: It was the president's special assistant for arms control matters.

Chenery: His name?

Cameron: Otis Jones.

Chenery: Otis Jones. Distinguished lawyer and public servant. Held high posts in many different administrations in this city going back to President Harry S Truman. And what did Aldrich Ames tell you, based on his unique access to the facts of this matter, about the secret conversations of Otis Jones and Frank Cabot?

47

What Brad Cameron wanted most was a red cowboy handkerchief and a moment alone to mop the sweat from his forehead, behind his ears, and down the back of his neck—perhaps followed by an hour's walk in the cool of a forest somewhere a long way from a paved road. His hands were sticky, his scalp was prickly, and he wanted to shut out the booming baritone of the moon-faced examiner who was dragging the Ames story out of him. Brad wanted to tell what he knew without inflection or bias, but Chenery's running commentary made every word seem like a pointed finger. Myrna had warned him they were going to hear only what they wanted to hear, and she was right.

Directly before him was an impassive row of dark figures, the members of the Senate Select Committee on Intelligence, in shadowy silhouette against the bank of television lights burning behind them. Just to the right of MacLaverty was the disk of Chenery's round face with its fiery halo of hair, ready with a new question the instant Brad paused for breath. All around him in the hearing room Brad felt the presence of his audience but the ones most vivid in his mind were the CIA staffers surrounding Cabot, Cabot's wife, Kitty—softened and worn by life, with an expression of quiet sadness about the eyes and mouth—and Cabot himself. Marching across the front of the room to his seat, Brad had caught Cabot's eye—not deliberately, but once he had it the two men exchanged for a fraction of a second a shared knowledge that this was personal and lethal, a duel that could only conclude with the public rejection of one of them. Cabot's cool gaze exuded a conviction that he would be the one left holding the field, but Brad knew Cabot pretty well by this time and he was sure the older man was sick with anxiety.

Brad had been testifying for about fifty minutes by the clock, but it felt like hours. Every word addressed to him by Chenery or MacLaverty had crystal clarity. Every word of his reply was freighted with import, as if he were declaiming and underlining and driving his meaning home with exclamation points. He not only felt upon him the eyes of the room and of everybody he had ever known, parked somewhere in front of a TV set. He also felt the whole world watching. He felt centered in a white beam of attention that could burn a man to a cinder.

Everybody had said don't do it, but it was Myrna and Hugh who had explained why: This is not going to be like anything you have ever experienced before; this can never be taken back or lived down; this will overwhelm your entire previous life; you will be changed, people will act strangely around you, people who don't know you will think they know all about you; this moment will mark you for the rest of your life like a port-wine birthmark. And he could feel it happening. But he was convinced he had no choice. He was like a kid walking out to the end of the high board at the swimming pool, with his friends and family all watching below. It didn't matter how high it was, he had to go off.

The last question from Howard Chenery was the one Brad had been waiting for. "And what did Aldrich Ames tell you, based on his unique access to the facts of this matter, about the secret conversations of Otis Jones and Frank Cabot?"

All these reflections occupied only a moment of anticipation between the question and the parting of Brad's lips to answer.

"He told me," Brad said, "that their discussions focused on two points. The first was how to find out if the report was true—whether an American really was being held prisoner in the Soviet Union. And the second was what to do about it."

"They debated how to handle the POW?" asked Chenery.

"No," said Brad. "According to Aldrich Ames, Mr. Jones told Mr. Cabot what the president wanted done. They discussed the best way to carry that out."

"And what did Mr. Jones say the president wanted done?"

It was well past dark by the time Jenny arrived, and Kitty had already changed out of her supportive-wife uniform, putting on a gray sweater and slacks. When Jenny found her, Kitty was in the room Frank called the library but which was really the TV room. The TV was on but not the sound.

"I'm better," said Jenny. "I can move again."

"Does that woman do deep-tissue work?" Kitty asked.

"Deep-tissue work is just the beginning of what she does," said Jenny.

She took her usual seat on the couch, lowering herself delicately. The room looked as it always did at the hour reserved for drinks: curtains drawn, lots of lights on, books and magazines piled on the coffee table, a drinks tray on the Philadelphia mahogany lowboy by the door. The tray was large, made of black tin, painted with floral loops and whorls. On the tray were a blue seltzer bottle, wine and highball glasses, bottles of The Famous Grouse, Bombay Gin, and Wild Turkey, and a bottle of Saint-Émilion with the cork half out.

"I felt terrible ducking out of the afternoon session," said Jenny. "I hope Uncle Frank will forgive me."

"Honey, his mind was on other things."

"I know. But I feel like this is all my fault. Was it awful?"

"Honey, it was beyond awful. But don't blame yourself."

"I thought maybe if I talked to Tater—"

"It was a dumb idea," said Kitty, "but in fact it probably helped. He hasn't been writing with his usual venom. But Jenny, darling, we're way beyond Tater now. You'll understand. They'll rerun Brad's testimony in a couple of minutes."

"I don't know how that business with Tater happened," said Jenny, filled with shame. "I don't think I could look Brad in the face if he knew."

"Are you planning to tell him?" asked Kitty.

"Should I tell him?"

"That depends," said Kitty.

"You think he needs to know?"

"No," said Kitty, "but maybe you need to tell."

"I don't know if I've got the courage for it," said Jenny.

There was a moment's silence while Kitty poured drinks.

"Bad, huh?" said Jenny.

"Trust me," said Kitty.

"Is Uncle Frank furious with Brad?"

"I suppose he is," said Kitty, "but I'm not. He did what he had to do, just like Tater."

"What's Uncle Frank going to do now?"

"I don't think he has much choice. He's going to have to withdraw his name and resign from the Agency. There's not a lot of ambiguity here. Harry Hawkins called earlier—he sounded very weak, as if he were on his deathbed. I told him Frank was still at the Agency trying to hold it together, but Harry said he'd wait till Frank got home. I think Harry will make Frank see it. With Harry against him, who's left?"

"What about you and the boys?"

"The boys will stand by him, they always do, but I'm sick to death of the whole thing. I'd like to pack an overnight bag and drive to New York and go back to painting. But I can't leave Frank beaten like this."

Kitty refilled her glass to the brim. As she turned up the sound on the TV, a woman in a white suit was saying, ". . . a day of charges and denials. It began this morning with a rumor that the Senate committee holding the hearings would be calling a surprise witness who would provide the real story behind headlines of recent weeks about an American army sergeant of the Vietnam era who was held in a Russian prison camp more than thirty years ago. This afternoon a young CIA agent told the committee that former President Jimmy Carter issued a tacit request for the murder of the American prisoner and said the Russians had apparently complied. His testimony provided quite a bombshell."

"This is it," said Kitty. "What the president wanted done."

The woman in white was replaced by Brad Cameron in the hearing room. The voice of the newswoman said, "The committee's counsel asked what role had been played by the president."

"God, he looks nervous," said Jenny. "He looks sick. He looks awful. How the hell did he get through this?"

"He looks better when it's over," said Kitty. "Dividend for you?"

. . .

Brad fidgeted head down at the witness table. His right hand was on a piece of paper. First he pushed the paper away, then pulled it back. "They were on the phone," said Brad. "Mr. Cabot had flown back out to Geneva from Moscow and was speaking on a secure phone from the consulate. Mr. Jones was in Washington—I think in the West Wing of the White House. Cabot had stayed on a couple of days after telling Jones that the report was true; he'd seen Kondrashov, and Kondrashov had confirmed that a U.S. Army sergeant captured in Laos was being held in a prison camp in Akmolinsk."

Cut to the moon face of Howard Chenery. He was leaning into the microphone.

"Jones told him to stay put. He'd seek guidance."

"Yes, sir."

"From the White House?"

"Yes, sir, from the White House. It was Cabot's understanding that Mr. Jones was handling this problem for the president. And after a day or so—I'm not sure how long it was—Mr. Jones called and told Cabot the president felt that discovery of the American prisoner would precipitate an outcry in the United States and jeopardize the status of nine separate negotiations with the Russians concerning nuclear arms and conventional force reductions and human rights and other matters."

"An outcry against the Russians?" asked Chenery.

"Yes, sir. For lying to the United States. They had already denied many rumors of American prisoners being held in Russia, and the president felt—Mr. Jones said the president felt—that the know-nothings in Congress—that was his phrase, the know-nothings in Congress—would say this proves you can't trust the Russians."

"And in fact," asked Chenery, "the Russians had been lying, is that not so?"

"Well, they hadn't been telling the truth. But it's possible that the people who weren't telling the truth didn't actually know what the truth was. That's often the way it works in situations like this."

"That is your opinion."

"Yes, sir, that is my opinion. What Jones said was that too much was at stake. And Cabot in Geneva said, 'Well, what are we supposed to do?'

"Jones said, 'The president hopes you will return to Moscow and see Kondrashov again and deliver the following message. Exactly these words: " 'The president is grieved to learn of the death of the American prisoner.' "

" 'Grieved to learn of the death of the American prisoner,' " Chenery repeated.

"Yes, sir," said Brad. " 'And in light of this fact believes that the cause of peace would be best served if neither side makes any public reference to this episode.' "

"The Russians and the Americans would agree to hide the truth?"

"Yes, sir. That's what Ames told me was on the tapes."

"Transcripts retained in the files of the CIA and the National Security Agency and sent to Rome in nineteen eighty-six?"

"Yes, sir, that's my understanding."

"And did you take notes of your conversation with Ames?"

"Yes, sir, I did. But I also remember his words vividly. Ames repeated them with a certain relish, I would say. And at the end he said, 'This is the organization I worked for. What do you think now? Does it deserve a decent man's loyalty?' "

The woman in white reappeared on the Cabot TV set. "Former President Jimmy Carter held a news conference in Plains, Georgia, this afternoon to say that he had already issued many denials over the last several weeks insisting he knew nothing at all about this series of events at the time."

The white-haired visage of the lined face and pained eyes of Jimmy Carter appeared on the screen. A forest of microphones was in front of him. "This new report—that I somehow encouraged or told the Russians to do away with an American soldier—is absolutely and totally false. I respect the right of the Senate fully to investigate any person nominated by the president for a job as important as that of CIA director, but I do not understand why any Senate committee would allow a charge of this magnitude to be made against any president before any effort, however perfunctory, has been made to confirm the truth of the charge. No one has spoken to me officially about this extraordinary claim."

The strong, patient voice of the former president went on to attack Senator MacLaverty without naming him for this inexcusable lapse. The denial was extended, detailed, lucid, passionate, and utterly unambiguous.

Kitty said, "They got Frank coming out of the hearing room and he denied it too, of course, but I can't say he put himself into it the way Carter did. And they caught Brad, who said he had told the committee everything he knew, but the media people were eating him alive until one of MacLaverty's people spirited him out the back. I hate to think what he's got ahead of him."

"Where is he?" asked Jenny.

"I have no idea," said Kitty. "They've already got camera crews staked out at his apartment." Kitty poured herself another glass of red wine. "He's completely unprepared for this," she said. "He needs a lawyer but he doesn't have a lawyer. He needs somebody to give him advice, but he arrived at the hearing completely alone, so far as I could tell. Frank's surrounded by highly paid professionals who would protect him even if he were a child molester. Brad is like a lamb in the lion house at the zoo."

"Did Uncle Frank ever tell you about any of this?"

"Not a word," said Kitty. "Sharing is not his style."

"The whole thing seems unbelievable," said Jenny.

"I'm afraid you haven't heard it all," said Kitty. "Brad was on for most of the afternoon. The committee dragged out all kinds of names and dates and other details to back up the story. MacLaverty said he was recessing the hearings for two days while subpoenas were served on the Agency, the NSA, the Carter Library, the FBI—you name it. There was a huge fight at the end. A couple of the senators wanted to question Brad right there, but MacLaverty was like a drill sergeant—he recessed the hearings with a pound of his fist on the table and marched out, while senators shouted and jumped to their feet. You missed a real spectacle, honey. I've never seen anything like it. It wasn't easy walking out by Frank's side."

"But he had to do it," said Jenny. "It was the president."

"No, honey, he didn't have to do it. He could have said no. He almost did say no. He listed all the awful things that would happen to him if it ever got out. They'll run the rest of Brad's testimony in a minute. Frank knew exactly what was going on."

It was hard to talk for a time. Jenny had an awful feeling of guilt: that she personally had done something terribly, terribly wrong. Then the woman in white surrendered the television screen to the hearing room again. Brad was telling the committee how Otis Jones persuaded Cabot to return to Moscow.

"Jones admitted all the dangers but he said it had to be done, and he promised Cabot that he would be rewarded for serving his country in this matter.

"Cabot wanted to know rewarded how? Jones asked him what did he want?"

"What did he want," Chenery repeated, "for conveying the president's message to Russia?"

"Yes, sir. Cabot said Jones already knew what he wanted—to be head of the Directorate of Intelligence, and someday he wanted to be DCI."

"Can you tell the committee," asked Chenery, "how Otis Jones thought he could promise any such thing as that?"

"Jones said he couldn't. But he said he thought Cabot was well suited for important jobs in the intelligence community. He said that the fast track in Washington ran through the White House. He said Cabot's career would get a big boost from a couple of years of detached duty with the National Security staff. And that, Jones said, he could guarantee. And he said he was a man with a long memory and many friends and he promised Cabot that his support would be steady and it would be effective."

"So Frank Cabot promised to convey this shameful message to the Russians in return for a promise of advancement in his career?"

"Yes, sir," said Brad. "Beginning with a jump in grade to GS-Fourteen as soon as he moved to the White House."

"Mr. Jones agreed," said Chenery.

"Jones promised the promotion at the end of six months. He said it would look fishy if Cabot got a promotion right away."

"Look fishy."

"Those might not have been Ames's words, sir, but that was his general meaning."

"All this was captured on tape by the NSA back in nineteen seventy-seven," said Chenery.

"Yes, sir."

"And conveyed to the CIA station in Rome nine years later. The NSA knew this and did nothing. The CIA in nineteen eighty-six knew this and did nothing. How do you explain this extraordinary inaction?" asked Chenery.

"Sir," said Brad, "the NSA hears a great many things it does nothing about. The NSA and the CIA aren't in the law enforcement business."

"So they sat on their hands."

"They probably breathed a long sigh of relief that Jones and Cabot weren't working for the Russians," said Brad.

"They shook hands and they had a deal," said Chenery.

"They were speaking on the phone between Washington and Geneva," said Brad. "But Jones said he knew he had spotted his man, and Cabot said he looked forward to crossing the river."

"Meaning the Potomac," said Chenery.

"Yes, sir. From Langley, Virginia, to the White House. And it all pretty much worked that way."

"Mr. Cabot carried out his half of the bargain," said Chenery.

"Yes, sir, he did. And Jones did the same."

"And this committee is in effect being asked here today," said Chenery, "to confirm Frank Cabot's reward for this shameful deed."

Brad groped for an answer. "I suppose," he said at last, "you could look at it that way."

It was a long evening. The only calls came from Kitty's two sons, who wanted to know if they could come down. Kitty said no, Frank wanted it that way, he'd call them when he got home.

Around nine they finished the bottle of red and opened another. They made an omelet and ate it in the kitchen. They wondered if somehow the law would become involved, if Frank would be arrested, if there would be a trial, a jury, time in jail. Kitty tried to explain the agonies marriage sometimes brought in its train, and Jenny tried to understand. Jenny tried to explain why she had been so angry with Brad even though she knew he was trying to do the right thing.

They switched off the news two or three times, but they always turned it back on, and every fifteen or twenty minutes they watched again as the sighing, squirming, agonized figure of Brad Cameron repeated what he had learned about the rise of Frank Cabot.

"Maybe it isn't true," said Jenny.

"Maybe I'll quit drinking," said Kitty.

48

From long experience Frank Cabot had learned there was no point in getting into bed when he was wound up and thinking twenty thoughts at once, which remained the case as midnight Monday came and went. He had done all he could do and he knew it, so he tried to read. He had no interest in the papers or magazines, and the spy novel he'd picked up and put down a month ago had faded from memory. If he opened it at the bookmark he'd have no idea what was going on, and if he went back to chapter one, page one, he'd feel futile. He knew this because he had tried to get back into it once or twice in recent weeks. His book of last resort in such circumstances was Winston Churchill's memoir, *The Second World War,* which for Frank Cabot ranked with the great expressions of the indomitable spirit of man. In times of trouble he liked to open volume two and read about the terrible spring of 1940 when France collapsed, Hitler was triumphant, and Britain stood alone.

But tonight, sitting in the library long after Kitty had gone unsteadily up to bed, even Churchill failed to come to the rescue. Frank Cabot was in no doubt about the reason why. Without putting it in so many words, he understood that doing a president's dirty work was hardly the same thing as fighting the Nazis on the beaches and in the hedgerows. So he settled himself in the library on his father's old couch, which he still hoped to move into his own private office on the seventh floor of the CIA when this painful episode was over, and tried to think of ways to block or deflect the course of events within the next few days, which he sensed were all that remained to him. If nothing changed by the end of the week, the president would simply call in the press and end the agony. But for the moment Anderson was still hoping somebody else—maybe Cabot himself—would do the job. So there was yet time for a miracle. Volume two, *Their Finest Hour,* Cabot's favorite, lay open across his stomach, and his eyes were closed.

During the hours between the recess of the hearings at five o'clock and Cabot's departure in an Agency car for home at ten, he had talked almost without interruption. First came a global denial to the reporters outside the hearing room. The crush was mad, the level of feeling close to hysteria. But the situation was not intrinsically hard to handle. The reporters were all shouting questions at the same time so each stinging query was drowned out by the others, and only Cabot's words made it to the evening news. In his office at seven and from the library couch at eleven he had watched himself holding up both hands palm outward and in two or three different ways reminding the people of the United States that a wise man once said it ain't over till it's over. Cabot was good at looking unruffled, and for what it was worth he knew the television audience had seen his own calm insistence that he was telling the truth in contrast to the hot-eyed hysteria of the shouting men and women who were thrusting microphones into his face. But Brownie points were not going to turn this around.

The serious work of shoring up a defense had begun only after he was back in his office at Langley. First came a brief meeting with the young intelligence officer, Larry Shedd, arranged by Weissberg. After that he took calls from a handful of close friends and fence straddlers who said he could depend on them. Cabot was warm in his thanks. For the next couple of hours he lodged denials with a string of individuals more or less close to the center of the Washington establishment, but of the twenty or thirty phone calls he made, only a handful counted. First among them was a brief, painful talk with Peter Schleicher at the White House, who asked nothing, barely acknowledging they were even in conversation, but simply listened to Cabot's solemn assurance that you could trust Aldrich Ames's version of these events about as far as you could trust him to stand by his pledge of allegiance to the flag.

"I'll pass along what you say," said Schleicher.

"We need to speak clearly, Peter," Cabot said. "I can't walk away from this, and the president can't either. If he runs for cover the first day, they'll be investigating this for the rest of his term."

Schleicher said nothing but he did not hang up.

"Better to fight them right here and right now," said Cabot. "Stand up and fire back."

Continued silence.

"I'm ready to go the distance for the president. I won't fold. But I need some word of support, Peter, some sign."

At last Schleicher spoke. "I'll be honest with you, Frank," he said. "I don't know how the president feels. I can imagine, but I don't know. But I personally feel you've dumped a load of horse manure right in the middle of this administration's whole foreign policy. In my opinion, the one thing you can do for your country now is withdraw your name. Step aside. That is only my personal opinion."

"Peter, they're not attacking me. They're attacking him."

"I'm speaking for myself," said Schleicher.

"Peter, tell him to wait forty-eight hours. Tell him they won't let you walk away from a fight in this town. Tell him things always look bad the first day. Tell him there is no way MacLaverty can prove any of this crap. He's way out on a limb. He hasn't got the paper. He's asking people to take the word of Aldrich Ames! Trust me on this, Peter. MacLaverty's going to be a whipped puppy before this is over. But the president has got to be willing to put up a fight."

"I can't speak for the president," said Schleicher, "but I feel personally betrayed by you. You assured us there was nothing in your past."

"Peter, this isn't helping—" Cabot began. But it was too late. Schleicher had hung up. For a moment Cabot was delirious with a bitter anger which included lurid mental images of physically disfiguring Peter Schleicher with his fists, but he understood fate would never give him a chance to settle this score physically, much as he longed to tear the bastard apart, so he told himself to calm down. He put the anger away forever and asked Jane to make the next call.

"Mr. Kiddle, forgive me, I can't talk long," Cabot said when he got through. "Someone's waiting to see me. But I want to say that it's very important for me to speak to Mr. Jones tonight, and I would appreciate it if you would give me a number where I can reach him."

As expected, Kiddle stonewalled: Otis was extremely ill; the doctors demanded complete rest; it was impossible to disturb him. Kiddle understood, he sympathized, but nothing could be done. This answer was delivered in a cold flat voice.

"If he dies, that's that," said Cabot. "But I've known Otis for a good many years, and there are two things he values as much as life itself—his reputation and his access."

"I'm sorry—" Kiddle began.

"This isn't Texas," said Cabot. "There are no appeals from a sentence of death in this town."

"Listen—" said Kiddle.

"If I can't tell him, you tell him," said Cabot. "Tell him I have no choice. I'm going to defend myself. If he wants to know what I'm going to say, tell him I'm going to stick to the facts as I know them. Tell him I won't say anything I can't prove. If I don't hear back, I'll assume he trusts me to handle this any way I see fit."

"That sounds like a threat."

"Call it a threat if it makes you feel better. I'm only stating the obvious. Unless you failed to notice, my name wasn't the only one in that young man's testimony this afternoon. Otis and I need to agree about what happened. I'm trusting you to let him know that."

"I can't promise anything," said Kiddle.

"I don't want promises," said Frank Cabot. "I've had promises up to here."

Jones would call, Cabot was sure of that. He wouldn't trust a delicate matter like this to Stanley Kiddle no matter how many people he'd put on death row back in Texas. But it might take a day. Otis Jones was a careful and deliberative man, and he fully understood the power of words. He'd want to know every detail of what Cabot planned to say.

Cabot picked up the Churchill and read a few pages about Dunkirk and the ghastly fate of the *Lancastria*, a troopship crammed with five thousand men that went down in a sea of burning oil. More than three thousand British soldiers burned or drowned. When the terrible news reached Churchill, he forbade all mention of it in the newspapers. "I had intended to release the news a few days later," the greatest Englishman since Wellington wrote in the calm after the war, "but events crowded upon us so black and so quickly that I forgot to lift the ban, and it was some years before the knowledge of this horror became public."

Cabot allowed himself to smile at this. It would be a great help, he reflected bitterly, if he too could tell the papers what they could print. But he had no such power. His only hope was to feed the media a better story tomorrow than the one they heard today. He believed this might be pulled off by his old friend Mikhail Kondrashov, once a handsome man in the rugged Russian way but a wreck now: blue-white in color, thin, white-haired, with an oxygen tube stuck to his nose.

He was trusting Larry Shedd to make this possible, but he knew it was a long shot. The young man had been waiting in his outer office when Cabot returned from the first day of his confirmation hearings. Shedd was a highly presentable fellow, young-looking but the sort who had never really *been* young. He wore a good English suit and gleaming cordovan shoes, had grown up in Washington, and had met most of the surviving great names among the intelligence old boys around the dinner table in his father's house in Georgetown.

"My bag is packed," he said, "and my passport is valid, sir. Mr. Weissberg arranged for a visa."

"Sit down," said Cabot, gesturing to the chair across from his desk. "This is a mission for a volunteer, and I want you to understand what's involved."

"Yes, sir," said Shedd. His face gave nothing away. There were lots of young men with advantages working for the CIA. Most of them would have middling careers and lose their luster. But some would make the right friends, find the right jobs, avoid the obvious mistakes—too much time in the field, too many failed operations—and rise as if called by God. Frank Cabot was about to give Larry Shedd the chance to be one of these favored mortals, and both of them knew it.

"I'm sure you watched the testimony today," said Cabot.

Shedd confirmed that he had. Cabot said only two people knew what he had discussed with Kondrashov in Moscow in 1977 and Aldrich Ames was neither of them. "I'm going to tell the committee what happened," said Cabot, "but my word isn't going to be enough. Senator MacLaverty is opposed to my nomination for what amount to personal reasons, and I'm afraid he has got the majority with him for the moment. So I want to bring Kondrashov here to Washington to confirm my version of events."

Cabot explained that Kondrashov was ailing and would need help, that he was living on a minuscule KGB pension and would require financial assistance to make the trip. Cabot said he had a few Russian friends who could take Shedd in hand and help him with logistics, but this trip would be conducted entirely outside normal channels. "Senator MacLaverty will block this effort if he learns about it," he explained, "and he *will* learn about it if I ask the station in Moscow to make the arrangements."

"How will he do that?" asked Shedd. "You're still running the Agency, sir."

"Our people there are mostly on the covert side," said Cabot. "They work for Joe Flint, and he sides with MacLaverty in this dispute."

"Sides with MacLaverty?"

"Flint hoped this nomination would be his."

"He thinks MacLaverty can make him DCI?"

"No, he just wants another chance, and next time he might actually get it. After a certain point everything in this world comes down to politics, Larry: who's on their side, who's on our side. I'm asking you to be on my side, and I'm asking because I need help. But I want you to understand what the dangers are."

Shedd listened.

Cabot explained that a law on the books gave the CIA the right to bring into the United States a limited number of people each year for reasons of national security without going through the usual red tape of visas and State Department approval. He proposed to bring Kondrashov in under those regulations. He would provide Shedd with the funds and several names he would need to get himself and Kondrashov to the port of entry at John F. Kennedy Airport in New York City. Cabot would make sure the gates opened when Shedd arrived.

"Once Kondrashov is in Washington, MacLaverty will be in a corner," Cabot said. "If he won't let him testify, we'll go public—call in the reporters. If he does let him testify, Ames's story will collapse."

"I understand, sir."

"If you pull this off I am going to be very grateful, Larry."

"I appreciate that, sir. I'll do my best."

"But if something goes wrong—if we can't get Kondrashov in somehow, or I lose in committee or in the Senate despite his testimony—then MacLaverty and Flint are going to be very angry with you, and they are going to make their anger felt."

"I appreciate that, sir. I've been thinking about this as we talked. The truth is I could use some help, sir. I got a new assignment a week ago and it's to Uruguay. I don't speak Spanish, I speak French. Do you think it would be possible to have me reassigned to Paris, where I know people and where there's something going on?"

Cabot couldn't have put it more gracefully himself, and he understood perfectly. Latin America was not where great issues were decided and great reputations made. He said Paris sounded like a very good idea, and Larry Shedd said he was ready to go to Moscow.

Cabot had put off calling Harry Hawkins, and now it was too late. He'd call in the morning and make his excuses. With any luck, Kondrashov would turn everything around.

Still restless, he cracked the book again. The dust jacket was in tatters, the page was stained where he had once spilled a drop of red wine, but the passage was as magnificent as ever. It was June 18, 1940, the day after the French collapse, when Churchill rose in the House of Commons and called on his beleaguered nation to fight on.

> . . . the Battle of Britain is about to begin. Upon this battle depends our own British life, and the long continuity of our institutions and our Empire. The fury and might of the enemy must very soon be turned on us. Hitler knows that he will have to break us in this Island or lose the war. If we can stand up to him, all Europe may be free and the life of the world may move forward into broad, sunlit uplands. But if we fail, then the whole world, including the United States, including all that we have known and cared for, will sink into the abyss of a new Dark Age, made more sinister, and perhaps more protracted, by the lights of perverted science. Let us therefore brace ourselves to our duties, and so bear ourselves that, if the British Empire and its Commonwealth last for a thousand years, men will still say: "This was their finest hour."

Cabot was a master of the confident exterior, but over the last two weeks his confidence had slowly eroded. Moments of conviction that he could still pull it off were increasingly replaced by a sense of the walls closing in around him. He still desperately hoped Shedd would find Kondrashov and the Russian would somehow turn the tide, but then he would remember the day's testimony—Brad's voice laying out the awful charges.

He had dreamed of doing something great for his country, making his sons proud, canceling the shame of his father's wrong turn. . . .

Hunger hit him about 1:00 a.m. He got up and headed for the kitchen, wondering if there was anything to eat. He flicked on the light in the kitchen and opened the refrigerator door. Inside there was only a half-empty quart of milk, a couple of bottles of white wine, an old box of Arm and Hammer baking soda, and a wilted head of lettuce in a plastic bag.

Staring into the fridge, an odd thought came to him. His life was like the maw of this refrigerator: cold, brightly lit, and empty. His wife was like a ghost in the house. The boys had grown up and moved away. If they took his job away there was nothing left. For a long moment Frank Cabot stood in his kitchen, hungry for something missing, knowing this was his darkest hour.

49

When the buzzer went off, Dean Cutter knew he was safe. He felt pretty smart; a smile found its way to his face. The security guard looked at him strangely. Cutter lifted both hands gently away from his body; he didn't want to overdo this, frighten the guards, conceivably even get himself shot. He tried to shift from smiling to worried. The guard gripped him by the upper arm and said, "I'm sorry, sir, but I'm afraid you'll have to empty your pockets."

Cutter felt eyes turning his way. A second guard approached. People in line stared. From the little knot of television reporters across the lobby a man watched, then detached himself from the group and headed for the barrier. Cutter saw all this in the moment it took the first guard to back him toward the wall and issue his request. Slowly, Cutter dropped his hand into the right-hand pocket of his parka and lifted out between thumb and forefinger the oiled metal clip for the .380 Beretta.

Cutter now expected two things: his immediate arrest and removal to the city jail for questioning and the helpless fury of Russell, the ex-marine, as he watched his efforts go up the chimney. Russell was inside.

Cutter couldn't see him but he knew Russell was nearby; he had a way of being just out of sight but right there.

"Excuse me, sir," said the guard, but he didn't wait for permission. He took the clip and began to pat Cutter down. The second guard had been joined by a third and a fourth. There was a buzz in the foyer, people pushing. Television lights went on.

Goodbye, Russell was Cutter's first thought.

The guard finished the pat-down. "Can you explain this?" he asked, holding up the clip between thumb and forefinger.

Explaining is what I do best was Cutter's second thought.

"It's an ammunition clip," he said. "I was practicing at the range yesterday and I forgot I had it with me. There's a club that meets every week. One of the guys is Michigan state rapid-fire champion."

Michigan ought to ring a bell, thought Cutter.

"You're going to have to leave this with us," said the guard, still holding the clip, "if you want to go inside. But I can't guarantee it'll be safe with us; I'm afraid we don't have storage facilities."

"I can go inside?" said Cutter, amazed.

This was not what he had expected. He had been counting on one night in jail at the very least, Russell in a panic, heading down the road as soon as he hit the street. "You take your problems with you," Lisa Benson had advised the group. "There is no geographical cure." Well, this was one problem Cutter was definitely planning to leave behind, but he had been counting on the cops to get him out of sight and scare off Russell. He felt trapped and dumb.

"Of course you can go inside," said the guard, "but you'll have to leave the clip with us. I'm sorry—it's regulations. No firearms, ammunition, explosives, inflammables, edged instruments with a blade longer than one inch—there's a whole long list, and I'm afraid firearms components are on it."

The television lights had gone out. The second and third guards had turned away. The television reporter was heading back to the knot of colleagues. The guard was giving him a look of rueful sympathy and embarrassment. *What's the matter with you guys?* thought Cutter. He wanted to write a letter of protest to somebody.

"That's all right," he said. "I'll take it home."

The guard handed him the clip. As he turned to leave, Cutter glimpsed Russell's gray ponytail and the green of his fatigue jacket inside the lobby and figured he had a couple of minutes to disappear at best. Distance was the only thing that could save him. He pushed his way back through the door, past the silent line of citizenry waiting to enter, took the flight of steps two at a time, just barely caught the light, and broke into a jog on the far side of the street. He checked behind him but Russell was nowhere in sight. Cutter began to think maybe he was pretty smart after all. A day in jail would have scared off Russell for good, he believed, but maybe an old-fashioned run for it would work just as well—wave goodbye and disappear. Wherever Russell turned up looking for him, Cutter was going to be somewhere else. The people in Michigan were going to have to find some other patsy to do the deed.

50

After an early phone call to Hugh Diamond for directions Tuesday morning and a couple of false starts before she actually got into her car; after several minutes of walking up and down the sidewalk in front of the old apartment building on 18th Street, and after riding the elevator to the top floor and back down to the basement, Jenny finally told herself she wasn't making a mistake, she was doing the right and natural thing. She got out on the third floor, marched calmly up to the door of 3E, rang the bell—and wished she hadn't.

But it was too late to change her mind yet again. She heard someone coming, the click of a bolt, and a woman's voice as the door came open with a tug: "Did you forget your key?" And then: "Oh."

"Myrna? I'm sorry," said Jenny.

"That's okay."

"I'm Jenny Moore."

"Ahhh."

"And I thought perhaps my friend Brad Cameron . . ."

"He's gone out for a run," said Myrna. "But it was a good guess. He said you were smart, and you are. He's hiding out with me. Come in."

Myrna turned and led the way through the living room to the kitchen, where she immediately turned on the stove and put a pot on to boil, chattering the while about Brad's failed attempt to sneak past the reporters the previous evening to get into his apartment. "But they were staked out front and back," said Myrna, "so he did exactly what you did. He thought of me.

"Sit down. Let me take your coat. When that boy goes running, how far does he like to run?"

"Thirty minutes of running, twenty minutes of walking—first ten and last ten."

"Do you run with him?"

"Sometimes."

"That's nice," said Myrna. "How do you like your tea?"

"With milk."

"I was afraid you'd say lemon. Milk I've got. I've been hearing about you for weeks, it's nice to meet you."

"Has it been weeks? So much has happened."

"It has," said Myrna. "And it ain't over yet."

By that time the water was boiling, and Jenny got a chance to look around. What she saw was a kitchen, neat but not recently painted, with a substantial bookshelf on one wall loaded with cookbooks; a couple of prints on the walls of gray European landscapes; some sepia-toned photographs of kids in overcoats beneath leafless trees, family groups in living rooms; and at the counter, pulling down cups and saucers, a gray-haired woman, short and solid, wearing a print dress and floppy slippers. When she had poured she picked up some knitting from a chair and settled back, needles clicking.

"What are you making?" asked Jenny.

"I'm making a sweater." She held it up. "For the runner. More sweaters I don't need. When I knit, I feel like the world's at peace. Not true, but."

"Is that your family?"

Myrna gestured with the knitting. "My mother. My little brother, Nathan. Some cousins. That one—honest, I don't remember. Probably an aunt or a friend of my mother. But I like the expression on her face. She looks intelligent, determined. What do you think?"

"Maybe a little angry," said Jenny.

"A little angry too," said Myrna. "Like you, maybe? Don't look surprised. The runner talks about everything. So tell me—have you come to make up or to give him hell?"

On her own, Jenny would have taken hours to reach that point, but asked point-blank she answered directly. "I'm tired of giving him hell."

"Me too," said Myrna. "I thought he was in too big a hurry. But now things look different."

For half an hour without self-consciousness Jenny tried to explain what she thought was going on and what she thought Brad ought to have done and what she thought she owed to her Aunt Kitty and to the man Kitty chose to marry. She told Myrna that she'd met George Tater, the *Times* reporter who had been pushing the story so hard, and that she had made a stupid, misguided, and completely futile attempt to slow him down or deflect him or soften his assault somehow. Despite everything Jenny had heard, and imagined Myrna had heard, Tater was in fact a human being and had a heart, but for him reporting was one thing and friendship was another and Jenny had learned there was no way Tater would ever for one minute let a friend come between him and what he thought he owed to a story. Jenny failed to mention that she had become Tater's lover but if Myrna had asked Jenny probably would have said yes, she had gone to bed with Tater, and she probably would have added that it was an ill-considered, impulsive thing to do and she was not at all happy about the prospect of explaining it to Brad, much less to the world, if it came to that. But at the same time, she probably would have also added, she wasn't sorry. There it was. Or would have been, if she had said any of the many things concerning Tater that had been forming in the back of her mind.

"Mm-hmm," assented Myrna, as her needles clicked, getting the drift of much of what Jenny wasn't saying.

"I was angry because it was my uncle, and Kitty means a lot to me. But now I don't know. What Ames told Brad is hard to ignore. And I've been so dumb myself."

"It's a complicated world."

"People keep saying that," said Jenny. "I try to understand what I'm supposed to do—what's right. But things never look the same two days in a row. How can you ever figure it out?"

"You can't," said Myrna.

"You can't?"

"You can't. What's right is about the tenth question on the list. This is how I look at it. My philosophy. You don't try to figure out who's right. The big question is, Who matters to you? Do you stand by your friend? Do you defend the man in your life?"

"Not always," said Jenny.

"That's true, not always. But the price is heavy when you don't. For me it wasn't so hard. I don't kid myself Cabot's a saint. But I work for this man. I understand what he's up against."

"It doesn't matter what he did?" asked Jenny.

"Well, that's the problem," said Myrna. "Sometimes it does matter. Brad tells me this is one of those times. I say give him a break, you don't know all the facts. They're trying to destroy Cabot so they can put in their own man. It's all politics. But he said—"

"He said he couldn't stop thinking about the man they left behind."

"Right," said Myrna. "Do I stand by Cabot or not?"

"Brad won't," said Jenny. "Is he doing the wrong thing?"

"I don't know. I know he's turned the town upside down, but I don't think we'll ever really get the whole picture about what happened back there in Russia."

"Even after today?"

"Especially after today. Brad says, Ames says, the secret transcript says . . . *oy.* But one thing I know," said Myrna. "That boy has stuck his neck out, and maybe I work for Cabot, but Brad I care about more. Very unprofessional. What about you?"

"That's it," said Jenny. "What about me?"

About the time they were finishing the third cup of tea, talking now about Myrna's early life in the Agency, when everybody was faced with hard questions about loyalty and Myrna's closest friend was being unfairly and unjustly banished for a human mistake in love, the sounds of a door opening and closing and somebody entering came from the living room. "In here," called out Myrna. "We're just having tea."

Brad appeared in the doorway, pulling off his sweatshirt. When his head emerged he was astonished to see Jenny. While they were saying hello, a little tentatively, Myrna put her knitting aside and started another kettle of water. "I'm going downtown," she said. "I got some errands to run. You two entertain each other. I'll see you later."

In a moment she was gone.

"How'd you know I was here?" Brad asked.

"I just asked myself where you'd feel safest," said Jenny, a little sadly.

51

"Don't acknowledge," said the voice on the phone, which of course Frank Cabot recognized immediately, despite the early hour and his groggy state.

Kitty murmured by his side.

"I'm going to give you a phone number; you know the area code. I want you to call me from a public phone in one hour. I know you have great confidence in the loyalty and security of your outfit, but I don't think it's possible to be too cautious in the present case."

Cabot wrote the phone number on a pad.

"One hour," said the voice.

"Honey," murmured Kitty.

"It's nothing," said Cabot. "Go back to sleep. I've got to get an early start. Long day."

Indeed it was. That Tuesday was the longest day of his life, starting with cornflakes and skim milk in the darkened kitchen and thence proceeding to the icy parking lot of a supermarket a mile away, where Cabot found a working pay phone. He bought a copy of *The Washington Post* from a machine and sat in the car until the appointed time, reading about his doomed appointment. Philip Macomber's story under a three-column headline related the basic facts: what Cameron said, what the former president said in heated denial, what Cabot said to the piranha school of reporters outside the hearing room, what Senator MacLaverty said about the oceans of corroborating testimony to come. Cabot skipped his way through the gray columns and then flipped pages to read a *Post* editorial advising against a rush to judgment ("Thank you," he thought) pending the administration's response to the extraordinary charges unveiled in the first day of the confirmation hearings for Frank Cabot.

"But"—new sentence, new paragraph—"if no convincing denial is quickly forthcoming . . ."

Convincing, thought Cabot. How am I going to engineer that?

But all the same, the case wasn't quite closed. The body language of the front page hinted at doubt. Big stories got banner headlines. Stories rarely came bigger than this, but it was not a banner headline; it didn't even lead the paper. Only one thing could explain the restraint: The editors were still not one thousand percent convinced the story was going to stick. Until that spark of doubt was extinguished, Cabot's nomination remained alive.

At the appointed time he got out of the warm car and punched in numbers. The charge would be billed to an account not easily traced to the Agency. The phone was picked up on the first ring. "We'll trust," said the voice, "that your colleagues are not listening in. My question to you is: Have they got the paper or not?"

"I very much doubt it," said Cabot. "There was a little flap about that investigation a couple of years back and it turned out the attorney general did *not* authorize the bugs and taps, and I think we all scrambled to sanitize the files at that time."

"You know or you think?"

"I think."

"Can you get your people to make sure?"

"My authority over that search is going to be limited at this point."

"Limited or zero?"

"Zero."

"Well, in that case, no matter what the bugs recorded and no matter what the transcripts say, our position is that we were misunderstood."

For several minutes while Cabot huddled and shivered and stamped his feet beside the frigid phone booth he negotiated a common version with Otis Jones of the sad fate of the inquiry about the American prisoner held in Akmolinsk: they asked, they were told, they certainly never gave any such order, et cetera, et cetera. "Carter says nobody spoke to him," said Cabot. "Do we contradict?"

"Nobody wins a pissing match with a president," said Otis Jones.

"But in fact he did know? You were getting your instructions from him?"

"I don't see how I could prove it. I wasn't bugging the Oval Office or the White House phones."

"But he did know?"

"That's certainly what I told you."

"But it's true?"

"Don't worry about that, Frank. Your instructions came from a lawful source; you're covered, relax."

"But tell me it's true."

"Of course it's true. I would never take anything like that on myself. But I don't want to get into an argument with a former president. I think what we should emphasize now is that this report from Israel was discreetly investigated, and once it was clear the prisoner had died no further action was taken, because what was the point?"

"And we deeply regret now that the family was not informed."

"Exactly. It was a judgment call, we had no proof, no body, nothing in writing, so we—"

"Said nothing," said Frank Cabot.

"Said nothing," said Otis Jones. "I think that's the best we can do under the circumstances. It pretty much explains what happened. If the transcripts are missing, so much the better."

"You're ready to come back here at the end of the week and take the stand?"

"Not this week. The docs have got me confined to bed rest at the moment, and it won't hurt if I hover between life and death for a couple of days. Nobody wants to harass a dying man."

"Okay. But I'd feel better if we had some sort of paper or a witness to prove we weren't off on our own. Wasn't somebody handling this for the president at the White House?"

"Frank," said Otis Jones, "that was me."

Cabot was back in the house by eight in time for a cup of coffee with Kitty before the Agency driver picked him up. She didn't ask where he had been and he didn't say. She asked if he was going to be home for dinner and he said he didn't know. She asked if he still planned on dinner with the Becketts on Friday and he said he didn't know.

"You don't make it easy, Frank," said Kitty. "I don't know what you're feeling or what you're thinking or how to help."

"It's not complicated," said Cabot. "I'm feeling trapped and I'm trying to think of a way out and I don't know how you can help."

"What should I tell people?"

"What people?" asked Cabot.

"People who ask. People I know. People I see."

"Tell them what they heard on TV isn't so. I wish I'd found that prisoner alive and brought him back to cheering throngs. But it wasn't possible. That wasn't an option. This wasn't easy."

Cabot told Kitty pretty much the story he'd worked out with Otis Jones. "That's what I'll say when I get back on the stand," Cabot said. "We tried and we failed, but we had nothing to do with the death of this man."

Cabot waited for a response, but it was a moment in coming.

"Could you call up the White House and withdraw your name?" asked Kitty. "Could you say this isn't worth it, you don't want this job or any job this much?"

"Is that what you'd like?"

"I'd like to get our life back. We have no life now."

"I think it's too late," said Cabot. "I think MacLaverty might start pushing the attorney general to bring perjury charges. I'd be on my own. I'd need a lawyer. At Washington lawyer rates, I'd be broke at the end of the first week, and no one's going to raise funds for me like they did for the Clintons. As long as I'm running the Agency I've got access to the files and I can get people to answer the phone."

"You can't cut a deal?"

"I haven't got much to bargain with, Kitty."

"So we've just got to live through it."

"There's no other way."

. . .

In his office before nine, having said good morning to the gauntlet of tentative faces that lined his route, Cabot asked Jane to place calls to the directors of the National Security Agency, the FBI, and the Justice Department, and to the CIA's chief archivist. To each of them, when Jane got them on the phone, he delivered opening pleasantries as appropriate and roughly the same message.

"As you know, yesterday during my confirmation hearing certain charges were made in the Senate by a very junior officer of the CIA concerning my handling of an inquiry about an American prisoner of war in Russia twenty-some years ago. Claims were made that conversations in which I participated were recorded by a branch of this government. Whether such recordings exist I have no idea. But I want to ask you, personally, to take an interest in the search for any records your organization may have about this episode, and to press that search to the utmost of your ability, and to let me know what has been found, if anything, as soon as possible but in any event before the close of business today."

While Cabot delivered four versions of this speech, stressing his desire that no stone be left unturned and how grateful he would be for an early report, Leo Weissberg sat patiently in a chair by the window.

"Have I left anybody out?" asked Cabot.

"I'd say you got the people you have to worry about most," said Weissberg.

"Who's next?"

"Friendly senators." Weissberg named the members of the Senate intelligence committee who would or at least might vote for him, suggested a couple of reporters he might give a few minutes on the phone and others he should under no circumstances speak to, and finally reminded Cabot of some longtime friends of the Agency in the Washington establishment. If he spoke to them personally, they might stand fast and even place a call or two of their own.

"But if I were you," said Weissberg, "I'd start with this list of MIA groups." He pulled a typewritten sheet from his pocket. "They're still mostly in shock, but when they start talking they're going to raise holy hell. I wouldn't put it off. You need to convince them to keep their peace till the evidence is in."

They went on talking damage-control strategy for another twenty minutes: Issue a detailed statement or wait for the next hearing (wait); give a talk to the assembled troops in the Bubble or send a one-page letter to the supergrades (letter); make a point of being seen around town or lie low (lie low); go on all the talk shows or give an interview to a friendly columnist (interview). Cabot wanted to charge out with guns blazing. Weissberg told him to sit tight until he had something to go out *with*—documents, witnesses, official reports slamming the Ames story, something with a little more substance than a claim of Scout's honor, it ain't true.

"But, dammit," Cabot said, "it *isn't* true."

"Of course not," said Weissberg. "People who know you will understand that. But the rest of the world is going to want to see some evidence."

"I hate doing nothing," said Cabot. "My instinct is deny, deny, deny."

"No," said Weissberg. "Let the rumor mill run wild for a couple of days; then attack the crazy ones."

Cabot pondered. "What I'd like to do," he said, "is go on some talk show like *Larry King Live* and explain what crap this is."

"How much time have you spent listening to call-in shows?"

"Not much," Cabot conceded.

"There's a guy who picks the phone calls, and he plays for the ratings," said Weissberg. "He can put on pussycats or conspiracy nuts, and what are you going to say to the guys who think you got paid millions of dollars for leaving the MIAs behind?"

"What are you talking about?"

"Check out Larry King," said Weissberg. "Or Rush Limbaugh or Gordon Liddy. The average American thinks government is a con game, the CIA killed Kennedy, they've discovered a cure for cancer but the doctors won't let it out, the State Department wants to turn the country over to the UN, the army keeps the bodies of aliens frozen in a secret lab at Fort Detrick, Maryland. You should see the mail we get.

"Frank," Weissberg continued, "let's look this in the eye. The only American who ever had a shot at bringing back an honest-to-God MIA was you. And the Russians let him die while you were talking. Think about it. You don't want to go on Larry King."

Cabot saw the point. But he was irritated. He thought he was pretty good at fielding hostile questions.

He worked the phone, ate a sandwich at his desk, gazed out the window, and wished he could have told his father he was beginning to understand what he'd been through. He resisted the temptation to phone Larry Shedd in Moscow, knowing it was much too soon for news. Shedd might still be hung up in customs at Sheremetyevo. Kondrashov was living in a dacha in

Peredelkino outside Moscow. He was probably very frail, and it would take Shedd another day to reach him. Cabot had to be patient.

He worked his way down his list of names, keeping the calls short. It was tiring work: trying to sound confident, cheerful, and upbeat while deep within he felt the cold onset of defeat. He wondered if the FBI was right and some crazy right-wing militia group was plotting to kill him. He half wished somebody had pushed his way through the crowd of reporters the night before. It might not be so bad, compared to what he was going through. Cabot could imagine it perfectly: the frightened people stepping back, the young man with wild hair and a pistol in his hand, the shocking crack of the shot, Cabot falling backward, his hand going to his ribs just beneath the heart, coming away wet with bright arterial blood. It would all be captured on video and played over and over on the news shows. The president would speak at his funeral. Kitty would stand weeping at the president's side.

Where was John Hinckley when you needed him?

Cabot's sad reverie was interrupted by the phone; it was Jane saying that one of the senators on MacLaverty's committee was responding to a roll-call vote and was unavailable to take Cabot's call.

"Damn," said Cabot quietly to himself. He crossed out the name.

"Jane? Would you try Harry Hawkins in Georgia? His wife called last night, and I promised to get back to them."

A few moments later he was on the phone with Lydia.

"It's been crazy here, Lydia," Cabot said. "I'm sorry to take so long getting back to Harry. Is now a good time?"

"The doctor's with him now. But he wants to talk to you."

"Did he tell you what's on his mind?"

"No," said the senator's wife. Her manner had softened. Cabot wondered what that meant. "I know he was terribly upset by that young man's testimony yesterday. I suppose it's about that. You might try again this evening but he's best in the morning. He wakes up feeling sixty again. Frank?"

"Yes?"

"Just tell him you did everything you could for that MIA, will you? Harry always thought the world of you."

"I'll tell him," said Cabot.

In midafternoon the director of the National Security Agency called to say that the NSA had, in fact, plucked from the air and recorded certain telephone calls between Cabot and Otis Jones during a security investigation of a White House aide in 1977. The original recordings had been destroyed and a sole set of transcripts had been surrendered to the Justice Department in 1986. "The cupboard's bare, Frank," said the NSA's director. "No logs, no copies of copies, nothing."

An hour later the director of the FBI reported that the Bureau had, in fact, placed listening devices in certain offices of the National Security Council in 1977 during an investigation of a White House aide. The original recordings had been destroyed and a sole set of transcripts had been surrendered to the Justice Department in 1986.

Shortly thereafter, the CIA's chief archivist informed him that all recordings, transcripts, logs, and intraoffice memoranda concerning the 1977 security investigation, along with correspondence with the Justice Department in 1986, had been destroyed in the mid-1990s at the order of Frank Cabot.

"Are you sure I gave those instructions?" Cabot asked.

"You gave them to me, Frank," said the chief archivist.

"And the files are clean?"

"Clean as a whistle," said the archivist. "I know because I ran all that paper through the shredder myself, and I put the litter in the burn bag, and I took it all down to the burn room. Just as you instructed."

After Cabot's third attempt to call the attorney general without success he summoned Weissberg and asked him to try the attorney general's assistant for internal security affairs. While Cabot listened, Weissberg punched in the numbers, asked for an update, said "Uh-huh, okay" two or three times, glanced at Cabot, and shook his head.

"He says he doesn't know," said Weissberg. "But he knows. My guess: They've sent the transcripts to the White House. The president can fight a subpoena better than the AG—if he's in the mood to fight. You could try Schleicher."

"I have tried Schleicher. He's away from his desk until the next millennium."

"Haven't you got any other friends at the White House?"

"Schleicher was never a friend," said Cabot. "And the answer is no. My other channels all shut down a week ago."

"No news from the Russians?" asked Weissberg.

"Not yet. I expect to hear something in the morning."

"Is there anything else you'd like me to do?" asked Weissberg.

"I wish I could think of something."

"In that case," said Weissberg.

They said good night. Cabot thought about calling a friend, but the only one he really felt like talking to was in Savannah recovering from a heart attack. He thought about going home but hesitated. He hadn't called Kitty, she'd have nothing planned for dinner, she'd be in the library with a scotch and soda making a ring on the end table, watching the news with the sound turned off. Tomorrow was going to be just the same. And on Thursday, barring a miracle, the Senate intelligence committee was going to peel the skin from his body, one strip at a time.

Outside it was growing dark. It wasn't late, but he could think of nothing useful to do.

Usually he was the master of his feelings and dismissed those that served no purpose. But at this moment he felt about three-quarters beaten, and he was sick of trying to keep it all going. He just wanted to get out of Washington. It wasn't hard to arrange. He kept a bag filled with overnight things in the office. The travel office could get him anywhere anytime.

"I'm leaving for the day," Cabot told his secretary on the phone. "Will you tell the night watch officer I'm going out of town? Just for the night—I'll be back by lunchtime tomorrow."

"Should I tell him where you're going?"

"Tell him," said Cabot, "I don't know where I'll be staying. But I'll check in when I get there."

By the time Cabot found a car and a reservation at a motel—a world trade conference had sucked up every room in downtown Savannah—it was past eight and he wanted a drink more than he wanted dinner. He figured there'd be some kind of local watering hole near the motel, but that guess turned out to be utterly wrong. The Motel 6 on the old road to Ossabaw was next to nothing but marsh grass and live oaks. The man at the desk, wearing a T-shirt and watching TV, told him the Krispy Kreme was closed but there was a 7-Eleven that stayed open all night a mile farther down.

Cabot dropped his bag in the room and drove down the road in the darkness past the occasional flash of an oncoming car until he spotted an oasis of yellow light ahead and the big red and green sign. A pickup was parked near the entrance. Inside sat two young men smoking cigarettes. "Evening," said Cabot as he passed.

"How ya doin'?" asked the driver.

Cabot looked around the store, rejected the potato chips and the doughnuts with pink frosting, bought a can of Planters cocktail peanuts and, after several moments of staring gloomily through the glass doors of the cooler, two six-packs of Budweiser in cans.

Back at the motel, Cabot popped a beer and turned on the TV. He called the Agency night watch officer and left his address and phone number. He called Kitty to explain he'd be away for the night. He called Lydia to say he didn't want to talk to Harry, he wanted to see him, and he'd drop by at nine in the morning if that was all right.

"Are you already in Savannah? Don't you want to spend the night here?"

"Oh, no," Cabot lied, "I'm very comfortable, I don't want to be any trouble."

He was not comfortable. The bed sagged deeply in the center and the springs creaked whenever he moved. He opened a second beer, took a handful of peanuts, and surfed channels until he ran into *Larry King.* This is what it's come to, Cabot thought. I used to be a rainmaker in Washington. Now I'm just another worn-out sonofabitch sitting on a motel bed watching TV and drinking a Bud.

> KING: Back with more on the dramatic story unfolding here in Washington this week. We've just been talking with Faith Osborne, star columnist for *The Washington Post,* who has been writing about the tragic human cost of living for decades with uncertainty. One day a telegram arrives to say a loved one is missing in battle in Vietnam, and then—nothing. Decades of not knowing. Devastating.
>
> We have with us now the sister of an MIA, a young sergeant in the Green Berets who disappeared on a hush-hush mission in 1970. Last week Stacy Dyer discovered that her brother didn't die in Vietnam; he died in Russia, eight years after he was first reported missing! Stacy—welcome to *Larry King Live.*
>
> DYER: Thank you very much.
>
> KING: Tell us. You watched the Senate hearing on Monday? You heard that young CIA officer describe what happened to your brother?
>
> DYER: It was awful.
>
> KING: Tell us, Stacy. How did it make you feel to learn your brother was a prisoner in *Russia*? How did it make you feel to learn your brother was alive when we first heard about him, and that reliable sources say he was left to die on American orders?
>
> DYER: At least now we know.
>
> KING: Yes?
>
> DYER: Now we know it's over. When I think of all those years. My

mother . . . Jason was her firstborn. He was her baby. I have children, I know what this means. To lose your brother or your child—to worry about him every night for thirty years. Is he locked up somewhere? Is he sick or injured? Is he hungry? Is he waiting for someone to come take him home?

KING: Devastating. Let's take some calls. The switchboard is lit up. Everybody has a question. Bill in Minneapolis. Bill? You're on the air.

BILL: Mrs. Dyer—you're a brave woman.

DYER: Thank you.

BILL: They've been telling us there are no MIAs alive in Southeast Asia. No prisoners in Russia. No confirmed sightings. And now this. I want to know—How many other American boys are in prisons over there in Russia?

DYER: Well, I don't know.

KING: Thanks for the call, Bill. We've got Terry in Battle Creek, Michigan.

TERRY: This country needs to wake up. What this shows us is the government is lying. It's been lying to us for thirty years. They said all the prisoners were coming home, but they knew it was a lie. Because they went back on the deal.

KING: What deal is that, Terry?

TERRY: The peace accords—you remember? The United States was going to help rebuild Vietnam with billions of dollars. Billions and billions. And the prisoners were all coming home. That was the deal. And we never sent them a dime.

KING: What's your question, Terry?

TERRY: Don't you see? No money, no prisoners.

KING: Thousands of prisoners did come home, Terry.

TERRY: And thousands didn't. That's my point. Now tell me this. Where did the money go?

KING: I wish I knew. Thanks for the call, Terry. Now Phil in Dearborn, Michigan. Lot of fans in Michigan tonight. Phil, you're on the air. Have you got a question for Stacy?

PHIL: That last caller, he had a point. Mrs. Dyer, why do you think they told us about your brother now? Why now, after all these years?

DYER: I guess . . . I don't know.

PHIL: This country is waking up, that's why. People won't take it anymore. That senator who ran the committee—the one they said had a heart attack. How many people know he didn't have any heart attack?

KING: What are you talking about, Phil?

PHIL: He was shot. Mrs. Dyer, that senator was shot by a member of the Ruby Ridge Brigade to wake up this country. That's why they're telling us about your brother; they're afraid.

KING: They're coming out of the woodwork tonight.

DYER: You know, what they say is right. I don't know about the Ruby thing, but this country is going through a whole shaking up. It's like it says in the Bible—you shall know the truth, and the truth shall make you free. And that's what's happening.

KING: You heard it here. The truth shall make you free. Are you listening, America?

When he opened his eyes Wednesday morning, Cabot knew what he was going to do. He had been back and forth on this but he was finished. Cabot was famous in Washington as a man whose composure never cracked, but now he felt he had run out of brave smiles. They had his balls in a vise and they were turning the handle, and Frank Cabot didn't want to fight anymore.

The sun was peeping in through the blinds. The clock radio said 7:45. The lights and the television were both on and he was still in his underwear on top of the covers where he had fallen asleep in the small hours halfway through the second six-pack. He rarely drank, he had never before in his life consumed nine beers in a single day, but aside from needing to pee in a desperate way Frank Cabot actually felt pretty good. He was at peace. He had decided to quit making up stories and tell Harry Hawkins the truth, every last painful bit of it.

It seemed so simple, so obvious and inevitable. Harry would help him through it. Cabot did it because Otis Jones told him that's what the president wanted. It was awful, it just about killed him, but he had no choice. The business about jobs? Cabot wasn't angling for anything. Jones kept telling him he wouldn't be forgotten. That's the way Cabot remembered it, no matter what the transcripts might say.

Feeling almost cheerful for the first time in weeks, Cabot shaved, showered, dressed, and departed. Outside, the morning was brilliant and mild and lush with the green of an early southern spring. The day was practically patting Frank Cabot on the back for the courage of his decision.

He drove back north to Savannah on the interstate, made his way through town to Victory Drive, and stopped at a place that looked as if it might serve a decent breakfast. "Honey," said the waitress, when Cabot put down a five-dollar bill as a tip, "something good must have happened to you because you are just all smiles."

It was true. He had quit agonizing; the cloud had lifted, he had known Harry Hawkins for twenty years and Harry knew how things happened in this town. Naturally, he'd be upset. He'd be disappointed. But Cabot felt he simply could not go through one more day without being able to speak honestly with someone about the terrible mistake he had made nearly thirty years ago.

He turned down Bradley, found Commodore Drive, and was soon pulling up a long curving driveway past noble oak trees to a white house with a broad porch and columns in the classic southern mode. He parked, his feet crunched on the gravel, he was met at the door by Lamarr Stebbins, Hawkins's driver, who took him into a sitting room. Lydia got up from a highly polished mahogany table in a sunny corner where she'd been drinking coffee and reading the paper. The ceilings were high, the windows tall. She gestured to a chair on the other side of the table, thanked Cabot for coming, offered him coffee.

"How's he feeling?" asked Cabot.

"When he first wakes up," Lydia said, "he thinks he might like to play nine holes of golf but it doesn't last long. The doctors say he suffered a lot of damaged heart muscle. He might fool us all and live another twenty years, but he's not the old Harry—you'll see. He frets and forgets. Right now he's just sick about these hearings. He reads the papers, he watches CNN, he wants to call everybody in Washington. I took the phone out of the room. Frank, I don't know what happened back there, but I don't want you fighting with Harry. He can't handle it."

"I won't fight," said Cabot. "I'm going to tell him anything he wants to know."

"He's been after me and after me to get you on the phone," said Lydia. "I told him you were coming and I'll be honest with you; he's in a state. Just let him speak his piece."

Cabot promised he wouldn't argue, he wouldn't raise his voice, he wouldn't interrupt, and he wouldn't stay long.

Lydia led him up a broad curving staircase to a large, brilliantly lit front bedroom overlooking a vast expanse of lawn with a view in the near distance of the Savannah River. Hawkins was sitting up in the middle of a huge canopied bed, wearing a bathrobe of freshly pressed seersucker. There was a television set on a bureau across the room, and as soon as Cabot entered Hawkins turned off the sound with the mute button of his remote control. He patted the side of his bed but he didn't say anything.

His face was grim, the eyes unhappy; Cabot was struck immediately by his old friend's pale skin, the blue-gray shadows beneath the eyes, the blue-pink of his trembling lower lip. He continued to pat the side of his bed, almost as a man might pat his leg to summon a dog.

While Cabot hesitated, Lydia drew up a chair near the bed. Cabot sat down. Lydia settled herself nearby.

"Harry," said Cabot.

Hawkins waved his hand to say no.

"Harry," said Cabot again. He was sure the best way was to plunge in—get it said, the flat fact of it, then fill in the details. Brad Cameron was telling the truth. That was the right place to begin. "Harry, I want to tell you—"

"No," said Hawkins. "No. I know what you're going to say. No."

"You don't understand, Harry—"

"Let me speak," said Hawkins.

Now Cabot was desperate to get it out. He couldn't keep the denial going another second. But just as he was saying, "It's true," Lydia laid a hand on his knee. She shook her head.

"I know," said Hawkins. "Listen. I've been thinking about this. I've been thinking about my whole life, Frank, my whole career—what I've stood for. I've been thinking about this country's promise to the boys who serve in the armed forces. I know that young fellow from your outfit, and I know he's a decent, honest fellow."

Hawkins paused. He seemed overcome by sadness. Cabot sensed that the moment of truth was near.

"When I think," said Hawkins, raising his head, his voice suddenly loud, firm, and clear, "when I think of the lies—the damnable lies—of that felon and traitor Aldrich Ames. He's trying to destroy this country.

"Frank," said Hawkins, "I don't believe a goddam word of it. He's trying to besmirch the honor of this country and of every American government since the Vietnam war. You wouldn't do that. No American would do what Ames is trying to say was done here. I trust you absolutely and completely. You don't need to explain anything to me. Please, not a word, I *know* this didn't happen. If there's anything I can do to help you get the truth out . . . God, Frank, if I could just get out of this damned bed."

His voice fell. There were tears in his eyes, but he was smiling and he had taken Cabot's hand in his own. "Don't lose hope," said Harry Hawkins. "We're going to find a way."

After a stunned moment spent collecting his thoughts, Cabot said, "I knew I could count on you, Harry."

52

Standing in line Thursday morning, waiting to enter the Senate Office Building where the second day of hearings in the nomination of Frank Cabot to be Director of Central Intelligence was scheduled to begin at 9 a.m., Dean Cutter felt invisible. Russell knew how to do things. First he'd used hair clippers to shave away the curls on the side and back of Dean's head. Then he'd showed him how to roll two pieces of well-chewed spearmint gum into tubes about the size of a piece of macaroni and slip them up under his upper lip, one on each side. Wearing a new blue suit, a white shirt, and a striped tie and carrying a hard leather briefcase, Dean Cutter looked nothing like last week's angry vet from Accokeek but like somebody getting ready to sell life insurance. There were a dozen people ahead of him and another dozen behind who all looked more dangerous. The side-cut guys with earpieces, walking slowly up and down the sidewalk checking out the crowd, paid no attention to Dean Cutter, who thought to himself, *It's almost over.*

Russell had turned him around. Russell and that bitch therapist Lisa Benson. He'd hit the street on Monday determined to get as far from Russell and the District as he could, but what he discovered in the day that followed was that he had just about nothing going for him: no money, no friend he could call, no plan. Putting the ammunition clip in his pocket was his last bright idea. He couldn't even go home for five minutes, for fear Russell would be there with that steely look and the promise that the guys in Michigan never forgave and never forgot. And now—

"Would you open the briefcase, please?"

Cutter's mind froze. He felt the prickly onset of sweat on his forehead, neck, under his arms. He had no idea what was in the briefcase. Russell had handed it to him, saying, "Don't worry, trust me, this will get you in."

"Sir, I'll have to look into that briefcase. Can you step to the side, please?"

Russell had fucked him. He was going down. His hand was shaking. His voice croaked when he said, "All right."

He stepped over to the counter, placed the briefcase on top, started to work the catches.

"I'll do that," said the guard. He turned the briefcase around, snapped the catches, raised the lid. Cutter could not see what was inside but he could see the face of the guard as he stared for a long moment at the contents, then slowly lifted his gaze toward Cutter. He saw it in the guard's eyes. He was dead.

The first night on his own Dean Cutter had found a warm corner in Union Station. He'd kept one eye open all night for the cops who patrolled the station hourly in pairs and rapped the feet of sleepers with their billy clubs. The floor was hard. He was dying in the groin area. In the morning Cutter's pockets surrendered coins enough for coffee and a sweet roll, and he faced the rest of the day with no plan. For two hours he pored over discarded copies of the *Post* and the *Times* and read every word of the long accounts of the young CIA officer's testimony. It was impossible not to see the image of Jason in Russia, thousands of miles from anywhere, wondering when his country would come to his rescue. Waiting all those years ago right up to the moment when the Russian guards came for him because he was no longer convenient to his country. It was impossible not to want to pay back the man who had done that. He'd like to hear what Lisa Benson had to say now.

But anger and the desire to kill had run thin in Cutter. He hadn't had a drink, he hadn't smoked up. He was nervous and shaking. Maybe Russell was right. Maybe the Ruby Ridge plan to wake up the country by shooting Frank Cabot would make some sort of difference, but Cutter didn't care. He didn't want revenge, he wasn't looking to be a hero; he just wanted the pain in his groin to go away, a place no one would bother him, a decent meal, a long sucking drag, and a chance to explain to Stacy Dyer he wasn't a creep and he had never stopped thinking about her.

Close to panic, knowing he had to stir himself, he pulled a paper coffee container out of a trash can and tried begging. It wasn't easy. The groin area didn't like standing in one place, and the men and women with briefcases sweeping through were blind to his need. He got a quarter. He got a dime and a nickel. He got a rattle of pennies. With mingled feelings of hopelessness and self-pity, Cutter reflected that he was asking but he was not receiving.

Cops, he learned, didn't mind sleeping in a public place so much, but begging they came down on hard. The third time, two cops hustled him out to the street and one of them gave him a parting tap on the elbow with a billy club that ached for an hour.

What could you buy with eighty-three cents? Where could you go?

It crossed Cutter's mind that he probably couldn't find Russell if he wanted to. But if he did find him maybe he could explain. Maybe Russell would lend him twenty bucks and say he understood, he could find somebody else, the guys in Michigan had plenty of other avenues. Back and forth it went in his mind. Hitchhike to Accokeek or go back to his apartment, maybe sell the TV, sell the radio and the microwave—talk a blue streak if Russell was there, but if no one was around sell what he could, pack some clothes, and clear out.

He wavered until it was dark, and then it was too late to try hitchhiking; nobody was going to pick up a guy in his forties with a two-day beard and his thumb out on the streets of Washington. So Cutter walked slowly back to his apartment, favoring the sore point in his groin. It was nearly seven as he passed the alley three doors up from his building, and his heart jumped when a voice whispered his name and Russell's right hand emerged from the shadows to stop him.

"Dean," came the voice; the hand was on Cutter's arm, not grabbing, just touching, resting. "The cops were here this afternoon. They must have put something together."

"I don't believe it. What could they know?"

"Maybe somebody ID'd you from last week. But they came by—twice. Two cops. They went upstairs. They talked to the people in the stores."

"You were watching?"

"I know how to watch without being noticed. I've been at this a long time."

"Well, I'm not up to it. Why the hell do you want me in this?"

"You're a good man. You're just a little strung out."

"All my stuff's in there. I've got nothing."

"Don't risk it," said Russell. "I have a place we can stay. We'll be safe there. I know what you need—a little smoke. Am I right?"

"You've got dope?"

"Hey, you're my man," said Russell. "I've got what you need."

Cutter was hungry, he was frightened, he was tired of trying to decide for himself, and he had the shakes bad.

"You can't take this in with you," said the guard. He turned the briefcase around so Cutter could see.

Inside the briefcase were four or five copies of *Playboy,* the top one opened to a full-page shot of a naked woman sitting on a motorcycle. Cutter didn't understand, and it must have showed on his face.

"The corkscrew," said the guard. "I'm sorry. No sharp metal objects. If you want to go in you'll have to leave that here with us. It's regulations."

So Cutter had another chance to back out. Russell was giving him an excuse if he wanted it. *Up to you,* he was saying.

"That's okay," said Cutter. "I can always get another."

Russell had advised against it but Cutter insisted; he was going to his anger management group on Wednesday night because he hadn't missed a session yet, he needed to get his license back, and if the cops were really after him it would be better to find out there than tomorrow morning wandering the halls with a pistol in his pocket. Cutter did not mention the name of Lisa Benson or cite his desire to put her in her place, but he did not bend so Russell said okay and backed off.

Wednesday dragged until the hour for group at seven. Cutter arrived a few minutes early. He'd been planning what to say to her all afternoon. He had an idea that going to the meeting was a kind of cover, and he was telling the truth when he said he wanted his license back. But what he really wanted was to confront her with her own misreading of the truth of his life. Maybe he didn't see action in the Gulf. But he'd lived for thirty years with the betrayal of his friend left behind in Vietnam. The papers had been full of it, and he wanted to see Lisa Benson's face when she admitted he had been telling the truth.

"You're early, Mr. Cutter. Is there something you want to tell me?"

"No," said Cutter, "I just want to make sure you understand that I was telling the truth."

"The truth about what? About your experience in the Gulf War?"

"Not that," said Cutter. "The truth about my friend from Accokeek, the MIA we left behind. You said I was making him up."

"I don't understand. What friend?"

"It's been in all the papers. I told you about him—Jason Dyer. He was killed in Russia."

"I don't remember that name. I haven't seen anything about that in the news."

"This was a guy I knew, he used to do things for all the kids in the neighborhood. I told you his name—the CIA had him killed."

"What are you talking about?" asked Lisa Benson. She wasn't looking at him, and she seemed nervous. "Can't this wait?"

"No, it can't wait. You called me a liar, but it's in all the papers."

"Mr. Cutter, I would never call a client a liar. I think I might have said you dramatize."

"Dramatize?"

"Make up stories. Create an imaginary history to explain your troubles with anger and alcohol."

"You think I'm making this up?"

"I don't want to get into it. I want you to sit down."

"Those bastards killed my friend—they're the liars. They're going to pay for this. You just watch the goddam TV."

"What are you saying?"

"They think nobody can touch them. Well, they're going to die surprised!"

"Do you understand what you're saying? Making threats is not an acceptable form of acting out."

"Acting out?"

"You're shouting. You're making threats."

"You're calling me a liar."

"You're threatening to kill somebody. I have no choice in the matter, I have to report that. Do you think you can just make threats and nobody will say anything?"

She was going to say something else but she stopped and shrank away as Cutter took a step forward and raised his hand. But three of the men in the group were on their feet before he could strike. "It's no threat!" he shouted at her. He crossed the room to the door and turned back. He had stopped shouting. His voice was strained. He held Lisa Benson's eyes with his own and knew she was really paying attention at last.

"Tell anybody you want," he said. "It's too late."

He told Russell none of this. But he asked if the guys in Michigan were still ready to go ahead.

"That was a neat trick," Cutter said to Russell in the men's room. "The *Playboys*, the corkscrew."

"If you were nervous the *Playboys* would explain it, and if you wanted out the corkscrew would open the door. This is something you've got to want to do. You've gotta have that desire in your gut to even the score."

"It'll never be even," said Cutter. "I just want to see somebody else squirm for a change."

"Okay, then," said Russell. "Let's tell 'em we're here."

53

One of the assets of any Washington reporter elusive enough to remain single was the gradual seeding in government jobs all over town of former lovers who could generally be counted on to take a call. In the top drawer of his desk, George Tater kept an old address book with a red leather cover containing the names and changing addresses, job titles, and phone numbers of all the women he'd ever spent time with, which, over thirty years, amounted to quite a few. Sometimes an ember of old passion still glowed, but even those for whom it was completely over generally retained a kind of liking for Tater. In matters of the heart he never made a promise, so he never broke one. Over the years he remembered birthdays, he sent a note when he saw a familiar name in the paper, and he touched base for a cup of coffee or lunch from time to time. When he wanted access to the deliberations of some government office, the back door was frequently opened by someone recorded in his red leather address book.

The morning after Brad Cameron's testimony, George Tater spent an hour at his desk, drinking black coffee and going through the address book page by page. The morning *Times* had run a strong story by Tater about the explicit denials of Carter and his national security advisor, Zbigniew Brzezinski, laying a case for arguing that in the matter of Sergeant Jason Dyer the CIA had gone off on its own. But Tuesday's paper was already old news. Morrie Bloom was after him for a follow-up, and he wanted specifics, not Tater's vague assurance he had something in the works.

"Maybe the man from Plains is telling the truth," said Bloom, "but maybe not. Maybe the kid has got it right, but maybe the creep in Allenwood is running some kind of scam. That's what inquiring minds want to know."

"Keep your shirt on," said Tater. "I'll get it. I've just gotta get a foot in the door."

"What door is that?" asked Morrie Bloom.

"I'm working on it."

"Clock's ticking, George. We've got a front-page conference coming up in a couple of hours. It would be nice to have a story for tomorrow's paper."

"I'm your man," said Tater.

He called MacLaverty, but MacLaverty was in a meeting. He tried the assistant counsel, and Michael Vose told him that subpoenas had been delivered to the CIA, FBI, NSA, and the Justice Department, but it would be a day before anything turned up. Tater could call again tomorrow. But tomorrow was twenty-four hours and a whole news cycle away, and he needed something now. So he began to brood, and then he pulled out the address book and began looking for someone—an old girlfriend would be perfect—who might be witness to the records search at the CIA, the FBI, the NSA, or the Justice Department.

The morning went slowly. Tater's luck was bad. People had moved on, they were in the wrong office, they did not feel like doing Tater any favors, but mainly, of course, they just did not know the answer to his question.

Twice as he browsed back and forth he came to the name of Jenny Moore. Every other name had one or more old phone numbers crossed out beside it, but Jenny was still a one-number girl. He called it and left a message: Hi, how's the back, hope you'll be free later, lot to talk about.

Tater had known many women, and he could generally tell when one was moving on. Jenny's departure last week—in too much back pain for more than the tiniest peck goodbye—had about it the air of something closing down. When he finally got Jenny herself on the phone to ask if she'd be free around eight, he was pretty sure she would say she was sorry, and that would be that. Tater was unhappy about this, but he prided himself on looking things in the eye.

Tater made his slow way on through the address book.

Then he came to the name of Alice Rowe, and his mind began to work.

Alice Rowe. Lawyer. Second or third in her class at Harvard. Married, two kids, sweet overweight husband who was on the road a lot, utterly faithful but perfectly comfortable about meeting an old boyfriend for dinner when Oliver was out of town.

Tater had known Alice for twenty years. They'd dated for six months way back when. She wasn't his type—too thin, too angular, too quick to call him a jerk when he was being a jerk. But George felt a lingering fondness for Alice because she was smart, knew what was going on, always said what she meant, liked hanging out, told him things he didn't know, and described the people and events of Washington in sharp, amusing words that often found their way later into his news stories. She knew this, of course, and kind of liked it. Occasionally, late at night or on a summer afternoon when Congress was out and nothing was going on and Tater was alone, he asked himself if Alice Rowe was the girl he should have married. The answer was yes. Big mistake. But on the other hand, you can't call up a wife and wheedle a story.

Alice was a partner in a major Washington law firm. She took home a godawful amount of money, but every few years she asked for leave and went to work somewhere in the government. At the moment, as Tater had been reminded on coming across her name in his address book, Alice Rowe was a lawyer in the office of the White House counsel. His mind was working now. Alice had once been involved in a big White House–Congress pissing match over subpoenaed notes of a presidential briefing on China trade policy. She was hired to come up with reasons for saying no, her reasons were solid, and the Supreme Court agreed.

Now she was in the White House.

Focused and in full operational mode, Tater called a name at the Justice Department and spoke rapidly. He needed a little background. Who adjudicated conflict-of-interest problems when the White House wanted to do one thing and Justice another?

Well, came the answer, that would probably be Julius Blount.

Would it be possible to have Mr. Blount's extension?

It would.

Hello, Mr. Blount, George Tater here, I'm working on the inevitable story, ha-ha! Just looking for a little background on the way things might play out. Can you tell me if I've been correctly informed that the White House counsel has requested early notice of any transcripts that might turn up following yesterday's testimony in the Senate? . . . No, no. I understand you can't tell me what you've found, if anything, but I've got a source that says Legal Affairs wants to be in the loop; are you denying that? . . . No, you're not denying that. Of course they're in the loop. Now, if you could help me with just one more thing here. Who should I call to follow up—?

Here George Tater ran down a few names listed under Legal Affairs in the White House phone directory: Lane Stevens? . . . Ralph Richmond? . . . Alice Rowe?

Do you know Alice Rowe? Do you have any reason to think she wouldn't be involved in this matter? . . . You don't. . . . You do know Alice Rowe and you agree she's an expert on subpoenas.

Mr. Blount, you've been very helpful.

George Tater got up, took the elevator, left the building, and went for a brisk three-block walk, boxing the compass and returning to his office breathing rapidly and invigorated by the cold air. He called Alice Rowe at the White House.

"Hey, Alice. George Tater."

"How'd you know Oliver's out of town?"

"Oliver's always out of town. You free for dinner?"

"You asking?"

"Let's make it tentative. I've got one thing to check first."

"Another woman, I suppose," said Alice.

"You're right. Very sweet girl."

"Woman, George."

"No, Alice, this one really is a girl. I'm amazed we even had ten minutes together. I'll tell you about it sometime."

"But not tonight."

"Maybe tonight," said Tater. "I think I'm being phased out, but I haven't been actually told it's over.

"Listen. I'm working on you-know-what," Tater continued. "I spoke to a guy at Justice, Julius Blount. You know him? He says he knows you. He says Legal Affairs has asked for transcripts, if any. He isn't confirming anything has turned up—"

"Me neither, George," said Alice.

"I know. I understand. Here's my question. Deep background." Tater was talking quickly now. "Who decides what goes to MacLaverty? CIA isn't going to find anything as long as Cabot's running the shop. If NSA finds anything they'll give it to CIA. FBI will deliver to Justice. So if anybody has anything it'll be Justice. White House insists on seeing whatever turns up. So who decides? White House? Justice? You in your little cubicle? Can you help me on that?"

Alice said nothing for a moment.

"Alice?"

"I'm here." Alice sighed. Tater held his breath. "You've got it backwards, George. The White House didn't ask for those transcripts. We don't want those transcripts. I don't know why Blount told you that but trust me—no way."

"But the transcripts are the only solid evidence," protested Tater.

"Who cares?" said Alice. "Listen, the source for this is triple deep background, George, okay? Think about it. You know what the president is like. He hates hard choices. If you offer him vanilla or strawberry he has to take both. You can guess what's in those transcripts. Where does that leave Anderson? He can shred them and risk impeachment to protect some

CIA policy wonk, or he can blow the whistle on a former president and go down in history as a rat fink. Making that choice will require many sleepless afternoons. Trust me. Nobody in the White House *asked* for those transcripts."

"I think I get the picture," said Tater.

"It's painting by the numbers, George."

"The attorney general," said Tater, "put those transcripts in a pouch, handed them to a courier, and the White House signed a receipt before anyone knew what they were getting."

"I didn't tell you that, George."

"Who has them now?"

"Who's the man closest to the president?"

"I would say . . . Peter Schleicher."

"That's a very good guess," said Alice.

"And he has already asked if there's any way he can just ship them right back?"

"Knowing who he works for, I imagine that's exactly what he would do."

"And you've told him, stop dreaming."

"That would have been my considered opinion," said Alice, "if asked."

"Let me make sure I've got this right," said Tater. "The hot potato is in the White House as we speak and the president is agonizing about what to do."

"You're a helluva reporter, George."

"You wouldn't want to characterize what those transcripts actually say, would you?"

"I would not, George."

"I owe you a dinner," said George Tater. "I'll get back to you."

At the end of an hour, following another dozen calls to muddy the waters, Tater punched in the number of Morrie Bloom on the national desk in New York. "Morrie," he said, "the transcripts exist and the White House has got 'em."

"That's my boy," said Bloom.

54

Next to an election upset, the citizens of Washington love a public bloodletting, and Senator Brian MacLaverty's upcoming execution of the president's pick for the top job at CIA, universally predicted by the morning papers and news shows, was drawing a record crowd. Well before 8 a.m. Thursday a triple line stretched from the front door of the Richard Russell Senate Office Building around the block. Double the usual number of capitol police checked bags and briefcases inside while their colleagues kept the lines in order on the street. In addition, numerous plainclothesmen with listening devices in one ear passed slowly up and down the sidewalks, scanning the crowd and the traffic for any small thing that might tweak a well-developed sixth sense—a glance, a posture, a too-baggy coat, a bundle, an arm in a cast, too many men in a car moving too slowly, anything that did not seem right.

Inside the building the lines slowly shuffled toward the metal detectors and the desks where guards squeezed purses, opened umbrellas, unzipped the inner pockets of briefcases. The assistant counsel of the Senate intelligence committee had called Brad the night before to ask him to come. Brad agreed but said he'd prefer to sit in the audience this time, not in front of a TV in the senator's suite. Jenny and Myrna, on either side of him at Myrna's kitchen table, had declared they were coming too, and together, on the morning the hearings were to resume, they spent twenty minutes in line before they even got into the building. Directly ahead of them were a man and two women loudly comparing the mild March weather of Washington to the subzero temperatures and freak snowstorm they'd left behind in Idaho. And in front of them bobbed the gray ponytail of a Vietnam vet, his U.S. Army parka festooned with pins and medals, making his slow, laborious way forward with the aid of crutches and a leg brace. Brad turned to Jenny and Myrna beside him and whispered, "How the hell is a man in a leg brace going to get through those detectors?"

The answer was: after a scrupulous pat-down of every fold and nook of the human anatomy where a weapon might be hidden. When the inspectors were satisfied, the vet clanked off down the hall with surprising speed and vigor.

Brad and Jenny got through without trouble, but Myrna's satchel-like purse kept the guards busy for several minutes. She quarreled with one of them about her Swiss Army knife, insisting it was a culinary tool used only for cutting hard Genoa salami or peeling apples. The guard was sorry but firm. Myrna asked if she could leave her knife at the desk. Yes, the guard said, but he couldn't accept responsibility for it and she had to leave it at her own risk because there was no system in place for checking personal items. He was sorry again.

"I love this knife," Myrna said to Brad, "but I'm not letting you go into that lions' den alone." She shrugged and placed the knife on the desk.

Once through the security checkpoint they found themselves in a new line, heading down the hall through a lobby filled with photographers, reporters, and television crews and turning into the rear doors of the huge hearing room. Most of the faces meant nothing to them, but they recognized a couple of local television reporters and the Capitol Hill correspondents from CBS and NBC, slender, impeccably dressed men talking to assistants in the manner of generals to their staff officers. "They're really turning out," said Myrna.

"I wonder if they already know what's going to happen," said Jenny. "I suppose they're here to see MacLaverty nail down the coffin lid."

A buzz and hubbub spread through the news gaggle in the lobby—everybody turning, talking, asking, telling, whispering into phones. "Something is going on here," said Myrna.

Suddenly a woman in red—red dress, red silk shoes, long red fingernails, lips the dark bright red of arterial blood—focused on Brad. "Mr. Cameron! Mr. Cameron!"

She was on him in a moment, one hand on his arm, a strong whiff of perfume rising from her like must. "Two questions? Only a minute? Please."

But Myrna was like an attack dog. "Later," she said firmly, stepping in front of the woman in red and pushing Brad forward. "Not now. Let's see who says what, then maybe."

Cameras and lights had swiveled around. Cameras flashed, microphones were pushed at him, the woman in red was suddenly ignited like a beacon and she spoke loudly and firmly into a microphone: "Can Frank Cabot survive your testimony?"

BRAD: I—
MYRNA: *Thank you! Later, please!*

WOMAN IN RED: Are you surprised Frank Cabot hasn't withdrawn his name?

BRAD: I—

Myrna was between them now. The woman in red said okay, later; it was a promise; she'd be waiting. The line—heads turning to watch, mouths whispering "Who's that? Who's that?"—parted to let Brad, Myrna, and Jenny push directly into the back of the big hearing room, where all seemed calm.

They got good seats on the right not too far back. Four or five rows, ahead in the center, Brad could see the figure of Frank Cabot, his wife beside him, aides and assistants around him like a praetorian guard. "Cabot's here," Brad whispered, "so what's all the hubbub back there?"

"Hold your horses," said Myrna. "We'll find out with the rest of the country."

But it was more than an hour before the rest of the country got the news. The scheduled gavel moment of 9 a.m. came and went, and the whispering level began to rise. A great stirring and craning of necks followed as the minutes went by while a constantly changing stream of assistants roamed the stage, filling water glasses, adjusting microphones, fiddling with lights, and above all—as was apparent even from the audience—asking each other what was up and receiving shrugs in return.

"What's taking so long?" asked Brad. "Do you think he's withdrawn?"

"He'd die first," said Jenny.

"You don't always get to choose," said Myrna. "When a president says you gotta, you gotta. This seat isn't comfortable. I wish I'd brought my Twinkle-Toes."

"Your what?" asked Jenny.

Brad started to laugh. He tried to outline Myrna's theory of air travel, but he was laughing too hard to get it out.

At last, a few minutes before ten, a door opened at one end of the stage and the hearing room erupted with excited words as a line of senators emerged, talking quietly, making their way slowly across the dais. One by one they reached their name plates on the table and took their seats. "Poor Uncle Frank," said Jenny. "They all look so grim."

Senator Blair of Alabama, a great shambling walrus of a man in a white suit that seemed to glow in the spotlights, slowly made his way down the line, speaking a few words into the ear of each senator before settling himself in the last seat but one. A moment later the junior senator from Massachusetts came in, face set, making no eye contact, striding forward to the chair in the center of the table, where he paused. He looked up, scanned the audience with deliberation, and then reached down, picked up the name plate boldly reading SENATOR MACLAVERTY, and carried it to the empty chair at the far end of the table.

A puzzled murmur began to spread.

Then from the side, tall and proud, entered just a trifle unsteadily the white-haired figure of the senior senator from Georgia. His skin glowed with an almost ghostly pallor, but he was smiling and his head was high.

"My God," said Myrna. "It's Hawkins. The *meshuggener* has taken his committee back."

HAWKINS: The committee will now come to order. This is the first session of the second day of hearings on the nomination of Franklin S. Cabot to be Director of Central Intelligence. I apologize for the delay this morning, but there was a little confusion. I have been away, as you know. I was ill. But I am much recovered.

I now call Mr. Cabot to take the stand. Mr. Cabot?

CABOT: Thank you, Senator.

HAWKINS: In this important matter of your confirmation as DCI, all testimony must be given under oath as you know.

CABOT: Yes, sir, I understand that. I welcome it.

HAWKINS: Please stand to be sworn at this time. [*Cabot rises to his feet and raises his right hand.*] Do you solemnly swear that the testimony you are about to give is the truth, the whole truth, and nothing but the truth, so help you God?

CABOT: I do.

HAWKINS: Please be seated. Earlier this week a witness appeared before this committee—directly following your opening statement, if I am not mistaken.

CABOT: That is correct, Senator.

HAWKINS: The previous witness testified that in 1977 you twice visited Moscow at the request of the White House.

CABOT: That was my understanding, yes, sir.

HAWKINS: And on the first visit you were informed that a sergeant in the United States Army—one Jason Dyer, captured in Laos in 1970—was being held.

CABOT: Had been held.

HAWKINS: Had been held; that is your testimony.

CABOT: Yes, sir. I was told he had been held.

HAWKINS: But the witness on Monday testified that you were told the prisoner was *being* held.

CABOT: With respect, Senator, Monday's witness was not there, he had not spoken to anyone who was there, he did not actually know what had happened, sir.

HAWKINS: Perhaps it would be better if you would now tell us what you yourself remember about this episode. Everybody knows what was testified to on Monday. The transcripts are available? Is that correct? Senator MacLaverty, you have made a transcript available?

MACLAVERTY: The transcript is available.

HAWKINS: We'll explore the details later. Just tell us in your own words what happened.

CABOT: Thank you, Senator. As everyone now knows, the CIA received a report in 1977 of an American prisoner being held in Russia. This was a delicate matter for obvious reasons. The first I learned of this came in a phone call from Mr. Otis Jones, who was then a special assistant in the White House for arms control. Mr. Jones relayed the report to me and asked me to go to Moscow to inquire, in as quiet and unobtrusive a way as I could manage, whether in fact this report was true.

HAWKINS: You didn't work for the White House.

CABOT: No, sir. I was an analyst at the time in the Directorate of Intelligence. But I had worked on arms control issues and I knew Mr. Jones.

HAWKINS: So you knew that Mr. Jones could in fact speak for the White House?

CABOT: Yes, sir, I believed that to be the case.

HAWKINS: Go on.

CABOT: In Moscow I contacted a man in the Soviet intelligence community whom I had reason to believe might be in a position to answer my question. He said he would get back to me in a day or two. When we met again he said the report had been true, an American *had* been held in a camp in Akmolinsk, but there had been an outbreak of typhus in the camp, the American was among several dozen inmates who died of the disease, and his body had been cremated with the others. The ashes were buried in a common grave. There were no personal effects, no identification papers or dog tags, no bones or ashes—nothing. That's what I was told. I then left Moscow for Switzerland, where I went to the United States consulate in Geneva to report to Washington.

HAWKINS: To Mr. Jones in the White House.

CABOT: That is correct.

HAWKINS: Why didn't you report from the United States embassy in Moscow?

CABOT: It was a question of communications. Moscow traffic passed through the hands of the CIA and specifically of officers in the Directorate of Operations, and it was felt—

HAWKINS: Excuse me. Do you mean that Mr. Jones in the White House felt?

CABOT: Yes, sir, it was a fear of Mr. Jones that this communication would or might get out unless I reported directly and personally to him through a secure channel in the consulate in Geneva. So that's what I did. I told him what I myself had been told.

HAWKINS: He was in the White House?

CABOT: Yes, sir. And he thanked me and asked me to stay where I was until he got back to me, which took, I believe, about thirty-six hours. I had spoken to him in the morning; he called back late the next afternoon, as I recall. He told me to return to Moscow and deliver two messages from the White House.

HAWKINS: Did he say "from the White House"? Did he use those exact words?

CABOT: No, sir.

HAWKINS: What words did he use?

CABOT: He said "from the president."

HAWKINS: From the president.

CABOT: Yes, sir, two messages from the president. First was a message of sorrow and grief, not only concerning the death of the prisoner but also for the fact that nothing remained to be returned to his family. And, second, a message of vigorous protest and anger that an American had ever been held in Russia against all precepts of international law and in violation of repeated pledges by the Soviet Union that no such prisoners were being held or had ever been held under Soviet control.

HAWKINS: Excuse me, I want to be clear about this. The president never said "We want that man dead," or words to that effect?

CABOT: I never spoke to the president.

HAWKINS: Mr. Jones never passed on any such words as coming from the president or the White House or any source at all, is that correct?

CABOT: That is absolutely correct.

HAWKINS: So this alleged report delivered by a convicted spy currently serving a life sentence in the federal penitentiary at Allenwood is completely false and without foundation?

CABOT: Yes, sir, completely and utterly. I never—

HAWKINS: And you are outraged.

CABOT: Very, very angry, yes, sir.

HAWKINS: That anyone would claim, or believe for a minute—

MACLAVERTY: Point of order.

HAWKINS:—that you or any American would allow himself to be party to any such—

MACLAVERTY: I must protest!

HAWKINS: You are out of order, sir. I will not be interrupted.

MACLAVERTY: You are putting words in Cabot's mouth.

HAWKINS: You have done damage enough, sir. Your hour upon the stage is at an end. I'll tell you what I am doing. I am quashing the ugliest lie ever uttered about this country, or about any American officials, that I have heard in more than thirty years of public service. That this man, this convicted spy, this traitor who betrayed his honor and his comrades and his country should be allowed to spread this poisonous untruth in this Congress . . . Mr. Cabot, I apologize to you, sir. You have been very unfairly treated and impugned.

And I want to tell this country something. We have not betrayed your sons. We have done everything in our human power to learn the fates of the boys who never came home from Vietnam, and no president, and no official of the CIA, has *ever* abandoned a single American soldier for any reason *ever.* I hope I am making myself clear. But this is not just my personal opinion. Mr. Cabot, please tell this committee. Is there is any other person who can testify to what happened in Moscow?

CABOT: Yes, sir. There was a witness.

HAWKINS: And who is that witness?

CABOT: My Russian friend, the man I went to see in Moscow because I knew and trusted him: Mikhail Ivanovich Kondrashov.

HAWKINS: Thank you, Mr. Cabot. We will ask you to continue your testimony later. You may step down now. Ask the sergeant-at-arms to call the next witness to the stand. [*Loud talking, shouts, persons standing on chairs to see*] We will have order in the hearing room! Take your seats. We will have silence. Bring forward Mikhail Ivanovich Kondrashov.

55

"You can't kill that guy," said George Tater. "I don't believe what I'm watching!"

"Just what is it," asked Morrie Bloom, "that you're having trouble with?"

"He's pulled Hawkins off his deathbed, and now he's got the KGB taking the stand."

"Why not?" asked Bloom. "The chief witness against him is a KGB spy. If you ask me, it just proves what I've been trying to tell you reporters for years—it's a complicated world out there. Don't try to figure out the heroes and the villains. Just tell me what's happening."

"What's happening," said George Tater, "is that Cabot now looks like even money to be the next DCI."

"You're telling me you've run out of curiosity on this story?"

"Morrie," said George Tater, "I'm tired of trying to get ahead of the curve on Cabot. Maybe a guy with this many tricks up his sleeve *ought* to be running the CIA. I think I'm going to send down for a cappuccino and watch what happens next."

"And you call yourself a reporter," said Morrie Bloom.

Several minutes passed before quiet returned to the hearing room. "I should have brought a cushion," said Myrna, stretching to get a glimpse of the stage. "I can't see over these giants."

Jenny was holding Brad's hand in both of her own. "I don't understand," she said. "What's going on? Who are they calling?"

"Jenny," said Brad, "I don't know how they managed it, but this is the guy your uncle talked to in Moscow. And I don't think he's been dragged over here to confirm what Ames told me."

"They're going to call you a liar?" asked Jenny.

"If I'm lucky," said Brad, "they'll just say I'm a gullible idiot. And God, maybe they're right. Maybe I've been wrong from day one."

"I thought that," said Jenny. "Now I've got an awful feeling."

A door opened at the far end of the stage and a tight knot of men emerged—a man in a wheelchair, hunched and shrunken with a blanket over his lap, hair white and wispy in the television lights; a man in the white coat of a doctor pushing the wheelchair; and a third man wheeling an oxygen bottle with clear plastic tubes running to a mask over the face of the shrunken man. The witness was wheeled to the front of the room, parked at the witness table, and asked by the chairman to rise and swear.

The doctor shook his head. The other man rose and spoke up. "Mr. Chairman, my name is Hollis Corbin. I have been asked to translate for Mr. Kondrashov. I am afraid he is too weak to stand, sir."

"Will you ask Mr. Kondrashov to raise his right hand, please?" asked Senator Hawkins.

Corbin delivered the message directly into the shrunken man's ear. The right hand rose slowly, palm out, and the witness began to talk—a raspy, halting sort of speech like a radio broadcast half obscured by static. The great room fell abruptly silent as the audience strained to hear.

KONDRASHOV: *Da.*

CORBIN: Yes.

HAWKINS: We have received testimony about your meeting in 1977 in Moscow with Franklin S. Cabot, who is here in this room today.

CORBIN: [*Words in Russian*]

HAWKINS: Can you tell us, in your own words, what it was that Mr. Cabot came to ask of you and how you responded.

CORBIN: [*Words in Russian*]

MACLAVERTY: Point of order.

HAWKINS: I will not tolerate interruption for polemics, Senator. Save your quarrels for the question period.

MACLAVERTY: Mr. Chairman, I would like to request you to ask Mr. Corbin to identify himself. Is Mr. Corbin an employee of this government? Was he retained by Mr. Kondrashov? Who is Mr. Corbin? It is customary for witnesses to identify themselves.

HAWKINS: Mr. Corbin, would you identify yourself for the record?

CORBIN: Yes, sir. I am a longtime resident of the District of Columbia and a graduate of the United States Army language school in Monterey, California. I was attached to the United States embassy in Moscow from 1992 through the spring of 1996, during which period I worked as a Russian language specialist. I then left the government, and I now do consulting work for American business firms as well as government agencies here in Washington.

HAWKINS: Thank you.

MacLaverty: Have you ever worked for the Central Intelligence Agency?

Corbin: I . . . [*hesitating*]

Hawkins: You may answer.

Corbin: Yes, sir.

Hawkins: Thank you.

MacLaverty: Is the CIA paying for your appearance here today?

Hawkins: That is enough, Senator.

MacLaverty: Mr. Chairman, how do we know that this man is accurately translating our questions and the answers of the witness?

Hawkins: The record will reflect your concern, Senator. The witness will proceed.

Kondrashov: [*Words in Russian*]

Corbin: I understand what has been said.

Kondrashov: [*Words in Russian*]

Corbin: None of it is true.

Kondrashov: [*Words in Russian*]

Corbin: Mr. Cabot came from the CIA to ask about the American prisoner. I was shocked. I did not believe such a thing could have occurred in my country. But I knew he was a serious man and would not raise a foolish question. So I went directly to the chairman of the KGB, Yuri Andreyevich Andropov, and he told me he did not know how this could be but he would have an answer in twenty-four hours.

Kondrashov: [*Words in Russian*]

Corbin: The fact is, there was such a prisoner.

Kondrashov: [*Words in Russian*]

Corbin: He was flown to Russia as a humanitarian gesture. He was rescued from danger in Laos.

Kondrashov: [*Words in Russian*]

Corbin: His papers were not in order, he had entered the country illegally, and he could not be returned to Laos.

Kondrashov: [*Words in Russian*]

Corbin: While the organs deliberated what to do with him, time passed.

MacLaverty: [*Rising to his feet*] For eight years?

Hawkins: You are out of order, Senator MacLaverty.

Kondrashov: [*Words in Russian*]

Corbin: Under the previous government, hygienic conditions under the Glavnii Upravlenie were not always of the best. We did not respect the concept of human rights at that time.

KONDRASHOV: [*Words in Russian*]

CORBIN: In short, regrettable incidents occurred. Comrade Andropov personally told me that the American prisoner died of food poisoning.

HAWKINS: Excuse me.

KONDRASHOV: *Da.*

CORBIN: Yes.

HAWKINS: It was our understanding that Mr. Cabot was told he had died of typhus?

KONDRASHOV: [*Words in Russian*]

CORBIN: I remember clearly that Comrade Andropov told me food poisoning. Maybe I told Frank . . . typhus.

HAWKINS: But in any event, you told Mr. Cabot—correct me if I am wrong—you told him the American had died. Is that correct?

KONDRASHOV: *Da.*

CORBIN: Yes.

HAWKINS: And you have no reason to believe he reported anything different to his superiors in Washington?

KONDRASHOV: [*Words in Russian*]

CORBIN: I *know* that is what he told Washington, because at that time the KGB had compromised the communications facility in the United States consulate in Geneva.

HAWKINS: Are you telling us that you yourself heard Mr. Cabot's conversations with Washington?

KONDRASHOV: *Nyet, nyet.*

CORBIN: No, no.

KONDRASHOV: [*Words in Russian*]

CORBIN: I read his remarks. I was provided with a transcript of the English and of the Russian translation.

HAWKINS: You were given a transcript? And is this transcript still available?

KONDRASHOV: [*Words in Russian*]

CORBIN: Oh, yes. I have brought it with me. [*Corbin pulls from a briefcase by his chair a thick sheaf of manuscript pages.*]

KONDRASHOV: [*Words in Russian*]

CORBIN: Perhaps this will help your committee in its work. [*Loud talking from audience. Several members leave.*]

HAWKINS: This hearing will come to order! The witness has not yet completed his testimony.

. . .

With his trousers around his ankles and his head in his hands, Dean Cutter sat on a toilet in the last stall of the brilliantly lit marble men's room at the far end of the hall in the Richard Russell Senate Office Building. He had been sitting there for a long time. It was Russell's idea—stay out of sight till the moment approached. Occasionally Dean heard the door open, feet crossing the tiled floor, the flush of a urinal or toilet, water running into a sink, the sound of paper towels being pulled from a wall dispenser.

Dean's elbows were on his knees, the palms of his hands were snugged into his eye sockets, and he was trying to think about his friend Jason, dead in Russia. For years he had remembered Jason's face perfectly, the smile when he teased the neighborhood kids or rumpled their hair. The summer before Jason went off to the army he was around a lot, driving the country roads in his pickup, chasing a blond girl named Trish who was a school friend of Stacy's.

Sometimes Jason took the two girls and Dean and maybe another couple of kids to the drive-in. He'd back into a space and set up folding chairs in the bed of the pickup, and they'd sit there in comfort, watching the movie and eating popcorn, until at some point Jason and Trish would disappear into the cab of the truck. Dean loved those summer nights, he loved playing baseball on the diamond at the Accokeek high school, he loved the big cookout on the Fourth of July. The big kids teased the little kids sometimes, but Jason never let it go too far.

But now, staring into the blackness, sitting in the last stall in the men's room, Dean couldn't quite remember Jason's face. He was trying not to think of the slow, throbbing pain in his groin. When he first came through the security barrier he felt like a kind of superman, ready for anything. But now, waiting for the moment to act, that feeling had disappeared, he saw things in a cold light, and he knew there would be no emerging at the end of this day with anything good in front of him. This bleak knowledge was so clear and so strong that Dean's body began to shake lightly—a steady little tremor, almost like shivering, and in fact he felt cold.

He heard the sound of the door open, then the squeak of rubber on tile, the rasp of a metal joint flexing, a second squeak, an answering rasp. Down the length of the men's room the sounds came. Then came a light tapping of a finger on the door to the stall in which Dean Cutter sat.

He got up, hoisted up his trousers, buckled his belt, and opened the door. Russell was standing in front of him, looking down at him. He didn't look fierce. He looked calm and friendly. "Dean," he said softly, "zip up your fly."

Dean zipped up.

"Is the gun in your pocket?"

"Yes."

"Is the safety off?"

"Yes."

"Okay," said Russell. "All you have to do is pull back the hammer when you see Cabot. Let's go out into the hall now. I'm going to turn right. You go left. Walk to the end. There's a big lobby there and lots of television people outside the hearing room. When the hearing is over the doors will open and everybody will come pouring out. Cabot's not going to be first, but he's going to be one of the first. I'll wait till I hear the shots. Then I'll pull the pin on the grenade. You'll have to take care of yourself for three seconds. After that, no one's going to pay any attention to you. You're going to make history, Dean."

"No more talking," said Cutter. "I don't want to think about it. I just want to do it."

HAWKINS: Let the record show that Mr. Corbin is handing the transcript cited by Mr. Kondrashov to the chief counsel of this committee, Mr. Armor. I direct that it be entered into an executive record of these proceedings and made available to the CIA for security vetting. After that it is my intention that this transcript be released to the media as soon as practicable.

MACLAVERTY: I object. We have no idea when this transcript was prepared or by whom or whether it is a faithful copy of actual conversations or a fabrication intended to deceive this committee and the American people.

HAWKINS: It says what it says, Senator. Any comments you may care to make will be entered into the record at the appropriate time.

MACLAVERTY: I am shocked at what is transpiring here.

HAWKINS: This shocks you? And the outrageous claim of a convicted spy that a president of the United States would ask a foreign power to murder an American soldier—that doesn't shock you?

Senator, I have been a member of Congress for many, many years, first in the House, now in the Senate. I do not believe I have ever allowed myself to breach the decorum of this august body by calling into question the motives of a fellow senator. But I want you to know that today I am tempted—sorely tempted—to describe your conduct in this episode as unfair and impetuous.

Let us proceed. Mr. Kondrashov, please tell this committee: What is your present status?

KONDRASHOV: [*Words in Russian*]

CORBIN: I retired several years ago. But the pension of a retired intelligence officer is very small. At current exchange rates, about seven dollars a month.

KONDRASHOV: [*Words in Russian*]

CORBIN: So I am working a few hours a week in Moscow on a committee that considers the requests of journalists and historians for declassification of records from the KGB in the Soviet era.

HAWKINS: And am I right in thinking that you have recently received a request for declassification of all records concerning the American prisoner we have been discussing?

KONDRASHOV: [*Words in Russian*]

CORBIN: Such a request has been received, and because of the extreme importance of this matter in the eyes of the present government our work has been conducted with unusual haste and thoroughness. In fact, all the files have been declassified, and I have brought copies of them with me today.

HAWKINS: Let the record show that assistants of Mr. Kondrashov are wheeling in a cart piled with boxes of documentary material and that these are being surrendered to Mr. Armor, the counsel of this committee. Mr. Kondrashov, can you summarize for this committee the most important of the documents you are delivering to us here today?

KONDRASHOV: [*Words in Russian*]

CORBIN: These documents conclusively show that everything reported about this American prisoner by the Soviet and now the Russian authorities has been frank, complete, and true—with one exception. The late Comrade Andropov was wrong when he told me that the American had died of food poisoning.

KONDRASHOV: [*Words in Russian*]

CORBIN: He did not die of food poisoning. It was only that certain of his records had been lost. But now they have been found, and I can tell you that the American prisoner did not die at all. He is alive and in good health. At one-twenty this afternoon at Dulles International Airport Mr. Jason Dyer will be arriving on the regular Aeroflot flight from Moscow.

56

After a moment or two of futile gaveling and calling for order, the chairman of the Senate Select Committee on Intelligence surrendered to the inevitable and declared a recess in the hearings. *Recess* was the last word heard above the tumult as the doors at the rear of the room burst open and a wave of reporters and other professionally interested parties made a break for the hall, pulling cell phones from their pockets or heading for the elevators.

"I can't believe it," said Brad, making his awkward way sideways down the row of seats toward the aisle.

"Believe it," said Myrna, all but shouting to be heard above the crowd. "I may live to be a hundred and never know how he pulled this off, but you can bet your pension your sergeant is going to step off that plane this afternoon."

"He can't be alive," said Jenny. "Everybody said he was dead."

"It's crazy," said Brad, all but shouting to be heard. "Where's he been? How'd they find him?"

"Anywhere else," said Myrna, "not in a million years. Russia's the answer."

Around them in the aisle, scores of people were shouting, pushing, shoving toward the big double doors at the rear of the room. Brad pulled Jenny close as Myrna slipped behind while other, bigger people elbowed their way forward. "Why is everybody pushing?" shouted Jenny.

"It's the television lights," said Brad. "They think something's happening outside in the lobby."

And in fact just outside the doors there was a breaking wave of excitement where television lights brilliantly illuminated the marble walls of the lobby. "Myrna?" Brad called. "You with us?"

"I'm coming," she called back. "Don't worry about me."

Brad caught a glimpse of her purple dress.

Once through the double doors the crush eased and the crowd spread out into the hall and the lobby, beyond where Brad could see the television lights like a stockade rising behind a semicircled phalanx of reporters focused on a lectern that the dark blue figure of Frank Cabot was slowly approaching from a side door. Cabot's head was bent to hear the whispers of an aide, but Brad couldn't make out who was hurrying by his side.

At that moment a firm feminine voice called out, "Mr. Cameron! Mr. Cameron!" Advancing upon Brad was the woman in the red silk dress, microphone in hand. The crowd melted back; the woman in red took Brad by the arm and pulled him forward. Brad in turn held on to Jenny's hand, and slipping along behind them both was Myrna, hurrying to keep up.

"Mr. Cameron," said the woman in red, parking Brad firmly next to the lectern, "stand here. Fred," she called over her shoulder, "are you getting this?

"Mr. Cameron. What is your reaction to the news we have all just heard that the prisoner is coming home?"

"I am astonished. And pleased. And eager to hear his story."

"Mr. Cabot," called out the woman in red. "Are you getting this, Fred?" She had control of the moment and was running with it; other reporters were trying to shout questions at the same time, but the woman in red was there first and had engineered a direct confrontation between Cabot and his accuser, who were now standing only a few feet apart. "Mr. Cabot!" shouted the woman in red, "this man accused you of leaving an American prisoner to his fate in the Gulag or worse. What do you have to say to him today?"

Brad turned. Cabot was at the lectern. He tapped his finger on a microphone. He was smiling. His glance flicked across Brad without anger. "Lorraine," he said, in a friendly, familiar voice. The microphone quieted the room. "I was young once. I've made my share of mistakes. I bear no grudges. My young friend did what he felt he had to do. But there is one thing I want to say."

Cabot's voice rose. He looked out into the sea of cameras. His eye caught no other eye.

"Today," he said, "is a great day for Americans. We've all—" He paused, looking around the now-silent room. "We've all waited for this day, when one of our boys would be miraculously restored to us. Sergeant Dyer—" He spoke the name loudly and firmly.

Then someone dropped a video camera, or a big spotlight exploded. There was a loud noise.

. . .

Uniformed guards stood in pairs at both ends of the hall and outside the big double doors of the hearing room, but none of them paid any attention to Dean as he let the high wooden door to the men's room close quietly behind him and headed for the light-filled lobby. He was limping, the pain in his groin almost more than he could stand. He saw everything clearly now. He wasn't waiting around for Mr. C.

The lobby was crowded but Dean had little difficulty slipping forward, saying Sorry, excuse me, sorry, leading with his shoulder, then wedging forward with small cool smiles right and left. He was in no hurry. He knew where he was going. There was a tiny opening in the wall of reporters to the left, not a dozen feet from the lectern, right in front of the wall of lights and cameras. Cabot's face and white hair were like the bullseye at the center of a target.

A woman's loud voice brayed at the front. He could see the flash of her red dress through the crowd. He wedged his way sideways between two men carrying heavy gear and wearing microphones and put his hand into his jacket pocket around the grip of the Beretta. It was cool to the touch. He wasn't waiting around to let the doctors cut him up. He was going to prove himself to Stacy Dyer. He was going to force an admission of error from Lisa Benson. He was going to show Russell he could do it. He was going to make everybody he had ever known see what had really been inside him all the time. It all seemed perfectly clear and simple as he eased back the hammer of the pistol with his thumb.

The woman in red was shouting now. She was hauling somebody up front to the lectern. With her free hand she pushed a girl to one side, tried to hold back an older woman in a purple dress. Cabot was backed up by a whole crowd of men in suits. But Dean had a clear shot at him. He was right there.

Now Frank Cabot was talking. Dean started to pull the gun from his pocket. It caught. He tugged. He felt the gun pulling at his jacket lining. He pulled harder but the hammer, cocked back, was caught under the hem of his pocket and he couldn't pull it out. He tried to wiggle it free.

"Hey," said a man at his side.

" . . . restored to us," said Cabot at the lectern.

Dean yanked the gun with all his might. There was an explosion in his pocket and a searing burning; something simultaneously like an ax and an ice pick raked his thigh. A noise burst from Dean's throat halfway between a shout and a groan. He had shot himself in the leg.

But his pocket had ripped open. The gun came free. The crush around him began to fold back with shouts and cries. Dean began to scream, raising the gun to aim.

Brad was confused. Someone was yelling. For the briefest fraction of a second it was silent, and then all at once, simultaneously, came a second crash, a third crash—shouts that were screams. The woman in red was turning. She was trying to get on the other side of him. Brad was pushed, Jenny's face started to twist in fear, he felt himself pulled, he heard Frank Cabot make a startled "Oh!" then a wincing "Oh!" and Brad saw Cabot settling back, as if in slow motion, his right hand coming up toward his shoulder, something wet on the blue suit, something red showing on his white shirt next to his tie.

Another crash—it was a shot. Somebody was shouting, "He's got a gun!" Cabot was going back and down. Brad started to turn, trying to see the danger, somebody was pulling on him. More shots. A man behind Brad fell to his knees saying, "I've been hit!"

"Over there!" came the shouts. "By the cameras! He's getting away!"

But then Brad lost all the detail in a sea of shouted questions and panicked answers. "Call a doctor!" he shouted. "Someone call a doctor!" He grabbed the arm of the woman in red, who was speaking into her microphone. "Have you got a cell phone?"

"There have been shots," said the woman in red. "A man has fired shots at Frank Cabot; I think he was hit. He went down. He's on the ground."

Brad was furious, but then someone said to him, "It's all right—help's coming."

Jenny's face was red. Brad saw tears. He saw Cabot sitting on the floor. His hand was on his chest near his shoulder. He was white but he was speaking; when he took his hand away briefly Brad could see red smeared on Cabot's palm and fingers but he was sitting up, he was okay; Brad started to tell Jenny her uncle was okay.

"Don't pull on me," he said angrily. Someone was pulling on his coat, pulling him down to the ground. He was irritated. He turned, ready to slap the hand away. "Don't pull on me," he said again.

Then he saw it was Myrna. A thick fold of his coat was clenched in her hand, but she seemed to be trying to kneel down. Then she fell on her knees, hard, onto the marble floor. She looked up. "I'm fine," she told Brad.

. . .

Dean wasn't sure how many times he had pulled the trigger. The pain in his leg was searing. Three times. Four times. He pushed the gun back into his tattered pocket. Maybe five times. He turned. There was no grenade. He couldn't see Russell. He was on his own. His leg hurt but he could walk. He looked down. His coat was torn and his pants were torn but he couldn't see anything else. Shouting people pointed at him. But Dean turned, took one step back through the wall of cameras, and found himself in a swirling crush of shouting people on the other side who paid no attention to him.

People were heading for the doors. Dean went with them. Others were pushing forward to see and ask questions. "What happened?" some people shouted. Others shouted, "Somebody's been shot!" They pushed right on by Dean. The guards who had been by the security desk were rushing forward. Their guns were drawn. They paid no attention to Dean. He reached the door. He was limping. His leg hurt more and more. It seemed to be quivering. He felt his leg getting weak.

Dean pushed through the door to the bright sun outside.

Everything had gone wrong, but everything was going right. He was just walking away.

Myrna went on falling, onto her hands, onto her side, finally over onto her back. "The wind," she said, "must've . . . got knocked out of me." Her head turned over to the right, then back to the left. "I'll be okay. Check Jenny."

Jenny was right there, she was all right. "Jenny's fine," said Brad.

"Unh," said Myrna. It was a sound almost of protest. "Unh. Unh."

"Where is it?" said Brad.

"I'm okay," said Myrna.

Then things began to happen, people rushing in, a new round of shouts, people getting up, people bending down. Brad saw white coats, a stretcher on wheels, a police uniform, more white coats, guns held up in the air. Cabot was still sitting on the floor nearby and the crowd around him opened to let in the white coats and the stretcher on wheels. Brad watched as the men in white coats put Cabot down flat, lifted him onto the stretcher, cranked it up even as they went over his body looking for wounds and asked him questions which he answered.

Brad turned back to Myrna just in time to see a spurt of dark blood thick as a rope pump up into the air from her rib cage. Then a big bubble formed, blowing up quickly, turning a lighter and lighter red as it expanded, till it was pink and big as an apple and it burst and a second spurt of blood jumped up into the air. Brad slapped his hand down on the bloody place and shouted louder than he had ever shouted any other word in his life, "*Medic!*"

It seemed as though an age was passing at a glacial pace while Brad pressed his hand down on the soaking mess of Myrna's dress trying to stanch the blood, feeling the viscous ooze betwen his fingers. Again and again he shouted for help in the loudest, firmest voice of which he was capable until Jenny said, "Someone's coming." Her hand was on his shoulder. It had been on his shoulder the whole time.

A moment later a child in white was on her knees by Brad's side. She looked eighteen, pale and frightened. "Keep your hand right there," she said to Brad. "What's her name?"

"Myrna Rashevsky."

"Myrna? Myrna? Can you hear me? Are you all right? Can you tell me how you're doing?"

"I'm okay," said Myrna. "Just tired. I don't know what happened."

"We're going to put on a C-collar, Myrna."

"Like a punch," said Myrna. "It was like a punch."

"I'm going to lift your head," said the girl in white.

A man was with her now, slender and dark—an Indian or Pakistani. The girl picked up Myrna's head and the man slipped a white collar around her neck and closed it with Velcro.

"We're going to move you to a spine board now, Myrna. Are you still hearing me?"

"I hear fine."

"That's great. Okay, we're going to move you over now. You," she said to Brad, "just keep your hand down tight right there. One, two, three." The two of them picked up Myrna, placed her on the spine board, and moved the board to the stretcher. Brad was amazed at how strong these two tiny people were.

"Uh-oh," said the girl.

Brad saw several big bubbles of blood oozing out around his fingers, expanding and popping. "Vaseline gauze," she said to the Indian. He handed her a packet. She ripped it open. "Put this under your hand," she said. "Hold it down."

"What's the matter?" asked Brad.

"Sucking chest wound. It's going to be okay. We're going to get her to the ER in about two minutes. You're going to be okay, Myrna. We're going to move you now. How are you feeling?"

"Feeling fine," said Myrna. "Feeling tired."

"Let's go," said the girl. "Keep your hand there and stay with us."

Jenny was beside them. “What hospital?” asked Jenny.

“George Washington ER,” said the girl as they pushed the stretcher on wheels across the marble floor and through the opening crowd of faces, row upon row, each expressing horror and curiosity.

Within moments they were out the door, down the few steps, and into the back of the ambulance parked by the curb. “All set?” asked the girl in white.

“Ready,” said Brad.

“You all right, Myrna?” asked the girl. “You still with us?”

“Feeling fine,” said Myrna.

But she didn’t look fine. Her face was gray, completely without color. Her eyes didn’t seem to focus. Her cheeks seemed to be sinking back into her head.

The ambulance began to move. Lights began to flash. A siren went *wheep-wheep* at traffic blocking the way, then fell silent as the ambulance sped up.

There was a window open to the cab and driver. “Get me Com Center on the phone,” shouted the girl.

The Indian had ripped open the sleeve of Myrna’s dress and was tying a brown rubber cord around her arm above the elbow. It was awkward. Brad was trying to give him room and still keep his hand pressed hard down on the gauze bandage.

“Give me an emergent line to George Washington ER,” said the girl on the phone.

Myrna seemed to be smiling. She seemed to be panting.

“Hang in there, Myrna,” said Brad.

“Fine,” said Myrna.

Something was wrong. Myrna didn’t look right.

The Indian slipped a needle into Myrna’s arm and hooked it to an IV bottle hanging from the roof of the ambulance. He clipped something onto her finger. “Uh-oh,” he said.

“What’s it read?” asked the girl, hand over the phone.

“Oh-two sat under ninety.”

“Coming to your facility with a white female seventy unconscious with gunshot wound to right anterior chest, no exit wound. Bilateral fourteens, eight hundred CCs anticubital infused. Oh-two sat under ninety.”

“Eighty-two,” said the Indian. He had slipped on a stethoscope, was listening to Myrna’s chest.

“Vitals seventy over forty,” said the girl into the phone. “Pulse one forty. See you in four.”

“Uh-oh,” said the Indian.

"Central, do you copy?" said the girl.

Brad pressed and pressed and pressed.

"Yes, that's affirm," said the girl. "Patient from the Russell Senate Office Building."

"I've got no breathing sounds on the right," said the Indian.

"We're going to intubate," said the girl. "Give me the crash kit."

"Where's the crash kit?" asked the Indian.

"Where's the crash kit?" shouted the girl.

"Is this it?" asked Brad as he pulled a black box from behind him.

"Thanks," said the girl. She opened it, pulled out a gadget. She opened Myrna's mouth. "Give me a seven-oh," she said. The Indian handed her a tube. Myrna's mouth gaped wide. "I can see the cords," said the girl. She was feeding the tube into Myrna's throat. "I think I'm in. Can you listen for me?"

With his stethoscope the Indian listened. "You're in," he said.

The girl put a hand on Brad. "Everything's okay," she said.

Myrna was no longer smiling. Sounds came from her throat. She was gagging, trying to cough.

Behind a white pleated curtain in Trauma One at Georgetown Hospital a nurse helped Frank Cabot into a hospital gown. His left arm was taped firmly down to his side, he was cleaned up, and his hair had been brushed, but his shoulder hurt where the bullet had nicked the bone. A generous injection of morphine had not yet begun to work.

Kitty was in a chair watching him. Doctors conversed in a corner. Leo Weissberg was by the wall speaking into a cell phone. Three men from the Agency's public information office were discussing a press release. "Frank," one of them called, "can we say you're resting comfortably?"

"In some pain," said Frank, "but otherwise resting comfortably."

The nurse finished buttoning him up, fluffed a pillow behind him, and said, "You look beautiful."

"Kitty," said Frank, "don't let anybody get rid of that jacket or my shirt."

Leo approached. "Frank," he said. "Schleicher says the president would like to call you in about ten minutes. They're setting up a camera in the Oval Office for a live newsbreak. Are you up for that?"

"Are you kidding?" said Kitty. "He's ready to sing 'America the Beautiful' on *Larry King Live.* Aren't you, Frank?"

. . .

Outside in the brilliant sun, Dean felt shaky. No one was paying him any attention, but his leg didn't seem to want to do what he told it to do. Something wet had got into his shoe. Only a few steps and the sidewalk separated him from the street, where traffic roared past. At the far corner people waited for the light. Among them he thought he saw Russell's gray ponytail.

Dean started down the steps. His leg hurt when he put weight on it. It seemed to shake and twist.

"Hey," said somebody. "Hey, buddy."

Dean looked around.

"You're bleeding," said a man. He pointed at the ground. Dean looked down and saw blood on his shoe and a smudge of blood on the sidewalk. He limped down the next few steps but the man was shouting, "Hey! Hey!"

Between the whizzing cars, among the people waiting across the street, Dean saw Russell's face, he was sure now. He was puzzled. How did he get out of the building so quickly?

Now there were no people around him on the sidewalk. Everyone had backed away. But two men were stepping toward him. They were in uniform, and Dean saw they each held a pistol in a two-handed grip, pointed up. They were shouting at him, "Stop where you are! Put up your hands! Don't move!"

Russell wasn't there anymore. He had melted away.

Dean put his hand in his pocket.

"Don't move! Show your hands!"

What did these assholes expect? Dean began to pull out the Beretta.

The police leveled their guns at him, shouting. But Dean wasn't going to put his gun down. He wasn't going to put his hands up. He was going to blow these bastards away and the whole rest of the world with them.

"This is where we take over," said the girl. A nurse was taking Brad's place beside the stretcher just inside the double slide-back doors. "We're going to be in Trauma Three. Go to the front desk—they need you there."

Brad had something he wanted to ask but the girl and her team whisked off with the stretcher. Another nurse led him through a couple of doors to a front desk, and Brad was soon telling a clerk that he did not have Myrna Rashevsky's insurance card although he was sure she was covered, she was not his mother, and he was not related to her at all. Her age he thought was seventy-six, she was a U.S. citizen for sure, her place of birth was Warsaw, Poland, and her legal address was on 18th Street in the District of Columbia. But he thought he knew how to locate her next of kin and he would get back to the hospital one way or another before the day was over.

In the waiting room after an hour or so, a young doctor appeared with news of Myrna's condition, which was critical but stable. He explained the path of the bullet and said it had been removed and the damage repaired. "This was a very close thing," said the doctor. "When you stopped that bleeding, you probably saved her life."

"Thank God," said Brad. "Is she awake?"

"Not yet. She's under heavy sedation. She'll probably be out for another couple of hours."

"Maybe I should go home for a while," said Brad.

"You might want to stop in the bathroom first," said the doctor, "and clean up a little."

He pointed down the hall and Brad went into a room marked with the signs for man, woman, and wheelchair. He locked the door behind him, stepped to the sink, and looked into the mirror. After a moment he held up his hands.

His hands were red with blood. There was blood on his hair and blood on his tie. There was blood on his jacket, pants, and belt. There was blood on his shirt. His right shirt cuff was black with dried, stiffened blood. One of his shirt buttons had been ripped off, and he could see blood on his T-shirt. There was dried blood on one side of his face from eye socket to chin, and through the blood ran the dry, smeared tracks of what Brad realized after a moment must have been tears.

57

In all of Washington, Jenny's favorite place outdoors to sit—on broiling days in midsummer, on crisp days in the fall, on the first days of spring sun in March—was on a bench in Franklin Park near the corner of 14th and K. The air had been stinging with cold when she'd been in the park last, on the Saturday she had quarreled with Brad and turned her back on him forever—or so she had thought at the time. But thinking back it was clear now that something quite different had happened there. When she asked what Frank had done, Brad's silence and the look on his face told her everything. She refused to admit it, of course, in her usual stubborn way, but from that moment she could no longer honestly claim she didn't know.

But now, on Friday, March 22, only two weeks later, it was already warm enough at ten in the morning to sit with her coat in her lap. Meg would be coming by in a few minutes, and Jenny was trying to remember how to pray. She knew the Lord's Prayer from Sunday school, although she sometimes forgot whether the giving of daily bread came before or after the forgiveness of trespasses. But what she wanted now was something powerfully focused and specific that would implore whatever God there was to come to the aid of Myrna Rashevsky.

Jenny wanted to approach the question seriously, and she knew there was a correct or at least an accepted way to proceed. You weren't supposed to pray for things; that point she remembered clearly. And you weren't supposed to bargain with God, and you certainly weren't supposed to threaten—but after that, what could you say that would do any good? Not knowing the right way, she prayed in the only way she knew, just as she had prayed long ago for a puppy, or a seat by her best friend in sixth grade, or a clear skin in ninth: "Oh, God, please, please, please, please, please. Give that woman a break."

"You okay?" were Meg's first words, taking a seat beside her in the sun.

Jenny said she was.

"I saw it all," said Meg. She meant on TV: the crowd in the lobby of the Senate Office Building, the television lights, the woman in the red dress, the sudden shouts, the popping sounds, the whirling of the cameras trying to find the gunman in the crowd.

"We got one glimpse of Brad and you—there was something odd, you could tell, as if that other woman was pulling on him. I thought maybe she was trying to get him down on the ground to protect him.

"But then," said Meg, "it was all hysterical, jumpy shots of Cabot and the medics and I was thinking, *Pan the fucking camera! What's happened to Brad and Jenny?* I can't even imagine what it must have been like."

"Like it was happening to someone else," said Jenny. "I saw this gout of blood; it spurted up. But Brad slapped his hand down on the place and I thought, *Everything's going to be fine. He's stopped the bleeding and it's okay.*"

"And?"

"I don't know," said Jenny. "Brad was there till past midnight and the doctors said everything was under control, but then he got called in the middle of the night. When I talked to him this morning he said there's some problem about the hepatic vein. He didn't understand and I don't either, but I'm going over there now."

"You okay?" Meg asked again.

"I'm okay," said Jenny. "I feel like hell, actually."

"That's natural."

"It's not what you think."

Jenny tried to explain. She'd been furious at Brad for attacking her uncle. She told him she'd never forgive him and she meant it. But then everything turned upside down. It was obvious Uncle Frank had done things Jenny didn't even want to think about, and Aunt Kitty said she wasn't sure she knew the man she'd been living with for thirty years. She saw that part of it, and once she admitted that she couldn't help thinking about what she had done to Brad—

"Is it Tater? Are you worried about Tater?"

"Tater," said Jenny, "and the way I just turned on Brad when he was feeling completely alone."

"He'll understand that. You're afraid to tell Brad about Tater, aren't you?" asked Meg.

"It's worse than that," said Jenny. "Somebody at the CIA told Brad about Tater."

"Then you don't have to. He knows. So what's the problem?"

"The problem," said Jenny, "is I told him it wasn't true. And I got furious and said if he believed anything some professional liar told him—"

"You denied everything?"

"I denied everything backwards and forwards," said Jenny. "I've been kicking myself all night. I feel like an idiot."

"He probably didn't believe you."

"Why wouldn't he believe me?" Jenny was a little offended.

"Because you were lying," said Meg, "and you probably got flustered and looked guilty as hell. Listen. This is a mess, but it's not complicated. Do you want Brad in your life or out of your life?"

"I don't want him out of my life."

"That's good enough. Tell him he caught you off guard. Tell him you were mad. Tell him you lied. And tell him Tater's over and that's that."

"Can't I get out of this?" asked Jenny. "There's no way he'll ever really know if I don't tell him."

"Jenny. Don't make your life complicated. He knows already. Just tell him."

"It isn't that easy."

"I know it's not easy," said Meg. "It's simple. Do it. He'll be hurt in some stupid male way but he'll get over it."

"What makes you so sure?"

"I'm not sure. But if he doesn't get over it, the hell with him."

"Just tell him," Jenny repeated. And then she said, "Okay."

George Tater managed to squeeze in a question during the twenty-minute news conference and photo opportunity presided over jointly in an auditorium at the Pentagon by the Secretary of the Army, the chairman of the Joint Chiefs of Staff, and the senior senator from Georgia, Harrison Hawkins. Flanked by these high officials and his sister, standing erect on aluminum crutches behind the spray of microphones, was the lean and worn figure, gray at the temples but snappy in immaculate dress greens and green beret, of the only honest-to-God POW/MIA to come back alive since January of 1973—Sergeant Major Jason Dyer. The sergeant had been promoted to the highest enlisted rank during his long captivity, the reporters were told by the Secretary of the Army, and the sergeant's back pay had been faithfully invested in an interest-bearing account. One by one, all the officials had expressed their gratitude at being able to contribute in some small way to welcoming home this inspiring example of old-fashioned American grit. Then it was the sergeant's turn.

"What I want to say to you," he began, "and to all my buddies back in Accokeek, and to the whole country is this." He paused for emphasis. "This is the greatest country on earth."

"Oh, God," moaned George Tater to Faith Osborne, standing shoulder to shoulder beside him in the crush of reporters.

"What did you expect?" Faith whispered back.

"All these people," said the sergeant. His gestured at the wall of officials squeezing into the photo opportunity behind him. "I can't thank you enough."

The thirty years in the Gulag seemed to have been forgotten. The sergeant had little idea where he'd been held and no idea why his incarceration had gone on after the end of the Cold War. It was flat where he was, the winters were cold and the summers were hot, and that was all he could say. Concerning the food he had strong opinions. Faith got in a question early on: Who had the sergeant missed most during the long years?

"My mom, my sister, my truck, the kids in the neighborhood," said the sergeant, "and a couple of girls I used to take to the drive-in."

As the laughter died, Tater found his millisecond of opportunity. "Sergeant Dyer—what would you like to say to Frank Cabot, the man who was sent to get you out thirty years ago?"

A groan of disapproval rolled through the room.

"I could be bitter," said the sergeant. "But what good would it do? So I guess I'd tell him, Better late than never."

Loud applause followed.

"Let me ask *you* a question," said the sergeant. "Maybe Mr. Cabot screwed things up a little. But who opened the door in the end?"

Laughter and applause.

"Isn't Mr. Cabot the one who got that Russian out of the old people's home and brought him over here? Didn't the Russian find out where they were holding me?"

There was silence in the room.

"You just want to knock guys like him down," said the sergeant. "I may have been locked up ever since Vietnam, but I see some of you reporters haven't changed one single bit."

Tater took it all with a smile.

"You should have seen it coming," said Faith, after the Secretary of the Army called a halt and the sergeant was led away across the stage, moving proudly on his crutches and followed by peals of applause. His empty left trouser leg with its knife-edge crease, pinned to his hip, would be on the front page of every newspaper in the country the next day.

"I thought maybe thirty years of gnawing his vitals might have pissed him off a little."

"He's giving them what they want," said Faith. "I expect he's going to have a pretty good time while the money lasts."

"God help the girls of Accokeek," said Tater.

Everybody was packing up and moving out.

"Speaking of girls," said Faith, "how's the new girl I met last week, Cabot's niece? That's cutting pretty close to the edge, don't you think?"

"She's the old girl now," said Tater. "Nice kid. Never told me a damn thing. No hard feelings, but I don't think she wants me in her obit."

"I haven't heard anybody talking," said Faith, "so don't worry about it."

"Don't worry about it?"

"Don't worry about it."

"You free for coffee?" asked Tater.

"If you give me ten minutes to capture this pathos on my laptop," said Faith, "I might squeeze in a coffee."

. . .

During the early morning hours the hospital had transferred Myrna from the intensive care unit to a large private room, where Brad now sat quietly on the edge of a metal chair, watching and listening to the machines that perform modern medical wonders—the *ping* of a monitor recording the beating of Myrna's heart, the *wheeze* and *whoosh* of the respirator, the slow drip of the IV, the flickering blue-green line of the electroencephalogram that made its quivering way across the screen with an occasional tiny flicker or sputter upward recording a random event—perhaps even a fragment of a dream—in Myrna's brain. Occasionally a nurse in white with a name tag reading BLANCHE CARTER, RN bustled in with a clipboard to scribble down numbers or adjust the drip. Brad was waiting for the arrival of Dr. Kaplan, specialist in the treatment of trauma victims. The nurse had promised that the attending physicians would be making rounds between ten and eleven and would explain Myrna's condition then. There was a TV set on a shelf near the ceiling, but it was off. There were copies of *The New York Times* and *The Washington Post* on the floor beside his metal chair, but Brad had hardly looked at the headlines. He was watching Myrna and the machines that held her to life, and he was thinking.

Brad had gone through Myrna's desk early that morning, looking for letters or an address book or anything else that might help him to contact her family. He had called personnel and the Office of Security at the Agency, and after a runaround they confessed they had no knowledge of next of kin. The guy who ran Myrna's shop at the Agency had the names of a couple of friends, but the friends, mostly retired in places like Tampa or San Diego, were sorry, but they couldn't help. That left Shulamith and Rachel in Israel, and Brad planned to telephone them as soon as he had talked to the doctor.

A little before eleven the door to the room opened behind Brad and Dr. Kaplan swept in at the head of a pack of seven or eight chattering young residents in white. One of them took the curtain, which half enclosed Myrna's bed in a kind of quiet twilight, and swept it around and back, letting in the morning sun. Myrna made no sign or movement but lay there motionless: tubes running into her mouth, cheeks shallow and sunken, arms flat on the bed by her sides, palms up.

"You're a son?" said the doctor, taking Myrna's wrist to feel for pulse. "A friend? I haven't met any of the patient's family yet."

"A friend," said Brad. "Brad Cameron. We work together. Her family's all in Israel and—uh, they've asked me to handle things."

"Have you got a medical consent form? No? Harriet, please help Mr. Cameron get a consent form faxed to Israel for signature. We do this all the time. It's not complicated. Then I can talk to you and you can make decisions. But there isn't any hurry—my practice in cases like this is a three-day delay before any decision about continuing medical support.

"Draw close, ladies and gentlemen. Mr. Cameron, did the doctor on night duty fill you in? No? Well let me explain what's happened here." He checked the clipboard carried by Harriet, standing at his side.

"Mrs. Rashevsky is a seventy-six-year-old woman—"

"She's not married," said Brad.

"I'm sorry," said the doctor. "Miss Rashevsky was the victim of a gunshot wound yesterday morning." The doctor placed his hand gently on Myrna's torso, just below the rib cage on the right-hand side. He spoke clearly but in a quiet, feeling voice. The residents stood silently around him, their faces blank. Brad occasionally noticed one or another of them giving him a quick look. Brad recognized the question behind that look; he had seen it often during his two years with the CIA: Does this guy understand what he's being told?

"She was given an IV and intubated on the way to the ER in the ambulance," Doctor Kaplan continued. "She suffered heart failure twice after getting here, but the ER staff quickly revived her both times so that was not a problem. But—and this is the core of the diagnosis, Mr. Cameron—in treating her gunshot wound, which was quite messy, probably owing to the use of some sort of expanding bullet, the ER did not at first . . ."

The door opened at the rear of the room and Brad saw Jenny come in. She gave him a smile and closed the door quietly behind her.

" . . . did not at first detect," the doctor was saying, "a secondary problem, not in the direct path of the bullet, here." He touched Myrna again, on a spot a few inches away.

"What probably happened is that the bullet broke up and a fragment deflected off a rib or just followed an errant path of its own up and to the right and nicked the hepatic vein just above the liver. Maybe it didn't even break all the way through. Maybe an embolus developed and burst later in the night at a moment when no one was around to notice.

"In any event, at some point the vein ruptured and Miss Rashevsky developed internal bleeding—quite severe internal bleeding. Eventually one of the monitors alerted the nurses and we managed to stabilize the patient once again, but as you can see"—the doctor pointed to the screen for the electroencephalogram with its quivering blue-green line—"this line is essentially flat, and it has been flat for nearly five hours."

Dr. Kaplan continued for another minute or two, pointing out additional details of Myrna's condition: the way she was breathing, vital signs, the mouth, the eyes, the various internal organs injured by bullet fragments. "I'll take questions outside," he said at last. He waited while the interns filed out through the door and then turned to Brad.

"Harriet will give you a consent form. When you get it back, please leave a message on my voice mail. We'll find a minute and talk."

"What, exactly," said Brad, "should I tell her family?"

"You didn't understand what I was saying?"

"I can tell them where the bullet went. But they're going to want to know what you think her chances are?"

"Miss Rashevsky is on life support," said Dr. Kaplan. "If we turn off the respirator, she'll die very quickly. I'm afraid you're going to have to tell her family in Israel that this wound was fatal. With a little luck we might have saved her, but she didn't have any luck. I'm sorry. If it would help, I can explain what happened to her family."

"No," said Brad. "If you're sure, I'll tell them."

"I'm sure," said the doctor.

When they were alone again in a visitors' waiting room down the hall, Jenny, as much to herself as to Brad, said, "It doesn't seem fair."

"None of it's fair," said Brad. "It's so far from fair it's in the next universe."

"Did you get a chance to say goodbye?"

"I didn't know it was goodbye," said Brad, "but I had a chance. She was awake and we talked last night before I went home. She said she'd never been shot before but now she knew why people died of it. I said, You'll be okay, don't worry about it; you're just tired, you need some sleep. I was worn out myself. I was trying to figure out why things turned out the way they did."

Brad remembered the moment clearly: the passage of rubber-soled shoes in the halls, the faint light, the low hum and flicker of machines. Myrna was fretful, uncomfortable, weak but eager to talk. She had many opinions to convey.

"You're a quick learner," she said.

"What have I learned?" Brad asked.

"It's never the way you think."

"You mean the intelligence business?" Brad asked.

"Life, love, politics, what we do at the cookie factory—all of it," said Myrna. "It's okay as long as you keep first things first."

"I try, but what's first?"

"*Mishpocheh,*" Myrna had said.

Jenny didn't understand. "*Mishpocheh?*"

"I think it means people you care about."

"Like children, lovers, family, friends—what?"

"All that," said Brad. "I don't think you can translate it exactly."

"Am I *mishpocheh*?"

"Of course. But I don't want to try to pin that down right now."

"I can wait," said Jenny. "But I want to get something straight. When you asked me about George Tater—"

"I know. It doesn't matter."

"Listen to me," said Jenny firmly. "I want to tell you something."

"All right."

"I lied to you. I'm very sorry about that. What they told you was true. It's over, but it was an affair while it lasted."

"Why are you telling me this now?"

"Well, why do you think? I don't want to lie to you. I want you to trust me."

"You think that's all you have to do—tell the truth and I'll trust you again?"

"I don't know what I have to do," said Jenny. "But I'm sure this is part of it."

Brad was sitting in the metal chair and Jenny was standing directly in front of him and looking at him fiercely. He reached over to a table by the couch and took the phone, cradled it in his lap, picked up the receiver. "The woman I'm about to call," he said, "is named Shulamith. She's the granddaughter of an old friend of Myrna's. She's a doctor, she's about two inches shorter than you, she's intelligent, and she's beautiful in a dark exotic way. When I was in Israel we went to bed together."

"Why?"

"Jenny," said Brad, "I guess it was the usual reasons."

"And now?" Jenny demanded.

"That's over too," said Brad.

"Where does that leave us?"

"I don't know," said Brad. "I thought you said you could wait."

He took a piece of paper from his pocket and began to dial.

58

It was just after two o'clock in the morning—ten o'clock in the Persian Gulf—when a night duty officer monitoring the Cable News Network in the communications center on the fourth floor of the CIA's headquarters heard the flash that a bomb had exploded on a downtown street in Doha, the capital of Qatar. The officer immediately placed a call to the chief of station at the U.S. embassy in Qatar but sounded no wider alarm pending news of some kind—at the very least a casualty count. The detonation of bombs in Arab cities was too common to justify waking from their rest such mighty panjandrums as directors of central intelligence or secretaries of state, not to mention a president as notorious for valuing his sleep as Norman Anderson. But within a few minutes the chief of station, an old Middle Eastern hand named Ratliff, had reported a death toll of four—three bodyguards and the Prime Minister of Qatar in a Mercedes-Benz limousine that had been blown more than sixty feet into the air despite two thousand pounds of armor plating. At that point the chief of the Agency's Middle East Division decided to sound the general alarm: the White House, the Pentagon, the principal deputy directors at the CIA, and Leo Weissberg, the personal assistant to the new Director of Central Intelligence, confirmed by vote of the Senate only the day before.

When Frank Cabot arrived at his desk at six that Tuesday morning, his left arm still bound tightly to his body in a canvas sling, he found a thick sheaf of cable summaries and reports from the deputy directors for Operations and Intelligence, all of which agreed in evaluating the assassination of the Prime Minister—and an equally successful assault on the director of the Qatari secret service, shot to death as he sat in a café having a morning coffee—as the beginning of a determined effort to overthrow the government. The Qatari military, such as it was, had been placed on high alert; tanks were dispatched to protect the palace of the sheikh and the television station; and the Qatari coast guard had put to sea. Cabot spent ten minutes with the action officer in charge of incoming information, twenty minutes reading, and an hour on the phone before driving to the White House with Leo Weissberg and another assistant, loaded down with charts and graphs for an 8 a.m. briefing of President Anderson and his principal advisors.

"How's the arm?" the president asked when Cabot entered.

"Not bad. It's quit hurting. The docs say I'll be out of the sling in a week."

"Any report on the shooter?"

Everybody was interested. They all knew they were potential targets.

"The Bureau says it was a man named Cutter," said Cabot. "The strange thing is he grew up in Accokeek down the street from the MIA, but exactly how that ties in they can't say. Somebody entered the building with him; they're sure of that. But it stops there."

The president and his advisors were thoughtful for a moment. "Bad luck about that Agency woman," said the president. "You going to give her a star on that wall of yours out there?"

"I hadn't thought of that," said Cabot. "Thanks for mentioning it. I'll see to it."

"If you have a little ceremony, maybe I could come out, say a few words."

"That would mean a lot to the troops," said Cabot. "We'd all really appreciate it."

"Okay," said the president. "Down to work."

The secretary of state, Walter Akins, wanted to know how long it would take for an American aircraft carrier task force to reach the scene in the Gulf.

"Walt, I'm not sure that's the way we want to go at this stage," said President Anderson. "Frank, what do we know about the people behind this effort?"

"So far no one's claiming credit," said Frank Cabot, "but our man in Qatar says he's pretty sure the people on the ground are connected to the Cambridge Group."

"The Cambridge Group?" said the secretary of state, baffled.

"A group of Arab students from the Gulf states who have organized a study group at Cambridge University in the UK," said Cabot. "Reformist, moderate in religion, Western in spirit, mostly engineers and economists who have been issuing papers over the last few years calling for an end to the hereditary rule of the sheikhdoms in the Gulf."

"Why haven't we heard more about them?" demanded Akins.

"They've been going about things quietly," said Cabot. "Besides, my predecessor, as you know, had many close friends in the oil industry who held a very negative attitude toward the Cambridge Group. The Agency kept a close watch, but Delaney decided not to circulate any of our reports. It was his opinion—and many of us tried to argue with him—that these people were trouble-making radical malcontents."

"And how does this administration feel?" asked Akins.

"Well, of course we deplore the use of violence," said President Anderson. "Let's issue a very strong statement to that effect. And then let's wait and see."

At the close of the meeting, Cabot lingered to accept the congratulations of the other participants as they filed out. All assured him they were extremely pleased by his confirmation and thought he had handled himself well.

The president held Cabot back with a touch on the arm. "Have you got a minute?"

"Of course," said Cabot. He asked Weissberg to wait for him at the car and followed the president down the hall to the Oval Office, where Anderson gestured to a chair in front of a mahogany desk that had once been used by Franklin Delano Roosevelt.

"I take it," said the president, "that you boys were keeping a close watch through someone in the group, is that right?"

"Yes, sir, that is correct. Do you want us to work that relationship at this point or let it lie until things are a little clearer in the Gulf?"

"Work it for all it's worth," said the president. "I don't support violence, but I'd like to see something good come out of this turmoil."

"The chances are good," said Cabot. "Sir, I'd like your okay for something else. I believe the Israelis know quite a bit about this group, and I think I might work a trade with sat photos. They're interested; we used to provide them on a routine basis. That's a very important intelligence relationship for us, and for them too, and I'd like permission to reach a quiet agreement on this."

"I trust your judgment, Frank. That it?"

"Yes, sir, that's all I've got."

"I want to say I'm proud of you. You got a lot of crap from the media and that idiot MacLaverty over the last month, and you took it like a man."

"Thank you, sir."

"Kitty get through okay?"

"Thanks for asking," said Cabot. "Kitty found it all very difficult—the accident, the innuendo in the press. But she's come through it fine. She's gone up to New York to spend some time with a friend and do a little painting. She was quite a painter when I first met her, and she'd like to get back to it."

"That's fine. I'm very pleased to hear all's well on the home front. Dust settling out at the Agency? They all know who's boss?"

"I may need to make a few changes and bring in a little new blood," said Cabot. "I think it's time to appoint a new deputy director for operations. That's a very sensitive position."

"Joe Flint a little burnt out, you think?"

"He's been talking about early retirement. He told me once his first love is sailing. He's had a fine career. But there's no point in making a man drag himself to work when the spark is gone."

"Have you got someone in mind?" asked the president.

"Somebody younger. Somebody comfortable with American power. Somebody I've worked with and trust."

"I leave this entirely up to you," said the president. "You pick the man you want. But when you've got a candidate, let Peter know, will you? I like Peter to be on top of things."

"Peter and I get along fine," said Cabot.

"I'll warn him to be ready for you," said the president. "Now I want you to rest easy on one point."

"Yes, sir."

"There's been some talk in the media the last couple of days that some kind of embarrassing transcripts or reports or something of the kind were delivered to the White House by the Justice Department."

"Yes, sir. I believe George Tater had a story to that effect."

"I've had Peter look into that, and I don't know where Tater got his information but he's dead wrong. We have no papers that fit that description. The search came up empty."

"I'm relieved to hear that," said Frank Cabot. "I was pretty sure Tater had blotted his copybook on that one, but you never know till you know."

"Well, you can quit worrying about it," said the president, rising and extending his hand. "Now get back across the river and do us some good in the Gulf."

Not twenty minutes after the Senate voted to confirm, the previous afternoon, Cabot's secretary, Jane, had called to say that the man in charge of the motor pool wanted permission to provide the director with a different car to take him around Washington—a bigger, somewhat more plush, electronically more sophisticated, and very much heavier car. It had tinted windows and Cabot liked tinted windows. He said he would be pleased to ride in any car the motor pool cared to give him, but he hoped it would include a small refrigerator, so he could pop a cold soda when he felt like it. Jane was back on the phone in a few minutes to ask what kind of soda? The answer was root beer, and now, as soon as Cabot and Weissberg had settled themselves into the gray plush, Cabot opened the little fridge and took out a root beer. He offered one to Weissberg, but Weissberg shook his head.

"Will you speak to security this afternoon?" asked Cabot. "The president's worried about that Ruby Ridge group. He doesn't like to think they can walk into the Senate and take potshots at his cabinet officers."

"They're working closely with the Bureau," said Weissberg. "The one guy had no history with militia groups. They just rounded him up somewhere. And their friends in Michigan—all we've learned is they know how to dial the phone. Morrissey says he hasn't got much hope unless someone comes forward."

"You know," said Cabot, "that was quite a neat little operation those Ruby Ridge people ran. Very tightly focused, and no mistakes that I can see."

"Lot of good it did them," said Weissberg.

"I disagree," said Cabot. "The point is to let people know you're around, remind us there's a real world out there beyond the Beltway. Maybe they didn't kill me, but Rashevsky is dead. Bodies get attention. We're all going to be looking over our shoulders until we get those Ruby Ridge people."

"Not me," said Weissberg.

"What do you mean?" Cabot had a feeling he knew exactly what Weissberg meant.

Weissberg pulled a white envelope from his jacket pocket. "I'm requesting early retirement."

"Now?" asked Cabot. "Why now? Everything went well at the meeting this morning. We're going to put all this behind us. Why now?"

"Now feels like the right time, Frank." Weissberg had the look of a man who has made up his mind.

Cabot was silent for several moments, looking out the tinted windows at the blue-gray world. He didn't like this one little bit. He wanted this whole story put to rest once and for all. He wanted people to say, Okay, let's get on with the job. But even in Cabot's mind things refused to stay settled.

Over the weekend he had called Otis Jones to give him hell, but it hadn't gone the way he expected. "It was you, wasn't it?" Cabot had said.

"You never talked to the president. You just made up your own mind and told me what you thought I needed to hear."

"I would never admit that," said Jones. "What good would it do you if I did admit it? You knew what we wanted. And you still went."

"I went for the president."

"No," said Jones. "You went because I promised you a big future. And we made good on the promise. We avoided a nasty little fight with the Russians back in nineteen seventy-seven, and nobody else really knows what happened. What are you complaining about?"

Cabot quit arguing. Jones was wrong. A lot of people knew what happened. That's what Weissberg was telling him, and he wasn't alone. Cabot had gone to Moscow twice, and he had done what he was told to do. No one was going to pat him on the head for letting himself be fooled by Otis Jones. It made him angry that Jones had sailed through this whole episode without a scratch. Cabot did not like that either.

"I take it," Cabot said to Weissberg, "that you don't approve of what happened in Moscow back in nineteen seventy-seven. Have I got that right?"

"It doesn't sit well, Frank."

"You don't know the whole story," said Cabot.

"What I know is bad enough," said Weissberg. "You can spare me the rest."

"Well, I won't argue with you. I can't change the way you feel. Go ahead and talk to personnel. Tell them you're leaving in a few weeks—but not until this flap in the Gulf is under control. I need you, Leo. You know what's what and you know how I operate. Stick with me till the war's over, agreed?"

"I don't think that's what I want to do. I'd prefer to move on now."

"You'd prefer to move on," said Cabot. His voice had changed; the old friendship had gone out of it. "Well, I don't care what you prefer. You didn't hire on to work for me. You hired on to work for the United States of America, and right now your country needs you—not me, your country. I don't have to explain this to you. I won't accept your resignation."

"I'm a free agent," said Weissberg. "I can quit when I want to."

"Yes, you can. But you know I'm telling the truth. I need your help to see this through. After that you can do what you like."

"You don't care what I think of you?" asked Weissberg.

"Of course I care," said Cabot. "But I can't do anything about it. When we get back to Langley, there are a couple of things I want you to do. I want you to check if there's any satellite imagery of the Gulf we've got to worry about—Iranian ships, Saudi aircraft, whatever. You know what questions to ask. Second, I want to know what NSA has got. Who's talking and what are they saying? Does anybody know what's going on who shouldn't know? Third, I want you to check with our friends in Tel Aviv. And I want you to send that young man to see me."

"Brad Cameron?" asked Weissberg. "I don't think he's in the building, Frank."

"Maybe not. But I'd appreciate it if you'd hunt him up. I don't want Jane to do this, or his boss, or security. Just tell him to come to my office. One final thing. I appreciate everything you've done for me. You won't be easy to replace. I will miss you.

"Now I've got some reading to do. We won't discuss any of this again."

Cabot pulled a thick sheaf of papers from his briefcase and flicked on the reading light in the back of the car.

Brad wasn't hard to find. He was in Myrna's office, filling a cardboard box with personal items. He'd already been through her apartment. A man from security was sitting on a chair reading the newspaper while Brad methodically took pictures down from the walls, went through the stuff in drawers, and checked the books on the shelves. He had spoken to Shulamith, and she said her grandmother would like to have a good picture of Myrna if he found one, but the other stuff really meant nothing to them. The red dress, the little Indian beaded purse Brad found in Myrna's apartment—Shulamith had no idea what that was all about. Myrna loved to talk about the old days with Rachel, but the truth was they hadn't shared much. They were some kind of cousins, they had attended the same school in Warsaw before the war, they could be found together in one photograph of ten-year-old girls standing in a line on a stage, tall ones to the right, short to the left, all dressed in white pinafores and singing in the chorus of some school show. But that was it. They never really knew each other till long after the war.

"Doesn't Rachel know of anyone?" Brad had asked Shulamith. "Some cousin or friend?"

"Not here," said Shulamith. "We thought she had people in America."

In Israel the story was not so unusual. Shulamith's great-aunts, Rachel's sisters, had all been older, and one of them had survived the war and still lived in Paris. But Myrna's brother was younger and had gone to Birkenau with their parents and whoever else there was, and that, Shulamith had said, was the sad truth of the matter. Of her entire family only Myrna, a skinny girl with a suitcase traveling east in the last weeks of peace in September 1939, had managed to find her way over the course of a year to Vladivostok, Shanghai, South Africa, the Dominican Republic, Brooklyn, and a home of a kind at last in Washington with the Central Intelligence Agency.

"You should give her things away," said Shulamith, "or keep them yourself."

There wasn't much. Except for a drawing of Warsaw, artist unknown, the child's dress of red silk, and the beaded purse it was mostly just stuff: clothes to give to the Goodwill, the usual kitchen equipment no one wanted, photos of people long dead. In the center drawer of her desk at the Agency, Brad found a bank savings account passbook and statements for a Keogh plan and a Merrill Lynch cash management account. Myrna had provided for herself very comfortably, but Brad found no will, no letter To whom it may concern, no key to a bank safe-deposit box. Myrna Rashevsky had apparently departed life without leaving behind an instruction of any kind.

So it was in a bleak mood that Brad looked up as Leo Weissberg made his way into the small room with a summons, softly worded but still a summons, from the Director of Central Intelligence.

"Sad work," said Frank Cabot, when Brad arrived half an hour later. "Has she got family?"

"Not really," said Brad. He explained that Myrna's closest living human relation was a woman she used to pass in the hallways of a Polish school more than sixty years ago.

"If that woman claims something a little closer," said Cabot, "there will be no quarrel at this end. They can probably find a use for the money. Otherwise the federal government will get it."

"I'm not sure they'll want to do that," said Brad.

"Ask, you might be surprised," said Cabot. "But that's not why I sent for you. I want to speak to you about your future at the Central Intelligence Agency."

"You don't have to worry about that," said Brad. "I understand how the game is played."

"Joe Flint was playing the game," said Cabot, "not you. He will be retiring at the end of the month, but you're a young fellow with a future, and I want to know what you'd like to do next. We've had our disagreements, but that's over. Obviously the MIA job isn't right for you anymore, but this is a big organization."

"Mr. Cabot," said Brad, "I don't know what Jenny might have told you, but I'm not trying to hold on to my job."

"I haven't discussed this with Jenny," said Cabot. "She has nothing to do with it. You're a young man. You did what you felt you had to do. If you're ready to forget all that, I'm ready to help you get back on track."

"Just go on as if nothing had happened?"

"Why not?"

"You don't understand," Brad began.

"I suppose," said Cabot, "you think this will poison your chances at the Agency. You're afraid I won't really give you another chance."

"No, that's not it," said Brad.

"If you don't trust me," said Cabot, "ask somebody you do trust. Ask your friend Hugh Diamond. I don't bear grudges. When it's over, it's over. We move on."

Brad tried to find words for what was going through his mind. He was thinking about all the people who had told him to keep his mouth shut. He was thinking about Golenpolsky and Aldrich Ames. He was thinking about the crazy chain of unraveling secrets that somehow in the end brought home an MIA. He was thinking about his face in the mirror in the hospital and what he saw in his own eyes there. He was thinking about Myrna in the hospital bed and the sound that came from her throat after the respirator was turned off: a long, rasping, coughing sigh. On the monitors at that moment all the green lines went flat. He was thinking about the thousands of people who got up the next morning and went to their desks at the CIA as if nothing had happened. How could he hope to explain all these things to this busy man who was now running the American intelligence empire?

"Sir," said Brad, rising from his chair, "without going into it, I don't think this is where I want to spend my life."

"I understand," said Frank Cabot. "It isn't for everybody."

The day was mild, sun flooded the Agency parking lot where Brad had put down his boxes of stuff next to his car, and Hugh Diamond had quit arguing about the brilliant future Brad might still make for himself at the CIA if he just wasn't so damned stubborn. He might have fought on if Brad had been ready to bend an inch, but all the bend had gone out of him. He said no and he meant no. "I'm done with the secret life."

Hugh said he hated to lose his friend; Brad had been the breath of fresh air in their musty corner. But all right. Inevitably, in time, he would find a way to give meaning to his life and make a career elsewhere. But under no circumstances should he leave the Agency in a bitter mood of self-reproach, feeling he had achieved nothing.

"You made Cabot sweat," said Hugh. "You made the Agency cough up some big secrets. You made those senators ask some hard questions. You had the whole country glued to the tube. You set an example for America's youth by putting conscience ahead of career."

"You're forgetting something," said Brad. "Cabot is DCI."

"Yes, and Sergeant Dyer came home," said Hugh. "Without the ruckus you made he'd still be eating potato soup in Akmolinsk."

"I'm happy about that," said Brad. "But the trade was Myrna."

"That was rotten luck," said Hugh, "but *you* didn't shoot her. Don't forget rule one in this business: Do what you can, then let it go."

"I don't like letting things go."

"We've noticed," said Hugh. "What now? Scholarship? The law? International banking?"

"Something like that," said Brad. "But first I think I'd like to walk home."

"Walk home? With all these boxes? All the way into D.C.? Are you crazy?"

"Probably," said Brad. "But I'm tired of trying to avoid reporters. I'm tired of people thinking I'm hiding the real story. I'm tired of being called up by security to remind me of my oath of secrecy. So I'm going to take a couple of months off and walk home—from Georgia to Mount Katahdin in Maine, on the Appalachian Trail."

"The whole way?" asked the amazed Hugh Diamond. "Alone? Jenny's not going with you?"

"We talked about it," said Brad, "but I'm not in the mood for hearts and flowers right now."

"I'm surprised," said Hugh. "I thought you two would survive this."

"Don't be in such a hurry to nail things down," said Brad. "Ask me in September."

59

In New York City, Kitty tried to pick up the thread of her life. She moved in with an old college friend, long single, living on Sutton Place. Despite the address, there was nothing posh about Mary's building. The lobby needed fresh paint, there was not much of a view from the third floor, and the only window in the dining room looked out on an air shaft. But Kitty had what she wanted: a room of her own, somebody to talk to, time to paint.

It was slow going at first. She rented space in the corner of a studio in Soho, got out all her old brushes, bought a lot of new paint, and stretched some canvases—not big ones, small ones. She had an instinct that the effect she was after was small, clear, relaxed, open. She visited the museums and galleries, usually one every afternoon, then went home for dinner with her friend, who taught history at the Nightingale-Bamford School on 92nd Street. Mary usually had a glass of wine with dinner, but Kitty declined. She had decided to quit.

She loved the sunny onset of spring in April and May. She loved seeing her sons, both of whom lived and worked in the city. They met her for lunch, said they got only cheerful letters and e-mails from Dad, didn't ask their mother too many questions. Every week or so Kitty got a letter from Jenny, who reported that she was fine, she was in the middle of *Anna Karenina*, which was maybe the best book she had ever read, she had received a couple of postcards from Brad as he made his slow way up the spine of the Appalachians. At first Kitty thought that was over, then wondered if they would get back together in the fall. Either seemed possible. Kitty liked Brad, but she knew he wasn't the only fish in the ocean. She was content to wait and see.

Frank wrote too, every Sunday, and Kitty soon learned to dread his letters. Every Tuesday evening a thick blue envelope addressed by hand was waiting for her when she got home from the studio. Its tone was friendly, news of the neighborhood was included, he asked about her painting. Once or twice Kitty cried over these letters; they were in Frank's hand but they might have been addressed to a college alumni magazine. He rarely alluded to anything that happened within the walls of the Agency, but he was full of comment on Washington politics, a squabble in the Senate Foreign Relations Committee, who was writing what in the papers, what it all meant. But in these longish letters he wrote nothing about Kitty's absence, expressed no anger or sorrow, made no demands. Even worse was the way he made excuses for her: my job is so demanding, I know it's been hard, you need time alone. Did he care at all? How could she possibly know?

Late one afternoon, staring at a canvas that did not seem to be going anywhere and glancing at her watch every few minutes to track the day's glacial progress toward five o'clock, Kitty realized she wasn't thinking about painting. She was thinking about having a drink. Two days of that told her what she had pretty well known from the beginning: moving to New York, picking up a brush, sticking to water for a few weeks was not going to be enough.

So she made some phone calls and at four-thirty, instead of heading home for dinner with Mary, Kitty went uptown to the Madison Avenue Presbyterian Church at 73rd Street. Inside she asked directions and proceeded to the second floor of the parish house. With a cup of black coffee in her hand, she took a seat in the rear and gave small frail smiles to people who caught her eye. Forty minutes later, trembling but determined, she rose, moved to the front of the room, and spoke to the assembled faces.

"My name is Catherine," she said. "I'm an alcoholic. I've been drunk for twenty years, and I want to know who I am when I'm sober."

When the room broke into applause and even a few cheers, Kitty began to cry. Much happened to her over the following weeks, but what surprised her most was the discovery that the secret she had hidden for so long was no secret at all. Everybody knew.

60

It was George Tater's idea of the way to start a perfect day, beginning at seven in the morning with a leisurely breakfast at the Mayflower. He sat at his regular table by one of the big plants where the light was good and he could see who came and went. He began with coffee and a large grapefruit juice, ordered a tomato omelet, and spread out the day's newspapers. He always read *The New York Times* first, then *The Washington Post, The Wall Street Journal,* the *Los Angeles Times,* and whatever else had tweaked his interest at the newsstand in the lobby.

First he scanned the page-one headlines to take the pulse of the world. All seemed placid and serene. Then, page by page, Tater moved inside. A story below the fold on page three of the *Times* held his eye for a moment. Something was going on in Qatar—there had been a murder, the sheikh had stepped aside, a nephew had abandoned his studies as an economist in England to head an interim government. Something about the story seemed slightly off, but Tater couldn't quite put his finger on it. He moved on.

All the papers were still running follow-up stories about last week's sensation in the Senate. Cabot's confirmation was already ancient history, but the *Times* and *Post* were in a horse race to fill in the blanks about the captivity of Sergeant Jason Dyer in Russia. It wasn't Tater's kind of story at all; the reporters weren't trying to identify the villains: the men who gave the orders, the men who lied about it, the men who looked the other way while Dyer rotted in the Gulag for all those years. Hardly. They were calling it "the Miracle of Akmolinsk." Russian stringers were tracking down fellow prisoners who remembered the courage of the mysterious man in the special annex. They were retracing the chain of discovery begun by Kondrashov in the files—how the KGB's yellowing flimsies, clumsily typed and boldly signed in broad strokes of blue ink, led step by step to the camp, the commandant's office, the special annex, the solitary cell where Dyer had been held since the collapse of the Soviet government in 1991. Tater muttered and growled as he read this breathless horseshit.

But Faith Osborne—Tater had to hand it to her—had done something quite different. They were meeting later for lunch, and he planned to tell her how much he liked this story. She'd gone out to Accokeek for the homecoming and had written a long restrained account of the return of a prodigal son. It was tough on him: he'd lost a leg; his sister was struggling as a single mother; his old friends were potbellied guys in their fifties driving trucks or hammering nails. Jason Dyer had spent thirty years in prison for no reason anybody could understand, nearly went mad from the solitude, and yet his old friends envied him. The back pay had accumulated into quite a little stash. By their lights, America's most famous MIA had come home rich.

"That's a really fine story by Faith," said Richard Kramer, pausing by Tater's table in the Mayflower. "Don't you think?"

"Hey, Richard." Tater folded the paper.

"If you see Faith before I do, tell her I said so."

"Okay," said Tater. "She'll be pleased to hear it, I know."

"She's covered the human angle," said Kramer, "but that still leaves the big picture—you know, what does it mean?"

"That's mighty deep water," said Tater.

"The way I see it," said Kramer, "this is the real end to the war in Vietnam. Now it's really over."

"Except for the two thousand guys still missing."

"Well, the true end to the Cold War, then. Putting things behind us—a new sense of trust. I'm trying to pinpoint the deeper meaning here. How do you see it?"

"Cabot lucked out," said George Tater.

Tater placed a twenty-dollar bill on his check, left the restaurant, crossed the lobby of the Mayflower, and took the stairs up to the barbershop. Cherry was sitting at the desk just inside the door, reading the paper. Tater noticed that she was wearing a new shade of lipstick, purple. Her nails were purple too, and her eyeshadow was a kind of lavender.

"Good morning, Mr. Tater," she said. "Manicure today?"

"Thanks, Cherry," said Tater. "I *would* like a manicure. It's been too long and I've been working too hard. I could use a little buffing up."

The senior Morelli brushed off a barber chair, Tater settled himself, and Cherry pulled up close. "A shave?" said Morelli. "A little trim? We fix you up fine."

The chair was cranked back, Tater's face was wrapped in a hot towel, Cherry's cool fingers worked on his right hand, and Tater drifted off lazily. When he was working on a story he obsessed about it every minute of the day, but he was between stories now and his mind wandered. The previous evening he'd met Jenny for a drink. She had called him, she had picked the place—the bar at Notte Luna near Dupont Circle—and she had opened the conversation by thanking him for going easy on her Uncle Frank.

"I thought I had him," said Tater, "but he was too quick for me."

"Stop it," said Jenny. "You backed off and I appreciate it. That's half of what I wanted to tell you."

The other half was to part on the right note. He had a right to know why she had ended it. Tater started to protest but Jenny insisted. It wasn't anything Tater had done, but some things are built to last and this wasn't.

At that point Jenny came up short for words. Tater came to her aid by saying he knew she'd spent most of a weekend at the hospital with Brad Cameron at the bedside of the woman who got shot. "I'm guessing," said Tater, "that the two of you sorted things out."

"Not really," said Jenny. "But at least we're talking about it."

"If you're worried he'll find out about us—" Tater began.

"He knows," said Jenny. "I told him."

"You told him?" asked Tater, genuinely surprised. "Why did you tell him?"

"I thought if I told him I wouldn't have to worry about keeping the secret for the rest of my life."

"You two were meant for each other," said Tater.

Morelli unwrapped the towel from Tater's face and began to lather his cheeks and chin. Tater liked the little trace of lemony scent that rose from the lather beneath his nose. While Morelli, using a straight razor manufactured in the last century in Torino, carefully scraped the stubble from his cheeks, Tater reflected that he had told Jenny the truth when he said he would miss her. But he was relieved, too. Girls approaching thirty wanted engagements, weddings, honeymoons, fixing up apartments, and, after a year or two, babies. The idea of children alarmed George Tater. He did what he did and he knew what he knew and none of it, he was sure, had prepared him to be a father.

Salvatore Morelli's long stainless-steel scissors, manufactured in the 1930s in Solingen, Germany, were flying around Tater's ears when the creak of the next barber chair announced a second customer. Tater opened his eyes. The gaunt frame of the senior senator from Georgia was easing itself down.

"Glad to see you out and about, Senator," said Tater.

Hawkins turned to peer at him.

"George Tater," said Tater.

"Ah, Tater," said Hawkins. "Yes, I'm feeling much better, thanks. I thought sure I was going to die, but I guess it's been put off."

"MacLaverty got over it yet?"

"Oh, he thought I might have been a little intemperate in my language, and he let me know it. But old warhorses like us don't take lasting offense at a few harsh words. I suppose you're on the prowl for another story."

"I try to keep my ears open," said Tater. "But that last story wore me out."

"It made me mad," said Hawkins. "Trying to besmirch the honor of the whole country like that. But we've been getting great press and bushels of mail saying Thank God for America. So it all came out well."

"I can think of a few loose ends," said Tater.

"Such as?"

"Well, do you think," asked Tater, "that Otis Jones really ran everything by the man from Plains?"

"Are we on the record or off the record?"

"You choose, Senator."

"All right," said Hawkins. "I want to be frank with you, George. I want to tell you exactly what I think with the bark off. But I don't want to see it coming out of my mouth on the front page of the *Times* tomorrow morning. Fair enough?"

"Fair enough," said Tater.

"That dog won't hunt. I've been a friend and colleague of the man from Plains for many, many years. We make our home in the same state, we're members of the same party, and we share common attitudes about God and country. And I can tell you right now he would never have sent some junior CIA officer to Russia to ask if they were holding an American prisoner. He'd have called in the Soviet ambassador, he'd have asked for the truth without varnish or delay, and if there had been any sort of waffling response the air in the Oval Office would have turned blue.

"In short," Senator Hawkins continued, "Otis Jones is a lying polecat with the moral character of an army mule."

"So far," said Tater, "we are in perfect agreement."

"Let me tell you a few things about Otis Jones," said the senior senator from Georgia.

"That's promising material," said Tater, when the senator had done. "It backs up a good deal of what Frank Cabot told me on the phone the other day."

Outside it was almost shirtsleeve weather: mild and sunny, with a gentle breeze and the grass a rich, almost luminescent green in the parks, buds on the trees, daffodils popping up everywhere. George Tater would be meeting the *Post's* leading lady columnist for lunch. Maybe they'd have seafood, maybe they'd share a bottle of white wine, maybe they'd go to a gallery and look at some pictures. Who knew where it might end? The only wisp of cloud on Tater's horizon was the need to tell Morrie Bloom that the Cabot story was over and Tater's vital juices had run dry; he needed a breather before he could return to the well.

"You're telling me you're dropping this story?" Morrie Bloom demanded when Tater reached him on the phone. "What about those transcripts the attorney general sent to the White House? What about the cover-up of the story from Aldrich Ames? If the man from Plains wasn't issuing the orders, who was? Come on, George."

But Tater insisted. Long experience told him it was over when it was over. Those transcripts had been deep-sixed. Cabot had been confirmed, and they were no longer fighting about anything. It was time to remove the dead from the battlefield and wait for a new day.

"Listen, Morrie," he said, "there comes a moment when you see every story from the outside. You step back. You ask, What does this add up to? Is this going somewhere or is it dead in the water?

"I thought this was the big one. I thought I was going to bring Cabot down. I was going to rip open the whole culture of secrecy in this country. I was going to put the CIA up against the wall and make it tell the truth for once. But let's be honest. The air has gone out of the balloon. We got dark stories from a convicted spy on one side, and we got an MIA coming home a hero at last on the other. I'm looking at this story from the outside now. You can't argue with success. Cabot had the horses. It's time to give it a rest."

"I don't like hearing you talk defeat like this," said Morrie. "It's upsetting."

"It's not defeat," said Tater. "It's the breaks of the game. He won this one. But hey, Morrie, buck up. Cabot's not going anywhere and neither is the CIA. We'll be back at 'em."

But Bloom was in no mood to be philosophical. He had a front-page conference in an hour, the rest of the week was still a cipher to him, there were going to be three hundred and sixty-five editions of the *Times* in each and every year until he retired or died, and he needed something to keep the upper middle classes laying down their shekels at the break of each new day.

"Don't worry," soothed Tater. "I'm on to something big. It's going to take some digging, but I've got a story brewing. You're going to be a happy man."

"So give me a teaser," said Morrie Bloom.

"Think back, Morrie. Who told me that cockamamy story about Nixon stealing billions meant for Vietnam? Who was the mastermind of those bank scandals back in the eighties, when we were lending billions to Saddam Hussein so he could build a giant army for Iraq? What Washington insider shook down the Arabs for the loot to pay the Contras in Nicaragua? Who was the go-between who got the Chinese army to put up millions for the reelection of William Jefferson Clinton?"

Morrie Bloom was an old lefty and George Tater knew him well. He knew the stories that could raise Bloom's blood pressure—dark tales of secret wars, hidden bank accounts, rumors of assassination, the world made safe for giant corporations, all the unanswered questions of the American century. "There's even a CIA angle," said George Tater. "A big one. Oil, politics, offshore banks, slush funds. Think back, Morrie. Frank Cabot wasn't the prime mover in all this hugger-mugger. Ask yourself: Who sent Frank Cabot to Moscow? I'll give you a clue. It wasn't the man from Plains."

"Otis Jones," said Morrie Bloom in a hush. "Billionaire cold warrior. Advisor to presidents. The ultimate insider. Never been touched."

"Till now," said George Tater. "He can run but he can't hide, Morrie. I've got him in my crosshairs. Trust me."

ACKNOWLEDGMENTS

I have learned that writing a novel, no less than a long work of nonfiction, runs up large debts of gratitude. Many people have helped me in the course of this book, some by reading the manuscript and offering advice, others by explaining the world to me. At the top of the list of advisors is my wife, Candace. Whenever I ran into trouble, which was about weekly, we went for a two-mile walk along Broad Brook Road and talked out problems of plot, character, and theme, a remedy which always got me going again. Others who contributed their time and attention are Fred Childs, Jennifer and Dennis Coombs, Chip Fleischer, Crystal Gromer, Sam Halpern, Burton and Ellen Hersh, Robert G. Kaiser, Jo Long, Priscilla McMillan, Sherry Merrick, Robert S. Norris, David Overton, Hayden Peake, Danny Rubinstein, Nicola Smith, Helga Schmidt, Winn Taplin, Lucian Truscott, Jonnie Weiss, Lee Whittier, and several persons in Russia and Israel who prefer to remain unidentified.

Powers is an Irish name. All I know of Yiddish I owe to Stefan Chodorov, Alan Lelchuk, and the late Leo Rosten, whose classic work, *The Joys of Yiddish,* was my guide.

I also want to express my thanks to Ash Green and Chuck Elliott, my editors for twenty years. They have always taken an interest in what I wanted to do and helped me to do it. Every writer hopes to find such support, but not all are lucky enough to get it.

A NOTE ABOUT THE AUTHOR

THOMAS POWERS is a Pulitzer Prize–winning journalist whose most recent book, *Heisenberg's War: The Secret History of the German Bomb,* was published simultaneously in four countries—the United States, Germany, France, and Britain—where it received wide notice and sparked a continuing controversy. He has written frequently about intelligence organizations since the publication of *The Man Who Kept the Secrets: Richard Helms and the CIA* (1979). His other books include *Thinking About the Next War, The War at Home: Vietnam and the American People,* and *Diana: The Making of a Terrorist.* He lives in Vermont with his wife. This is his first novel.

A NOTE ON THE TYPE

This book was set in Minion, a typeface produced by the Adobe Corporation specifically for the Macintosh personal computer and released in 1990. Designed by Robert Slimbach, Minion combines the classic characteristics of old style faces with the full complement of weights required for modern typesetting.

Composed by Dix, Syracuse, New York
Printed and bound by R. R. Donnelley & Sons, Harrisonburg, Virginia
Designed by Anthea Lingeman